Steeples

W.D. Walters

WestBow
P R E S S
A DIVISION OF THOMAS NELSON

WestBow Press books may be ordered through booksellers or by contacting:

WestBow Press
A Division of Thomas Nelson
1663 Liberty Drive
Bloomington, IN 47403
www.westbowpress.com
1-(866) 928-1240

Because of the dynamic nature of the Internet, any Web addresses or links contained in this book may have changed since publication and may no longer be valid. The views expressed in this work are solely those of the author and do not necessarily reflect the views of the publisher, and the publisher hereby disclaims any responsibility for them.

Any people depicted in stock imagery provided by Thinkstock are models, and such images are being used for illustrative purposes only.

Certain stock imagery © Thinkstock.

ISBN: 978-1-4497-0874-0 (sc)
ISBN: 978-1-4497-0875-7 (dj)
ISBN: 978-1-4497-0873-3 (e)

Library of Congress Control Number: 2010940645

Printed in the United States of America

WestBow Press rev. date: 11/19/2010

Dedicated To

Katherine, Jonathan, and Liam –
Time and distance can never diminish love.

Prologue

Confusion reigned. The crowd of onlookers fled from the site fearing for their lives, fearing the bullets, the canisters of tear gas, and the canisters of smoke that turned the sounds of applause almost instantly into cries of terror. Blood pooled a few feet from the podium and out of the left ear of the lifeless body. The round from the rifle had penetrated its target with trained accuracy bringing instant death on impact. The chaotic response to the attack by the huge crowd was unabated by the attempts of security and police to contain the thousands fleeing in every direction. Like a stampede of wild animals, survival of the fittest had replaced the unity of the political rally.

The attack was well planned and synchronized, clearly the work of professionals. Simultaneously, canisters of tear gas and smoke were fired into the crowd while a sniper fired the lethal round into the intended target. The angles of attack had been selected to confuse anyone attempting to determine the source and location of the assassination. The strike was decisive - the timing clearly meant to send a message to a nation that was divided.

As rapidly as the attackers struck, equally fast were they gone from the scene leaving only frantic onlookers and security. Sirens blasted as additional police and other emergency personnel rushed to the area. Limousines rushed the various dignitaries present for the rally away from the scene. Bodies were strewn all over the park where the event had taken place, innocent people trampled in the stampede of a horrified crowd. Security had already taken up positions around the podium while paramedics were permitted onto the stage to attempt to revive the target.

Anthony Mason, a member of the security team stood just a few feet from the dead body. Nine-millimeter pistol drawn, he was the antithesis of the chaos occurring around him – calm, confident and clear in his responsibility. John Luther, on the other hand, was a rookie with very little experience, clearly the opposite of Mason.

"Mason, man what's goin' on here? This is insane." That nervous kind of sweat formed above Luther's upper lip as he continued to point his pistol in every direction not really aiming at anything in particular. He was no Anthony Mason. Luther looked up above the tall buildings that encompassed the area surrounding the site of the rally. News helicopters hovered overhead before peeling off to the west and flying away, undoubtedly ready to enter the race against other television stations determined to report the tragedy first. Luther was less than three months on the job. He wasn't prepared for what had just occurred.

"Put your pistol away, rookie," Mason said with a calm, almost monotone voice. "This was the work of pros. They won't get caught!" Mason was fully prepared. None of what was happening seemed to shake his nerves.

"Mason, what are you talkin' about?" Luther continued, "I don't get this. How could this happen? We were here! We had the place covered! I don't get any of this."

Mason calmly knelt on the stage and holstered his pistol. He slowly turned his head and looked at the dead body as paramedics were preparing to move it. He glanced back to the rookie security agent then out into the still dispersing crowd. "America, Luther. America."

Chapter One

A small house in Lumpkin County, Georgia

Summer

Several years passed since he'd searched for a place to settle. Paul Atkinson moved to a quiet part of northern Lumpkin County, Georgia just a few years earlier after over eight years in the military. His first experience in that part of the country had been during the mountain phase of the United States Army's famed Ranger School. Despite the demands placed on him during that phase of the nearly seven week school, Paul took some time to absorb the absolute beauty of the mountainous area that served essentially as the southern start of the Appalachian Trail. He'd decided to revisit the area some day to consider settling there following his military career. Nearly four years into his career as a young first lieutenant in the 75th Ranger Regiment, Paul took twenty days leave and spent the entire time staying in a bed and breakfast located in Dahlonega, the largest town in Lumpkin County, an opportunity for him to look around the area. Following his leave, he was adamant in his desire to someday live there.

And, he did, indeed. Paul left the military after four years in a covert unit within the Department of Defense that consisted of elite soldiers from all of the branches. He arrived in Dahlonega with a duffel bag, a mountain bike and a 1993 Chevrolet S-10 pick-up truck that had seen its better days. After a few days in the same bed and breakfast where he had spent some leave time nearly five years earlier, Paul found a small two bedroom home for rent located in a valley on a farm in the northern part of the county. Charlie and Anne Taylor owned the house that Paul rented.

Following their wedding in the summer of 1957, the house had been their first purchase along with two hundred and fifty acres of mostly grazing land for Charlie's small herd of cattle. The couple lived in the same house on the property for nearly five decades until their daughter Dianne finally talked them into building a more modern home on the same property. It took some convincing to get the couple to spend a dime of their wealth – and there was plenty of it – but Charlie could be worn down by his little girl's sweet pleadings despite the fact that she was twenty-five and lived in Atlanta at the time when she convinced her father to build the new home. Charlie was retired from the postal service, a twenty-four year career that followed two tours in the Marines. Anne was a retired schoolteacher. The two had amassed considerable wealth from intelligent investing and frugal spending. The farm was more or less a hobby for Charlie. It kept him busy. With Dianne in Atlanta working as a pediatrician at Northside Hospital, Paul was a fresh face and a welcome arrival for the Taylors.

Paul had a full-time job at a warehouse in small but growing town southwest of Dahlonega. His weekday hours allowed him the freedom to spend his weekends just the way he had wanted when he moved to that part of Georgia. Saturday mornings were his favorite times, particularly during the summer months. The house he rented was situated at the bottom of a large, open pasture behind the house that sloped upward to the east and was bordered by a thick wooded area with huge trees that created a horizon. Paul's house had a small back porch where he could sit on those beautiful Saturday mornings and usher in dawn with a glass of freshly made orange juice.

The summer mornings in northern Georgia were unmistakable and unique in their profound beauty and Paul soaked in every available moment. The sounds of the mountain community created a natural symphonic concert that could make city symphonies seem cheap. Paul awakened early on those Saturday mornings to enjoy the sweet melodies of his self-proclaimed paradise. It was a dichotomy of the life he'd lived as a soldier. Glass of orange juice in hand he would take a seat on the back porch and listen to the orchestra introduce a new day and the day's star. Night still prevailing, the concert would begin on those mornings with the sounds of frogs and crickets, chirping and bellowing seemingly in unison. A slight breeze would occasionally move through the trees adding to the beautiful melody while bright stars and the occasional visit by a full moon provided the lighting for the stage. As the night gave way to the dawn of a new day, more of nature's musicians joined the concert, and slowly, as if perfectly planned, the chirping and bellowing faded and were replaced with the beautiful songs of the vast variety of birds singing such happy songs, one could not help but smile and assume the rapture had come. The crescendo of the melody ushered in the star of the show as the curtain of darkness began to lift and the sun entered stage right signifying the success of another morning concert in the mountains of Georgia. Paul took great comfort and serenity in those special mornings.

Following nature's concert Paul enjoyed a brisk ride on his mountain bike. He learned just shortly after moving to Lumpkin County that biking was extremely popular in that part of the state. His bike, a purchase made in Roswell, Georgia, was more valuable than his truck. Paul cared little for his truck, but cherished the bike and would never part with it. His ride usually took him north on a rural mountain road with steep climbs and sharp turns. Very few guardrails lined the road and less experienced riders had suffered serious injuries, even death at the hands of mountain biking rural North Georgia. Paul really pushed himself on his rides enjoying the speeds reached coming down the steep sections of the roads. He had no fear of the ride or the treacherous road.

His rides took him through some of the most beautiful scenery in the United States. Mountain rivers with rushing currents and occasional waterfalls, huge trees serving as a canopy for the road, and open valleys with plush green pastures providing the perfect background for the avid mountain biker. Paul usually rode thirty miles on Saturdays during the summer stopping halfway at a tiny country store for a Gatorade. He enjoyed the atmosphere of the rural setting. On those summer mornings the country store could always be counted on to have its usual cast of characters – two elderly men sitting outside at the entrance to the store on a bench, usually debating the state of affairs in the world, a thirty-three year old woman behind the counter always ready to greet the customer with a genuine, "howdy, sir". Her two young sons could be found riding their bicycles in the parking lot, a necessity for them to be there because their single mother was on a fixed income and couldn't afford a sitter. Yes, the familiarity was intriguing yet comforting to Paul. It represented to him the heart of America and a change from the horrors he had witnessed as a combat soldier and covert operative.

Gatorade consumed, Paul mounted his bike and rode back to his house to continue his Saturday routine. The rest of his day was usually left open with one exception. Those mornings represented the pinnacle of life to him and he was sure that there would never be an ounce of regret for moving to the area.

"Mornin' Paul. You look a little spent." Charlie knew Paul's Saturday morning routine. His comment was more tongue and cheek. "You know you're getting up there in age. You might want to ease up a bit."

"You're right, Charlie," Paul replied with a slight, sarcastic grin. "I'm thinking of tradin' in my mountain bike for one of those mobility chairs. You think I can get around the farm and feed the cattle on one of those?"

Charlie lifted his hand to his chin and looked up in the sky. "You know, I think we might be able to pull some parts from that ole John Deere to make that thing work."

The two stood silent for a moment staring at each other. Almost simultaneously, both began to laugh.

The relationship and genuine friendship between the two men had grown during the two years since Paul's arrival. Charlie's life always had that missing part, like a piece in a puzzle. He'd always wanted a son but after Dianne's birth, doctors informed Charlie and Anne that having another child would be impossible, too risky. The chance of the couple ever having a son was gone forever. Dianne became Charlie's little angel, as he called her. He doted over her constantly and always wanted the best for his little angel. He certainly made that happen, all the way through Emory University. His love for his daughter was undeniable, yet there had always been that empty space in his heart still remaining for a son. He dealt with it well, with deep love and care for his wife and daughter. When Paul came along, if only in a small way, some of that empty space in his heart was filled.

Paul tackled rural life with the zest of a child opening a gift. Living on Charlie's farm gave him an opportunity that he had never dreamed of before. Charlie taught him about raising cattle, how to run some of the various pieces of farm equipment, and how to be patient, an essential in farming as he told Paul. Of course, it took some prodding from Charlie to get Paul to take a peek out of his shell. Paul was, initially, very distant and hard to reach. Charlie was careful but persistent in drawing him out. He did it with nothing more than a John Deere tractor. Paul enjoyed the privilege of those evenings hopping on the new John Deere tractor that Charlie had purchased and hauling hay out to the cattle. He was intrigued with the cows, how they seemed to know just where to be and the time to be there. Paul liked predictability, and the cows were predictable. With childlike enthusiasm Paul went about the tasks of feeding the cattle like a seasoned farmer. Charlie proudly watched his pupil learn the trade.

"Anne's cookin' for you tomorrow. You comin'?"

"How could I ever turn down Anne's cooking? She should be in 'Better Homes and Gardens'." Paul had retrieved another Gatorade from the kitchen of his house and took a drink.

Charlie stepped over to Paul and placed his hand on Paul's shoulder. "What about church? Can you make time for that tomorrow?" Charlie knew that Paul was not particularly religious but always encouraged him to go to church with him and Anne. He didn't push Paul, though. He believed that Christians should never force their religion or beliefs on others. The true mark of a Christian in Charlie's mind was to lead by example, Christ's example.

Paul indeed wasn't religious. It wasn't that he had no belief that there was a force of creation out there somewhere. He had simply grown cold to organized religion after having seen major battles fought and innocent people die in the name of religion. But, Charlie and Anne were two people he had grown to love and care for, people he cherished and wanted to make happy. He looked at Charlie and replied, "You know I'll be there, but you'll have to overlook my growling stomach while we're in there waiting to get out for lunch."

"I'll toss you a biscuit during the sermon," Charlie replied with a satisfied grin. "Well, I'm goin' to get back to the house. The Braves have a one o'clock game today." Charlie's love of Atlanta Braves baseball bordered fanatical. "You want to come down for some lunch?"

"No thanks, Charlie. I'm going to Frank's for one of those burgers." That was the Saturday exception. Paul was a creature of habit, and after finding Frank's and his hamburgers, Paul had made a habit of being there every Saturday, rain or shine. "You know, the gift that keeps on giving," Paul said as Charlie began to walk away. Despite Paul's insistence on a healthy lifestyle, he couldn't resist the Frank's Bar and Grill famous one-pound hamburger and fries plate. The meal had become a Saturday mainstay for him.

"Alright, son. We'll see you in the mornin'." Charlie turned again and began his walk home. The pride in having a young man like Paul living on his property was obvious to all who came in contact with him. He couldn't wait to tell Anne that Paul was coming to church. He also couldn't wait for the ballgame.

Paul stored his mountain bike and got ready for a shower. He was an example of perfect health. At six feet and 175 pounds with short cut blonde hair and blue eyes, he could have been the poster child for the all-American boy. He had recently turned thirty and prided himself on his level of physical fitness and what it accomplished for him. He cared nothing at all that he was an attractive man and that most agreed. He simply wanted to keep his body in great shape, and by doing so he knew that life would become more fulfilling. He wasn't grateful for everything he experienced as a soldier, but he was grateful for the discipline the military instilled for getting fit and staying fit, and to be elite at doing so.

Shower complete, Paul put on his favorite pair of Wrangler jeans and the torn t-shirt that he felt just seemed to go with them and grabbed his keys. He went out to his S-10 pick-up and said to his self, "let this thing start one more time." Paul had purchased the truck six months before ending his military career. A smalltime used car dealership in Roanoke, Virginia where Paul had gone for a weekend, tried to up-sell the soon to be veteran. Paul had no interest. He cared nothing for flashy vehicles and high car payments. He paid cash for the truck - $1100 plus taxes and title. The 1993 truck had 102,000 miles on it when he purchased it in April of 2006. Now, nearly two and a half years later mostly due to his long commute to Cumming each weekday, the Chevy was limping at 208,000 miles. It had had more than its share of repairs, but Paul knew the end was near. He justified the purchase by dividing the amount of the purchase into the total miles that he had put on it since the day he drove it off the lot in Roanoke. But, now it seemed each time he put the key in the ignition the chance of it actually starting was like playing the lottery. He had decided, though, that he would drive the truck until it could no longer be driven.

Fortunately on that warm Saturday, the truck started and Paul drove off for Frank's Bar and Grill. Frank's was more of a bar than a grill located three miles south of Paul's home. Most people that visited Frank's were regulars making the place kind of a rural Cheers. Saturdays, particularly in the summer, were busy – if you can call thirty to forty patrons busy. Paul, however, liked to get there before the crowd arrived. At one o'clock in the afternoon at Frank's, the place only had three or four patrons, mostly all at the bar, perhaps one throwing darts. Few came in on Saturdays for the food, only to drink. Paul was the exception. He visited Frank's Bar and Grill for one thing and one thing only: one of the thickest, juiciest hamburgers to be found anywhere and exceptional fries as well.

Paul arrived at Frank's right on time, as punctual and routine as ever. He switched off the ignition of the Chevy and sat staring at the ceiling of the truck while he waited for it to stop sputtering and coughing. "I may have to get a pistol and shoot this poor thing," he said out loud yet to himself. If a truck could hear, then the Chevy pick-up heard what Paul said. It shut right off after his comment. He got out and walked into Frank's.

"Well, well, well, if it ain't Paul. Momma don't cook for you?" Frank, a retired Army master sergeant was always happy to see Paul, despite his relentless teasing about the differing generations of soldiers and who was superior to the other.

"Momma took the day off," Paul replied as he grabbed a seat at the bar. "She told me to let dad cook for me today." Paul gave Frank a slight, sarcastic smile. "Hi dad."

Everyone at the bar broke out in laughter. It was always entertaining to the few there at one o'clock on Saturday to listen to the sarcastic verbal exchanges between Paul and Frank. Of course, it was all in good fun since the two truly liked each other and admired their dedication to serving the nation in the military.

"Well, I see the gang's all here," Paul said as he took a sip of the water already waiting for him before he had mounted his bar stool. He sat in the same place every Saturday and needed neither a menu nor suggestions. Frank usually had his order placed before Paul arrived knowing how punctual he was. "Tom how's your wife? Is she out of the hospital yet?"

"Yeah, Paul. She was released on Tuesday. I was goin' to stay home with her today but she said that if she had to spend another minute with me she might have to use that ole twelve gauge on me." Tom, a six foot three inch tall homebuilder, took a sip of his beer.

"Well, from what I hear, she would've done it," Paul replied with a grin. "Hey Pete, are you going to put my truck out of its misery or repair it?" Pete was the owner of Pete's Auto Repair and Salvage in Dahlonega and was the only person Paul allowed to work on his truck.

"Paul, the best thing you can do for that truck is have a funeral, let me crush it and cut it into little ashtrays for Frank."

"No thanks," Frank said as he came out from the kitchen with Paul's meal. "I've seen that thing and rode in it. Those ashtrays would give a bad reputation to the, how do you say it, décor of the bar."

"Hey, don't knock my poor truck," Paul said attempting to hold a straight face.

"We hear it knock every Saturday at one o'clock," Frank replied as laughter filled the bar again.

Paul's attention had now officially shifted. Placed in front of him was his idea of culinary paradise. The hamburger was one pound of ground beef cooked so as to keep the juices on the inside. Under the bun were lettuce, fresh tomato and red onion. Mustard and ketchup added to the flavor. Next to the sandwich were piping hot freshly made fries. Paul never wasted time digging into his Saturday lunch. He eagerly lifted the sandwich and took a bite. Juice flowed from the meat and down the side of his mouth. Perfect, he thought.

Conversation continued while Paul finished his lunch when suddenly he felt a tap on his shoulder. He turned to see who it was and smiled.

"Why am I not surprised to find you here," the gorgeous woman said. "Like clockwork, Paul Atkinson is on his favorite barstool."

"Dianne," Paul said with a look that spoke for the beauty of this young woman standing beside him. "How are you? I didn't know you were going to be in town. Have you seen your parents yet?"

Dianne seated herself on the stool next to Paul. "No, mom and dad don't know that I'm here. I kind of wanted to surprise them. I'm going to church with them tomorrow."

Paul thought briefly that Dianne might be his way out going to church with Charlie and Anne. He quickly shunned the thought knowing how much his going meant to the couple. He nodded at Dianne and replied, "Well, I guess there'll be four of us."

"You're going Paul?" Dianne's smile was illuminating. "That's great!" In addition to her striking beauty, Dianne was a devout Christian having been raised by her parents in a Southern Baptist church. She had always been the daughter every couple would want, studious, athletic, and always courteous to others. She was the valedictorian of her high school graduating class and the top female runner on the cross-country team finishing fifth individually in the state finals. Dianne stood at five feet six inches tall with that familiar build that female runners have. Her brown eyes seemed to be accented by her medium length straight blonde hair. She had clear, light skin that seemed as smooth and soft as a baby's. She needed no make-up with her natural beauty. Paul, a man who had sworn off any relationships, recognized the inner and outer beauty of this woman and always enjoyed her company, as rare as it was. With Paul's insistence on remaining a bachelor, and the fact that everyone in the county seemed to know it, he and Dianne had developed a deep friendship. Over time, though, Paul's brick wall of denial had eroded and he found himself more and more attracted to the gorgeous, intelligent daughter of some of the kindest people on earth.

With a reluctant shrug, Paul told Dianne that he was indeed attending church with her parents. The two continued their conversation with Paul prompting Dianne to do most of the talking. The chemistry between the two was obvious, and the regulars at the bar left them to their conversation. Many in the small community had whispered their desires to see Paul and Dianne wed.

The glaring summer sun illuminated the darkened barroom as the door suddenly opened. Three men walked in and up to the bar. No one had seen these strangers before, but Frank did his best to make them feel welcome.

"Good afternoon gentlemen. Glad to have some new faces in here. Mold's beginnin' to grow on these folks." Frank approached the left side of the bar where they were sitting. "What can I get for you?"

"Two pitchers of draft and three shots of Jack," one of the strangers replied.

"Alright gents, I'll have it right up." Charlie began setting the three strangers up with drinks, while trying to engage them in some friendly conversation. The strangers, however, showed no interest in talking to anyone in the bar. No one had ever seen these men in the bar before, but Charlie did his best to make them feel welcome. Unfortunately, the three men had other intentions. "Do you need menus," Charlie finally asked.

"Nah man, we look hungry to you," a second one answered.

Frank gave him a quick hard stare. "I wouldn't know partner. Maybe momma didn't breast feed you this mornin'."

Paul was now zeroed in on the conversation, concerned that trouble was just about to begin. Frank was an incredibly kind and generous person, but he had a flashpoint temper when the right buttons were pushed. It appeared at least one of those buttons had just been pushed. Paul pushed his plate forward and leaned back in his barstool.

"Hey man, who you think you talkin' to, cracker?" The tension was growing as the three strangers were now standing.

"That's it," Frank replied. "Get out. There's no way I'm servin' you."

"Oh, that's where you're wrong." The third one was now speaking up. "You goin' to serve us whatever we want, cracker."

Frank was now yelling in an octave he had never before experienced. "Get out before I throw you out."

One of the strangers turned and smiled at his cohorts, one gold front tooth showing. He bowed his head slightly and nodded before looking back at Frank. "You, old man, you goin' to throw us out?" The young stranger pulled out a pistol and laid it on the bar.

Suddenly, there was a tap on the shoulder of the stranger with the gold tooth. He quickly turned to see who it was. "No, I'm going to throw you out," Paul said as he delivered a choking punch to his gut. The gold-toothed stranger went to his knees immediately while the two others attempted to grab Paul, but before they could make a move Paul landed a high kick to one's jaw. The bones shattered on impact. To the other stranger, Paul delivered an uppercut that knocked him unconscious. In just a matter of seconds all three strangers were laying on the floor, one out cold, another with a broken jaw, the third feeling like he may never eat again.

Paul picked up the stranger with the gold tooth. He was coughing and heaving, barely able to breathe. "Are your friends carrying any weapons?" The stranger shook his head. "Well, you know, safety first. Tom, search the other two." Tom did as he was told, but found no weapons. Paul looked angrily into the stranger's eyes. "Now I'm going to give you a chance to leave, that is, unless you want me to finish the job. Pick up your sleeping friend and get out of here." The young man tried to reach for his gun but Paul reached over and pounded the stranger's hand onto the bar with his fist. "Leave the pistol right where it is." Paul began to walk away but turned and said, "And don't ever let me catch you in here again."

Two of the strangers picked up the now groggy third and stumbled toward the door. As the door opened, Frank couldn't resist the chance. "Thank-you for visiting Frank's, and have a nice day." The shock of the event turned to laughter. Frank could always be counted on to lighten any situation. He walked to the door and got a look at the car driven by the strangers as well as the tag number. After they were gone, Frank took the pistol back to his office and called a friend on the police force in Dahlonega. He gave him the details of what happened and asked the officer to come by and keep an eye on the place in case the thugs decided to go for round two. He gave his friend the tag number of the car to have it checked.

Paul walked back to his spot at the bar and sat back down next to Dianne, sitting motionless at the bar staring coldly and silently ahead. He seemed to have what appeared to be a dejected look on his face. Meanwhile, everyone around the bar was hailing his lightning fast fighting skills. Hearing these types of accolades bothered him.

"What's wrong, Paul?" Dianne leaned over and placed a hand on Paul's right arm.

He turned and looked into her beautiful eyes. "Let's get out of here."

"Alright, where to?"

"Home," Paul replied with a look of longing in his eyes that would make one think he had been away for years.

Dianne smiled and said, "Fine. Let's go."

The two got up from their seats, and Paul left the cash for his meal on the bar. "Have a good one, Frank."

Frank recognizing something in Paul's voice replied, "Uh, yeah, okay Paul. We'll see you next Saturday, right?"

"Right," Paul replied as he attempted to muster a smile. He turned and followed Dianne to the door.

Dianne, driving a royal blue 2005 GMC Envoy followed Paul who was in his limping Chevy truck. Ten minutes after exiting Frank's, the two vehicles pulled into the driveway of Paul's house. Dianne switched off the Envoy and got out while Paul remained in his truck with the engine still running.

"What's wrong," Dianne asked Paul as she approached his vehicle. "Why are you still sitting in your truck?"

Paul looked straight ahead through the front windshield. "Get in. I want to show you something." Dianne said nothing, but walked to the opposite side of the truck and got in. It was a bit of a task finding room for her feet with what appeared to be twenty or more Gatorade bottles on the floorboard of the vehicle.

Paul drove the truck along the makeshift road that Charlie had cut with a backhoe for easier access to parts of the farm. Reaching the cattle gate, Paul got out and opened it allowing access into the pasture and onto the trail made by the tractor. He got back in the truck, pulled forward, got out and secured the gate. He drove through a flat area on the path, then up a steep hill. Reaching his desired destination, Paul turned the truck 180 degrees leaving it facing downhill. He shifted the gears into park and switched off the ignition. He was surprised when it didn't sputter and cough after being switched off.

Paul sat silent for a moment, staring through his windshield out into the beauty of the land below. A quiet minute passed before he finally spoke up. "Look!" Paul said, pointing down the steep pasture toward the homes below. "Do you see your parents' house?" Dianne felt the need to simply listen. "They have a beautiful home, and they deserve it. I really care for both of them very much and would do anything for them. I've never been very good at loving people, but it's hard not to love Charlie and Anne." Paul paused for a moment, eyes fixed on the scenery below. "If you look to the right you can see my place. Can you see the back porch? That's my favorite spot – you know, that place where everything seems good." Paul paused for a moment, then glanced at Dianne. "Things didn't feel so good at Frank's today. I came here because this place, my house, your parents – all of this is the way I want life to be."

Dianne finally spoke. "You know something, Paul? My parents care deeply for you, too. You're like a son to them. You've been living here for awhile – surely by now you know how much they…how much so many around here care for you." She reached over and held his hand. "What happened back there at Frank's?"

"A fight – that's what happened." Paul pulled his hand back from Dianne. He knew where she was going with her inquiry.

"I think you know what I mean, Paul. No one blamed you for the fight, as you call it; although, I choose to call it defending the safety of friends. Those men were clearly dangerous. One of them pulled a gun. There's no telling how serious the situation could have been for everyone there had it not been for your good old Saturday feeding frenzy at Frank's. You know, you can show kindness and love to some people and go as far as giving them the shirt off your back, but no matter what, they choose anger, hatred, and violence. Those men certainly appeared to be those types. They could have hurt Frank and others, possibly worse. You stepped in and dealt with the situation. I'm sure those men are licking their wounds somewhere right now questioning their bravado. Paul, when you returned to the bar you had a look that seemed to say you'd been defeated."

Paul turned his gaze onto the beautiful face of Dianne and replied, "In some ways I was beaten in that fight."

Dianne appeared puzzled. "What? What do you mean by that?"

"Did you watch? Didn't you see what happened in there?" Sweat formed on Paul's brow as his heart rate increased. He began ringing his hands nervously. "That guy – me, that guy is just the person I've tried so hard to get away from. I thought he was gone when my orders were cut releasing me from active duty."

Dianne responded in a soft, caring voice. "I know what I saw. Right, wrong or indifferent, we are, at our deepest core, who we are. God formed us individually, and individuals we are. I'm a doctor. You are a man who may have been trained to do just what you did, but what really came out was just who God made you to be. You are a man who believes in right and wrong – you defend right and care for others. That's what I saw in there."

"Dianne, I spent nearly eight years of my life training to kill people like those guys. Our philosophy was that anyone that posed a threat had to die. It seemed like every day of my military life was surrounded by this idea of training, traveling, finding and killing the enemy. Kill, kill, kill – that's all we ever seemed to talk about, the next mission, the previous mission, the number of kills. After a top-secret mission in Russia I decided I had had enough. I couldn't take it anymore. I hung it up and moved here to this place. I guess you could call this place my dreamland. Today at Frank's I felt like I was back in Russia."

"Can you tell me what happened in there?" Dianne was a believer in the government's need to protect important information. She wouldn't dare press Paul to tell her things about his experiences she wasn't supposed to hear.

Paul stared into Dianne's eyes. He wondered if he was falling in love, something he swore he would never do. Months had passed since they first met during a cookout at Charlie's house. The self-sworn bachelor was stunned by her beauty then. The friendship had grown and now he was experiencing emotions he had never allowed before. Nearly a minute passed before Paul finally leaned over and gently kissed Dianne. Her kiss was soft, her lips soft. He wanted to kiss her longer but he pulled back. Dianne smiled in a way that said she approved.

Chapter Two

Covert Operative

"I was in a covert unit based in Quantico, Virginia. After training at a top-secret facility at Fort Bragg, I spent the better part of four years in Quantico, at least on paper. We spent most of our time overseas on missions that you never hear about in the news. We answered only to senior personnel at the Pentagon. All missions were classified top secret. This small covert unit consisted of what the Pentagon considered the nation's most elite soldiers. It's true. There were some awesome fighters in the unit.

"We were placed on full alert one December after our commander was informed that one of our F-16's flying in Russian airspace had gone down in northern Siberia. The pilot had been extricated but the aircraft, somewhat intact, was still on the ground. We were called in for two reasons: to destroy the evidence of any American fighter having been in Russian airspace and to prevent the Russians from capturing the aircraft to study it. People think the Russians have an air defense detection system equal to ours. Not even close – especially in areas of the country like desolate Siberia. It had been two and a half hours since the crash when we got the alert and there was no hint that the Russians had any idea one of our aircraft was on their soil and a successful extrication of the pilot had already occurred. Our flight to the site was relatively quick since we were already in northern Germany training.

"We flew in a stripped C-130 at thirty thousand feet and jumped in HALO to the wreckage. HALO stands for High Altitude, Low Opening. You jump at or around thirty thousand feet, burn in for over three minutes

14

and pop the parachute at less than a thousand feet. We were a team of eleven from every branch of the armed forces, highly trained for just this sort of mission. Our job was to secure a perimeter around the crash site and send in our demolitions expert to destroy what was left of the mangled aircraft.

"So, we hit the ground and proceeded with the mission plan. It went according to training and took very little time. The perimeter was secured in less than ten minutes and within - I think it was twelve minutes the explosives were rigged and ready. The order was given to detonate, and the remains of the plane were destroyed. Those demolitions guys are really good or really crazy. There was almost nothing left of the aircraft. We knew the snow would cover any of the charred remains of the F-16. Mission accomplished. I linked with the team leader to get the coordinates of our pick-up by a Blackhawk helicopter.

"Then one of the team members surprised us all when he approached the team with a man, a woman and two children. I dreaded what was about to come. You see, we were ordered to kill anyone and I mean anyone we found near the site that could confirm the wreckage of the F-16. This looked like an innocent family who had stumbled onto the site after hearing the crash. Why they were just reaching the site is still beyond me. Maybe they had come to the site, witnessed the extrication of the pilot, hid and decided they would return to the site again. I'm not sure. But whatever the case, there they stood with terror written all over their faces.

"Our team leader was a guy named Lowery, but we called him 'Ace'. He was a stickler for the details. I knew he was going to follow the mission plan in dealing with this family. Three team members forced the family toward the site of the crash as they kept their M-16 assault rifles poised on the family. Our Russian interpreter questioned the father asking him what he knew and if he had informed anyone. The children clung to their mother crying, while the father begged the guy, telling him he knew absolutely nothing, that his family lived near. The questioning proceeded but the father continued begging for his family's life. Finally, the Russian begged us to kill him but let his wife and children live. The interpreter relayed the request to Ace but he just said, 'Nope, can't do it. Mission first.'

"I watched this stuff going on and decided I couldn't do it any longer. I wasn't going to continue traveling the world as a trained killer, especially one that would kill an innocent Russian family. I stepped between the interpreter and the family and told them I wasn't going to let it happen. Ace ordered me to back off, but I refused. I told him we were Americans. We were supposed to be representing right. Ace reminded me of the mission orders, and I told him that I had just changed those orders. I wasn't going to let that family die.

"I turned around and told the interpreter to translate what I wanted to say to the father. I told the father that we were under orders to kill his entire family. I asked him if he understood what I said. He nodded. I looked at the two children, two little girls, maybe five and six. They were still clinging to their mother's legs crying. I told the father to calm the children. He tried but with no success. I pulled my knife from its case and pulled up my left sleeve. I told the father to pay close attention. You could tell the interpreter was puzzled. I took the knife and sliced the upper part of my arm. The family watched in shock as if I was completely insane. The team members thought I had gone off the deep end. I handed the knife to the father and told him to do the same to his arm. He was a brave man. He had no hesitation in doing it. If it meant saving his family, this man probably would have sliced up both arms. He finished and started to hand me the knife but I told him to keep it. I ordered him to do the same to his wife and two children, a slice with the knife at the same spot as his and mine. He began crying, begging me not to make him do it. I told him that if he wanted to save his family he would do what I told him to do. One by one, he followed the order, beginning with his wife and finishing with the youngest child. It was hard for me to watch the children scream in pain but I felt this was the only way to save their lives.

"The Russian father handed the knife back over to me. I put it back in its case and rolled up my sleeve again. I showed the family the wound on my arm, still bleeding, and I told them that we all had something in common to remind us of the night when an American soldier put his career, even his freedom on the line for them. I told them that their scars would remind them that they could have been killed and buried in the snow, and I said that the scars would also remind them never to speak to anyone about that night. I warned that compromising this treaty in blood would bring death. Then much to Ace's dislike, I told them to leave and return to their home. The family left the area, one child in the mother's arms and the other in the father's. I still have no idea why Ace let the family leave.

"Most of the team congratulated me on what I did, but not Ace. He swore he was going to have me tried and put in prison for compromising a top-secret military operation. I told him that he couldn't prosecute a flea and that I was done anyway. I was resigning upon our return to Quantico. I knew I'd had enough.

"We flew back to Quantico and Ace kept his promise in trying to have me prosecuted. It didn't work. The Pentagon didn't want any of what had happened to get out into the media. I kept my promise, too. I turned in my resignation. After I pushed someone I knew in the Pentagon, the resignation was finally approved and I got out. One advantage of being a member of an elite unit was access to high level personnel in key positions. The orders for my resignation and release from active duty were cut in less than two weeks. Once everything was final, I loaded my truck and came here. I came here to put those years behind me, to start life fresh.

"That fight today made me feel that those days aren't behind me at all, that I'm that same soldier that nearly took the lives of an innocent family. I don't' need that kind of stuff in my life. I came here to put that part of my life to rest forever."

Dianne slid over on the bench seat and laid her head on Paul's shoulder. "You saved that family, Paul. And what happened today only goes to show that you care for the members of your community, your home. You care for others. And they care for you. In fact, they love you. Your life has started fresh. Those days are over."

Paul was amazed with Dianne's genuine care. There was nothing false about this woman. Despite Paul's insistence on a solitary life, he had impacted the lives of people in the community that he had adopted. Though he would never admit the change, a transformation had quietly taken place within Paul, and his dream of leaving the past in the past seemed to be coming true. Telling Dianne a little about his past seemed therapeutic, seemed like a healing salve and seemed to make the incident at Frank's easier to stomach. Paul gave Dianne a quick kiss, smiled, started his truck and began driving down the steep hill. After getting through the gate and securing it, he surprised Dianne by driving to Charlie and Anne's house. "Work with me on this," he said with a cunning smile.

"What are you up to," Dianne asked, knowing a good laugh was in store.

"When we get on the back porch, wait outside while I go in." Paul, clearly cheered up after his time with Dianne, rubbed his hands together. "This'll be fun." Dianne did as she was asked and waited on the porch while Paul walked inside. He always had an open-door invitation into the Taylor home. Charlie was sitting in his favorite recliner watching a post game interview of the long time manager of the Braves who had just managed the team to a two to one victory over the New York Mets. Paul circled around the recliner and took a seat on the couch. He had a serious expression on his face.

"Well, hello Paul. What's goin' on this afternoon with you?" Charlie was bewildered by the expression on Paul's face.

"Charlie," Paul began with a tone that expressed concern, "do you allow stragglers on your property, especially those that are lost and hungry?"

"He's lost?"

"She's lost," Paul replied.

"She? She? Well, we can't let her starve. I mean, there's no tellin' why she ended up here, but I sure don't want her to go hungry." Charlie, Paul thought, was falling for this hook, line and sinker. "Did she tell you where she's from or how she got here?"

"Well Charlie," Paul continued, "it was kind of hard getting anything out of her, but she finally said she's from Atlanta."

Charlie was extremely intelligent and was beginning to smell a rat. "Is that right? Wonder if she knows Dianne?"

Paul vigorously shook his head in response. "Seriously doubt it, Charlie."

"Well then," Charlie said, ready to launch his counterattack on the prank, "if she's from Atlanta and doesn't know my little angel, I don't think I can have her in my home or on my property. You better ask her to leave."

"Oh, oh, maybe she does know Dianne. You know what they say: 'It's a small world'."

"Paul, son, I was pullin' better pranks than this when you were in diapers. How about tellin' my daughter to come inside?" Charlie tried to maintain a straight face as Paul stood and walked toward the front door.

Paul mumbled as he left the living room. "Can't beat him in chess, can't beat him fishing, he has better jokes than me. I don't get it." When Paul was out of the room a smile broke out on Charlie's face along with a laugh.

Paul dejectedly opened the door and ushered Dianne inside from the porch. She laughed when his expression told her that he failed to pull off the prank.

"Better luck next time," she said. "You know you're dealing with a pro don't you?"

"I do now," Paul replied as he put his arm around Dianne and led her to the living room.

Charlie was always elated to see his daughter, especially when he didn't expect the visit. The two embraced in that unmistakable father and daughter way that reminds one that this man would go to his grave protecting his little angel. He invited her to take a seat on the couch and catch him up on everything. Dianne asked about her mother, and Charlie told her that Anne was shopping but would return soon.

"Well, I'm going to get out of here," Paul politely interrupted.

"Don't rush off," Charlie said. "Stay for dinner."

"No thanks, Charlie. I think I'll save some space for the Sunday feast. You want me to check on the cattle?" This was less of a question and more of a request.

"Sure, son, if you feel up to it, but we'd sure love for you to stay." Charlie loved Paul's company and always wanted him to feel welcome.

"No, no thanks. I've got some stuff in the fridge I need to eat before it turns into some evil creature." Paul cooked very little. He felt little need to with a Whole Foods just a few miles from where he worked. He could purchase all the food he wanted there without ever having to heat up a stove.

Paul began to leave the room for the door. "Hey Paul," Charlie said, "next week I'll spend some time teachin' you the finer points of pullin' off a good joke." Paul had no response. How could he? He simply shook his head, smiled and left for his house.

Chapter Three

A Sermon

Nature's orchestra ushered the following Sunday morning in again, and Paul was up before dawn as usual. Glass of fresh orange juice in hand, he sat on his back porch relaxing before sunrise attempting to wipe the dread of going to church out of his mind. He did so by reminding himself that Dianne was going to be there. His time with Dianne the day before had meant so much to him. He had no idea that he could allow himself to develop such affections for her. Of course, with Dianne it was not that difficult. He hoped that Dianne was planning on spending the day there before driving back to Atlanta.

A few hours passed, and Paul began to get ready for church. He owned no suits, only a single pair of light brown slacks and a blue button down shirt. No tie. He never felt a need for dressy clothing since he had moved to Lumpkin County after his military career. It took little time for him to dress for church – shower, shave, dress and out the door for the Taylor's. He was arriving a little early, but his stomach was growling and Paul knew that Anne would have something waiting for him to eat.

Paul walked into the Taylor's and found Charlie in his recliner watching the morning news and sipping on a cup of hot coffee. "Good morning, Charlie."

"Well, good morning, Paul. You're lookin' sharp this mornin'. Had any breakfast?" Charlie sat up in his recliner ready to get up and walk with him to the kitchen.

"No, Charlie, actually I haven't," Paul replied.

"Well, let's go in and eat," Charlie said as he stood. "I think Anne's already made somethin' for us anyway."

The two went to the kitchen and had one of Anne's famous breakfasts. The Taylor home was immaculate yet simple and unpretentious. With the guiding hand of Dianne, the home was constructed with all of the comforts. She knew that her parents had been hesitant to build anything and that they were content on staying in the original house where Paul now lived. Charlie and Anne wanted to keep things simple so they could leave everything they had to Dianne. She wouldn't have it. Dianne wanted her parents to have a beautiful home with all of the modern conveniences that the other house didn't have.

Paul especially liked the kitchen. It was perfectly designed with cedar cabinets and tile floor. It had a center island with a stove, even an indoor grill and an extra sink. As much as Anne enjoyed cooking, the kitchen of the house seemed to have her name on it when it was constructed. Paul's favorite spot in the kitchen was a built-in breakfast nook that had a sort of picnic table that sat in front of large bay windows facing the back of their beautiful property. Any meal eaten at that table was enhanced by the view.

Paul and Charlie enjoyed their meal and even more than the meal the conversation. Paul was intrigued with Charlie. Charlie was a youthful sixty-seven with the sharpest mind Paul had ever been around. His insight was amazing while his unique brand of humility was alluring. Though not formally educated beyond high school, Charlie possessed the intelligence, even the knowledge that rivaled those who had spent years in a formal educational setting. He was the most giving person Paul had ever met. He was reminded of the failed prank the day before. Paul remembered that Charlie was ready to feed the phantom straggler without hesitation. Paul realized that few people possessed the true care for others like the Taylors. Charlie's sense of humor was utterly undeniable. When Paul was with Charlie he always felt that things were right in the world. He wondered if anything could ever upset this living picture of peace and contentment. Then he thought, yes. God forbid anyone ever try to hurt his daughter. Paul feared few people. He knew that as it related to Dianne, he feared Charlie. Not that he would ever harm her, and Charlie knew that; but Paul realized that he feared for any person that would even attempt anything that could bring harm to Dianne. Charlie was a devout Southern Baptist where family is always considered first priority and the father is the head of the family, responsible for the well being of his household. Paul knew that

Charlie had always taken that responsibility seriously, and that he deserved an award for his success. His small family was special.

"You know there's a Braves game today." Charlie said to Paul as he took the last bite of his scrambled eggs.

"No, I didn't know that," Paul replied sensing where the conversation was going.

"Game two of the series against the Mets. The Braves have a young prospect from double A coming up to pitch." Charlie took a final sip of his coffee.

Paul knew that Charlie wanted him to stay after lunch and watch the game, and he knew that he was going to be asked. He wasn't much of a baseball fan, but he was a fan of Charlie. "Well, if you have no objections Charlie, I'll stick around after lunch and watch the game."

"No objections here," Charlie replied with an almost childlike smile.

"But, if I pass out on the couch after Anne's meal, don't blame me."

"Don't worry," Charlie said. "I'll wake you for the seventh inning stretch."

"My two favorite men." Dianne walked into the kitchen dressed and ready for church in a light gray skirt and white blouse that accented her beautiful figure. She gave Charlie a kiss on the cheek and sat down next to Paul.

"Had breakfast yet sweetheart?" Charlie was so happy to have his daughter home.

"I got up early with mom and had a light breakfast," Dianne replied. She looked at Paul who was still trying to recover from seeing her in the outfit, how beautiful she looked. "How are you this morning, Paul?"

"Couldn't be any better," Paul replied. He meant it. He may have been dreading attending church services but he really felt great. He was with a family he loved and who loved him. He lived in what he considered to be paradise. He was far away, he felt, from the life in the military he once lived. Paul felt at least cautious content for the first time in his life. He could only hope that the cautious part of his contentment would someday disappear.

"Well everyone, church starts in thirty minutes," Anne said as she walked into the kitchen, Bible in hand. Anne's beauty defied her age. It was clear where Dianne received her beauty. Exceeding her sixty-five year old beauty was her gracefulness. She possessed all of the qualities of a refined southern woman. Her hospitality was perhaps her greatest trait. She knew no strangers and like her husband Anne had genuine care for others. She truly loved her husband and said many times to Paul that her love for Charlie had never diminished through the years but had grown stronger. She always respected his role as husband and father in the household. "Good morning, Paul. I'm delighted you're coming to church with us this morning."

Paul stood and kissed Anne on the cheek. "Good morning. Thanks for inviting me. I'm looking forward to it."

Charlie cleared his throat and responded with some of his patent sarcasm. "Lookin' forward to what's in that oven over there."

"Oh, Paul, don't listen to the old man over there." Anne replied. "You know that we would love for you to attend with us every weekend."

"I know," Paul said as he took her arm and began leading her out of the kitchen. He glanced over his shoulder toward Charlie and winked.

The Taylor house had a large two-car garage and a second garage for Charlie's bass boat. Charlie owned a 2007 GMC Yukon that had it all. Another purchase urged by Dianne. It was, as the automotive industry likes to say, fully loaded: heated leather seats, a third row seat, a navigation system, XM radio, DVD/Television system, OnStar, traction control system, a 5.3litre V-8 Vortec engine with a fuel management system. Dianne was with Charlie during the entire purchase process reminding him that he had worked too many years not to deserve a vehicle that deep down he knew he would enjoy. Charlie really did want the vehicle. Other than the house, he had never really purchased something extravagant for himself. Anne had encouraged Charlie to splurge a little and to buy a new vehicle. He deserved it. The salesman at the dealership just southwest of Dahlonega asked Charlie to fill out a credit application and nearly choked when Charlie said that it wouldn't be necessary. The sale would be a cash transaction. Needless to say the now fidgety salesman quickly put the application back in his desk and moved on with completing the purchase. Charlie commented to Dianne after all was final: "You think that salesman's wife will get some roses tonight?"

With everyone loaded inside the Yukon, Charlie drove to the church. Spring River Baptist Church was situated in a small valley six miles north of the Taylor property. The Taylors had been members of Spring River since moving onto the land they now owned. The congregation was somewhat small – nearly 150 active members. It was a very traditional Southern Baptist church – Sunday school, deacons, choir, and Wednesday night meals. It had everything that would be expected in a rural Baptist church. The pastor, however, Dr. Matthew Rodgers was not perceived at first as typical of a rural Baptist church. He was a highly trained minister who had come to Spring River Baptist Church from a six thousand-member congregation in Nashville, Tennessee where he had served as associate pastor. It was easy for people in the congregation to question why a pastor living in a large city like Nashville serving a congregation numbering into the thousands and certainly earning a much higher income than any pastor at Spring River ever had would come to rural North Georgia to head up a tiny congregation and take a huge cut in pay. Rumors were numerous when he first arrived. He quickly dispelled all rumors on his second Sunday leading the church when he explained his reasons.

Dr. Rodgers, in a sermon format using scripture as his background, explained how he had such a zest for his calling after graduating seminary. He had one desire and one desire only: to preach the gospel for the rest of his life. He wanted to share with others the hope he found through his faith in Christ. After seminary he set out to do just that. He began by pastoring a small church in Corryton, Tennessee where he was warmly welcomed and accepted. With Dr. Rodgers as pastor of the small church near the base of House Mountain, the struggling congregation grew from twenty-five active members to nearly two hundred in less than three years. During his time as pastor he worked on and earned a doctorate in theology. Dr. Rodgers went on to tell his current congregation that he had had every intention of staying at that church in East Tennessee his entire preaching career. He felt alive, vibrant. He felt like his passion was being fulfilled. He said, however, that while in his office one day, he received a call from the senior pastor of a very large congregation in Nashville. The pastor from Nashville phoned Dr. Rodgers to congratulate him on the growth of his church. He had heard about the success from a fellow pastor in Knoxville. Dr. Rodgers appreciated the compliment but told the congregation at Spring River that he knew that there was another reason for the call.

Dr. Rodgers went on to explain that he was offered the position of associate pastor at that very large church in Nashville. He said at first he refused to accept the offer but after considering the fact that he and his wife were expecting their first child and that the income they currently had was barely enough on which to survive, he accepted the position. He said that he and his wife packed their belongings and headed for Nashville leaving the church in Corryton in the hands of the senior deacon until a new pastor could be found.

The pastor said that the first few years at the large church were exhilarating. Activity was constant. Dealing with such a large congregation was a daunting experience. He told of how nervous he was on that first Sunday when he was asked to preach. With a beautiful baby boy having been born, he said it was nice to have an income that allowed him to provide some of the finer things for his wife and child. He thought all was well. He was convinced that he had made the right choice in moving to Nashville.

But, Dr. Rodgers explained, after the newness wore off he realized that there was something missing. He felt disconnected from the congregation. He never wanted to feel that way when he ventured out of seminary to pastor a church. He had a congregation, he said, but he didn't. It lacked the closeness of leading a congregation like the one back in Corryton. He was also becoming disgusted with the politics of a large church. He became concerned that money and growth were becoming more important than ministry. He finally reached a point where he realized that the large congregation might be good for some but not for him. He worried about telling his wife of his desire to resign, how she would respond but was happily and gratefully surprised when she told him that she had been unhappy for some time and that she longed for the days of living in Corryton. So, he said, he resigned, began looking for another church and was finally led to Spring River Baptist Church where he, his wife and their little boy were elated to be. That was all the explanation the small congregation needed to hear, and they accepted Dr. Rodgers with open arms.

Six years later he was still pastor and the congregation was proud to have him. He had made a huge impact on not just the congregation but also the entire community of northern Lumpkin County. Paul had visited the church several times with the Taylors and was pleasantly surprised with what he experienced. He expected one of those fire and brimstone sermons often heard in small, rural churches, but Dr. Rodgers' style was refreshing. His style was calm but not boring. His sermons were educated and challenging. He didn't, however, compromise scripture with his style. Dr. Rodgers had his own style of fire and brimstone, and he could deliver his sermons in a way that would challenge a person to always keep a look in the mirror and to never forget the face staring back. Paul was impressed with Dr. Rodgers despite his disdain for organized religion.

The Taylors sat in the same pew every Sunday. This particular Sunday was no different. They were mainstays of the congregation and had humbly donated much of their time and money to the church. On Dr. Rodgers' first Christmas, Charlie appeared at the Rodgers' residence and gave the family $500, knowing they were on a limited income. The pastor and his wife were amazed at the generosity, but Charlie swore them to secrecy.

Sunday school having finished, the sanctuary opened for services. Following hymns and the offering, Dr. Rodgers delivered his sermon.

"Good morning, friends and visitors. I'm glad each of you could be here this morning. You'll notice in your bulletin that no information was provided concerning the sermon I will be delivering today. There's good reason for that, which I think you will learn during the sermon. What I will preach today is not a popular sermon, a feel good sermon. No, it's a sermon of warning. It's a sermon to remind us of the times we are now in and the days ahead that we are facing. So, let's begin by reading from the scriptures, II Timothy, the third chapter, beginning with verse one.

"The scripture says, 'This know also, that in the last days perilous times shall come. For men shall be lovers of their own selves, covetous, boasters, proud, blasphemers, disobedient to parents, unthankful, unholy, without natural affection, trucebreakers, false accusers, incontinent, fierce, despisers of those that are good, traitors, heady, high-minded, lovers of pleasures more than lovers of God; having a form of godliness, but denying the power thereof: from such turn away.'

"Now, I'm not a genius but that sure sounds like a place I know. That sure sounds like a place that once held the love of God in the highest regard. That sure sounds like a place where at one time the centerpiece of town square was the church and not the courthouse. That sure sounds like a place that believed the union of man and woman in holy matrimony, and the growth of a family was vitally important to survival. Yes, those verses sure do sound like a place I know."

Paul listened intently to the sermon. Dr. Rodgers had struck a nerve, so much so that the palms of Paul's hands began to sweat as he listened.

"I think we all know where this place is. We should. We live in it. Stop and look at those verses for a moment and tell me if you can find even one from that list that our nation is not guilty of. Hence, the perilous times that the Apostle Paul mentioned in the first verse. Can anyone in this church today deny that these are perilous times? I think you would have to be in a coma not to see the rampant turmoil that plagues this nation today. Why?

"It goes back to the idea of foundations. A house without a foundation will eventually fall given the right conditions like a strong storm. I could bring Tom up here to confirm that. This nation was founded upon a solid foundation – a belief in God in the person of Jesus Christ. Faith in God was paramount to the early growth of our country. If you don't believe me, read many of the documents written by our early leaders. In them you will find clear expressions of faith in God. Did I say a higher power? Did I say Buddha? Did I say Allah? No, I said God. Not a generic god but God in holy trinity.

"Nearly all of our nation's early settlers were people of faith. They came to this land to worship, to worship freely. We talk about freedom of religion and have completely misinterpreted what our forefathers had in mind. They didn't envision a melting pot of many religions at all. Look at the Middle East and tell me if you think that religious diversity has worked. How many millions upon millions have been killed over thousands of years due to varying religions living in the same region? Am I saying that I'm intolerant of other religions? Not intolerant, but realistic. My desire is to convert the Muslim, to convert the Buddhist, not to shun them. Yet, I realize that mankind has been unsuccessful at living peacefully for any significant length of time when there are differing religions.

"But, back to our soil. Why is there such denial in our nation as to the design of our foundation? We are indeed a Christian nation, first and foremost. Or, at least, we were; for now there is an eroding away of our foundation. Liberalism has reached such a fanatical frenzy as to encourage gay rights activists to invade a church during a service and throw fliers everywhere and chant for their rights. I don't know about you, but for me that's where free speech goes too far. Gay rights. Can you find that in that list from the scriptures? You can if you look hard enough.

"Who's most guilty for a gay rights movement that would grow to a point where activists would invade a church and spew their point of view by throwing papers everywhere? You may be surprised with the answer. The church is the guilty party. There are, as we all know, congregations out there claiming Christ and the Holy Scriptures yet accepting homosexuality as permissible behavior in their congregations and even in the pulpits. I would love the opportunity to ask a minister from one of those denominations if the pages in the scriptures concerning homosexuality and its consequences were missing from his Bible. If a homosexual came to our service at this church would I expect this congregation to receive this person with compassion and Godly love? Yes. Would I compromise the Word of God to appease this person? Never! My desire, as with the differing religions, is that this person be converted, and conversion for this person signifies an end to the gay lifestyle that has invaded our nation and eroded our foundation.

"It's not, however, only homosexuality eroding away our nation's foundation. We are a nation of greed. Can you find that anywhere in the list? Of course! When we have a burdensome tax system that encourages debt and puts families onto the streets while billions are spent in places thousands of miles from our border - that smells of greed. This nation has reached a pinnacle of greed with corporate executives caught up in scandals that defraud investors of their life savings while politicians are caught up in taking bribes. I'm glad I'm pastor of a church that leads the way in generosity in this part of our community. I've experienced that generosity first hand.

"We've lost our sense of community. Prisons are going to have to install revolving doors. Did you know that this state has one of the largest prison populations in the nation? Who's to blame for this? Can you find at least one from the list that tells us why this is happening? Sure you can if you look hard enough. I'm not saying that many, many men and women serving time in prison don't deserve to be there; but I am saying that there are countless others that don't.

"We wonder why our teenagers act the way they do today. Turn on a television and I think you'll find out why. There seems to be no standards for conduct any longer for television material and our children are being exposed to this. Now you may say that you have strict control in your household, but what happens when you let your teenage daughter sleep over at a friend's house? Immorality is so rampant in this country that I'm afraid to watch a football game. I'm afraid of what my little boy might see on a commercial. Since when did being conservative become such a wrong, backward way of thinking?

"So, where do we stand as Christians in a nation facing perilous times? While the foundation of a once great nation crumbles and a nation descends into obscurity, where is our place? Do we even have a place any longer? Is this a doom and gloom forecast? Not for us who can be found in Jesus Christ having been cleansed of our sins by his blood and reconciled by his faith. We do have a place. Jesus said that we are to be lights on a hill. Our churches are to truly become sanctuaries. Many in this nation are searching for answers. Who can give it to them? The government? The television? The financial adviser? The answers can be found in only one place: God's Word. And, it's our responsibility to carry this spiritual torch God has given us that can bring this nation back from the brink. I pray this morning that each one of us will show ourselves worthy of our calling.

"The Christian church has become passive and of little effect in a society that is being overrun by immorality and greed. When Jesus ran the greedy moneychangers out of the temple, was he passive? No! Did he try to coax them out of the temple with meekness and gentleness? No! He carried a whip and he turned over tables, screaming at the greedy men telling them that they were staining the temple with their greed, that they had turned the temple into a den of thieves. We can no longer stand by and remain passive. Christianity is all about stepping into the light and shining. We need to light those candles within us." Dr. Rodgers paused and stared from the pulpit as the somewhat stunned congregation. He closed his Bible and finally spoke. "Let's pray."

It was one of Dr. Rodgers' shortest sermons but to the congregation it packed a powerful punch. He had never delivered that type of sermon. Paul was affected by it. He was basically a "live and let live" kind of person, but something inside him wouldn't let him escape the fact the nation was indeed in perilous times. The sermon shook his idea that things were just the way they were supposed to be. After the sermon, he agreed that life in the United States wasn't the way our forefathers had dreamed. Paul cared nothing for the gay rights movement. He wasn't gay, and he couldn't understand how anyone could be. If a man or woman chose homosexuality, he or she had the right to do so. But, he did agree with the sermon about the idea of free speech going too far. He suddenly had a vision in his head of armed guards posted at the entrances of these churches and the guards blasting away at protesters trying to enter the services to cause havoc. Had the nation actually come to that point? Paul, despite not being a professing Christian, questioned how a person who believed in the Bible and claimed to be a Christian could just gloss over parts of the scriptures in order to preserve a certain lifestyle. Paul's way of thinking on the topic was that if you were going to preach and accept every word of the Bible then homosexuality had to be considered unacceptable behavior. Paul had decided years before that he would never do anything halfway. He viewed a practicing homosexual Christian who refused to try to change as going about religion halfway. This was Paul's first time in a church service where a sermon left such a mark on him. It provoked consideration and debate from within.

"You sure are in deep thought," Dianne said as she nudged Paul. "What's going on in that brain?"

"I turn my brain off on the weekend." Paul smiled at Dianne as the two headed for the exit. "I don't reboot it until Monday morning at five."

"Let's go outside while mom and dad talk to Dr. Rodgers. I want to ask you something." Hand in hand, the two walked out to the front of the church.

"We're at a church," Paul said ready to deliver another of his sarcastic comments. "Don't let the atmosphere affect the type of question you want to ask me."

"Oh, Paul," Dianne responded with the quick wit of her father. "You figured it out. What do you think mom and dad are talking to the pastor about? We're going ahead with the wedding ceremony in fifteen minutes. They're getting rice from the pantry in the basement."

"Easy, easy." Paul was nearly completely sure she was joking.

Dianne grabbed Paul's other hand and held it. "Paul, everyone in Lumpkin County knows that you are the eternal bachelor."

"Hermit I think better describes it."

Dianne gave Paul one of her soft kisses that made the knees of the former Army Ranger weak. "I want to invite you to come to my place next Saturday for the night. Spend the night, and on Sunday we'll surprise my parents with a trip to Lake Lanier for the day."

Paul saw his Saturday routine going up in flames. It was a constant in his life and the highlight of his week. "Dianne, what do you think your father would say to this? I love the man and never want to disappoint him. Besides, you're a Christian. How do you think this would look to members of this congregation?"

"First of all, Paul, I've already told dad that I was going to ask you down for one night. He trusts me and he trusts you. I have a guestroom in my condo where you will sleep. Secondly, I was raised partially by this congregation. They trust me as well. I only want you to come down so that we can spend an evening seeing some sights. You've spent no time in Atlanta since arriving. You've never seen Atlantic Station. It's a great place. I can get some tickets to the Georgia Aquarium and I'll get to buy you dinner at the Oceanaire."

"I don't know, Dianne," Paul responded still looking for a good reason why he should turn down the invitation of the most beautiful woman in the world. "You know, I ride on Saturdays. Then at one I'm at Frank's."

Dianne was persistent. "Do those things. Just bike a little harder and eat a little faster. Please, Paul. It would make me so happy."

There went the final nail. She just had to pull that line, Paul thought. How could he say no now? "Alright, we'll figure out all the details this afternoon."

A mischievous smile appeared on Dianne's face. "There's a bonus."

Paul turned and looked at Dianne wondering what could possibly be coming next. "What?"

"Dad's giving you the Yukon to drive for the weekend."

Paul stopped abruptly. "What?"

"That's right," Dianne replied. "He's worried about you driving your truck down that far. He's afraid you might break down."

Paul, not accustomed to such care and generosity, a consummate loner, tried to squeeze out of this one, too. "No, no, no. I can't take your dad's truck. I can't do that."

"Paul," Dianne replied, "you know that it will break dad's heart if you don't accept his offer. I've told you that he loves you like a son and wants to do things for you."

"Well, you did it again," Paul said as he sarcastically clutched his chest.

"What are you talking about?"

"Never mind. I wonder when your parents are coming out."

Dianne pointed at the front entrance. "There they are."

"That was some sermon," Charlie said as he and Anne approached the two now standing by the Yukon. "Here, Paul. You drive. I want to sit in back and talk to Dianne about the sermon on the way home." He tossed Paul the keys. Paul said nothing, but simply unlocked the doors for everyone, got in and drove to the Taylor farm.

The rest of the afternoon went as planned. Lunch by Anne was as superb as ever. Charlie enjoyed having Paul watch the ballgame with him. Paul's mind, however, was distracted by the sermon he had heard earlier in the day. He might have had some bad experiences during his military career, but he always thought America was a great nation. Dr. Rodgers seemed to be saying that the days of America's greatness were over. Charlie interrupted his thoughts.

"You know Paul, I read a book a few years ago that described the fall of major empires throughout history."

Paul stared at Charlie for a silent moment. "Charlie, are you psychic?"

Charlie leaned forward in his recliner. "Son, it wasn't hard to figure out what you were thinkin'. How could any sane person with a conscience listen to that sermon, however brief it was, and not be affected?"

"You know, Charlie, you're right. Honestly, I've never been to church and been affected like that by a sermon."

Charlie leaned back in his recliner. "Well, do you agree with what Dr. Rodgers said?"

"It's hard not to. He wasn't preaching fiction or theory. He was preaching fact." Paul got up from the couch and walked to the fireplace.

"Then you might find this historical fact interestin'. You know that sayin', 'there's nothin' new under the sun'?" Paul nodded as he took down a photograph of Dianne from the mantle. "Well that originated in the Bible. The history book I'm referrin' to was given to me by a kid who was takin' a college class in military history. It maps out the rise and fall of some of history's greatest world empires. The book says that certain signals are always found in the fall of these empires. It says these signals are found throughout history and the patterns are always the same. The signals are high taxation of the citizens, an overextended military force, a weakened economy and rampant immorality. Sounds a little like home, don't you think?"

Paul lifted his stare from Dianne's photograph and looked at Charlie without speaking. Had he served eight years of his life to see his country collapse? Rome, he thought, one of the greatest empires in history had been reduced to a tourist attraction after ruling the world two thousand years earlier. Paul put the photograph back on the mantle and sat back down on the couch. "What inning are we in?"

"The sixth," Charlie replied. "The Braves are goin' to need a comeback. They're down three to one."

Paul had no sooner gotten comfortable again when Dianne walked in and informed the two men that she was leaving for Atlanta. She said that she had a very early Monday morning shift at the hospital and needed her rest. Paul offered to help her with her bag as the two walked out to her Envoy. Paul placed the bag in the back seat and closed the door. He was feeling emotions that he had never experienced and didn't want Dianne to go. He turned and stared into Dianne's eyes. Neither said a word. The two embraced in a long, sensual kiss. When it was over Paul knew that he had fallen in love.

Dianne flashed Paul one of her patent smiles. "Can't wait to see you Saturday."

"We never got to make the plans. I don't even know where you live." Paul was actually trying to keep Dianne there longer.

"Mom's got all the details and dad will show you how to use the navigation system in the Yukon. I better go. I'll see you Saturday." Dianne got in and started the Envoy. She gave Paul another smile and drove away.

Paul went back inside and informed Charlie that he wouldn't be able to stay for the remainder of the game. He needed to ride for about an hour. Charlie knew the reason why. He realized that Paul was falling in love with his daughter, and he also knew that these unfamiliar feelings were confusing the young man who had sworn off relationships. The ride would do him a great deal of good. It would ease the pain of separation and the conflicting thoughts. Paul had always promised himself that he would remain single, saying he had no interest in the complications that come with relationships. Yet, in a matter of twenty-four hours he had gone from a man with a mild affection for Dianne to the beginnings of falling in love with her. Charlie understood this all too well. He had fallen in love with Anne the same way. He had no intentions of doing so but before he could actually realize what was happening, he had fallen deeply in love with her. From the first day, Charlie couldn't imagine life without Anne. Paul was bound to be feeling the same way. Charlie only wished that mountain bikes had been available to him in the early days of his relationship with Anne.

Paul quickly changed and retrieved his bike before filling a water bottle. The temperature that day was a hot and humid ninety-three degrees. He would need to stay hydrated. Deciding he would follow his usual route, Paul started the ride at a relative mild speed, but five miles into the ride his speed increased. Paul leaned forward on the bike coming off the seat and pedaled harder than he had ever pedaled on the course. On downhill slopes during the ride he even managed to pass a few cars taking a Sunday drive. His weekend had been extremely unorthodox from his usual routine. He needed the ride to clear his head and to get Dianne off his mind, if only for a moment. He reached the halfway point in his fastest time since riding the course. This time, instead of stopping for Gatorade he turned around and immediately began the ride back. He had so many questions going through his head. He asked himself if he was making a mistake going to Dianne's. He wasn't sure if Dianne felt the same for him as he did for her. Could he handle a serious relationship? After all, he was very independent, not accustomed to the strains that sometimes come with relationships. Paul pedaled harder in an attempt to put all of the questions out of his mind. In record time, Paul arrived at his home. Mission accomplished. The ride helped. He decided to spend the rest of the afternoon and evening on the couch. After such a weekend, he thought, he deserved to do just that.

Chapter Four

A Weekend in Atlanta

The workweek had passed and Saturday had arrived. As usual, Paul followed his typical Saturday routine. Dianne had plagued his thoughts the entire week. He was excited and anxious to see her despite the fact that he had no interest at all in spending time in Atlanta. Having disposed of another hamburger at Frank's, he was back at his place packing a bag.

"Well, you look as though you're just about ready." Charlie had walked in the house through the back door. The hinges on the back door alerted Paul to Charlie's arrival. The door made an awful sound that could wake the dead when it was opened, and Paul still hadn't gotten around to repairing it.

"Yes sir. I've never spent any time in Atlanta. This will be interesting." Paul zipped closed the bag that carried the small amount of clothing he was taking.

"You'll be fine," Charlie replied. "At least the traffic won't be as bad on a Saturday."

"Relative to what," Paul retorted. "Tokyo's bikes? I despise Atlanta's traffic."

After Charlie finished laughing about the "Tokyo's bikes" comment he handed Paul the keys to the Yukon. "It's already full of gas and is in excellent health. I had it checked at the dealership this week. When you get ready I'll show you how to activate the navigation system. A six year old could do it. The directions along with a map from Mapquest are already on the front seat just in case you have problems with the navigation system. Oh, and Anne made you a couple sandwiches for the ride down." Paul slowly looked up at Charlie with a grin that he couldn't hide. Charlie laughed. "I know Atlanta's not that far, but she doesn't want you gettin' hungry on the way. You never know. You might end up in some Tokyo style gridlock." Paul dropped the shoe he was trying to put on and started laughing. Once Charlie joined in, the laughing had become uncontrollable, tears streaming out of their eyes. They truly loved each other like a father and a son. With personalities that were so similar any stranger meeting the two of them would automatically think that they were, indeed, father and son.

Moments later Paul was en route to Atlanta and Dianne's condominium located in Buckhead. He had a chance to reflect on some things on the way, things like how far away he had come from the soldier who had traveled the world with his covert unit performing missions under the orders of Pentagon senior personnel, missions that often meant assassinating certain key people who were threats to American security. He felt that that man was fading away, and he was glad to see that chapter closing. As he drove he thought about the changes that had come in his life. Moving to northern Lumpkin County, Georgia signaled a turning point in his life. Without even realizing it, the move to Dahlonega had changed him. He admitted to himself that finding the house on the Taylor's property was the key catalyst in the metamorphosis that was taking place in him emotionally and psychologically. Charlie, Anne, and Dianne had had a profound impact on his life. He felt good about himself for choosing the area years before he actually arrived and settled. He thought that if there was a God then certainly he must have led him to where he currently lived and to the people in his life. He thought about those people, so many more than he had ever become acquainted with during his life as a soldier. He never dreamed that he would develop so many friendships, real, meaningful friendships. He asked himself if life could get any better.

The Yukon's navigation system accurately led him right to the condominium where Dianne lived on the fifteenth floor. Paul parked the GMC in the building's garage and walked into the lobby. Dianne was waiting for him. He was surprised. The two embraced, and Paul asked her how long she had been waiting.

"Not long – about five minutes. You are Paul Atkinson. The world can set its clocks by you." Dianne led Paul to the elevator. "I'm so glad you're here."

Dianne pressed fifteen on the elevator panel and the door closed. This was a modern high-rise condominium in Buckhead that had been completed for three years. It had all of the modern conveniences of living in a large city along with great security. Charlie had insisted on excellent security when Dianne began searching for a place to live in Atlanta. He purchased the condo for his little angel after coming down with her and looking at it. He personally preferred being on the ground, but Dianne told him that she really liked the condominium, and he wanted to make her happy. She had been such an incredible daughter, and she was following her dream of being a doctor and succeeding at doing so.

"You know something, Dianne?" Paul said as turned to her and took her in his arms. "Last Sunday I really didn't want to do this for many reasons – fear mainly. I've been single so long; I never wanted a relationship. But, I'm glad I came, if for no other reason than it tells me that I'm growing, that I'm no longer the man I used to be. I've left him behind. You, your parents, so many others in the community who have received me with open arms – all of you make me feel so alive for the first time in my life. I feel like I've been reborn."

"The man you are today," Dianne replied, "is the man you've always been. That man just needed help coming out. You are special – special to me, to my parents, to so many who have come in contact with you." Paul looked into Dianne's eyes and at her incredible smile. The two stood holding each other on the elevator with the door open at the fifteenth floor. Suddenly, the elevator door closed while they were engaged in a kiss, and Dianne quickly tried to press the open door button but to no avail. The elevator began going back down. It reached the lobby, and the door opened again. The security guard at the front desk turned and gazed at Paul and Dianne with a look of bewilderment. He had just seen these two. Paul and Dianne gave a quick wave and a smile that attempted to convey to him that they meant to come back down. It didn't work. The door closed and the guard shook his head before going back to the sports section of his newspaper. With the door closed and the elevator climbing again to the fifteenth floor Paul and Dianne spent most of the ride laughing.

The two finally got into Dianne's condominium. It was small but plush with all of the modern conveniences. The view was incredible. The condo faced downtown Atlanta and from that height the city skyline was clearly visible. Dianne had a Maltese puppy she had named Wilson. The snow-white purebred dog was purchased from a breeder in Jasper, a town north of metro Atlanta. The tiny puppy was undeniably cute. When Dianne entered the condo he ran to her and began trying to leap into the air begging her to pick him up. She did so and he greeted her by incessantly licking her face. Dianne introduced Wilson to Paul. The puppy knew no strangers and as Paul held him he was greeted with the same licking of the face from the excited little dog.

"How long have you had him?" Paul asked while holding and petting Wilson.

"About two months," Dianne replied. "The breeder in Jasper said he had to be weaned before I could pick him up."

"What do you do when you're out of town?" Wilson was licking Paul's face as he was talking.

"Oh, they have someone here that checks in on tenants' pets if someone's out of town." Dianne went to the kitchen and opened the fridge. "I know how much you like your bottled water and Gatorade, so which will it be?"

Paul placed the Maltese back down on the floor. "Thanks for thinking of me. A Gatorade would be fine. You know I go to Frank's every week – a rural bar with tons of booze there, but I've never wanted to drink. I got drunk once. It was after airborne school. It was at a blood wing party."

Dianne walked into the living room from the kitchen and handed Paul the Gatorade. "What's a blood wing party," she inquired as the two sat down on a sofa.

"Well, tradition says that you're not really airborne qualified until someone blood wings you. You take off your shirt. The airborne wings you receive at graduation have two pointy prongs on the back that allows them to be pinned onto a uniform. The person that blood wings you sterilizes the prongs with a lighter first and lets them cool. Then he holds them up to your bare chest with one hand and with the other hand pounds the wings into your chest. The prongs break the skin easily and the wings stick to your chest." Dianne was now cringing in disbelief. "The night I got blood winged was at a retired colonel's home. He had done four tours in Vietnam. A friend from college lived in Columbus near Fort Benning and informed the colonel that I was graduating. Anyhow, the colonel insisted on throwing me a blood wing party. It was a big party, too. The colonel didn't throw small ones. I was so drunk when the colonel blood winged me I walked around with those wings in my chest for at least an hour. That was the first and last time I ever got drunk."

Dianne was, at first, speechless. "You soldiers are a fraternity of psychos."

"All kidding aside, I think to be in that fraternity you have to be willing to be a little crazy, to take risks that the average person would never take. When you jump out of an aircraft that's thirty thousand feet in the air and you've got to wear oxygen because of the altitude that you're jumping at, and you can't pull your parachute until you're less than a thousand feet from solid ground, you need just a touch of insanity to do it. It defies all logic why anyone would do that, but I've done it more than a few times."

Dianne reached over and held Paul's hand. "Guess what? You're not that guy anymore. There's not an ounce of insanity in you. There never has been. You had to live a life that was dangerous, but you live another life now." Another kiss and growing confirmation for Paul that he was in love with Dianne, but should he tell her. It was difficult for him, but she needed to know. He wanted everything out in the open at all times in their relationship. He didn't want to hold anything back from her.

"Dianne, I have to tell you something. If I don't say it now, I may never say it." A pause. "Dianne, I swore that I would never let it happen to me. I never wanted to get involved in a relationship. I thought all relationships were complicated. Now, I'm not sure of anything I've ever assumed about relationships. I mean it looks like I've been wrong all along and just never realized it. Maybe I'm just a loner and used all that as an excuse to -"

"Paul, I'm deeply in love with you."

Paul let out a short laugh. "I guess I was rambling. Dianne, I'm in love with you, too." Dianne led Paul out onto her patio where the two held each other and stared at the Atlanta skyline.

The remainder of the afternoon and evening had been well planned by Dianne. She was a very meticulous woman. The first stop was Atlantic Station, a successful Atlanta development that consisted of various restaurants, stores, town homes and other businesses. There was an ice cream shop she wanted to take Paul at Atlantic Station. After ice cream, the couple drove the short distance to the Georgia Aquarium. Paul was impressed with the immensity of the place and the variety of fish and other animals. After the aquarium, the two took a walk in Centennial Olympic Park and into the CNN Center. Paul, despite living in Georgia both as a soldier and now a civilian, had never actually developed any interest in seeing Atlanta, but now he was impressed. He could never live in the city, but he was impressed with its beauty as well as the incredible variety of activities that seemed to be a constant. Following the CNN Center, it was on to the Oceanaire Restaurant in Midtown. It's paradise for the seafood lover, especially the one that enjoys raw oysters from all over the world. The two sampled a variety of oysters before moving on to the main course. After the meal, Paul and Dianne walked outside to enjoy the warm, summer air.

"There's one more place I want to take you," Dianne said as the two retrieved the Yukon from the valet. "We'll have to have to take a small detour on the way."

She had Paul's curiosity aroused. "No problem. Just tell me where you want me to go."

Dianne directed Paul to take Peachtree Road, and just past the Fox she showed him where to turn left onto Ponce de Leon Avenue. They drove another mile and she had him turn left into a McDonalds. She asked him to pull up to the drive-thru. Paul had grown increasingly curious as the ride progressed but now his curiosity was off the charts. He drove the Yukon up to the drive thru speaker and following the customary McDonalds greeting Dianne ordered forty cheeseburgers. The girl taking the order had to ask her to repeat her order twice. It wasn't every day that someone ordered forty cheeseburgers at one time. Needless to say they had to park the Yukon and wait fifteen minutes for the order.

"Alright, I can't handle it any longer. What's going on?"

"Be patient Paul," Dianne replied. "You'll know very soon."

"What? Is this one of those things you don't know about a woman until you fall in love with her? Let me guess. You get the late night munchies and just have to have a cheeseburger – or, maybe it's forty cheeseburgers."

Dianne laughed. Her laugh was so beautiful to Paul. Everything about her was beautiful. "Paul, you're hilarious. No, I don't get the cheeseburger munchies late at night. You'll find out in a few minutes. I work with a nurse. Her name is Gail. I hang out with Gail and her husband often. They're Christians on very solid ground and I really enjoy being with them. Anyhow, they took me to where I'm taking you tonight."

The order was finally brought to the vehicle and the two drove back onto Ponce de Leon headed toward Peachtree Street. This time, however, Dianne had Paul turn left onto a small street and right onto North Avenue. They crossed Peachtree and the Interstate 75/85 downtown connector just past the world famous Varsity and followed a route that took them barely onto the Georgia Tech campus. Dianne directed Paul to turn left on one street, another left after a quarter mile and to keep straight until she told him to stop. Upon reaching the intended destination she told him to park on the street in front of a building. Paul looked at the name on the building: The Atlanta Union Mission, a well-known homeless shelter and recovery program in the Atlanta area.

"Gail and her husband brought me here several months ago when it was still cold outside. We brought cheeseburgers and some faith to these desperate men. I've been coming with them once a week since that first night."

Paul stared into Dianne's eyes. "How much more are you going to do to show me just how incredible you are?"

"Paul," she replied, "I get more out of this than these guys do. You'll see - they can be a bit vicious when we hand out the burgers, but invariably one or two of them will show genuine gratitude and spend some time allowing you to minister to them."

The two got out of the Yukon and carried the cheeseburgers around to the gate that led into an asphalt courtyard. A man was passed out on the sidewalk right outside the gate. Paul picked him up and carried him inside to the courtyard. He sat him down by the building and leaned him up against the wall. It wasn't difficult for the men that were in the courtyard waiting to get in the shelter for a night to figure out that the casually dressed man and woman came bearing gifts. A crowd formed around Dianne. Hungry men started pushing and shoving trying to be the first to get a cheeseburger. One bumped Dianne.

"Hold it!" Paul shouted and everything came to a screeching halt. "You want to eat, then form a line and act like human beings. There's plenty to go around."

The group of men did exactly as told. Dianne was amazed. It appeared that Paul had a gift for dealing with the men. The cheeseburgers were handed out in an orderly fashion and most of the group dispersed. Just as Dianne said, a few hung around to talk and to show some gratitude for the meal.

Paul was engaged in conversation with a man by the name of Thomas. He seemed intelligent and, to Paul, didn't seem to belong at a homeless shelter. Thomas explained to Paul that he was an Army veteran and had reached the rank of staff sergeant. He was married with two daughters. While in the Army he worked on his bachelor's degree in business administration and needed only three more semesters to graduate when everything stopped after he was sent to Iraq. He said he wasn't prepared to see some of horrors of war that came with the job and admitted that when he returned from the war he wasn't able to cope. He sunk into depression and started drinking. His wife tried to help but no matter how hard she tried nothing seemed to work. He went on to say that he had attempted suicide twice. He sunk to an all-time low after his wife left with the children. The drinking finally led him to the streets and to the Atlanta Union Mission.

"Do you want to die this way?" Paul's question was direct and to the point.

"No," Thomas replied.

"Then why not the VA Hospital? There's one not that far from here."

"I've tried to get into the program they have there, but there's always a wait. I've tried three times in the last six months."

Paul said, "So, you're really willing to go through that program and stick with it?"

"Yes," Thomas replied, "if I could only get in."

"Dianne, do you have your cell phone on you?" Paul led Thomas over to Dianne who was talking to another man.

"Sure, Paul," she replied. "Here it is."

Paul took the phone, dialed a number and pressed the call button on the phone. A short moment passed before his call was answered. "James, Paul Atkinson, how are you? Good. I'm great. You know, a mountain man now. Listen, I have a favor to ask. I have a soldier that needs to get off the streets. He's tried to get in the recovery program at the hospital three times but has been told every time that there's a wait. I want him in there tonight. Can you make the call? Great! One hour? He'll be there. Hey, semper fi you sick Marine." Paul handed the cell phone back to Dianne who was now suddenly speechless. "Alright Thomas," Paul said. "If you're as serious as you said you were then get your things and come with us." Thomas paused as he stared at Paul. Who was this man? When he came to his senses he rushed over to a fence where he grabbed a small bag that contained a few meager belongings and rushed right back over to Paul.

Dianne walked over to Paul and put her arm around him. "What about you?" Paul gave her a puzzled look. "How much more are you going to do to show me how incredible you are? For a hermit, you sure do seem to have a few connections."

"The fraternity. Remember? And Thomas is a part of that fraternity." Paul put his arm around Dianne. "Can we make one more stop – the VA?"

She flashed her patent smile. "Absolutely!"

On the way to the VA Hospital Dianne spent some time sharing her faith with Thomas. Paul listened and was amazed by the genuine love in her way of talking to Thomas. She certainly didn't come off as someone looking down on another. She talked to him as an equal. She shared her faith in a way that was inviting. It was not overbearing. It was masterful the way she talked to him. A stranger walking up on the conversation would have thought these were neighbors or co-workers having a casual chat. She was really good at taking the person, this one being Thomas, out of the mindset of failure and making that person feel human, to feel like someone. Thomas smelled badly from being on the streets. His clothes were dirty. He wasn't clean-shaven. Yet, suddenly he was feeling like a person of worth. The two strangers with cheeseburgers were about to change his life.

"Alright, we're here." Paul was really beginning to like the GPS system in the Yukon. They parked the GMC and walked into the facility. Paul was able to find out how everything had to proceed. First, Thomas was going to be admitted through the emergency room. The following day, assuming his health checked out, he would immediately go into the recovery program. This would be a great opportunity for Thomas to restart his life. The program even allowed the people in it to work at the hospital. It also had a housing program. Thomas couldn't believe what was happening to him. He felt good about life for the first time in years.

"Thomas, it's up to you now," Paul said as he shook the veteran's hand.

"Man, I can't believe this," Thomas replied. "There is a God after all, isn't there?"

Paul took a glance over at Dianne and back at Thomas. "Yes Thomas. There is a God. Take care of yourself."

"God bless you Thomas. Never forget that He is always with you." Dianne hugged Thomas.

Thomas now had tears flowing from his eyes. "God bless you both."

Paul and Dianne made their way out of the hospital and back to the Yukon. Paul glanced at Dianne and noticed tears flowing from her eyes. He stopped and looked at her. "I told you I get more out of this than those guys do." When she said this Paul pulled her close to him and kissed her. "Well, what do you think of the weekend thus far," Dianne asked as she continued to hold Paul.

"Incredible. I'm really glad I thought of it." Both laughed as Paul opened Dianne's door.

"Are you sure someone didn't clone you from my father?"

Paul looked up into the now dark sky. "You never know. Sometimes I feel like I was poured out of a test tube."

Dianne grabbed both of Paul's hands. "Well, it appears they got it right."

Paul and Dianne spent the rest of the evening and night on her sofa watching movies. She fell asleep during the second movie. Paul switched off the television and stood up from the sofa, walked into her bedroom and pulled down the comforter. He came back to the sofa and picked up Dianne and carried her to her bed. She had already changed into the clothes she slept in – a pair of cotton sweat pants and an Emory University t-shirt. Paul pulled the comforter up. He leaned over and kissed her on the forehead. "Thank-you for one of the best days of my life."

Paul went to the guest room and for the first time in his life he knelt by his bed. "God, I have never really known if you're there. I think I believe you are now. If I'm right, then I want to thank-you for everything that is happening in my life right now. I've never been this happy. I will try to learn more about you. Amen."

Morning for Dianne came very early in the condominium. Paul woke her up at seven-thirty. "Wake up and lets get ready to go."

"Paul, what's going on? It's still very early." Dianne usually slept in on Sundays when she was in Atlanta.

"I want to go to church with your parents and we have to get ready to go. We should have plenty of time to get there." Paul pulled the comforter back and off of Dianne.

Dianne sat up in her bed. "Did I hear that right? You actually want to go to church with mom and dad without anyone asking you to go?"

"What? Are you that surprised?"

Dianne nearly jumped out of her bed. "Uh, yes! To say the least, I'm surprised. Alright, let me get ready." She could not believe that Paul had developed a desire to go to church, to actually go without being asked. This was going to be quite a day for her parents, a day that was sure to make them very happy. They had wanted Paul to come to faith in God since meeting him. Thirty minutes later Paul was in the Yukon and Dianne was in her Envoy and on the way to Lumpkin County. One hour and forty-five minutes later, the couple pulled into Charlie and Anne's driveway. They got out and went in surprising Charlie who was reading the newspaper. He was worried that something might have gone wrong.

"Good morning, dad," said Dianne as she leaned over and kissed Charlie on the cheek.

"Well, good mornin'. I'm surprised to see the two of you."

"Paul woke up early this morning and told me he wanted to go to church." Dianne turned and looked at Paul who was standing in front of the fireplace.

A smile filled Charlie's face as he stood up from his recliner and walked over to Paul. The two said nothing. On cue, they embraced each other. Charlie had wanted this day to come since meeting Paul. He didn't know what had happened in Atlanta to bring this on but whatever it was, he was grateful. Anne walked in from the kitchen and learned of Paul's desire. She walked over to Paul and gently kissed him on the cheek. "Paul," she said, "now that you've made this choice, I encourage you to give God an opportunity to reveal himself in his way to you. If you're patient, he will." Paul responded by hugging Anne.

Church came and went. Paul was amazed that suddenly he seemed to absorb more than he had before. His faith in God was growing it seemed with each new experience. As planned, Paul and Dianne treated Anne and Charlie to a day on Lake Lanier. They didn't spend much time on the water due to the excessive heat. It was difficult for Anne to be in those types of conditions for extended lengths of time. After an hour and a half on the water, they loaded the boat back on the trailer and headed for dinner at Longhorn Steakhouse. Paul usually didn't eat red meat two days in a row, but he simply couldn't resist the prime rib. All four spent that time together growing in their love for each other, as if it wasn't already full. Charlie and Anne were elated to see Paul and Dianne together. It was a dream come true. Most parents would want their daughter to marry someone else with a little better career path. Paul earned twelve dollars an hour in a warehouse. Charlie and Anne cared nothing about where Paul worked. They knew his character and hoped he would become a permanent part of their lives. Of course, he had never shared with anyone that during his four years in the covert unit, he spent absolutely nothing out of nearly all of his earnings. He wasn't wealthy especially when considering that including the land Charlie was worth millions. Paul, however, since his pay was much higher than others with the same rank due to being in the covert unit, had put away a larger amount of money. He had kept it in a CD and never touched it. It was enough to build a very large home and pay cash. He never saw the need to touch the money, however; in his mind, he was living very comfortably.

"Well, I'm stuffed," Charlie said as he patted his stomach. "Paul you might have to get that bike out for a midnight ride. I watched how much you ate."

"I think I will," Paul replied. "Don't you have one of those little red wagons in the barn? I think we'll hook it to the back of the bike and take you along."

"Sounds like fun. You'll be doin' all the pedalin'"

Dianne leaned over to her mother and whispered. "Here they go. Full stomachs and a valiant attempt to see who's most sarcastic."

"Charlie, I already had that figured out. Pedal fifteen miles out, get off the bike and make you pedal back. And, if you refuse? Well, I guess we would have to sleep with the crickets." Paul wiped his mouth.

There was a short pause before Charlie responded. "Who wants ice cream?" The two men shared in a laugh.

Dianne leaned back over to her mother. "Score Paul one, dad zero."

"Don't worry, we have the ride home," Anne replied.

Getting back to the Taylor property had always been a pleasure for Paul. He loved the place. That night, however, getting there brought on a feeling of dread. Dianne would be returning to Atlanta. Another early shift awaited her on Monday. He had never felt such an ache in his heart. He longed to be with Dianne. The friendship had quickly grown into deep affection. When he garnered control of his emotions, he realized that he must grasp that the relationship had to take its own course. He couldn't push it. Doing that would only bring him heartache. Not that Dianne would ever hurt him, but he knew that the harder he pushed the more he would be disappointed. There were aspects of this relationship that were completely out of his control. Pushing those aspects would be futile and emotionally exhausting. Charlie had the new house built in such a way that would allow easy access to all three garages. The driveway was built to allow him to back the boat trailer right into its space without having to unhook it. He had become extremely proficient at backing the boat into the garage. Paul had seen him do it numerous times and each time grew more amazing. It was done with the accuracy of a professional over the road truck driver.

Dianne could only stay a few minutes before needing to leave. It was already past eight o'clock and the nearly two-hour drive would put her back at her condo just before ten. There was still some light, so she wouldn't have to drive the winding mountain roads in the dark. She escorted her parents inside and told them when she would return. Paul waited outside. He needed a moment to gather his thoughts before having to tell the woman he was in love with that he would see her in a week. He paced around by her Envoy trying to figure out how in just a matter of hours he had become so weak. What had become of the independent, self-sufficient bachelor? Love, he thought. If he had to choose, now that he was in its clutches, he would choose love with all of its aches.

Dianne walked up from the house to where Paul was now standing. He had walked over to a fence that bordered one of the pastures. "Well, I have to go," she said trying to hold back her own emotions.

"I know," Paul replied as he looked out at the pasture. "Why didn't you tell me that love was this painful?"

"Because, I've never been in love either." Dianne reached out and took Paul's hand.

Paul turned from the fence and looked at her. "You've never been in love?"

"No. I thought I was once, about nine years ago." Paul released Dianne's hand and knelt to the ground, finding a pecan on the grass below the huge tree it had fallen from. "Now, I've met you. Now I know what falling in love means. Yes Paul, tonight it is painful, but that pain is even a sign of the love that is there. The pain will fade because we know we will spend time together soon. We have to hold onto those thoughts and not the pain of separation. We are not worlds apart. We are not far from each other at all. You have your job, and I have mine. Your paying job is important, but the main job God has given you – I think you know where I'm going with this – your job is to be the son to my parents that they never had. I'm amazed at the similarities between you and dad. Don't you see God in that? They need you. If you left this property it would leave such a void that I don't think my parents could handle it – especially my father. I'm their daughter and I couldn't imagine life without them. I want them to be happy. You are the man I've fallen in love with. You make me very happy by being here for them. Is that selfish of me?"

Paul stood and hugged Dianne. "Absolutely not, Dianne. One of the many things I love about you is your care for your parents. You would do anything for them. Guess what? I would, too. I used to get squeamish at the idea of anyone thinking of me as a son. I don't get that way with your parents. I love them very much and never want to be away from them or you. Each of you has changed my life. I'll never be the same." Paul paused and appeared to be in deep thought. "I'm going to do it. I'm getting a phone in the house."

"You already have one." Dianne backed away from Paul and grinned.

"What? No I don't."

"Yes you do. Dad had the line turned on last week." Paul appeared bewildered. "Paul, my father never misses anything. He knows we are in love with each other. He hid the phone in one of the closets."

"That man never ceases to amaze me. They don't really make fathers like that, do they?"

Dianne kissed Paul. "They did with my father. I have to go. I'll see you next weekend. I'm coming up Friday evening with Wilson and spending the entire weekend."

A smile returned to Paul's face. "I like that idea. Maybe I can turn you on to one of Frank's famous hamburgers."

"I don't think so. I've seen you eat one and it was a nauseating site to behold." Dianne hit the auto start button on her Envoy remote. The GMC fired right up. Paul thought after seeing all the fun components of the Yukon that perhaps he needed to catch up with the times. The two embraced and kissed one last time. "Guess what Paul? I'll call you when I get home to let you know that I got back alright." Dianne opened the driver's door and got in.

"Don't worry. Your dad's getting a bear hug after you leave."

"I love you Paul Atkinson." Dianne had no real desire to leave, but knew she must. Paul needed to say something to get her to laugh.

"I love you Dianne Taylor. I'll wait for your call right by my new modern phone system. You see, my previous system consisted of a very long string and two Styrofoam cups. The sound quality wasn't that good, but it sure was cheap." Dianne was looking out of her front windshield as he was talking. He wondered if it worked. She turned and looked at him with her gorgeous smile.

"Do you and my father ever stop?"

"We can't," Paul replied. "It's an illness." He walked over to her and the two kissed again. "Be very careful going home. Crazies like me are biking on that road."

Dianne drove away. The pain in his gut wasn't as bad as he thought it would be. Dianne was so intelligent. She knew all the right things to say to ease his pain. Paul went in to see Charlie and Anne. The two of them were in the kitchen pouring a glass of iced tea. They didn't hear Paul come in so he just stood and observed them. They were clearly best friends with a love for each other that couldn't be put into words that would appropriately describe their deep affection. Their way of communicating with one another was the stuff of marriage therapy textbooks. Charlie and Anne had taken Paul under their wing. They had invited him into their lives and accepted him as if he was their own son. They were gracious, intelligent, witty, giving, spiritually sound people. Paul decided to go in and talk to them.

"I'll bet that tea tastes great," Paul said as he walked into the kitchen.

"Well," replied Anne, "let me pour you a glass so you can find out."

Charlie placed a hand on Paul's shoulder. "Son, you've had a long day. You must be exhausted."

Anne handed Paul the glass of tea. "No, not really. I'm going to stay up and wait for Dianne's call. A certain someone had the phone turned on."

Charlie looked over at Anne who was grinning. "Well, I was goin' to tell you about that. I know that you and Dianne are gettin' closer. I just thought it might help you while she's out of town. We wait for her call at six o'clock in the evenin' every day while she's gone. I was goin' to tell you. I know how you've not wanted one." Charlie was rambling.

"Charlie, thank-you. I appreciate you both – everything you have done for me. Do you know that?" Anne put her arm around Paul. He felt the need to share his feelings for their daughter, despite the fact that they already knew. "I think you know I love Dianne very much. I can't imagine having to go a week without hearing her voice. Thank-you very much for the phone. When Dianne told me that you had the lines turned back on after I told her I was going to get a phone, I was, as I am often with you two, overwhelmed. I'm very grateful for you both. It's going to be great to have a real phone. The Styrofoam cup and string thing just wasn't working anymore. Do you know how hard it is to stretch a string from Lumpkin County to Atlanta?"

Charlie laughed and shook his head while he wiped tears from his eyes. Anne turned and faced Paul. She put her right hand on his jaw. "We love you. You have become a special part of our lives and have meant so much to us. You do so much for us and bring so much joy to this home – we want to do things for you."

"Thank-you both." Paul drank down the last of his tea.

"You know when I was in the Marines we used to use those styro cups and strings to communicate between foxholes." It was Charlie's turn.

"How did it work out for you guys," Paul replied waiting to see what Charlie would come up with this time.

"Not so good, Paul. The enemy kept shootin' the string and breaking our line of communication. Get it? Line of communication?" Anne rolled her eyes and grabbed the container of tea to put back in the refrigerator.

"I heard how primitive you Marines were. You should have asked one of us in the Army for a radio. We had radios."

Charlie walked over to the sink with his glass and turned on the faucet. "We didn't need to ask for a radio. We just took it from one of those boys in the Army. The soldier always ran back to his unit cryin'."

Paul had no response for that one. Score Charlie one, Paul one for the day. "Well, on that note, I think I'll head over to the house."

"Paul, if you'll look in the utility closet, I think you'll find a phone," said Charlie.

"Thank-you again. I look forward to hearing Dianne's voice." Paul walked out of the kitchen and outside toward his house. He walked to his house and went inside to the utility closet. There it was, a box in a plastic bag. Paul rarely went into the utility closet, so he hadn't noticed it. He reached up and pulled the bag from the shelf. The phone was a cordless with a built-in answering machine. He immediately went into his living room and hooked the phone into the phone jack and plugged the base unit into a wall outlet. He looked for the instruction manual that would assist him in setting up the answering machine. He found them and followed the instructions to get to the point where the greeting could be recorded. He hit a button and suddenly a message began playing: "Hello, you've reached Paul's phone. Yes, he finally got a phone. Please leave a message and he'll call you back. God bless." It was Dianne's voice. The beautiful prankster was more like her father than Paul had imagined. Paul decided he would leave it just the way it was.

After getting the telephone set up, Paul decided he would have some orange juice and lift some weights. He wasn't that big on watching television. Despite being in love with Dianne, Paul enjoyed his time alone. He mostly read. Like a dry sponge soaking water, Paul's love of education led him to all types of books. He particularly enjoyed books on psychology and anatomy. His evenings after a day of work consisted of hours of reading. Paul kept notes in files. People always wondered what made Paul Atkinson tick. What did he do in the night hours, this somewhat mysterious anomaly? He carried himself in a way that defied logic in such a chaotic world. Where was all the stress? Where was the anger when someone on Georgia Highway 400 cuts another off in a vehicle? No one ever heard a negative word from his mouth. He was quiet, unassuming but didn't avoid conversation. He wasn't arrogant yet he was incredibly intelligent. Not even Charlie, Anne and Dianne really knew everything about him. He was even more complex than anyone really knew. Dianne had not really reached the depths of the man with whom she had fallen in love.

At 10:15pm Paul's telephone rang for the first time. He was reading from a psychology text and quickly laid it on the coffee table so that he could reach for the phone. "Dianne's residence, how may I help you?"

"Very good, Paul. You're learning. How's it feel to be in the modern age?" Dianne's voice was as beautiful over the phone as it was in person.

"I'm not sure," Paul replied. "I kind of miss the styro phone. How was the trip back?"

"Uneventful, which when driving in Atlanta, is a good thing. How are you?"

Paul sat back on his sofa to enjoy the conversation with Dianne. "I'm better than I thought I would be. I spent a little time with your parents after you left. I'm not telling you anything you don't already know, but the more I'm with them the more incredible they become to me."

Dianne was holding Wilson who was, as usual, licking her face. "My parents are incredible people. They always tell me how God sent me to them, but I mostly think he sent them to me. I couldn't be where I'm at today without them. Please say nothing of what I'm about to tell you to them. When any big decisions are about to be made in the family, we have always had a rule of getting together as a family and praying about it. Like or not Paul Atkinson, you're a part of this family now, so I'm going to tell you what we prayed about last Sunday. The church needs some upgrades and some expansion, but lets be real. Most of the congregation doesn't have a great deal of money. Dad didn't want us to pray about whether we were going to give, but just how much we were going to give. As usual he insisted that everything be done anonymously. We're giving $50,000 to the church for renovation and expansion. The church really needs to grow and it won't in its current condition."

"You Taylors are incredible people," Paul replied.

"Paul, I don't think we're doing anything that God doesn't require of all who believe. If you have, give. God has blessed my family with a great deal of financial success. My parents are two brilliant people. Yes, they worked for many years, but they invested wisely and made the right choices. Most important to all of the success was that they have always been a praying couple. The formula works. Now my family is doing what we must do. The church needs help, and we can be there to do it. I thank God we can be. We're not in Thomas' shoes tonight."

"Dianne, do you realize just how much I love you?"

"Yes Paul, I do. I will love you always. You've changed my life." Wilson barked. "Wilson agrees."

Paul laughed. "Well, I'm glad I have Wilson's blessing."

Dianne yawned signaling to Paul that it was time to let her get some rest. He told her to sleep well and to call whenever she had time. After they hung up the phone, Paul realized that he had an errand to run during the coming workweek.

Chapter Five

Love Grows

Another workweek came and went. Paul's routine had been changed in a good way by the nightly calls from Dianne. He was always excited to receive her calls. Charlie was, as usual, right. Paul and Dianne never had a boring conversation. With his interest in anatomy, Paul was always intrigued by the conversations they had about her job as a physician. Dianne arrived at 9:00pm on Friday with an excited Wilson. She couldn't tell anyone when exactly she would be arriving since she had a strange shift at the hospital. Paul wasn't at his house at the time to receive her call that she was on the way. He was completing his errand. When Dianne arrived, Paul still had not returned. She worried about him – not whether he could take care of himself, but she always worried about the truck he was driving. She wondered when it was going to leave him stranded. She had thought about surprising him with a new truck, but she knew that such a thing would be going too far. Paul was a man and Dianne never wanted to invade the territory of his rights to make certain decisions. Paul had no interest in a new vehicle. He wanted to squeeze every mile of life out of his truck before making another purchase. Dianne would never make him think he was less than a man by purchasing him a new truck without his permission. Nonetheless, she was worried about him. He was always home right after work.

Charlie came out and greeted Dianne when she arrived. He also received the customary greeting Wilson gave to anyone the little puppy met – incessant face licking. Charlie instantly fell in love with the dog. He handed off Wilson to Dianne and grabbed her bags. The two went inside where Anne was completing the late meal the family would be having. Dianne let Wilson down on the floor, and the curious puppy, intrigued with his new surroundings, scampered off to look the place over.

"Hello mom," Dianne said as she embraced her mother. "It's so good to see you."

"We are so glad you're home for an entire weekend. Your father and I want to take you and Paul into Dahlonega tomorrow for lunch at the Smith's House, then a walk on the square. Is that alright with you?"

Dianne grabbed a piece of fresh, raw broccoli from a bowl sitting on the counter of the kitchen island. "It sounds great, mom, but where's Paul tonight? Has anyone heard from him?"

Anne stopped what she was doing. She realized that she hadn't heard from Paul the entire day. He usually enjoyed feeding the cattle on Friday evenings after the workweek was over. "No, as a matter of fact I haven't, and I don't think your father has either."

Dianne had a look of real concern. "This is not like him. You can set your clock by his routine. I hope he's alright. I really wish he would get rid of that truck." Dianne paused, then looked at Anne. "Mom, I'm really worried. He doesn't have a cell phone to call us if he's stranded."

Anne hugged Dianne. "Now don't get worried, Dianne. I'm sure he's fine. Paul could stand in the middle of a tornado and not get hurt."

"Good evening, all." Paul walked into the kitchen startling the two women. "I'm sorry I'm late. I had something to do after work that couldn't wait."

Dianne walked over to him and hugged him. She held onto him. He could feel her concern in the way she held him. "You know, mister independent, a call would have been nice."

Paul kissed Dianne on the cheek. "I know, Dianne, but it was difficult for me to do that. I'll explain it all at dinner." Paul walked over and kissed Anne on the cheek. She was equally relieved to see the usually prompt Paul. "How long before we eat?"

"Oh, about ten more minutes," Anne replied.

"Great. Ladies, I'll be right back." Paul rushed out of the kitchen and the house.

Dianne noticed Paul was acting a little strange. She was becoming legitimately worried about him. The sound of the John Deere tractor cranking up added to her concern.

Charlie walked into the kitchen. "What's goin' on with him tonight? He's as giddy as a schoolboy."

"I'm not sure dad," Dianne replied. "He's acting a little strange."

"Oh, angel, I'm sure it's nothing to worry about." Charlie hugged his daughter.

With the headlights on and the tractor at full throttle, Paul had a large bale of hay on the forks of the tractor headed as fast as the tractor would run to the back pasture where Charlie's cattle waited every Friday for Paul's appearance. He reached the pasture and dropped the large, wheel-shaped bale on the ground. The cows began gathering, happy to receive the hay however late it was. Paul jumped off the tractor, and with a knife, he cut the strings on the bale. He pushed against the bale to loosen up the hay and got back on the tractor. "Sorry guys, can't hang out with you tonight." Paul backed the tractor away from the bale, turned it around and headed back to the barn. He parked the tractor in its stall and returned to the Taylor house. The dinner table was set and ready. Charlie greeted Paul at the door. "I'm sorry for feeding the cattle so late. I had something I needed to do after work today."

"That's alright, son, but that could have waited until mornin'." Charlie was amazed with Paul's insistence on keeping his commitments. He found few people like that anymore. "You ready to eat?"

"I'll tell you Charlie. I am hungry enough to eat your cooking right now." Paul put his arm around Charlie's shoulder.

"Then you must be pretty hungry. Anne normally uses my cooking to kill rats around the barn." The two men shared a laugh as they entered the kitchen. Anne and Dianne were already seated having a conversation.

With everyone seated at the table, the meal began. Charlie did most of the talking. Anne chimed in as well. Paul told Charlie that the cows gave him dirty looks for being late with their evening meal. Dianne, though, didn't speak. She was concerned with Paul's behavior. He just didn't seem himself. Paul recognized her concern and decided it was time to clear everything up.

"I have something I need to say to everyone. Charlie, Anne, I'm going to tell you something that I've only told one other person. That person is Dianne. What I'm about to tell you is classified information. I've been told I'm a part of this family, so I trust my family with what I'm about to say. I've told you both that I was an army ranger, a member of the 75th Rangers and that I was based at Fort Benning. That is true. What isn't true is that Fort Benning was my last duty station. It wasn't. I was selected by the Pentagon to be part of a highly secretive covert special operations unit based out of Quantico in Virginia. I served in that unit during the last four years of my career. We traveled the world performing top-secret missions for the Pentagon. We answered to very high-ranking officers and a few politicians, but few others in the military knew anything about us. I got out of it after four years." Paul paused and stared into Dianne's eyes. She understood that he had difficulty talking about his time in the covert unit. She reached over and held his hand. "I couldn't take it anymore. Some of what we did or we were ordered to do seemed so senseless. After a mission in Russia, I resigned. You all have become a very special part of my life. In fact, I can't imagine my life without you. While I was based in Quantico I managed to save some money. Nearly all four years of that time in my life was spent traveling from one place to another. I had no need to spend money. I decided when I got to Quantico that I would use the money I saved while I was in the Rangers to spend as needed, which was rare. Nearly all of the money from my service in Quantico would go into an account, then into a CD. Because of the type unit we were in, we were paid more than our peers outside the unit. I accumulated quite a savings in four years.

"I hope you don't mind what I'm about to say, but again, I've been told that I'm a part of this family. Dianne told me what you're doing for the church. It's an incredible thing, especially the humility you show by wanting it to remain anonymous. I was late tonight because I have a personal banker with Bank of America that met with me at the branch I use after work. My CD is with them. He had to pull some strings to get some money that I wanted him to get for me. That's why it took so long. Here's a cashier's check for the church. I want to do my part." Paul handed the check to Charlie.

Charlie's hands began trembling as tears flowed from his eyes. "Son," he said in a shaky voice, "this is a check for $5,000."

"I have one real positive thing I can take from my time in that unit. I have nearly a hundred thousand dollars saved. I want to do this for the church. I was a part of something that took lives for four years of my life. Now I want to be a part of something that saves lives. The church needs to grow." Charlie, Anne and Dianne sat silently staring at this mystery man who had swept into their lives bringing with him so much happiness. Now they were witnesses to the transformation that was taking place in him, a transformation from a man who came to Lumpkin County to live a quiet, easy life as a single man into a man that wanted to be a part of a family, a part of a church, a part of a community. Paul looked at Dianne.

"So, I was late. I didn't call. I'm still not getting a cell phone." He looked at everyone. Sudden laughter erupted around the table.

"Paul," Anne said, "God has a way of using certain times in our lives to get us ready for another phase. Thank-you for trusting us enough to share about your time in that unit in Quantico. When you came to live here, you rarely spoke to anyone. You were very isolated. Charlie did everything to reach out to you. The ice broke when he asked you to help him on the farm. You found people like Frank where you like to eat on Saturdays. When you first got here, you would have never gone to Frank's. You began opening up like a flower. When the bloom of a flower is closed it's still attractive, but when it opens up completely, it's magnificent. Your time in Quantico allowed you to save enough money just for this day. Now, out of faith and generosity, you have given to the church. Why? You have opened up completely. You are magnificent – yes, to us, but most importantly to God. We are so proud of you, but there is no one prouder of you than God."

Paul smiled. "Anne, I guess I have changed. I've felt it and have been amazed by it. I believe in God for the first time in my life." What he was about to tell them he hadn't told anyone since getting out of the military. "I lost my parents when I was four years old. They were killed in a car crash just outside of Raleigh, North Carolina, where I was born. My older brother and I wound up in Durham with some very distant relatives but we remained foster children. All was well in the beginning, but after those first few years, something happened to our foster mother. She suddenly became mentally and physically abusive toward my brother and me so much so that my brother ran away and joined the Marines. I stayed. I received an academic scholarship to the Citadel and never returned to my Durham home. In fact, I wouldn't even know if she's alive today. Living in that home is where I decided that the only way for me to live was independently, on my own. Trusting someone else to help me in any way was out of the question. Those conditions became the makings of the perfect candidate for the covert unit I qualified for years later.

"When I met this family, I saw something that I envied. I was even a little jealous. But, slowly with Charlie's promptings, I've allowed myself to be accepted by the family. I had to sit down and look at all of this – at how it transpired. It most definitely sounds like God." Paul turned again and stared at Dianne. "Now, not only do I feel a part of this family, I've fallen in love with the jewel of the family."

"You can be sure Paul that it is all part of God's plan," Charlie said. "Your entire life has God's hand written all over it, despite the fact that you recently came to faith. Life with God is wonderful. It doesn't mean we don't get tested from time to time, but he is always with us through everything good and everything bad."

"I want to say this to you in front of my parents so you know that I am sure of everything I feel." Dianne moved closer to Paul. Her eyes were so clear and beautiful. Her skin was radiant, and her lips were a soft red. Her straight blonde hair hung down barely touching her shoulders. Her beauty, Paul thought, was further evidence of God. "I am completely in love with you. You have brought me happiness, laughter, and a feeling of being protected. My love for you is beyond words."

Paul was moved by what she said. "Dianne, I never thought I would fall in love, but I have with you, and I never dreamed that I would ever find someone like you."

"Well, all we need now is one of them tear jerker movies and this night will finish just right." Charlie's timing was always perfect.

"Charlie, I thought Patton was a tear jerker movie for you?" Paul was ready to lighten things up, too.

"Yes, Paul, you're right. For those of us that served as Marines, a movie like that is a tear jerker, but for the ones in the Army what was it – that's right, The Wizard of Oz."

Dianne looked at her mother. "Here we go."

Anne responded. "Let the boys play. I'm going to get the kitchen cleaned up."

"Charlie," Paul continued, "you would cry too if you were a tin man."

"Why cry? It would take an armor piercing bullet to bring the tin man down."

"No, the tin man's hollow. He doesn't have a heart. The round would go right through the tin man and knock Dorothy right out of her magic slippers." By now, the ladies at the sink were laughing at the comical verbal exchange going on a few feet away. Any stranger might come up on Charlie and Paul and think they were having a serious conversation, insane as the conversation sounded. Anne and Dianne knew that these two loved to see how far they could take their sarcastic tennis matches.

"Who knows," Charlie continued, "the round might knock her over the rainbow. That's a quick way back to Kansas."

"And they think we in the military don't care about getting people home." Paul lifted his glass of tea as if to toast.

Charlie did the same. "Here, here!"

Following dinner, Paul and Dianne took a late night walk. The sky was clear. There was no moon, so the stars were very bright. The star seemed so close to be able to reach up and snatch one out of the sky. The couple talked until one in the morning before Paul escorted Dianne back to her parent's home.

"I think what you're doing for the church is incredible. The church will never be the same again because of what you're doing." She kissed Paul with her soft lips.

"You told me why your family chose to do it. Those that can need to give, especially when there's a need like this. It's what I'm supposed to do, right?" Paul gazed into the sky as if he was looking for an answer in the vast heavens above.

"I can't say it enough. I love you so much Paul."

"Please don't stop saying it," Paul replied.

Dianne kissed him again. "Good night."

"See you in the morning. I understand your parents have a big day planned for us."

"You know mom and dad," Dianne said. "They want us to be very happy and always enjoy ourselves when we're with them."

"I'll see you in the morning," Paul said as he turned and headed for his house.

The weeks that followed were never routine anymore for Paul. He publicly confessed faith in Christ at the church. Two weeks later Charlie asked him to serve on the planning committee that would be in charge of the church renovation and expansion project. The one routine that Paul would never change, though, was his Saturday routine. He still enjoyed nature's symphony, his fresh orange juice, the thirty mile ride on his mountain bike and the ultimate reward that came at one o'clock sharp – a hamburger at Frank's. Frank did notice the difference in Paul. He was really proud of him for coming out of his shell and become a bigger part of things. Frank was particularly proud that Paul and Dianne had become so close. Everyone at Frank's had been hopeful that it would happen.

Paul looked at the changes in his life with a new perspective. He was, as Anne said, opening up, becoming the man God had called him to be. He wasn't passive with his role in the church. He really wanted to help plan the expansion. The other members didn't take him lightly either. When Paul spoke up at meetings everyone listened. He was very humble but assertive.

The relationship between Paul and Dianne grew with each moment they were together and even in the many hours they were apart. They loved each other, they respected each other, neither was selfish. The old phrase "a match made in heaven" seemed extremely appropriate for the two. Paul occasionally went to Atlanta to spend time with Dianne. She came up often with Wilson. Paul volunteered to keep Wilson for a week because Dianne was going to be at Emory for some training then off to the hospital. She wasn't going to be able to spend any time with Wilson, so Paul kept him for her. Wilson was growing fast and becoming more agile so Paul played with him quite a bit in the evenings after work. Wilson particularly liked it when Paul would take him on the tractor back to feed the cows. Paul wouldn't let Wilson run free near the cows for fear of him getting stomped, but he laughed each time Wilson would bark at the cows. Paul and Dianne seemed destined for the altar, and in his mind, life couldn't be any better.

That was until an October afternoon after Paul returned home from work. He noticed Dianne's Envoy parked in her parent's driveway. He stopped his truck and ran into the house to make sure everyone was alright. When he got to the living room where everyone was, the expression on the faces said something was wrong. Charlie was not seated in his recliner. He stood by the fireplace holding a portrait of Dianne and Paul. Anne and Dianne were sitting on the couch. Dianne stood and approached Paul, holding his hand upon reaching him.

"What's going on?" Paul wanted answers fast.

"It's your brother, Paul," Dianne replied. "Mom and dad received a collect call from a correctional institution today. It was your brother. The only number he had to reach you was mom and dad's. He was jailed by a judge in family court for contempt of court."

"Well, contempt of court. Isn't that one of those things where you spend one night in jail and they let you out?" Paul was pacing the floor now.

"No, Paul," Dianne replied. "The judge sentenced your brother to ninety days in jail."

"What!" Paul stopped pacing and threw his hands in the air. "For what?"

"Your brother told dad that he had his daughter for visitation and that the baby got sick. He had to rush her to the emergency room where she was treated. He said the court order required him to contact his ex-wife within four hours of a medical emergency. He told dad that he tried but the only person he could reach was her elderly father. When his daughter was released from the hospital, he continued trying to contact her but to no avail. It was always her father. He was worried that she had relapsed back into drinking, so he took his daughter home with him. It was a technical violation of the court order. Your brother said he was concerned for her safety. His ex-wife's family hired a high dollar attorney and next thing you know the judge was sentencing him to 90 days in jail. He's in jail right now in Dallas, Texas."

"Who is this judge? Mickey Mouse? My brother has had his struggles but he wouldn't lie about something like this. I've got to go there." Paul was pacing again.

Dianne went to him and stopped Paul. "I understand you're angry about this, and I agree that you should go to Dallas, but please don't let this tear your world apart."

"Dianne," Paul replied, "Christopher is it. He's the only link I have to any real family. He's the only link I have to my parents. This is earthshaking for me."

"I want to go with you." Tears were forming in Dianne's eyes.

"No, I think I better handle this alone."

Charlie held up the portrait of Dianne and Paul so that Paul could see it. "No, son, I don't think you should handle this alone."

Paul was stopped dead in his angry tracks with Charlie's wise move. Seeing the portrait immediately brought him back to his senses. He stared at the portrait. He loved it and the woman in it. He couldn't let this situation change any of that. He turned and held Dianne. "Please, come with me. I need you."

"I'll get the tickets purchased," she said.

Paul pulled out his wallet that held his Bank of America card. "Use this."

"Neither of you are paying for those tickets. I have sky miles. We'll use my card." Charlie was more authoritative than usual, but Paul understood that he just wanted to take care of the two of them. He would see to it that everything was paid for. Dianne got on the family's computer and looked up availability on Delta Airlines out of Hartsfield International Airport for the following day. She found a flight to Dallas leaving at 10:15am and arriving at 3:05pm Dallas time and made reservations for a joint suite at the Ritz Carlton in downtown Dallas. Paul asked her to keep the return date open. Dianne took emergency leave from Northside Hospital in order to make the trip with Paul. Paul was outside when she finished with the reservations. Her father had given her his American Express card to complete the reservations and made her keep it for the trip.

"Dad, where's Paul?" Dianne had printed off the boarding passes for the flight and a copy of the reservation at the Ritz and wanted to show them to Paul.

"He went outside, angel," Charlie replied. He stopped Dianne as she was heading for the door. "He's goin' to need you more than ever right now, sweetheart. This is not goin' to be easy for him."

"I know, dad. I won't leave his side."

She left the papers she was carrying on an end table and went outside. A few minutes later she found Paul out by the John Deere. He had turned the lights on in the stall and was checking the oil in the tractor. It was late in October and the temperatures were in the lower thirties. "That's one of the many reasons dad loves you. Who else would check the oil in the farm equipment at night in thirty degree weather?"

"I just want to make sure everything's good before we go. I don't want Charlie to have to do it." Paul knew that the John Deere didn't need to have anything checked on it. The tractor had just been through a major maintenance check-up at the dealer two weeks earlier. He just needed somewhere to go to clear his head and something to do to help him accomplish it.

"I love you Paul Atkinson. Please don't let this situation pull you away. Trust God in this. Everything will work out just the way he wants it to work out."

Paul laid the oil rag on one of the tractor tires. "Let's go to my place." The two, holding hands in the brisk October air, walked to Paul's house. They entered the house through the back door. It no longer had a horrendous noise when being opened. Paul replaced the door a month earlier. The couple went into the living room and sat down on the sofa. Paul gave Dianne a short kiss.

"My brother's a good guy. He's three years older than me. Chris and I didn't have the best of beginnings, but we both picked ourselves up by the bootstraps and kept going. When Chris ran away and eventually joined the Marines his life stabilized at first. He tried to stay in touch with me as much as possible while he was in the service. He even sent me a few dollars every now and then. Most of the time, if I could get to the mailbox in time, I could prevent my foster mother from stealing the money. Anyhow, while he was in the Marines, Chris started drinking. The drinking increased to a point where it was causing him problems in his unit and, of course, with the chain of command. He got out when his enlistment was up to avoid getting thrown out.

"After getting out of the Marines he drifted around quite a bit and finally settled in Lexington, Kentucky where he found work. He got sober going to AA meetings and got promoted at his job. The longer he stayed sober the more his life grew. He was promoted again at his job to senior supervisor in a huge warehouse in Lexington and afterward purchased a house along with a brand new car. He was asked to fly to St. Louis to speak at a big AA convention. Everything was going really well for him.

"Then he met this woman who was a few years younger than him. Her name is Amy. He met Amy at another AA meeting that was across town. Chris had never been to a meeting there but was on that side of town and decided to go. He and Amy were talking outside when several people who were going out for coffee after the meeting invited Chris and Amy to join them. It seemed some of the people there recognized him from the convention in St. Louis. After coffee, Chris invited the woman to go for ice cream. You know how it goes. One thing led to another and next thing I knew I was getting an invitation to his wedding. He wanted me to be his best man but he knew my military commitment could prevent it. And, of course, it did interfere. We were called out on a mission in Africa while his wedding was taking place. He sent me pictures from the wedding and I saw his bride for the first time, an attractive brunette. He called me, and I asked him how long she had been clean. Chris had five years. As it turned out, she had more time clean than him – 8 years. That made me feel a little better.

"As it turned out, the woman Chris married was the daughter of a very rich and powerful attorney in Dallas. Chris wasn't immediately accepted into the family. Chris said the attorney did a background check on him without him even knowing it. Pretty sick and egotistical, isn't it?" Dianne nodded. "Well, after three years together in Lexington, Chris said that they decided to move to Dallas because she was expecting. They wanted their child to grow up around the grandparents. Chris found a job in Dallas before arriving.

"When they got to Dallas the new surroundings really played with Chris' head. It wasn't long before he relapsed. After the baby was born, he stayed sober but he and his wife weren't getting along very well. Amy had a great deal of exposure to her parents, and they were extremely controlling. One evening in a heated argument, Chris walked out and got drunk. She filed for divorce and the war was on. It was an extremely bitter divorce.

She told horrible lies on the stand about him. Fortunately, he didn't lose custody of his child. Unfortunately, he was limited on the amount of time he could spend with his little girl. All of that lead us up to this. It's all insane.

"Why would two sane people ever fight like this over a child they both brought into this world? I just don't get that. Divorce is outrageous."

"You're right, Paul," Dianne said and she leaned her head against his chest. "It's ripping the country apart little by little. I can't tell you how many divorced moms and divorced dads I deal with at the hospital every day. It's very sad. I know it breaks God's heart to see these things happen. We just have to pray that we can make something happen in Dallas."

Paul and Dianne fell asleep on the sofa. An hour later Paul woke up. He woke up Dianne. "What do you want to do? Do you want me to walk you over to your parent's house?" The exhausted Dianne could do little more than mumble before drifting back to sleep. Paul lifted her from the sofa and carried her into his bedroom. The blankets were already pulled down so he was able to lay her down and cover her with the blankets. He grabbed an extra blanket and pillow he had in his closet and went back out into the living room. He laid out the blanket on the sofa and put the pillow on the end that he always put his head. Paul had another bedroom but he had converted it to an exercise room. He went back to the doorway of his bedroom and stared at Dianne as she slept. She was beyond beautiful. Paul would climb mountains and fight wars for her. He wanted badly just to lie beside her and hold her all night, but the two of them had decided that such a thing would be too much temptation. They promised to wait until after they were married. He went back out to the sofa, knelt and prayed. The prayer relaxed him so much that when Charlie woke him up the next morning he didn't remember falling asleep.

"We got to get you two ready for the ride to the airport. Is my little angel still asleep?"

Paul sat up on the sofa and rubbed his eyes. "Yeah, she was really exhausted last night. I'm sure she's still sleeping."

Charlie opened the door to Paul's exercise room and pulled it shut again. "When are you goin' to let me build you a room for you to exercise in? Every time she falls asleep on your couch, she ends up in your bed and you out here. How can you get a good night sleep out here?"

"Easy," Paul answered, "I sleep well knowing that the world's most incredible woman is in there asleep on my bed and that she's in love with me."

Charlie smiled. "Well, I can't argue with that. Since she's in love with you, you wake her up and both of you come up for some breakfast." Charlie left the house and Paul got up and went to the refrigerator for a glass of orange juice. He thought he would give Dianne a few more minutes to sleep. With glass of orange juice in hand, Paul returned to the living room and sat back on the sofa. He had a daily devotional that he had begun reading each morning. The devotional for that day was from Proverbs, verses five and six:

> "Trust in the Lord with all thine heart and lean not unto thine own understanding. In all thy ways acknowledge him, and he shall direct thy paths. There are times in our lives when God takes us to a place that causes us to begin to question Him. It is at those times that real faith is shown. For it is not when things are clear in our lives and God's direction is obvious that our faith is proven. It is, however, in those times when we are not sure why He is leading us in a certain direction, a direction that shows no logic – human logic, that we, if we remain faithful, receive the great blessings of faith from walking through adversity."

Paul closed the devotional, prayed and went to his bedroom to wake Dianne. She was still sound asleep. She always bragged on how comfortable Paul's bed was to sleep in. Charlie began joking that Paul would never know since he never got to sleep in it when she was visiting. Paul wouldn't have it any other way. If she had to sleep somewhere and she was too tired to make it to her parent's house, Paul would have slept on a cold concrete floor to have her near him in his room. He felt a great deal more peace when he was with her.

Paul sat on the side of the bed and ran his hand through Dianne's soft hair. He sat there nearly a minute before Dianne began waking. She was laying on her right side when she woke, and when she realized that Paul was there she rolled over on her back. "Good morning, beautiful angel," Paul said. She said nothing – only smiled. "I could look at this angelic face every day for the rest of my life and it still wouldn't be enough."

"I love you, Paul. Thank-you for waking me. There's no other way I would want to wake up." Dianne sat up and kissed Paul.

"Your dad gave me the wake-up call this morning. He wants us to come up for a bite of breakfast before we head for the airport." Paul stood up from the bed and from the bedroom closet he grabbed a suitcase that he had purchased a year after arriving in Lumpkin County. It still had never been used. "I'll be packed in five minutes."

"It must be a man thing. How is it a man can pack in five minutes when it takes a woman at least an hour?" Dianne was up and out of the bed now.

"It's genetics. We're wired differently." Paul was already tossing socks into the suitcase. "What are we going to do about getting you packed?"

"Not sure how all of this was going to play out, yesterday after my parents called me I went ahead and packed a suitcase just in case." She was looking in the mirror on the dresser checking her eyes. Paul was beside her busy throwing t-shirts, sweatpants and whatever he thought he might need for the trip into the suitcase.

"That's why you're the doctor and I'm the lowly warehouse worker. You think ahead." Dianne bumped Paul who had knelt down to pull some more clothes out of the dresser. Unable to keep his balance, Paul toppled over onto the floor. Dianne went over to him, got down on her knees and leaned over him. "You are no lowly warehouse worker. You are my hero."

Paul, in lightning fast speed, grabbed her and rolled her over on the floor. Dianne began to laugh as he held her down and tickled her. "Alright, alright, please Paul, let me up." Paul finally relented and Dianne got up off the floor still laughing. "How about heroic lowly warehouse worker?"

"How about round two?" Paul picked up Dianne and threw her on the bed and began tickling her again.

"Paul, Paul, alright, you win. Please, let me up." Paul stopped, gave her a quick kiss on the forehead while she was trying to catch her breath and quickly went back to packing.

Dianne got out of the bed and made her way for the door. Just before she reached the back door she teased Paul. "You're lucky I didn't give you a round three. You would have been the one pinned down laughing, buddy." She turned and ran for the door knowing that Paul would be coming after her to do it all over again, and he was. She ran laughing and screaming toward her parent's house, Paul in tow. Paul was barefooted while Dianne had slipped her feet into her shoes before making her daring comment. She was still a fast runner eight years removed from being on the track team at Emory. He laughed listening to her scream and continued laughing all the way to her parent's back door. Dianne ran into the kitchen still laughing, knowing that Paul would be close behind. Paul came in about fifteen seconds behind her. He found Dianne clinging to her mother.

"You don't think attaching yourself to your mother will stop me do you?" Paul began walking toward Dianne who was still laughing but begging Paul not to tickle her.

"Well, Anne, I see the kids are playful this mornin'." Charlie walked in with his newspaper and coffee. "I think it's time we build them a romper room."

Paul was in good spirits. "As long as you make it all cammo, that'll be great Charlie."

Charlie shook his head. "Then how will we find you two?"

"That's the point." Paul replied.

"I think we better get some breakfast so that we can get you two to the airport on time." Anne having been released by Dianne who was drinking a glass of water had prepared a light breakfast for everyone. The family sat down for the meal.

Charlie brought all of the early morning antics back to reality and said a prayer of thanks for the food, a prayer of divine protection for Dianne and Paul for the trip to Dallas and back home again, and a final prayer for Chris, a prayer that he would find peace in the midst of all that he was facing. Paul was particularly moved by Charlie's request of God that he bring back home the two most important people in the world to him and Anne. Paul was always impressed with the power and conviction of Charlie's prayers.

Breakfast and showers for Dianne and Paul complete, the Yukon was loaded for the ride to the airport. They wouldn't actually be going to the airport but would instead drive to the North Springs MARTA train station and let Paul and Dianne ride a train to the airport. With morning rush hour in full swing, MARTA would be much faster. During the ride to the train station, reality began setting in for Paul. He and Dianne were traveling to Texas to see his brother who was in a jail cell for keeping his daughter because he feared for her safety. He prayed silently that the trip wouldn't become a contentious nightmare, despite his burning desire to see the judge who had jailed Chris and find out exactly why such a decision had been made.

They arrived at the train station and parked in temporary parking. Paul and Dianne got out and Paul grabbed the luggage. Charlie and Anne got out to see them off. Dianne kissed her parents while Paul, loaded down with luggage, could only nod and say "goodbye". Anne walked over and kissed him on the cheek. Paul and Dianne headed into the station while Charlie and Anne got back into the Yukon and left. After purchasing two passes to ride the train, Paul and Dianne took the elevator up to the platform. A train was already waiting. The North Springs station is the last stop on the north line of the MARTA rail system. It is a convenient way to get to the airport in Atlanta, a straight shot to Hartsfield with no needs to board any other trains. Paul had been on mass transit trains in other cities throughout the world, but never on MARTA. He was impressed with how clean and organized it seemed to be.

At 8:55am, the couple arrived at the airport and checked in their luggage. Boarding began forty-five minutes later and like clockwork, the Delta 747 jet lifted off the ground at 10:15am. Next stop – Dallas, Texas. During the flight, Dianne read her Bible. Paul followed along with her, and the two discussed the passages they were reading. Paul, already an avid reader, had become an avid student of the Bible. He spent very little money, but since becoming a Christian he had purchased a computer and signed up for high speed internet through Charlie and Anne's satellite plan. With the computer, he was doing all types of studies of scripture and purchasing various textbooks on different Biblical topics. He was becoming quite the biblical scholar and was doing so in a relative brief time. Anatomy texts were collecting dust, having been replaced with texts on Bible history, concordances, and essays by C.S. Lewis. Now he was on a plane headed for Dallas, Texas, sharing scriptures with the woman he loved.

Chapter Six

Dallas, Texas

The plane touched down five minutes ahead of schedule. Paul and Dianne retrieved their bags, rented a car, and started the drive for the hotel. Paul was getting anxious, and Dianne was noticing. She tried to get his mind off the situation by talking about how flat and boring the terrain appeared in Dallas as opposed to Atlanta. Paul agreed. To him, Dallas looked like just one huge open prairie with a city stuck right in the middle of it all. The most notable difference between Atlanta and Dallas to Dianne was Atlanta's abundance of trees as opposed to Dallas.

The airport in Dallas is west of the city, quite a distance from downtown as compared to Atlanta's Hartsfield, which is extremely convenient to the city. The drive to the Ritz took Paul and Dianne forty-five minutes. They finally arrived and checked into their adjoining suites. A bellman carted their luggage and took it on up to the seventh floor where they would be staying. Paul and Dianne followed on another elevator after purchasing some drinks for the suites – the usual for Paul, bottled water and Gatorade. Dianne teased Paul saying to him that if there was a blood/Gatorade test like the blood/alcohol test, he would fail it every time.

The bellman was waiting for them at the door to their suites. His name was Marvin, an elderly man in his late sixties. He had graying black hair and amazingly clear eyes. He had an incredible smile and a very kind disposition. Marvin had been at the Ritz for fifteen years, starting the job some years following the passing of his wife. His only requirement for working at the Ritz was that he didn't work on Sundays. He was a deacon at a small Methodist AME church in Oak Cliff, a suburb of Dallas, south of the city. Marvin described his church to Paul and Dianne with obvious enthusiasm and love for the position he held.

Reaching the room, Paul keyed the door with the card and opened it for Marvin and Dianne. Marvin pushed the luggage cart into the suite and unloaded their bags. "Sir, is their anything else I can do for you fine folks?"

"No," Paul answered, "Marvin you've done enough to make us feel welcome."

"Well, if you need me you know where you can find me. Just call down to the front desk and have them send for me." Marvin began to turn and head for the door.

"Marvin," Paul said stopping the bellman in his aging tracks.

Marvin turned back to Paul. "Yes sir."

"Here, take this. The fifty dollar bill is for your church. The twenty dollar bill is for you." Paul walked over to Marvin and handed him the cash. Marvin's infectious smile appeared and he reached out and shook Paul's hand.

"Thank-you very much, sir. I will mention my friends from Atlanta who gave this money to the church when I'm there this Sunday. Remember, if you need anything at all, just call down to the front desk and I'll fetch it and bring it right up to you."

"Thanks again, Marvin," Paul replied.

After Marvin left, Dianne went over to Paul and put her arms around his waste. "Your heart's bigger than this state, do you know that?"

"I'm just following in the footsteps of my mentor," Paul said.

"Who's that?" Dianne kissed Paul on the cheek.

"You should know him pretty well." Paul returned the kiss. "He's your father."

Dianne went into the other suite where she found a vase of flowers and a card. She opened the card and read it out loud to Paul: "Dear Dianne and Paul, We trust you made it safely to Dallas and to the hotel. You both are in our prayers. We look forward to the both of you coming home. We love you. Mom and Dad." Dianne set the card on the table that held the vase of flowers and looked at Paul who was standing at the door smiling and shaking his head. Dianne was speechless.

Paul broke the silence and summed it up in one word to Dianne: "Incredible."

The word broke Dianne's silence. "I think you could also say, 'incredibly blessed', because that's what we are to have them in our lives."

Paul walked over to where Dianne was standing by the flowers and placed his hands on her shoulders. "You are right about that. We are blessed." He began looking around the suite. "Nice room. It reminds me of one I stayed in while in London chasing down an international counterfeiter with the unit. The Brits aren't quite as gracious, though, and the food in the hotel was really bad. But, it was fun playing a civilian for a few days. Maybe that's where I got the itch."

Dianne laughed. "You got the itch when you saw the absolute beauty of Lumpkin County, Georgia." She had retrieved one of her suitcases and had it opened ready to unpack.

Paul grabbed his bag and went back into the other suite to unpack. He really didn't see the point of unpacking since he wasn't planning on being in town more than a day or two. He grabbed the suitcase stand, placed his suitcase on it and opened it up. Good enough, he thought to himself – as quick as I can board a plane for Atlanta and my house I'm going to do it.

Paul called the city jail where his brother was being held to find out when he could see Chris. Visitation, he was told, would begin at 5:00pm that day. Paul had to be on the visitor's list. He was sure he was. The problem was that it was already fifteen minutes before five and Paul had no idea where the jail was located. Marvin. Marvin would know. Paul called down to the front desk and asked that Marvin be sent up. He was at their door four minutes later.

Paul inquired of the location of the jail. Marvin eased Paul's tension by telling him it was only five minutes away. The downtown area of Dallas is relatively small in comparison to Atlanta with everything practically within walking distance. Marvin gave Paul directions, and Paul and Dianne rushed down to their rental car. Marvin was correct; the jail was only five minutes away. Paul parked the rental at a nearby parking garage. It was ten minutes after five when they arrived. He hoped that there wasn't some strange rule that said you had to be standing in line at 5:00pm sharp. The couple walked into the area where visitors enter and approached an officer.

"Mr. Atkinson?" A tap on the shoulder and an unfamiliar voice prompted Paul to turn around abruptly - so abruptly that the sudden turn startled the man who had just tapped him on the shoulder. "I'm Jensen Parker, an attorney here in Dallas." Great, Paul thought, Chris' ex-wife sent her attorney down to intimidate them. "Mr. Charlie Taylor retained me on behalf of Mr. Christopher Atkinson." Paul slowly turned his head and looked at Dianne who simply smiled and shrugged her shoulders. "I'll be representing Christopher in this matter. We're going to try to have the judge's decision reviewed and overturned. Then we're going to ask the court to remove the judge from the case." Paul was still staring at Dianne.

As it turned out, the judge that presided over Chris' case was Dallas' first openly gay judge on the bench in family court. He ran on the democrat ticket and promised to clean up the family court if elected to the seat. In reality, he had very little experience especially at that level but the fact that he was openly gay garnered him an incredible amount of financial support from the gay community. He won the position in a landslide, unseating an aging republican who many thought was out of touch with the changes in the social structure of Dallas. Paul didn't care who he was, how he got elected or that he was gay. He vowed that he would speak to the man face to face before he left town.

Charlie never ceased to amaze Paul. He had called his attorney in Atlanta the day prior and asked him if he new any good attorneys in Dallas that could look into the situation. His attorney called him back ten minutes later with the name Jensen Parker, a graduate of the Steadman School of Law, an excellent law school at Southern Methodist University in Dallas. Jensen was still relatively young at thirty-two, but he already had a reputation of ripping into the cases of opposing attorneys. He had yet to lose a case, mostly due to the fact that most opposing attorneys didn't want to venture into the courtroom with him and face his fiery style. He never let a witness for the opposing team get a breath. As a result, most of Jensen's cases ended up in mediation. He was a devout Methodist, married and had a young son. Paul was never very fond of attorneys, but after some time and some conversations, Jensen seemed to be very genuine to him.

"Nice to meet you," Paul finally answered. "Maybe you can help us find out how we go through visitation."

"That's handled," Jensen replied. "Attorneys are allowed direct access to their clients. We're going to be seeing him in a private conference room inside the jail. Let me get us escorted to the conference room so you can see your brother in better surroundings." Jensen turned and walked away.

Dianne walked over to Paul who was still somewhat in a state of shock and grabbed his hand. She whispered to him. "This guy's good."

"Your dad's good," Paul replied.

A few minutes later, Jensen returned and told them to follow him and not to say a word. He had pulled a few strings to get them back there to see Chris, but no one really needed to mention anything. The three of them were escorted back to the conference room by a jail guard. Chairs were already set up when they entered the room. Chris wasn't there yet, so Paul, Dianne and Jensen sat down and waited for him to arrive. It was an awkward setting to say the least. Jensen decided to break the ice.

"Did you have a good flight to Dallas?" He was removing a legal pad as he spoke.

"Yes," Dianne replied. "It was a good trip. I've never been to Dallas."

"I've traveled to Atlanta several times," said Jensen. "I have a friend I graduated from law school with who's in a law firm right in the heart of the city. He's in contract law. Atlanta's a great town. I always have a good time when I visit. There's so much to do."

"It is an active city. I live in Buckhead."

Jensen, having placed the legal pad on the table was now fumbling with his pen. For a man who was rumored as being a confident fireball in the courtroom, he sure seemed nervous in front of Paul and Dianne. "I've eaten at several restaurants in Buckhead."

"There are some good restaurants in Buckhead but I prefer the hamburgers at Frank's just north of Dahlonega." Dianne was looking out of the corner of her eye to see what kind of response she would get out of Paul.

"Frank's? I never heard of it." Jensen was simply making conversation. "I'll have to check it out next time I'm in Atlanta. What part of Atlanta is Dahlonega in?"

Paul looked at Dianne and shook his head. She had a sly smile on her face. "This woman wouldn't eat a Frank's hamburger if he gave it to her on a diamond studded gold platter. I'm the one who frequents Frank's, and the burgers are fantastic. That is, if you don't mind getting a little of the burger on your shirt. And, Dahlonega isn't near Atlanta. It's a foothills town in Lumpkin County that's about an hour and a half from Atlanta. If you're ever in the area, look me up and I'll treat you to one."

"That's all he needs Jensen – an enabler to support him in his Saturday addiction to Frank's hamburgers." Dianne placed her hand on Paul's shoulder.

Jensen laughed. The ice had been broken. "Well, who knows? I may have to visit Dahlonega someday."

The door to the conference room swung open and Chris walked in with a guard. Paul and Dianne remained silent. The guard told Chris to sit down in the chair on the opposite side of the table. Jensen looked up at the guard, smiled and nodded. Understanding the nod and the fifty-dollar bill that had found its way to his pocket, the guard turned and left the room. Chris and Paul were obviously brothers. The only differences were Chris was slightly shorter and a little overweight. He appeared tired and disheveled.

Paul stood up from his chair and walked over to Chris. Chris seemed terrified to get out of his chair. He looked at Paul, then at Jensen and finally at Dianne who was smiling at him with one of her warm smiles. Finding the courage in that smile, Chris stood and faced his brother. Chris was wearing a black and white striped jail uniform. Paul grabbed his brother and hugged him, and Chris began to weep. "I did nothing wrong, Paul. I did nothing wrong. I only wanted to protect my daughter."

"I know," Paul said as he released his brother. He returned to his seat while Chris sat back down in his. "We're working on getting you out of here. You just have to hang in there. How are you holding up?"

Chris wiped the tears from his face with the sleeves of his jail uniform. "Not very well. I haven't slept in three days. There's constant noise. I have to get out of here or I'm going to go crazy. I can't handle it."

"Chris, you've got to hang in there. I know you're feeling trapped. I was trapped inside a cinderblock well house in Saudi that had no lighting, no fresh air and no room to lie down and rest. My unit came under fire and we got separated. I wound up in that well house after chasing an arms dealer with the unit through the desert for four days. I stayed in that well house with no food and very little water before I decided to make a run for it." Jensen looked over at Dianne. Who was this guy? She knew what he was thinking. I'll bet you would like to know, she thought.

"I just don't think I can handle much more of this," Chris replied as he scratched his head with his left hand.

"You're a Marine. Yes, you can handle this. Besides, you may be out sooner than you think." Paul pointed over to his right. "This is Jensen Parker, an attorney that is going to be working on your case and working on getting you out of here."

"Hello Chris," said Jensen as he reached across the table and shook his hand. "I promise you, my assistant is already working on two separate motions for the court."

Chris looked over at Paul. "Did you do this?"

Paul sat back in his chair. "Can't say that I did."

"Well then, who did?"

"That person wishes to remain anonymous." Paul looked at Dianne whose face was glowing with pride in the man seated next to her.

Jensen tapped his pen on the table. "Chris this isn't going to happen overnight, but I can assure you that I'm going to do everything I can do to have you out of here soon. And, upon your release we're going to move forward with some more action. I promise you that I'm completely devoted to your case. To be quite honest, I've been well-funded in order to discharge my duties." Paul looked at Dianne and slowly shook his head. Charlie Taylor.

"What can we get for you?" Dianne finally spoke up.

"I'm sorry," Chris said, "but who are you?"

Paul realized that he hadn't introduced Dianne to Chris. "This is Dianne Taylor. Her parents own the property where my house is located."

Paul didn't need to say anything else to Chris. "You mean Paul Atkinson, a man who had no fear in jumping out of an airplane at thirty thousand feet, who could hit a target a mile away with a sniper rifle, who is an expert in martial arts, but despite all of that, was terrified of a relationship; you mean that same Paul Atkinson has finally fallen in love?"

Only Chris could get Paul to blush. Dianne noticed and laughed. Jensen just wanted to know whom this guy was that had done all of those things.

Paul squirmed somewhat in his chair. "Yes, Chris, you could say that."

Chris was actually smiling. "Well, well, well. If only I had a way of calling some guys I remember from high school in Durham. They would like to know this information."

Dianne laughed again and Paul squirmed a little more in his chair. Even in a jail uniform Chris was good at needling Paul. He always had been. "Back to the topic at hand, do you need anything," Paul said in order to change the subject.

Dianne couldn't resist keeping it going. "I'm rather enjoying this. I've never seen you two together and I've never seen Paul blush. This is entertaining." Jensen laughed as he continued nervously tapping the pen on the table. Paul thought about it later that evening. He assumed that Jensen did not like the jail interviews. He felt, Paul thought, confined like the prisoners he represented.

Chris relented from the teasing of his younger brother. "I have everything I need."

They chatted a little more before they had to leave. Jensen gave Chris his card and told him to call him collect if he needed anything. Paul hugged his brother before the guard was called back in. Chris was led out and back to his cell. He dreaded going back but he was feeling a little more human now that he had spent some time with his brother, Dianne and Jensen.

Paul, Dianne and Jensen were escorted to the lobby. As they were walking toward the exit, Paul turned to Jensen and said, "I want to talk face to face with this judge."

Jensen stopped walking. "That's not as easy as it sounds."

"What's so difficult about it? You just get me an appointment." Paul was using some of his assertiveness.

"Alright, be at the family court tomorrow morning at 8:00am, and I'll see what I can do. Meet me on the fourth floor." Jensen began walking away then turned back to Paul. "But I'm not going in with you. I have to try cases in front of this guy nearly every day. I don't want to be on his bad side."

"We'll see you at eight in the morning." Paul turned back to Dianne satisfied with the results thus far.

"Be careful with this judge," Dianne said. "He doesn't sound like he really cares that much about law. It sounds to me like he only wants to make a statement that he is all powerful on the bench."

Paul didn't respond to Dianne's request. "Let's eat. Do you want to eat out?"

Dianne didn't push the issue any further. She believed Paul knew what he was doing. She pulled out her Blackberry and started looking for a restaurant. "This is great. They have an Oceanaire here. It's at a Galleria Mall. How about that?"

Paul put his arm around Dianne. "As long as I'm with you, I don't care where we eat."

"But is that alright with you?" Dianne ran her hand through Paul's short hair.

"Absolutely," Paul responded. "It's a great restaurant."

"Excellent! I'll call and see if we need reservations." Dianne dialed the restaurant and found she could reserve a table. She did so and ended the call.

Paul and Dianne had a quiet dinner at the Oceanaire before returning to the hotel. Upon returning to the adjoining suites, Paul asked Dianne if she would call Delta Airlines to check on space available for a flight back to Atlanta sometime after 3:00pm Dallas time the next day. She called and got seats for a 3:45pm direct flight. Paul and Dianne would only fly Delta. Paul always flew Delta during his military career, that is, when he wasn't in a massive C5 transport aircraft or some other military aircraft. Charlie insisted on supporting the Atlanta based company, and, of course, his loyalty had rubbed off on Dianne.

After everything was set up for the flight back to Atlanta, Dianne phoned her parents. Both got on the phone to join the conversation. They wanted to know how things were going thus far. Dianne told her how everything went and how much she was impressed with Jensen. She thanked them on Paul's behalf for what they were doing. Charlie said that it sounded as Chris may have been jailed wrongfully and that he was just doing his part to help the situation right itself. Final arrangements were made for the time Dianne expected to arrive at the North Springs MARTA station. Dianne told her parents that she loved them very much and would see them the next day.

After the phone call, Dianne found Paul lying on the bed in the other suite reading. She walked over to the bed and laid next to him. The two of them spent the next hour reading together, talking and mostly laughing. Afterward, Paul decided to get a late night workout in the hotel's exercise room while Dianne made some calls to Northside Hospital to check on a few patients. Paul returned an hour later drenched in sweat.

"Want a hug?" Paul found Dianne in her suite on her blackberry typing an email to someone at the hospital.

"I don't think so," Dianne replied as she completed the email and sent it to the recipient.

"Come on, Dianne. I'm feeling extremely vulnerable right now. I really need a hug." Paul walked over to where she was sitting. "I need a hug from you."

"You need a shower." Dianne stood up and backed away from Paul. "You take a shower and you can have all the hugs that you could ever want."

Paul, who was following her as she was backing into the other suite, suddenly stopped and brought his right hand to his chin. "It's hard to argue with that deal." He paused. "I don't know though. I'm really feeling the need for one now."

"Paul."

"Well, alright. I'll take the shower. But, don't forget the deal." Paul grabbed a towel and headed for the other suite and the shower. Dianne let out a sigh of relief. Paul had done that once before in Atlanta. He had come down for a weekend and competed in a five-kilometer road race that began and finished at the Georgia Dome. Dianne didn't compete. She still ran and occasionally competed in local races, but she decided to sit this one out. Paul did very well for someone who only ran occasionally. He finished tenth with a time of seventeen minutes and thirty-nine seconds. After the race, drenched in sweat – it was a mid-September event with humid temperatures in the seventies - Paul walked over to Dianne and said he needed a hug. This time he delivered, and as hard as she tried, Dianne couldn't break his sweaty hold. She insisted on going straight to her condo and getting a shower. They didn't even stay for the post race festivities. Back at the condominium, while Dianne showered, Paul rushed out to a street vender who was selling roses and bought two dozen. When he returned, Dianne was still in her room getting ready for their afternoon. Paul found two vases for the roses. He was in a hurry pouring water into the vases and arranging all but one rose. After setting the vases on Dianne's coffee table, Paul waited at her bedroom door with the other rose.

Dianne finally emerged from her room looking breath-takingly beautiful as usual. There Paul stood, trying to appear as innocent as possible, single rose in hand. He handed Dianne the rose. He asked her if she was upset with him. "You're amazing. Do you know that," Dianne said with a smile as she sniffed the rose. "I love you so much Paul, pranks and all." As the two embraced, Dianne noticed the two vases full of roses sitting on her coffee table. She looked at Paul. "Your love for me gives me so much joy. I hope you know that I wasn't angry with you. Actually, while in the shower, I was laughing and planning on how I could get you back."

"I would consider it an honor and a privilege to be surprised with a prank by the most beautiful and the most loving woman in the world." The two embraced before leaving for lunch.

Back at the hotel in Dallas, Paul finished his shower and put on some army sweatpants along with a Citadel sweatshirt. He found Dianne lying on her bed in the suite opposite his. She had the television on and was surfing the channels for something to watch. Like Paul, Dianne watched very little television. She was disgusted with much of what she had classified as filth that had invaded modern programming. Paul came over and sat on the bed facing Dianne. He began running his hand through her beautiful soft hair. She turned and looked into his eyes. "Your beauty is stunning," he said. "I'm so glad you came here with me. I'm so glad to have a family that cares. I'm so glad to have a home, a place in the church that makes me feel a part of rather than apart from. I'm so glad to have found Lumpkin County, Georgia, and I'm so glad God sent you, an angel, to me, a man lost in a desert of denial, a man who refused to believe he could ever experience meaningful love with anyone. Most of all, I'm so glad I've found faith in the Son of God. He has sustained me through this experience with Chris. I pray that our life together only continues to grow." Tears formed in Paul's eyes. Dianne had never seen him cry. To her the tear was a sign of his strength, character and the joy he had in his heart.

"I love you Paul. If God sent me to you, then he did so knowing I needed you. You are the man of my dreams, and nothing will ever change my love for you. It will stretch into eternity and beyond." Dianne sat up in her bed and gently wiped the tear from Paul's face. She leaned over and kissed Paul. Her kiss was like a magic potion that relaxed his body. Everything about it felt right. "You are no longer that loner in the dark, walking alone in a world conquering enemies and living in the shadows. I am with you, and when the days turn dark and life's enemies creep in, I will be there with you to fight those enemies. We carry the mightiest sword the world has ever seen – the Holy Bible."

"I could ask for no better partner in this life than you. You are an incredible woman." The two embraced and kissed again. The remainder of the night was spent watching a very old situation comedy on one of the cable channels. Dianne, as usual, fell asleep. Paul covered her up, switched off the television and went to his suite to pray and climb into the bed. He was exhausted. It took a great deal to wear him down. That day had accomplished it.

The 6:00am wake-up call came and Paul got out of his bed refreshed and ready to meet the judge. He woke Dianne and asked her if she wanted him to order anything from room service while she got ready. She wanted a plate of fresh fruit and some juice. Paul ordered the same for both of them. Each got dressed in their individual suite and after eating they spent some time in prayer before leaving for the court. Arriving at the courthouse at 7:30am, Paul and Dianne went through security and up to the fourth floor. Not seeing Jensen anywhere, they decided to wait near the elevators.

At five minutes until eight o'clock, Jensen didn't greet Paul and Dianne coming off of the elevators. He had just come from the judge's secretary and walked down the hallway to where they were standing. "Good morning, both of you. It's so good to see you again."

"It's good to see you, Jensen," Dianne replied.

"Hello Jensen," said Paul. "Did you get everything worked out?"

"Yes," Jensen replied somewhat nervously. "I need to warn you that this judge has a temper, and when he gets angry, he doesn't always respond in a, well, let me just say if you anger him it could be a bad day for you."

"Well, what do you say I go in and find out?" Paul had been in some of the fiercest firefights in Afghanistan. This judge didn't strike fear in his heart. He was determined to make it clear to the judge that he was convinced a tragic mishandling of the law had taken place putting his innocent brother behind bars.

Jensen escorted the two down the hallway to a door. He told them that that was as far as he was going to go with them. He wished them luck and promised to keep them updated on Chris' case. Paul asked Dianne to wait in the hallway. He wanted to handle this alone and didn't want her getting involved. She agreed, and Paul entered the secretary's office and introduced himself to her. The secretary instructed him to go right in, that the judge only had a few minutes.

Paul walked up to the door that led into the judge's office. The placard on the door read, "Judge David Simpson". Paul knocked and walked in. The judge was seated behind his desk with a newspaper in his hand. He laid the newspaper down on his desk when Paul entered the office. "Judge Simpson, I'm Paul Atkinson."

"I know who you are. I hope you have a good reason for interrupting me before court." The judge appeared tall behind his desk. He had a slender build with black hair, dark brown eyes and a moustache. He was everything Paul expected he would be – rude and to the point. Paul's desire to be as diplomatic and decent as possible had suddenly dissolved into anger toward a person who in just seconds appeared extremely egotistical and uncaring.

"You bet I do. I want to know why you decided to put my brother in jail for ninety days." Paul could feel anger rising.

"I don't have to speak to you about this case, but since you traveled so far to see me, I'll fill you in. Your brother violated a legally binding court order, an order I signed. He broke the law and now he's paying for it in jail." The judge leaned back in his black leather desk chair.

Paul let out a sarcastic laugh. "Well judge, first of all, let me tell you not to flatter yourself. I didn't come to Dallas to see you. I came to see my brother. You're not worth my time." The judge's face was turning red with anger. "Secondly, when a weak, pathetic, unqualified parasite like you gets power to jail men like my brother who was only trying to protect his daughter from a potentially drunk mother, then there's something terribly wrong with our system today. My brother had every right to keep that child. If you had read the court order you signed, you would know that. He followed the order. His ex-wife was no where to be found."

The judge, now filled with rage, leaned forward in his chair. Paul had struck a nerve with the comment about reading the order he had signed. "Mr. Atkinson, how would like to spend some time in that jail with your brother?"

Paul thought he would take it to another level. He knew with his connections the judge couldn't hold him. Paul also figured out that the judge had an ego the size of Alaska. He wanted to push those ego buttons to see what he could get out of the judge. "Simpson, you arrest me and I'll have twenty federal investigators down here from D.C. raiding your office and investigating you. I'm sure you have a few things to hide. Don't you know who I am?"

"You don't intimidate me," the judge replied. He wasn't being exactly truthful. The judge was intimidated by Paul. "I know who you are. You came up during the trial. You are an ex-army ranger. What connections in Washington is a ranger going to have?"

"Did you find out what I did during my last four years, Simpson?" The judge remained silent, face still red, sweat now forming on his forehead. "You don't want to know, pal. You're a tiny little judge in a tiny little court. You don't want to play the game with me. I'll take you into a world where you'll wish you could get out every second you're in it. But if you want to try me, let's go. Come into my world, Simpson."

"Are you threatening me, Mr. Atkinson?" The sweat was now dripping from the judge's face.

"Yes, Simpson. I'm threatening you. I'll tell you what I'm going to do. I'm going to fly back to Atlanta. I'll be contacting some friends in Washington. Now that I've met you I now know just how pathetic you are. My friends will be paying you a visit real soon. In the meantime, if anything happens to my brother while he's in jail, I'm going to pay you another visit. I'm sorry though. It won't be a nice, quiet social visit like we've had today. Give your lover my best." Paul tapped his hand on the desk, stood and left the judge's office. Paul realized on the way out of the judge's office that his disgust with the judge might have caused him to go too far. He felt no guilt for standing up to the judge, but he knew that he was developing a real hatred for the man, a level of hatred that could come back to haunt Paul. He stood at the door that led out into the hallway. Paul turned his head and stared at the secretary. With a shrug of his shoulders and a smile, he left the room.

Dianne was waiting for Paul in the hallway. "How'd it go in there?"

Paul took her hand and they began heading for the elevators. "I think the poor guy has a blood pressure problem. I've never seen a guy sweat so much during a kind, jovial conversation."

Dianne shook her head and laughed. "Paul, you can be completely crazy at times."

"At times? You're just being nice." The two headed for the rental car and back to the hotel.

Back at the Ritz, Marvin greeted Paul and Dianne at the door. "Good mornin' folks, how are you today?"

"We're doing good, Marvin," Paul replied as he reached out and shook his hand. A twenty-dollar bill was in Paul's hand, and it wound up in Marvin's.

Marvin looked at the money then at Paul. "Sir, you've done enough. Please, take back your money."

"You're a deacon. We have to take care of our leaders in the church." Paul put his arm around Dianne. "Besides, we're checking out. That's a down payment on the best bellman in the history of the hotel industry."

"You're leavin' already sir? You just got here. You didn't even get a chance to see our city."

"Trust me Marvin," Paul replied. "We've seen enough. We're going home."

Marvin walked over to Paul and Dianne and placed his hands on their shoulders. In an inexplicable way, Paul could feel the power of this holy man. "I want you both to be blessed. There is somethin' very special about both of you, and the Lord is goin' to bless you mightily. You could say I've only known you for a few minutes, but I feel like I've known you a lifetime." He looked directly into Paul's eyes. His stare was magnetic and powerful. "Remember what I'm about to say to you: when the rains come and the storms knock you down, you need to know where to go for God to pick you back up and put you back on the path." Marvin's words shook Paul. What was he saying?

"May God bless you richly Marvin," Dianne said. "May he give you everything you need to continue to be the holy leader he has called you to be."

"Marvin, we'll call for you when we get packed," Paul said, still somewhat shaken by Marvin's words.

"Yes sir. I'll be right here waitin'."

Paul and Dianne returned to the suites and packed. They wasted no time in checking out. Georgia and a thirty-mile bike ride were calling out to Paul. Dianne had gone down to the hotel office and printed their boarding passes off from the Delta Airlines website. It was a convenient way of speeding things up at the airport. Marvin had the valet bring the rental car to the front entrance and made sure to take care of the valet's tip before Paul could get to him. He escorted Paul and Dianne out and loaded the luggage into the roomy trunk of the Malibu Max before turning and asking them if he could say a quick prayer on their behalf. They, without hesitation, agreed. Marvin prayed beautifully a prayer asking God to bless their return to Atlanta and asked God to use them for kingdom work. He hugged them both and disappeared into the lobby of the hotel. Dianne thought to herself of the scripture in the Bible that says: "Be not forgetful to entertain strangers: for thereby some have entertained angels unawares."

Chapter Seven

Back to Atlanta

The couple made excellent time driving to the airport. The rental car was fast and easy to drive in heavy traffic, and Paul wasted no time in reaching his destination. Additionally, the airport in Dallas is much easier to get into than Atlanta's. It's not as crowded and has much more space. Paul and Dianne knew that they would be home soon when they returned the rental car. They had been gone about twenty-four hours, but it felt like a lifetime. They both loved living in Georgia. It was home.

The airplane reached Atlanta airspace right on schedule. It was a clear day, so Dianne could see downtown from the right side of the aircraft where she had a window seat. It was beautiful from the air. The pilot made a hard left and the plane leaned as it descended toward the runway. Paul, despite the thousands of hours in aircrafts of all types, really didn't like flying, mostly due to the landings. He would have preferred parachuting from the side of the aircraft with his luggage tied on. Dianne had traveled quite a bit and had flown many times. She enjoyed every aspect of flight, except the packs of nuts handed out during the trips. The plane landed smoothly on the runway and eventually stopped at its designated terminal. Paul and Dianne gave everyone else a chance to grab their things in order to rush to the luggage carousel where they would have to wait ten minutes or so for their bags. Paul looked at Dianne who was watching the bustling passengers engaged in a race to be the first off the plane. "A rat race to nowhere, he said."

"What's insane about it," Dianne added, "is that most everyone in here has traveled many times. They know by now that they're invariably going to have to wait for their luggage. We live in a world like that today. We rush around getting this and getting that and one day we wake up and realize that we've let life pass us by. We sit down on a bench and ask God where all the time went. I'm glad my parents have never made that mistake. They've savored every moment of their lives, especially their lives as husband and wife."

"That's obvious when you meet them and get to know them. There's nothing false about Charlie and Anne. What you see is what you get. Two content, mature, faithful adults who have decided to maximize life to its fullest. I'm sure they've succeeded at doing so far beyond their expectations." Paul was finally able to scoot out of his seat and open the overhead bin.

"And I'm sure they thank God every day for it all. I've never seen a couple who have prayed together so fervently as mom and dad." Dianne followed Paul out of the seats. She stood and stretched. The three-hour flight had tightened her muscles. She needed a nice run in Piedmont Park.

Paul and Dianne exited the plane and entered the concourse. They would have to take the airport train to the luggage carousel. Twenty minutes later, luggage in hand, the couple headed for the MARTA rail platform. Dianne called her parents on her Blackberry to inform them that they were preparing to board the train. Anne told her that they were already in Cumming traveling southwest toward the station. Just over a half hour later, Paul and Dianne left the train at North Springs and rode the elevator down to the exit. Waiting on them in temporary parking were Charlie and Anne. The four exchanged hugs and generic conversation. Paul whispered in Charlie's ear, "You're incredible, do you know that?" Charlie, usually easy with words, could only respond with a smile. Charlie was giving. He cared, yet was never careless in his giving. He always assessed any situation he was facing where giving may be required and decided through intelligent thought and prayer whether he should give. He felt confident that he was doing the right thing in trying to help Chris. A stranger could be walking along the road in front of Charlie's house and he would offer to feed the person. Giving was just a part of who Charlie was.

Charlie had brought Wilson with him. The little puppy had grown into a small dog now and he loved riding in vehicles. Wilson was excited to see Dianne; he climbed up on the console and jumped onto the back seat to greet her. Wilson was the most energetic dog Paul had ever seen.

Of course, finishing greeting Dianne, Wilson greeted Paul – the incessant licking of the face. Paul didn't mind at all. It was just more proof that he was home. He was not impressed with Dallas, Texas, and he had no desire to ever return. With Jensen working on Chris' case, Paul hoped that he would never have to make a return to Texas.

The ride back to the Taylor residence was pleasant for everyone. No one talked much about the situation back in Dallas. Paul kept to himself his encounter with Judge Simpson. He wasn't sure he did the right thing by trying to intimidate the judge. Not because he thought the judge did the right thing – Paul thought the judge was either inept or corrupt or both – but because he had to consider the idea that what he was doing wasn't what a Christian man does. He was torn with that. So, he simply decided to keep everything about the conversation to himself.

"I'm surprised you didn't come back with a ten gallon hat on," Charlie said as they passed through the northern part of Alpharetta.

"I wanted to but they said that you couldn't wear a Texas cowboy hat unless you chewed tobacco." Paul was ready for this exchange with Charlie. "Couldn't see that happening."

"You obviously don't know about the new law on the books there. You can wear one of their cowboy hats if you can wrestle a steer." Charlie glanced at the rear view mirror.

"I did wrestle a steer and won," Paul continued. "But, when I picked the steer up and carried it out on my shoulders they tried to arrest me for cattle rustling. I thought if I wrestled the steer and won I could keep it. I was going to check it in at the airport and bring it back to Frank's for hamburgers."

"Did you tell them that's the way we do it here in Georgia?" Charlie was enjoying this creative exchange of foolishness.

Dianne rolled her eyes and said: "Now I know I'm home. The two kings of sarcasm are back at it again."

"Come on Dianne," Paul said. "Can you imagine the number of burgers I could have eaten out of that cow?"

"Please, you two," Dianne replied, "your sarcasm has become a little stale. It's time for some better material."

"Little angel," Charlie said, "it works for us."

They passed through Dahlonega nearly thirty minutes later and drove another twenty minutes or so to their home. Charlie pulled the Yukon to Paul's house first and let him out. He grabbed his bag, gave Dianne a quick kiss, and went inside his place. It was good being home. He called his warehouse foreman and told him he would return to work the following day. After the call, he grabbed the pitcher of orange juice he made just before the trip to Dallas and poured his self a glass of the liquid vitamin C. He changed into one of the outfits he wore when he rode his mountain bike, retrieved his bike from his exercise room and hopped on the bike for a short ride. He wanted to give Dianne some time with her parents, and he wanted to ride.

The cool mountain air felt great against his face. His pedal turnover and strength on the bike was amazing. He pushed the bike up to thirty-five miles per hour and covered three miles in seven minutes and forty-five seconds, before turning and heading back to his place. Upon arriving at his house, he stored the bike in his exercise room and showered. He decided the unpacking could wait a day. He walked over to the Taylor residence and found Charlie, Anne and Dianne in the living room chatting. Charlie had a great fire going in the fireplace. Paul felt somewhat awkward walking in on their family time. He knew that he had been accepted as a part of the family, but he never wanted to invade those intimate times of father, mother and daughter conversation. Of course, no one in the Taylor family considered Paul anything less than another member of the family. When he walked into the living room, everyone perked up and was glad to see him.

Dianne got up from the couch and walked over to Paul. "Where have you been," she asked as she gave him a quick kiss on the cheek.

Paul put his arm around the woman he was so deeply in love with and replied, "I decided after our trip that a quick ride on the mountain bike was in order. I took it out for three miles. My bike gets a little emotional when I haven't taken it out on the road for a few days."

"I think you get a little emotional when you haven't been on that bike for a few days," Charlie said as he cracked a pecan shell and opened it up.

"Charlie, I can't argue with that," replied Paul with a laugh.

"Have a seat," Charlie said. "We were just making plans for thanksgiving."

Paul sat on the couch next to Dianne and joined in planning the upcoming Thanksgiving weekend holiday. It was difficult for him to imagine that just a year before he had turned down an invitation to thanksgiving dinner with the Taylors and opted for driving to a spot on Lake Lanier where he rode his bike forty miles. From a child into adulthood, Paul had always felt a void in his life, especially during the holidays. With his parents gone and Chris living his life in his way, Paul felt a little cheated by life at times. Of course, he would never project those feelings. The outer shell he had created was designed to make others think that he was a happy and content man. Of course, while others celebrated those special occasions with family, he had, by design, spent eight years of his life in the military covering up the pain by becoming one of the most prolific soldiers throughout the armed services. When he arrived in Dahlonega, it was a gradual process for Charlie to bring this broken soul out of his shell and into a state of willingness – a willingness to let someone in, to let someone love and care for him. A few years later, Paul found himself very comfortable in his role as surrogate son and to be in complete love with the daughter of the two people who had encouraged him to come out of the shadows of isolation.

Following the conversations on what everyone wanted to do at Thanksgiving, it was decided that they would all travel to Atlanta and spend the night at Dianne's. The next day, they would go as a family to one of the shelters and help feed the homeless. Afterward, the four of them would travel to Helen, Georgia, for the remainder of the weekend. Paul looked forward to spending four consecutive days with Dianne. The couple had yet to be able to do that. With Dianne's responsibilities as a doctor and Paul's job and commitment to being near Charlie and Anne, they usually only saw each other on the weekends. Four days together was something he could look forward to while waiting the four weeks for Thanksgiving. The holidays of 2008 were, in Paul's thoughts, going to be the best of his life.

Chapter Eight

Washington, D.C.

The election was finally over. Most were glad to see it off the television screen and out of the newspaper. The outgoing republican president still seated had wearied an already tired America with his inability to control a spiraling economy. The war in Iraq was another sore spot for many. Why were we giving so many American lives for a people and a nation that really hated us? People were tired. Gas prices were falsely inflated to a point where some people were forced to park their vehicles while others had to adjust their spending in ways that hadn't been seen since the great depression: buy bread or buy gas to get to work so the same question could be asked a week later. Pleas for help were coming from banking institutions that had been foolish with their spending, primarily in home loans. These same institutions were getting bit by their own policies. They expected their customers to be good money managers, but had failed to do so themselves. Now, they were asking the government to bail them out. The government did, signaling the end to a true free market economy. It was no surprise to many that the democrats won the White House in a landslide. People felt betrayed by an outgoing administration that failed miserably to do the things necessary to promote a strong economy.

The president-elect was a little known senator from Cedar Rapids, Iowa named Nathan R. Grigsby. He had very little international experience, very few leadership roles as a senator in Washington, and a relatively young career. What he did have was superior intellect to his opponent. He was eloquent. Finally, he guaranteed change. The campaign trail had not been kind to him. He had to endure criticism about his announcement that he was an atheist. He had to endure claims that while in Harvard Law School he got caught using cocaine. And, he had to endure accusations from his opponent's camp that he had been illegally funded by a Muslim organization out of New York. He was resilient though. He never seemed to let the attacks shake him despite the fact that some of them were true. On election night, his opponent accepted defeat before half the nation's votes were counted.

Grigsby ran on the platform of change. He vowed to create a health care program that would help the poor in the United States, a plan that frightened most established health care givers. He also vowed to end the war in Iraq and bring the troops home. He preached the idea of equality for all, vowing to protect the rights of minorities, gays, and the poor. The silent majority feared the president-elect, but the silent-majority felt it couldn't take four more years of what they felt the Republican Party had done to their lives. So many had lost their life savings in investments, and they blamed the republicans for it all. Many of the silent majority simply stayed home on Election Day while the democrats turned out in historically record-breaking fashion.

Now, the president-elect was putting together his staff. He angered some while received cheers by others by reaching across party lines for the Secretary of State seat. He frightened many by promising peace in the Middle East through diplomacy. The president-elect wanted to have open-dialogue with key leaders in the region – Iran, Pakistan, even Hamas. Many questioned the failure to include Israel in all of those speeches. With the continued instability in the West Bank, the president-elect was questioned numerous times as to why he rarely mentioned the problems in that unstable area of the world. He always responded the same way with his view that open dialogue was the first step in bringing peace to the region. Many said that his response was nothing more than another way of saying he had no idea how to deal with the West Bank or any other part of the Middle East. One staunch republican said that the United States was bound to experience buyer's remorse with the young president-elect once he was in office.

Numerous press conferences were held giving President-elect Grigsby an opportunity to map out to the viewers his plan for a better America. Evangelicals were paying close attention to everything the president-elect was saying. In some of his public speeches, he hinted to the idea of limiting the rights of institutions such as religious colleges to refuse entry into the school based on religious affiliation. For example, he hinted to the idea that it would become illegal for a Baptist college to refuse entry to a Muslim despite the fact that the Baptist college was a private institution. This, some claimed, was an invasion by the government into the lives of its citizens and their right to worship as the constitution allowed – freely, without interference by the government.

For the most part, President-elect Grigsby was considered a ray of hope in Washington, at least to the left. He stayed on course during the entire election, and nearly two months following his victory he was still on that same course, promising big changes in Washington and big improvements for the lives of Americans. He had the country's attention for a myriad of reasons, some out of fear that he would tax the nation into a depression, others out of fear that he would only stir up the terrorist pot and bring another huge attack to American soil, still others who had great hopes that they could keep their homes that were nearing foreclosure and finally be able to have health care for the family they worked so hard to care for. Time would tell.

President-elect Grigsby was planning a huge celebration on the day of his inauguration. Thousands upon thousands were expected to descend on Washington, D.C. Homeland security was keeping tabs along with the CIA and FBI on any suspicious activity with people they believed to be involved in terrorism. No chances were going to be taken and no stone would be left unturned in an effort to make the event safe for everyone. It was going to be an historic event for the nation, and the security side of the government would not allow either foreign or domestic terrorism to invade that day.

Chapter Nine

Atlanta, The Holiday Season

Paul despised shopping as much as he hated eating liver. He didn't like crowds, and Phipps Plaza in Buckhead, Atlanta's most prestigious mall, was packed with shoppers a week before Christmas. Paul always got turned around in malls despite the numerous directory stations located in various locations. Here was a man that could read and dissect a topographical map in a rain shower at mid-night with enemy fire coming in on his position and never blink an eye, but he couldn't find his way around a mall. He just wanted to get what he came for and leave.

He wound up at Bailey, Banks and Biddle Jewelers. Looks like a nice place, he thought to himself. He approached one of the cases and began looking at jewelry. This was an absolute first for Paul. He had never in his life shopped for jewelry for two women. Paul had already shopped for and purchased on-line a gift for Charlie. That had been relatively easy. This, however, was a new challenge. Fortunately, the store had an excellent staff member who assisted him with everything from choice, style and purchase. He was glad to find the guy. Paul felt truly like a fish out of water in there. The sales representative calmed him down and assured him that he would walk him through it all, that he would know exactly what he was getting for his money. In the end and $3500 later, Paul walked out feeling very good about his purchase. It wouldn't be ready for three days, but he felt better. The amount didn't bother him. Nothing was too good for the two women in his life. He was just glad he found a jewelry expert in the store who got him through it all. Paul would have paid extra for that kind of help – he despised shopping that much.

Dianne had no idea that he was in town. He thought he would drive over to Northside Hospital and surprise her. On the way over, Paul thought about how much fun he had at Thanksgiving. It was the Thanksgiving that he dreamed about as a child missing his parents. As planned, the weekend began on Thanksgiving morning with a trip to a homeless shelter where a hot meal was being served to at least five hundred persons. Charlie had acquired six hundred of the small New Testament Gideon Bibles and purchased six hundred pairs of new socks and six hundred sweatshirts. Among the myriad of equipment he had on his farm, he owned a twelve by six enclosed trailer that had all of the boxes in it. He pulled it with the Yukon to the parking lot of the shelter and kept it padlocked until the meal was done. After the meal was served, Charlie and Paul set up tables in the parking lot behind the trailer. The large table covers were embossed with "Spring River Baptist Church". Lines formed at the tables as the people who had been served began emerging from the large dining area. The usual dog-eat-dog pushing and shoving started, but Paul was there.

"Hey, everyone listen up. We all have nice full stomachs; now we want you to come through the line in an orderly fashion and receive a gift from our church. I'm going to be watching the line. If I see someone trying to cut in or push someone out, I'm going to remove you from the line and you can go to the back and pray in hopes of finding anything left when you get to the table. Fair enough?" Most everyone nodded approval of this assertive stranger who had a knack for being able to communicate with the people in line. Charlie who was seated and ready with the Bibles looked over at Dianne who was in charge of socks. He had never seen this side of Paul. She had. She gave her father her patent smile and shrug of pride in her hero.

Everyone went through the line in a polite, orderly fashion. Nearly everyone that came by the tables thanked them for their generosity. Dianne said the same thing to everyone that came through the line: "God bless you. Have a great thanksgiving."

This angel in blue jeans, an Emory sweatshirt and ball cap could bring a smile to the most desperate person going through the line.

Thanksgiving couldn't have been any better for Paul, Dianne, Charlie and Anne. It was a dream come true for each of them each in a very personal way. Their time together in Helen was fantastic. They were able to take four rolls of pictures while there, but the time spent there paled in comparison to the absolute satisfaction they all got by being a part of helping others in need at the homeless shelter in Atlanta. Charlie's idea would hopefully become a family tradition for many years to come. Another highlight of the weekend was a phone call from Thomas. Dianne had insisted that he take her number when they dropped him off at the VA Hospital in Decatur. He finally took it but had not called, that is until the Saturday following Thanksgiving.

Paul and Dianne had a chance to speak with him at the same time. Dianne put his call on her speaker and the three chatted for just under an hour. He said he was doing great, that he had sort of graduated to a point where he was actually working full-time in the hospital while living in a VA funded halfway house just a few blocks away from the facility. He was making four AA meetings a week. Dianne raised her hands in the air and thanked God with tears flowing from her eyes when Thomas told them that his wife and children were right there in the room with him as he was talking. Slowly, he said, God was repairing some of the breaches caused by his depression and subsequent alcoholism. Seeds planted, Paul thought. He felt great.

Dianne asked Thomas' wife, Amy, if she could get her phone number and call her sometime. She did not hesitate giving her number to Dianne. Amy continuously thanked Paul and Dianne for what they had done for Thomas. She said that he was a different man. Thomas said that he was so glad that his children didn't have to live in fear of what he might do next. Now he could be a dad. Of course, he was very realistic in understanding that the restoration of his family would happen one day at a time. When the phone call ended, Paul and Dianne sat next to each other on the bed in Dianne's hotel room and stared at each other. They said nothing, only stared, each admiring the other. After a romantic kiss, the two celebrated with a banana split at an ice cream shop near the square.

Now, Christmas season had come and Paul was happy that his shopping was done. He pulled the poor old Chevy S-10 into the parking garage at the hospital and parked the aging truck. Dianne had snuck out of her parent's home one evening a few weeks earlier when she was visiting Paul and tied a large red Christmas bow on the grill of the truck. Paul rode around in the truck for three days before he found out that it was there. Some of his co-workers started teasing him about it in the warehouse. He stopped what he was doing and walked outside. When he saw the bow he shook his head. "Dianne." He left it on the truck, telling Charlie every time he laughed at it, that the bow gave the truck some Christmas character. Additionally, Paul swore the truck had been running better since the bough had been put on the Chevy.

Now, just several days before Christmas, Paul was riding the elevator to the ninth floor of the hospital to surprise Dianne. He approached the nurses' station and inquired of Dianne's whereabouts. One of the nurses said that she would page her. Paul thanked her, smiled at the gawking nurses and walked over to a small waiting area.

"Is that the 'Paul' Dr. Taylor's been talking about?" One nurse whispered to another.

"I guess, unless she's stepping out on him." The other replied.

"Yes, that's Paul and no I would never, as you say, step out on him." Dianne came into the nurses' station quietly after seeing the nurses looking at Paul and whispering.

"Oh, uh, Dr. Taylor, uh, we were just talking about. I mean we were just."

"Gossiping?" Dianne held a clipboard to her chest.

"Uh, no, no. We were just bragging on how well you've done." The nurse was fishing for a way out of this.

"Thank-you for the compliment Bernice, but I think you have some rounds to make, don't you?" Dianne knew just how to remedy such situations. Break up the culprits.

"Yes I do Doctor; I'll get right on it." Bernice stood, grabbed a sheet of paper with patient names and room numbers on it and headed out of the nurses' station, embarrassed, a little shaken, but glad she was escaping the wrath to come.

Actually, Dianne was the most well respected doctor in pediatrics. She was liked by every shift of nurses. She was approachable about any topic work related or not. However, she would not tolerate incidents like the one she had just walked in on.

"Well," Dianne said as she walked up on Paul who was looking out through a window, "this is a great surprise."

"I was in the neighborhood." Paul scratched his head. "Is that how you're supposed to say it when in actuality you're stalking a beautiful doctor?"

"I think you're just supposed to give the doctor a kiss and say 'hello'."

Paul stepped away from the window and stood in front of Dianne. She was as stunning in her scrubs as she was in anything else she wore. He kissed her beautiful lips first, then moved to her forehead and kissed her again. "So, this is where you work?"

"This is where I work," she replied. "Would you like the speedy doctor tour?"

"Sure, if you have a minute to spare," Paul said. "It's certainly much more intellectually stimulating than the warehouse where I work."

"It's not made for television up here, Paul." Dianne began leading him down a hallway. "There's some heartbreaking tragedy on this wing of the hospital. Come with me. I want to introduce you to a little boy."

"Sure. What's his name?"

"Jerome," Dianne replied. "He's seven years old. His mother works two jobs – one full time and the other part time at a shipping warehouse that provides its part-time people full benefits. She was at work and her live-in boyfriend lost his temper with Jerome. The man threw the child down a flight of stairs. The tumbling fall broke his right leg, his left arm and three of his ribs. One rib punctured his lung. The boyfriend told police that the little boy had been nagging him all night long and he simply lost it and threw him down the stairs. Of course, this came after three hours of interrogation. The boyfriend initially claimed that Jerome fell on his own down the stairs. Things only changed after Jerome's mother arrived at the hospital and just before surgery Jerome asked his mother why the boyfriend pushed him down the stairs. Police went right over and arrested the guy. He's still in jail. And, they arrest people like your brother for caring for a child. I just don't get it, Paul." They were standing at the door that led Jerome's room.

"I don't either, Dianne. I don't either." Paul pushed the door open. "We have a real problem with our system today."

Paul and Dianne entered the room. Jerome's mother was seated by the bed reading to him. She was struggling with guilt for allowing someone like the man she had been letting live at her place to spend any time around her son. Her name was Paula, very attractive at five feet four inches tall with jet-black straight hair and dark brown eyes. Her skin was a very light brown color and she had an athletic build that would make heads turn of the young and of the old. Dianne had grown fond of her and Jerome from the first time they met.

"Paula, how are you tonight?" Dianne walked over to Paula and placed her gentle hand on Paula's shoulder.

"I'm holding up, Dianne," she replied. "How are you?"

"Excellent. I'm very blessed, especially every time I see this cute little boy." Dianne tickled the bare foot of Jerome's good leg.

He began to playfully giggle. "I'm not little," he said.

"You're right. You are a very big boy. Right?" Dianne moved to Jerome's bedside to check his vitals.

"Right!" Jerome replied.

"Paula, I'd like to introduce someone to you." Dianne walked over to where Paul was standing.

"You don't need to. I'll bet you're Paul."

Paul took a quick glance at Dianne. Does the planet know who I am, he thought to himself? "Yes, I'm Paul. It's a pleasure to meet you. Anything that I can get for little superman over there."

"No, thank-you," Paula replied. "I only hope that I don't lose my part-time job. The benefits that are paying for this came from that job. It will be an interesting Christmas this year."

"I'm sure everything will work out just fine," Paul replied. Paul looked at Jerome, wondering what could possess any adult to hurt a child. The two women talked for several minutes while Paul entertained Jerome with a few knock-knock jokes. Bland as his jokes could be, Jerome was all giggles just having someone visit him in the hospital.

"Please don't worry, Paula. God is with you and Jerome right now, and he is watching over this situation. Your job will be there when you get back. You told me how they were begging you to come on-board full time. That must mean something."

"I'll be right back." Paul interrupted. He quickly rushed from the room. It puzzled Dianne. She was worried that he might have been a little embarrassed about her sharing with people about him. Dianne knew how private Paul could be. She quickly shunned the thought, knowing truly that Paul loved and cared for her.

Paula continued talking. "You're right Dianne. This just seems like a bad dream."

Dianne, now somewhat distracted by Paul's quick exit, tried to remain focused on the conversation with Paula. Several minutes later, Paul re-entered the room, breathing somewhat heavily. He had Dianne's curiosity aroused.

Paul walked over to where Paula was sitting. "I know you don't know me. I don't know you. I don't know your beautiful son. Don't ask me why I'm doing this. It's not important. Maybe it's because you're Paula and I'm Paul. No, not the reason. Just accept this and have a blessed Christmas." Paul handed Paula two hundred dollars in cash. He had made a dash for an elevator, down to the hospital lobby and to an ATM. He pulled the money out of a savings account that he had with his bank.

Dianne sighed, then walked over to Paul and put her arm around his waist. He had done it again. Dianne had always tried to dig down into the depths of the man she was in love with, but each time she thought she had him figured out, he would do something like what he did that night and she would have to admit that she didn't have him figured out at all. It was obvious Paul cared about people, no matter the size, shape, color or language. He simply cared. Perhaps that was why he had to finally give up his military career. He cared more than the military could allow a soldier in his position to care.

Paula's eyes filled with tears. "Are you an angel?" She stood and took Paul's hand.

"No," Paul replied. "It took me five minutes in here to realize that if the tables were turned, you would do it for me or for Dianne." He looked at Jerome. "So, Jerome, what do you want for Christmas?"

"I want mommy to be happy," Jerome replied.

Paul took a step backward and turned away from the child. It was the second time Dianne had seen him shed a tear. He was amazed at the child's response. Children can be naturally selfish, only thinking of what they want. It's never their fault. It's just life sometimes. Paul was taken by this child's unselfish desire for his mother to be happy. Paul realized that underestimating the wisdom of a child could be a colossal error. Jerome knew his mother was blaming herself for what happened to him. He wanted her to be happy so that she would know she was forgiven, that he loved his mother, certainly more than a Christmas present. Paul gathered his emotions and turned back around. "I'm sure your mother is happy tonight. With a handsome little boy like you, how can she not be happy?" Paul took a quick glance at Paula. She was looking at him. She got the message.

"I'm not little," Jerome insisted.

"That's right, Jerome. You're not," Paul said. "Well, I have to be heading home. I have a long drive ahead of me."

Paula stood and gave Paul a kiss on the cheek and a hug. "Everything Dianne has said about you is true."

"Did she tell you I have a paper route up in Lumpkin County? I deliver papers on my mountain bike to all the farms up there." He gave a quick, sarcastic smile in Dianne's direction.

"Uh, no. That sounds interesting," Paula replied.

"Then she didn't tell you everything. Take care of yourself Paula. Merry Christmas! Ho, ho, ho and all that other Christmas jargon." Paul took Dianne's hand and began leaving the room. Dianne looked back at

Paula, rolled her eyes and smiled. Paula got it. She laughed as the couple exited the room.

"You know, you just made her entire year," Dianne said as they headed for the elevators. "You have a way of making someone feel really good about life."

"I just wanted to help. She needed help. Sounds like her boyfriend needs another kind of help."

Dianne stopped in the hallway, turned and looked at Paul with a mild look of concern. "Paul, I share with people around here about you because I'm so happy. People have seen it in me and want to know what's going on with me. I wasn't unhappy before, but I wasn't content. With you my life is complete. I love you so much that I just have to share it with others. I never thought I could meet someone like you. I thought it was only a dream. Please forgive me if that upsets you."

Running his hand through her soft hair, Paul stared at Dianne and shook his head. "How could I ever be angry with you? Yes, I admit that I'm a work in progress. For so many years because of what I did for a living, I lived in the shadows of anonymity. Dianne, your love for me has brought me out of that shell. I can assure you, it's no fun being in that shell. I'm not angry with you. I'm flattered that you would think of me. I really do love you." Paul kissed the love of his life. "Now, I've got to be going. Can't wait to see you this weekend." They were celebrating Christmas a few days early because Dianne had to work on Christmas Eve and Christmas day. Paul pushed the elevator button and began his wait for the door to open.

"Wait," Dianne said as one of the six doors opened. She walked over to Paul, dropped her clipboard on the floor, wrapped her arms around his waist and kissed him. She held the kiss long enough for the door to the elevator to close and move from the floor. "I need you. I will always love you, Paul Atkinson. Drive safely going home. Please call me when you arrive."

"I will," Paul replied. "I'll see you Friday night." The elevator door opened again and Paul boarded. He gave a short wave to Dianne as the door was closing, and she gave him her stunning smile. She never found out what he was doing in town. She was so excited to see him that it never crossed her mind to ask him just what he was doing there anyway.

Friday arrived and Dianne drove from her condominium to her parent's home. As usual, she brought along Wilson. Charlie had grown so fond of Wilson that Dianne knew not bringing the dog would hurt her dad's feelings. Wilson spent much of the time in Charlie's lap while Charlie watched football, basketball, and practically any sport on television that he could find. Upon arriving, she greeted her parents, went to her bedroom and changed, unpacked the few items she brought with her – she already had another wardrobe at her parent's home – and walked down to see Paul. He was usually waiting for her while watching television with Charlie, but he wasn't this time.

She walked in and found him asleep on his sofa. Sitting on the coffee table were three wrapped gifts. Two of them were obviously professionally wrapped. Her dad's gift was a different story. Paul had never wrapped a gift before, and after attempting to wrap Charlie's gift, he swore he would never wrap one again. It was a pathetic site to behold. Dianne, however, was more impressed with his attempt at wrapping a gift, than with the professionally wrapped gifts. That poorly wrapped, pathetically sad looking gift spoke volumes about this man who would never have attempted to wrap a gift for anyone a few years earlier. In fact, the first Christmas that Paul lived in that house he purchased restaurant gift cards for everyone. He politely refused to attend Christmas dinner with them, opting instead to stay in his house and read. Just a few years later, he was actually shopping for gifts and attempting to wrap one. To Dianne, the change was God. There was, in her mind, no other explanation.

Dianne tried to squeeze onto the sofa with Paul. He woke up briefly to make room for her and put his arm around her before falling back into a deep sleep. The workweek had been fast and furious, a great deal of product moving from the warehouse. Paul was one of the top producers in the warehouse, an extremely hard worker. He was counted on every time a period of heavy shipping and receiving rolled around to work a great deal of overtime hours. On that particular week, he worked sixty-five hours. He worked late on that Friday because he had taken a two-hour lunch to go back to Phipps and pick up the Christmas gifts he had purchased for Anne and Dianne.

Dianne enjoyed just laying there on the sofa with Paul. She felt safe in his arms. She laid next to him and remembered when she was a teenager. She was outgoing in so many ways, except when it came to boys. Charlie and Anne never pushed Dianne. She was such an excellent student, a great athlete and a wonderful daughter they saw no need to question why she refused to attend her senior prom. Dianne was only interested in going to college and becoming a doctor. She enjoyed being with her parents. She enjoyed the simple life of the farm, having been taught by her father how to operate every piece of equipment Charlie owned. She enjoyed her involvement with the church. Dating in high school seemed a bit infantile to her. However, while in college at Emory, she met a fellow student. The two of them began dating. She thought she loved him, but when he continuously tried to take things too far sexually, she finally broke things off with him. She returned home a weekend or two later and sat in her father's lap crying, saying she was never going to find someone. He assured her that she would find that right person if she would listen to God and not her emotions. After that bad experience, Dianne threw herself at her studies and graduated with honors. She went directly into medical school and never looked back. She saw the young man from time to time on campus. It seemed each time she saw him he was walking with a different girl. She realized that she had been somewhat shallow in getting into a relationship with a person like him.

Now, nearly a decade later, the man of her dreams was fast asleep holding her close. Paul was different. She had never met anyone like him. She was coming to the conclusion that the depth of who Paul was for those trying to understand the complexities of this man was essentially unreachable. He lived a very simple, humble, quiet life, yet he was an extremely multidimensional person. He never flaunted his intelligence. Paul graduated the Citadel with honors with a degree in Philosophy. He could read a person in a matter of seconds, as he had done with Paula days earlier. He cared nothing for pomp and circumstance, yet his accomplishments while in the military were the stuff of legends, though by choice he rarely talked about any of those years. Paul found nothing meaningful about being in the spotlight. He wanted no applause, no recognition, and certainly no awards. He had grown to a point where he considered life a quest that simply amounted to one basic principle: treat others with dignity and kindness, give when the opportunity presents itself, and try to live life as peaceably as possible.

One example of Paul's humility and character was shown several weeks prior to Christmas while Dianne was helping him move a new dresser that Anne purchased for his bedroom. The house had been mostly furnished when Paul arrived a few years earlier, and Charlie and Anne felt that it needed a few minor upgrades. Dianne needed to take the clothing out of the old dresser and exchange it over to the new one. While unloading one of the top drawers she accidentally came across a stack of certificates of achievement of various types from the military. One was a certificate for a commendation for a medal of valor given to him. There was a letter along with the certificate that read: "For outstanding duty and uncommon valor in a combat zone. Captain Paul D. Atkinson performed above and beyond the call of duty by withstanding an enemy platoon during a combat situation. Captain Atkinson thwarted the attempts of the enemy platoon to overrun his position and take civilians captive and as a result of his bravery he inflicted twenty-seven casualties on the enemy who retreated. It is for this reason that Captain Atkinson is receiving the Medal of Valor." Dianne found the medal in a plastic case under Paul's socks. When Dianne found those certificates and the medal, she realized that those things placed in a meaningless spot under socks were the essence of who Paul was. He didn't go for the spotlight. That was one of the many reasons she loved him so much. He just didn't fit the mold of anyone. As the old saying goes, Dianne felt that Paul Atkinson indeed marched to the beat of a different drummer.

Paul woke up at three in the morning with Dianne in his arms. She had rolled over while they were sleeping and was facing Paul on the sofa fast asleep. She had her head buried in his chest and was holding tightly to his left hand with her right. In some ways, this brilliant, talented, strong woman of faith seemed so fragile to Paul. He was reminded of the beautiful roses he had purchased for her just months before when he had competed in the road race at the Georgia Dome. He examined the flower, its beauty, its fragrance, yet with all of the rose's incredible characteristics, it remained extremely fragile. Dianne, in some ways, was fragile as well. Paul laid on the sofa next to Dianne for a moment and examined her face. She seemed so peaceful as she slept. Dianne awake or asleep was always the walking, talking definition of serenity. Paul had never seen her lose her temper or get angry. She would look at a situation, assess it and respond. He had never met anyone who seemed to have such tight reigns on her emotions. As he had done many times, Paul lifted Dianne from the sofa into his arms and carried her to his room. He laid her on his bed and covered her with the comforter. He returned to his kitchen and grabbed a glass of orange juice. After donning a hooded sweatshirt, Paul walked out on the back porch. He had seen some clear Georgia nights, but this one seemed incredibly clear. The night air was a biting cold forcing Paul to pull the hood up onto his head. He had slept so soundly on the sofa that he felt no need to try for any more sleep. He never heard or remembered Dianne coming in. He was just glad to have her at his side when he awoke.

After some thinking, Paul decided to fire up the John Deere and haul a bale of hay out to one of the pastures. It was four in the morning and the racket could wake Charlie, but Paul knew that Charlie wouldn't mind him taking out the tractor so early. He went back inside and grabbed a pair of gloves. The tractor was equipped with a heater that would blow warm air on the legs of the operator, but Paul knew that his hands would get very cold in the early morning winter air. He reached the stall where the tractor was parked and started the engine. Paul had his own key that he kept in a drawer in his kitchen. The engine cranked right up – more than I can say for my truck, Paul thought. The tractor only had about sixty hours of use on it, so it was in great condition. Plus, Charlie always maintained his equipment; every piece was in immaculate condition. After giving the engine a few minutes to warm-up, Paul climbed up into the seat and pulled the tractor out of its stall. He drove it over to the location of the hay bales and loaded one on the forks of the lift. Paul backed the tractor up and turned it onto the path that led to the pasture where he planned to drop the bale. On the way, he thought about Chris. In a matter of hours, Paul would be celebrating Christmas with his family, a family that had treated him as one of their own, and with a woman with whom he hoped to spend eternity. But, Chris, he thought, was in a jail cell serving time for something so ridiculous that it defied logic. Anger welled up inside Paul; he wanted this judge to admit to his mistake, but he knew the pride of Judge Simpson would prevent that from ever happening.

Paul had heard from both Chris and Jensen several times. The holiday season was slowing down the process of pushing through the motions that Jensen had filed. With each passing day, Chris was getting worse. His hopes of anything good happening had long since faded. He had lost faith in Jensen even though Jensen was working diligently on his case. Jensen was disgusted with the judge's decision to jail Chris based on the facts of the case. It sounded to him as though the judge turned a deaf ear to the facts and allowed his pride to rule his decision-making. Chris told Paul on numerous occasions that he didn't know how much more he could take, that his nerves were on the brink. Despite Paul's strong words of encouragement and his promise to walk through the entire legal process with him, Chris' hope faded. The phone conversations had become negative and hopeless. As Paul drove the tractor, he wished there was something he could do to get his brother out of that jail cell and to Georgia. For one of the first times in his life, Paul felt helpless.

Reaching one of the pastures that was situated mid-way across the farm, Paul dropped the bale of hay and switched off the tractor. He stared into the early morning dark sky. While many questions in his life were being answered through his newfound faith and the love he had experienced being a part of the entire community, there were still many questions in Paul's life that remained unanswered. Many in the community asked each other why Paul had yet to ask Dianne to marry him. She was never going to push him to ask. Perhaps the reason lied in the fact that Paul still wasn't fully sure of himself. Did he really know how to be fully committed? The pain of never really knowing his parents had kept him in the dark so long, there were times that Paul thought that he could never fully escape that dark pain. He had isolated for that very reason. He never wanted to get hurt by loss again, and if something happened to him, he didn't want to have someone mourning him. Yet, when he was in Dianne's presence he was sure of himself. He was sure of what he wanted out of life. He wanted her. She brought meaning and purpose to his life – love, laughter and a sense of security.

Paul got off the tractor, knelt in the grassy field and prayed: "Dear God, I know don't pray as often as I should. I know that I am but a child in faith, that I know very little of whom you really are. I only want to ask you to help me become the man that you want me to be, not for me but for the woman I love. I want to be everything she wants and more. I want to be everything she needs and more. I don't think I can do it without you, though. Please help me to put the past in the past and to move on with my life today. Amen." Paul stood up and stared at the clear sky and the bright stars that seemed to be hanging only a few feet from his head. A shooting star shot across the dark sky at an incredible rate of speed, moving from the northeast and headed in a southwesterly direction. Paul loved living in north Georgia for reasons just like that one – the night skies were often filled with shooting stars, especially during the late fall and winter months. He climbed back onto the tractor, started it and headed back. It was 5:00am and the sun would be rising in a few hours. He had had his Saturday morning quiet time. Paul decided that his thirty-mile ride would start a little early. As soon as the sun came up, he would begin his ride. With the tractor parked in its stall, Paul returned to his house. A few hours later, with Dianne still asleep in his room, Paul began his Saturday ride. He followed the same routine, biking fifteen miles out, stopping at the little country store and returning the same way he came. All of the usual cast of characters obliged. The two children of the cashier were bundled up in their winter coats. They had made a small ramp and were pretending to be stuntmen by jumping the ramp with their bikes. Their mother was as cordial as usual, while the two tobacco chewing gentlemen had moved to a bench on the inside away from the cold air, but the conversation was the same. All is well in the world today, Paul thought as he gulped down his Gatorade, threw the bottle in a trashcan by the gas pumps, and took off for home. He walked back into his place at 8:35am. Dianne was gone, obviously waking while he was on his ride and deciding to walk to her parent's to get ready for the day. Paul found a note from her on his kitchen counter that read: "Dear Paul, Thank-you for being the ultimate Christmas gift to me. God has enriched my life through you, and I will never be the same. See you at breakfast. I love you. Dianne." Paul could only shake his head and smile. What an incredible woman.

Paul arrived as the table was being set for breakfast. Charlie had warmed up in the bullpen and was ready for Paul when he walked in. "Anne," he said, "did you get that number of that psychiatrist for Paul? Only an insane night owl would be up before sunrise hauling hay around."

"Charlie, you haven't heard of the new farming methods? That's called stealth farming. No one can steal your top secret farming methods when you're feeding cattle at four in the morning." Paul grabbed a slice of cantaloupe from a plate that Anne had set out on the counter of the kitchen island.

"Oh, so that's the new method? I need to read more." Charlie took a sip of his coffee.

"You don't want me to give away our deepest farming secrets to our neighbors, do you?" Paul took a bite out of the cantaloupe.

"No, Paul you're right," Charlie replied. "I don't want our good friends, Fred and Linda Jenkins, who live a mile away stealin' our farmin' secrets. Anne, cancel the psychiatrist. This man's brilliant."

Paul walked over to Charlie and placed his hand on his shoulder. "Charlie, flattery will get you nowhere with me."

Dianne was assisting Anne with the final preparations for breakfast. She whispered to her mother. "Please, let's get some food in their mouths quick." Anne laughed.

Charlie and Paul were eating five minutes later, sarcastic jabs put on the sideline, at least momentarily. Breakfast completed, the four decided it was time to open gifts. Charlie and Anne had decided years before that for Christmas, they would simply exchange gift cards. They were more interested in shopping for their daughter and providing for the community's needy than spending hours trying to figure out what the other wanted or needed. Paul handed Charlie his gift. He opened it to find an interactive history book on disc. Paul explained to him that it was extremely advanced and that it would actually ask the participant questions. The participant could vocally answer without having to type a word. He also said that he would receive new discs every quarter. Charlie loved it, wanting to go right to the computer and start on it but refraining for the sake of everyone else.

Anne gave Paul his gift from her and Charlie. He couldn't believe his eyes when he opened it up and found two open airline tickets, a flier for a four star hotel in Paris, and a flier for the Tour de France. "Go when you're ready. The extra ticket is in case you decide you want someone to go with you."

Paul glanced at Dianne and back at Anne. "No, I think I'll go alone. You can have this one back." He looked back at Dianne.

She wasn't going to fall for his sarcasm. "I don't think so. You might want to hold onto that ticket – or else." Everyone laughed. Paul hugged Anne and Charlie for the incredible gift.

It was Dianne's turn. She opened her gift from her parents. It was an incredibly advanced Hewlett Packard laptop computer that had every feature available including a camera for those out of town teleconferences. This was top of the line. She didn't own a laptop. Her only source of communication with her work when out of town was through her Blackberry. Now she could dial in to her computer at the hospital and check on various patient issues.

Dianne gave her parents a four-day trip to Washington, D.C. Charlie was constantly talking about visiting again. The last time the family had been to Washington was when Dianne was in fifth grade. She purchased open-ended reservations for rooms at the Mayflower in the heart of D.C. and tickets for all of the major attractions. Charlie immediately began asking Anne when she wanted to go. He said he would brush up on American history with Paul's gift and afterward they could travel to the nation's capital. Anne said she was excited about the trip, that she would join Charlie studying the history lessons on the computer.

Paul handed Anne her gift. She opened it to find a stunning necklace. It was a white gold cross with five small diamonds – one in the center of the cross, the other four on each end of the cross. On the back of the cross the words, "He is risen" were engraved into the gold. The necklace was thin and medium length. It truly was a beautiful necklace. Anne, with a tear in her eye, hugged Paul and thanked him for the gift. Dianne helped her put the necklace on.

Dianne gave Paul her gift. He opened it up to find the latest edition of the Garmin athletic watch. He had seen these watches before. It actually links with a satellite during a workout: it monitors speed, different elevations, heart rate, has a map of where the athlete has traveled, and various other features. After a workout, the information could be downloaded to a personal computer where graphs of various types could be viewed as well as a map of the course. Paul had been riding some different courses lately and wasn't sure of the distances. The Garmin watch would solve that. He absolutely loved the gift. She also gave him a gift card to a well-known athletic apparel store in Atlanta. He thanked Dianne with a kiss.

Paul finally gave Dianne her gift. She opened it up to find the most stunning earrings she had ever seen. They were incredibly clear diamonds set in platinum. They were not too big, but just right for Dianne's face. The sales representative at the jewelry store had helped Paul with deciding on the size. They were beautiful. She was amazed at the quality and the fact that Paul had put so much effort into traveling to Atlanta for the purchase. Anne told Dianne to go ahead and try them on. Once the earrings were on everyone took a look at her. Not one said a word. The diamonds simply accentuated her incredible beauty. Charlie looked at Paul and joked. "Son, you are good!"

Dianne hugged Paul and kissed him on the cheek. "They are beautiful, Paul. Now I know why you were in Atlanta."

"Somehow I didn't think I was going to find earrings like those up here in the mountains," Paul replied.

"I absolutely love them, and I absolutely love you." She kissed him again.

"I love you, too. I'm glad you like them. That was a first for me."

"Why couldn't I be that good the first time out?" Charlie was looking through his history discs. "I bought your mother a pair of hose on our first Christmas together."

"Sure dad, I'll bet," Dianne said.

"No, he's telling the truth. I was speechless." Anne looked up at her husband and the two began laughing. Dianne and Paul joined in.

The early Christmas celebration came to an end later in the afternoon with Anne's incredible turkey dinner. Afterward, since there were always leftovers, Charlie and Anne followed their usual tradition of making plates for some of their less fortunate neighbors and set out to deliver them to their homes. The homes with young children received toys, while the elderly received supermarket gift cards for food and other needs. Charlie and Anne had been doing this for nearly eighteen years. They did it alone. Not even Dianne went with them on these outings of mercy.

Paul and Dianne walked over to his place to spend some time together. Paul was reading the instruction manual to his Garmin watch when the telephone rang. He picked it up and heard a recording instructing him that the call was collect from a correctional institution – Chris, he thought. He accepted the charges and said, "Chris, is that you."

"Yes, it's me, Paul." Chris sounded terrible. His depression level had reached an all-time low.

"Chris, how are you holding up?" Paul placed the instruction booklet on the coffee table. Dianne had been in the kitchen microwaving popcorn for a movie they were going to watch.

"Hey, how do you think I'm holding up?" Chris' voice was shaky. "You come here with some attorney who makes all kinds of promises, gets my hopes up, and I'm still sitting here in hell rotting."

"Chris, take it easy. I've been in touch with – "

"Been in touch with who, Paul? Jensen's worthless. I haven't seen him do anything except come here and talk to me for an hour at a time."

"Listen Chris, that's more than most attorneys with clients in jail would do. I've talked to Jensen and he is doing his best. The holidays slow the wheels of justice to a crawl." Paul was trying to stay calm. He understood that his brother was under a great deal of strain.

"I just don't know how much more I can take," Chris continued. "Can you hear all that racket in the background?"

Paul could here it clearly. It was incredibly loud. He could barely make out what Chris was saying. "That's what I have to listen to twenty-four hours a day."

Paul stood and began pacing the floor. Dianne knew what that meant. He was growing anxious as a result of the phone call with Chris. "Look Chris, I'm sending you money every week. I stay in contact with Jensen every week. I try to be here when I expect to receive calls from you. What more do you want me to do?"

"Did you have a good Christmas today?"

"Chris, please." Paul was rubbing his forehead now.

"Did you? I won't be having much of a Christmas. I'm glad you can though."

"Chris, I can't talk to you when you get like this," Paul replied.

"Good. You won't have to."

Paul heard a click on the line and then a dial tone. He slammed the phone back on the base and rushed outside pushing the screen door with such violence that the bottom hinge broke. Dianne followed him. He walked over to the fence and picked up a rotting tree limb that had fallen to the ground. He swung the limb like a bat plunging it into the bark of the trunk of the large tree it had fallen from shattering its aged wood into splinters sending pieces of the limb flying in every direction. Dianne had never seen him so angry.

She approached Paul cautiously and placed her hand on his back. He turned and stared into her concerned eyes.

"What can I do?" Paul pulled Dianne close to him. "Dianne, what can I do? He's alone there and I can't do anything to fix the situation."

"Pray," Dianne responded. "Pray."

"Do you think Jensen is on our side?"

Dianne looked intensely into Paul's eyes. "I'm convinced Jensen is on our side, and you are, too. He can only do so much. We're dealing with a judge that is playing god, and right now he holds all the cards. Stop blaming yourself for this. Don't blame Jensen either. Chris has to make a choice to stay strong. It's up to him. Our job is to pray and to try to help Chris any way we can."

"That's easy for us to say," Paul said. "We're not sitting where he is today."

"I know. It's got to be a very trying time for him." Dianne kissed Paul. "But, you can't carry that world on your shoulders. Please Paul, pray."

Dianne calmed Paul enough to where he was finally able to go back inside and watch the movie with her. He apologized for his outburst. She told him that she understood his frustration. She was frustrated, too. The couple sat on the sofa eating popcorn and watching a comedy on DVD. Paul, however, had his mind on Chris and his anger aimed toward a Texas judge.

The next day the family attended church. Paul stood and asked the congregation to remember his brother in prayer. After church, Paul and Dianne spent a few hours together. She had to get back early. There were some critical patients that she had to check on. She was extremely dedicated to the children that were placed in her care.

After Dianne was gone, Paul hopped on his mountain bike and tried his Garmin watch out on the road. When he returned, he set the watch in the pod that was hooked via USB to his computer. Graphs of various types popped up on the flat screen monitor that he owned. He loved this watch. He tried to call Dianne and tell her how much he liked the watch but only got her voicemail.

As it turned out, Dianne's day had turned challenging with a ten-year-old patient that had been in a severe automobile accident. The little girl had been thrown from the car that was driven by her father. Her parents did not have her buckled in and when someone pulled out in front of their car, the father of the child swerved, went into a skid, overcorrected and went off the road. The car flipped ejecting the little girl through a window that shattered as the car flipped. Amazingly, the little girl's parents survived with cuts and bruises, saved by their seatbelts and airbags. Their little girl was not as fortunate. With multiple broken bones, excessive blood loss and a severe brain injury, Dianne wasn't sure she would survive. Her heart had stopped and Dianne was performing resuscitation efforts, following hospital protocol. She managed to bring the little girl back. Once the ten year old was stable, Dianne walked to her office. On the way, the little girl's mother, still bruised and limping from the accident approached the doctor.

"Is my little girl going to be ok," she said reaching out and grabbing Dianne's arm.

Dianne pulled her arm away and with tears in her eyes said, "How could any parent allow a child to ride in a car without seatbelts? Tell me that." Dianne looked away from the lady. "I don't know if your daughter will survive or not. That's between her and God now. Please have a seat in the waiting area. A nurse will see you soon." Dianne walked away from the woman and to her office. She closed the door and locked it. After sitting down on a small couch that sat under a bookshelf, Dianne began weeping. "Why God? Why at Christmas? Please, please don't let this little girl die. Please, show me what I can do to help her." As tears continued flowing from her eyes, Dianne noticed that she had a missed call. It was from Paul. Paul – her love and her best friend. She returned his call. He noticed she was crying and asked what was wrong. She explained to him the series of events that led up to the little girl being placed under her care. She also told Paul how she responded to the hurting mother, who was most assuredly paying for her mistake with a ton of guilt on her shoulders.

"I'm sure she feels guilty," Paul said. "I'm sure her husband feels guilty. But, none of that guilt changes the fact that they have a ten-year-old daughter laying in a hospital bed fighting for her life. That doesn't change the fact that they carelessly allowed the little girl to ride in the back seat without seatbelts. Ten-year-old little girls are fragile. Their bodies aren't designed to handle such trauma. I'm sorry for the parents, but they need to feel some guilt. In this case it's a necessary evil. You did nothing wrong,

Dianne. You had just come out of a room where you had to bring a little girl back from the gates of death. Your adrenaline was at max level and your emotions were right there, too. If you feel compelled to apologize to the mother, then don't shun it, but if you don't, then don't. God may just want those two parents to sit awhile and think about their carelessness. In the meantime, I will be praying for the little girl. Will you keep me posted?"

"Of course," Dianne replied. "Thank-you, Paul. I love you very much."

"I love you, too, Dianne. Never forget that."

"I will never forget it. I better get back to work." Once the two hung up, Dianne went to the mother and had a talk with her. She did apologize to her and promised that she would do everything she could for her daughter including a great deal of prayer. The mother of the ten year old said she understood Dianne's anger, that she and her guilt-ridden husband had made a terrible error. She had never allowed her daughter to ride in the vehicle without a seatbelt, but they had just come from a movie their daughter had been begging them to see and she was still very excited about it. She unbuckled herself and was leaning against the front seats joyfully sharing with her parents the movie experience when the accident occurred.

"Isn't it amazing," Dianne said to the crying woman as she held her hand. "That one time that seems so innocent. One lapse turns tragic." Dianne paused. "We will have to trust God with this. We have to trust him to pull her through. Can you put your trust in him right now?" The mother nodded as tears continued. "Good. I'll be by later to talk."

Later that night, the little girl went into cardiac rest again. Dianne had to shock her to bring her back. After the little girl was stable, Dianne repeated under her breath the same prayer she had prayed earlier that night asking God to spare her during this Christmas season. The next day, surgeons performed a necessary procedure on the little girl to relieve pressure from her brain. Given the little girl's instability, the surgical procedure was somewhat risky, but the surgeon felt he had no other choice. If he didn't perform the procedure, with the swelling continuing, the girl was sure to die. Dianne assisted in surgery. She was going to do everything she could to see that this girl lived through this Christmas and to have an opportunity to enjoy many more after. Assisting the surgeon gave her a feeling that she was still fighting for the ten year old and that she wasn't helplessly sitting on the sidelines watching.

It was a miracle indeed. One week later, the little girl was actually awake, alert and talking. Everyone involved in the case was amazed. The surgeon had all but counted the little girl out after the operation. He said that if she did wake up from the coma, she would never be able to communicate again, that she would essentially be an invalid for the rest of her life. The little girl defied all of the odds. Despite the long road of recovery that still lied ahead, she was not going to die. Her mother was feeding her some ice cream when Dianne walked into the room.

"Well, how is my little miracle patient doing today?" Dianne moved to the side of the bed and checked her vitals.

"Fine," the little girl said in a quiet, sweet voice.

"I'm so proud of you for being so strong." Dianne wrote the vitals on her chart.

"Thank-you." The little girl took another bite of ice cream. "I saw angels."

Dianne stopped writing and looked up at the little girl. "Did you say you saw angels?"

"Uh huh. I saw them. They were beautiful. Then a man told me that I couldn't stay, that I had to go back to mommy and daddy. He was beautiful, too. Light was all around him everywhere he went. And, and, when he came to me, the angels all got on their knees and sang to him. He said they were singing to me, but I didn't believe him. They only talked to me. They sang to him."

Dianne knew that this little girl had had a spiritual encounter with Jesus. She had read about and even witnessed too many cases where people of all ages talked about actually entering a realm, a place of perfection where angels were present. Some saw Jesus, while others didn't, but they that didn't still knew exactly where they were. This little girl had witnessed something that few ever witness. She was a miracle, indeed. "Promise me when your arm gets better, you'll color me a picture of what you saw, alright?" The little girl nodded as her mother gave her another bite of ice cream.

The mother stood and limped over to Dianne. She hugged the beautiful doctor. "Thank-you for everything you've done. We will never forget you."

"There are many to thank, and I hope you have a chance to thank them all, but the one deserving the most thanks is God. I really believe he pulled her through this. We had reached a point of just having to let go and wait. Your little girl will not die. I wish your entire family blessings and happiness." Dianne turned and walked from the room. She had no doubt that she had witnessed a miracle. She called Paul and told him everything. He was amazed with the little girl's recovery. She told him about the little girl's heavenly encounter with Jesus. Paul asked Dianne if she thought it was real or imagined. Dianne said she thought what the little girl witnessed was indeed an encounter in heaven. She believed the little girl had actually seen angels and Jesus. It was settled in his mind, then. If Dianne felt that way, then he agreed with her.

Chapter Ten

A New Year's Tragedy

Christmas day had come and gone along with all of the New Year's celebrations. Dianne talked Paul into going down to Underground Atlanta to watch the Peach Drop, an Atlanta tradition mirroring, somewhat on a much smaller scale, the New Year's celebrations in New York. As much as he despised crowds, Paul told Dianne later that he had an excellent time. The next day the couple drove to his house. The plan was to have dinner out with Charlie and Anne. Paul and Dianne decided they would spend the day on the couch watching college football. They walked into Paul's living room to find Charlie and Anne seated on the sofa. Anne had obviously been crying.

"Mom, what's wrong." Dianne ran to her and sat beside her.

Charlie spoke up. "Paul, I received a call from Jensen an hour ago. I can't say it." Charlie began weeping.

"It's about Chris, isn't it?" Paul stood directly in front of everyone. "What is it?"

Charlie looked up at Paul and nodded. "Last night, after he had a mental breakdown, he was locked in a cell by himself. He somehow managed to hang himself in his cell. He was pronounced dead when paramedics arrived."

Dianne began crying while Paul simply stood and stared into nothing. She stood and went over to him. "We can get through this Paul. God will bring us through this."

Paul looked at Dianne. The rage behind his eyes was something she had never seen in him before. It terrified her. Was this the trained killer that spent years traveling the world in a covert unit? "God! God! Let me show you what I think of your God." Paul grabbed his Bible from the coffee table and began ripping pages from the book. Then he threw what was left of it against the wall behind him. Grabbing his keys from the kitchen counter, he ran out of the house and got in his truck. Dianne tried to go after him, but Charlie stopped her. He told her to leave him alone. She was weeping and screaming, "Paul, please come back! Please don't leave me! Please!" Charlie held his daughter as tightly as he could in his arms. Anne, too, was weeping. She knew that Paul had just lost the last link to proof of a family. Now Chris was gone, Paul felt alone, and a rage like no other consumed him. The Chevy S-10 started on the third try, and Paul disappeared into the night.

Dianne wasn't able to sleep that night. Anne sat by her bedside most of the night trying to comfort her. She couldn't, not with generic talk, not with Bible scriptures, not with prayer. Dianne was in a semi-state of shock. She simply laid in her bed and stared at a picture on her nightstand of her and Paul. She wouldn't speak. She only stared.

The next morning Charlie found Paul curled up on the front seat of his truck. He was parked at the top of the hill where he and Dianne had spent hours talking months before. It was twenty-eight degrees outside and Paul was shivering from the cold. Charlie opened the door and got him out of his truck and into the Yukon. Once he got him inside the garage of his house, Charlie led Paul to the guest room and got him into the bed. Paul was still shivering. Anne came in the room with two comforters and covered Paul with both. Once Paul's body temperature began rising the shivering subsided and Paul fell asleep.

Anne went to Dianne's room. "Paul is here Dianne. Your father found him on the property in his truck."

Dianne slowly turned her head and looked at her mother. "He's here? How is he?"

A tear fell from Anne's eye. "He'll be fine. He's asleep." Dianne got out of her bed and went into the guest room. Paul was in a deep sleep. Sitting next to him on the bed, Dianne ran her hand through Paul's short hair. Anne left the room to leave her daughter with Paul. Only her daughter with God's help could pull Paul through this experience, Anne thought. Dianne laid her head on the same pillow Paul was using, staring at him, saying silent prayers asking God to help her help him. She finally fell asleep.

Two hours later Charlie was shaken by a scream that came from the guest room. He rushed to the room to find Paul sitting straight up. He was breathing heavily and sweating. "Where's Chris? I can't find Chris. Get me my M-16! They've got him. Where is he? I have to find him. I have to find him."

Dianne was crying. Charlie moved her out of the way and sat down on the bed next to Paul. "Son, listen to me. Listen to me, Paul. Chris is dead. He's gone. You have to accept this. He's gone."

Paul came out of his state of shock. A single tear rolled down his face and dripped onto the comforter. He looked at Charlie. "I have to make funeral arrangements."

"Paul, it's done. I've already done it." Charlie stood back up.

"What? Charlie, that was my responsibility." Paul became angry. "That's my brother. He's not your son. What right do you have invading our privacy?"

Charlie was hurt by Paul's words, but he tried to keep the situation in perspective. "Paul, you are in complete control. Jensen called me and said that Chris left a suicide note, sayin' he wanted to be buried next to your parents. I only made arrangements to have his body flown to a funeral home in Raleigh. The rest is up to you. I'm sorry for upsettin' you more than you already were." Charlie turned and left the room.

Paul got out of the bed and followed him. "Charlie, please forgive me. I know you were only trying to help. I'm not upset with you. I'm just confused. I can't believe he's gone."

Charlie turned and looked at this young man who had become the son he never had. "I know. Listen, we love you very much." The two embraced. Dianne came behind Paul and wrapped her arms around his waist from behind while she turned her head and laid her face against his back. Paul turned to her.

"You look exhausted," she said.

"So do you," Paul replied. "I'm sorry I left last night."

"I understand, Paul. I completely understand."

Paul kissed Dianne and said, "I need some sleep, but I don't want to be alone."

"Paul," Dianne replied, "I'll be right here with you."

Paul returned to the guest room and removed one of the comforters. He laid down on the bed. Dianne covered him then sat down beside him. She gently ran her fingers along the curvature of his face. Paul smiled and finally fell asleep. Thirty minutes later, Anne walked by the room and found Dianne sleeping next to Paul on top of the comforter. The two each had an arm around the other. Anne went to Dianne's room and retrieved an extra blanket. She returned to the guest room and covered her daughter. Anne was wise. She feared that the worst was yet to come.

The next day, Charlie, Anne and Paul made the drive north toward Raleigh. Dianne had to return to Atlanta for one day. She could not miss work. Following her shift that afternoon, she flew to Raleigh-Durham's small airport and was picked up by her father. Paul had rented a car once they got into town in order to make it easier for funeral arrangements to be made.

Paul finally visited the funeral home and saw the body of his dead brother. The veteran had seen numerous dead and mangled bodies during his military career, many upon whom he had inflicted the deadly blow. But, seeing his only remaining blood relative, his brother lying in a casket made him nauseous. He quickly headed for the men's restroom where he threw up three times before he was able to return to the funeral director.

"I know how difficult this must be for you. Believe it or not, I knew your parents personally before they passed away. We attended the same church together. You were very young and probably don't remember. Your brother will be at rest beside his mother and father. You should take comfort in that." The funeral director was certainly old enough to know his parents. Paul understood that this man was only trying to comfort him. It didn't work.

"When will the funeral begin?" Paul wanted to clear up the details.

"A service will be held here tomorrow morning at 10:00am. Then the casket will be moved to the cemetery where you brother will be laid to rest next to your mother and your father. Your brother, as you may know, had a small life insurance policy that paid for nearly everything."

"Fine. I appreciate knowing that. Thank-you sir." Paul turned and quickly left the funeral home and drove to the cemetery. He had not seen his parent's gravesite in over twelve years. After arriving at the cemetery and the graves of his parents Paul simply stood and stared at the headstone. It had their names, date of birth and date of death on it. Under his father's name the words, "Loving husband" were engraved. On his mother's side, "Loving wife". At the bottom of the tombstone were the words, "Loving, devoted parents".

Paul noticed that there were weeds growing up around the gravesite. He got back in his rental car and drove to the cemetery office. He stormed into the office and approached a desk where a large, burly man was going through a site map. "Can I help you sir," the man asked Paul.

"Yes. Can you tell me why my parent's gravesite has weeds growing all around the headstone?"

"Sir, what's the last name?"

"Taylor," Paul replied in a raised voice.

The man stood from his desk. He was at least six feet five inches tall and must have weighed three hundred pounds. "Mr. Taylor, I know who you are, and I know about your brother. We are waiting until later this afternoon to make final preparations at the gravesite. That way it will look better tomorrow."

Paul turned away from the desk, took a few steps toward the door and stopped. "I'm sorry," he said.

The cemetery manager walked over to him and put his huge hand on Paul's shoulder. "I'm sorry about your loss, my friend." Paul did not respond but only left the building. He got in his car and returned to the hotel where Charlie, Anne and Dianne were waiting for him.

"How'd everything go?" Charlie met him in the lobby.

"Please, Charlie. I just want to be alone right now." Paul walked past him and took the stairs up to the third floor. He quickly disappeared into his room.

Charlie could not keep up and finally gave up trying. He returned to his room where Anne and Dianne were waiting. "Where's Paul," Dianne asked.

"He's in his room. Dianne, I don't think you should try to go over there. He walked right past me and told me he wanted to be alone." Charlie sat down on the edge of the bed and sighed. "I wish there was something I could do for him."

"Well, I've got to try to talk to him." Dianne stood and left the room. When she arrived at Paul's room she found the "Do not disturb" sign hanging on the handle of the door. She knocked twice. "Paul, please open the door."

A few minutes passed and the door opened. Paul would not let Dianne in. "Please Dianne. I just want to be alone right now."

"Are you sure that's the best thing for you right now?"

"Yes," Paul replied. "I'll see you in the morning."

Dianne returned to her parent's hotel room and sat back down in front of her mother. "I think I'm losing him," she said as she began weeping.

Anne stood and walked over to Dianne. She knelt down next to her and put her arms around her daughter. "You're not losing him, Dianne. Love doesn't work that way. If it did, then it was never real to begin with, and I know the love between you and Paul is real. You must give him time to heal right now." Dianne hugged her mother then her father before going to her room and falling asleep.

The next day, the funeral service was held. Noticeably absent were Chris' ex-wife and daughter. Nearly thirty people, however, attended the service, mostly friends from Chris' high school days. Chris was much more outgoing than his younger brother Paul, and he managed to make many friends while in school. What Chris lacked in academic skills he made up for in social skills. Paul was a classic introvert spending most of his time studying or running. He had always been envious of Chris' gift of gab. Dianne noticed how distant Paul was during the service. He barely said two words to her. However, Paul did speak at the service about his brother and did his best to share some of Chris' humorous side with some stories, but it was as if Paul was detached from the entire affair.

Later, at the cemetery, Paul simply sat and stared as the Marine color guard carried his casket from the Hurst to the gravesite. He didn't flinch as the others did when the riflemen fired their rounds as a tribute to a fallen soldier. He only stared. As everyone else left following the minister's benediction, Paul remained. Dianne came to his side. "Paul, we have to go."

Paul continued staring off into the distance. "You go home with your parents. I'll be there in a few days." Dianne didn't respond. There was nothing she could say to him. She turned and walked to where her parents were waiting. The three got in the Yukon and drove away. Paul finally left the gravesite, got in the rental car and drove to the hotel. He rented the room for two extra days.

After retrieving his things from the car, Paul went to his room and fell asleep on the bed. Several hours later with the sky now dark, he awakened in a pool of sweat. He was being tormented by nightmares about Chris. In the dreams Chris was calling to him, begging Paul to save him. Paul, in the dream, tried to reach Chris, but something seemed to be weighing down his legs. He couldn't move. He yelled for Chris and tried to get him to come to him. Chris couldn't. Then, suddenly, hands and arms began scratching and clawing at Chris, pulling him into the darkness that was behind him. Paul screamed at the faceless captors, begging them to let his brother go. Slowly, Chris disappeared into that dark place. Paul could hear him crying for help as he disappeared.

After waking drenched in sweat, Paul got up from the bed and took a shower. He went out and drove north out of town on a rural highway. He kept driving, actually winding up in Virginia before turning the car back around and returning to the hotel. He fell asleep again and woke again drenched in sweat. With the sun beginning to rise outside, Paul decided he would not stay another day. He turned in his key card and got a refund for the extra day he didn't use.

Paul's thinking was confused; his usually keen focus was off. He decided to do some more driving, this time west on Interstate 40 finally winding up at a truck stop just outside of Knoxville, Tennessee. Exhausted and bewildered, Paul parked on the huge property and decided on a nap in his car. Evening began to approach when a knock on Paul's car window startled him from his sleep. He looked up at two men staring at him with huge grins. He rubbed his eyes and looked again. They were still there. So much for the theory of hallucinations!

Paul rolled down the window to find out just what these strangers wanted. One of the men spoke up with a significantly southern accent. "How are ya," he said with a smile. "I'm Pastor Ricky and this here's Jerry. I saw ya restin' here and thought ya just might want to come inside for a cola. We're havin' a Bible study in ten minutes and would love to have ya." The pastor pointed toward a small chapel located to the right of the truck stop's main restaurant.

Go figure, Paul thought. A truck stop chapel. "I'll think about it," he replied as he began rolling the window back up.

"Well, you come on in if ya feel like it," the pastor said before turning around and walking away.

Paul leaned back in the driver's seat, clasped his hands and placed them on his head. Why would I ever want to go into a church again, he asked himself. The internal committee began debating. One voice was determined to stay put. Another voice said, "What's the harm". Finally, the voice of thirst prevailed, and Paul got out and walked to the tiny chapel. He opened the door to find two men and a woman seated with their Bibles open. The pastor was standing up front looking at his Bible. When Paul walked in and sat in the back, Pastor Ricky glanced at Jerry with what seemed to be a knowing smile.

"Welcome, friend," the pastor said. "You mind sharin' your name with us?"

"Paul."

"Well, Paul. We're kinda informal here. Jus' help yourself to a drink from the fridge and we'll get started."

"Thanks," Paul replied as he stood and opened the nearby refrigerator door and retrieved a soda.

The pastor began his short introduction. "Well, I thought we might talk a little about road construction tonight. Turn to Matthew seven, verses thirteen and fourteen. I'm goin' to read that, and I want you to decide just what kind of road you're buildin'. Are ya buildin' a wide road that leads to destruction, or are ya buildin' a narrow road that leads to life with Christ. What are ya buildin' for the Kingdom of God? Runnin' from Jesus sure ain't buildin' a road to abundant life which is what he wants for all of us."

Paul listened cautiously to this rural pastor with a passion for his calling. While he appreciated the zeal of this man, the pastor's love for those he took time to minister to, Paul had given up on believing that God was good in any way, if there was a god at all.

After filling the tank with gasoline at the truck stop, Paul drove the rental car back to Georgia. After sleeping through the night at a rest area just inside Georgia, Paul woke the next morning and drove straight to Frank's. Word gets around fast in small communities, and Frank was already aware of what happened to Paul's brother. Paul walked in. It was two in the afternoon and only three patrons were seated at the bar. Despite the fact that it was a weekday, Paul recognized the faces of each of the three. He said nothing to any of them. Seated at the bar, Paul pulled out his wallet and waited on Frank to come to him.

"Paul, how are you," Frank asked. "You want the usual?"

"No, Frank. Pour me the stiffest drink you can make." Paul leaned back in his barstool.

"I can't do that Paul. I won't do that to a friend that's hurtin' the way you are." Frank sat a glass of water on the bar in front of Paul.

"I can just get drunk somewhere else." Paul picked up the glass of water and threw it toward the back wall. The glass shattered into what must have been a thousand pieces while the water drained off the wall and formed a puddle on the floor. Paul walked out before Frank could say anything. A few of the people at the bar made a few comments about the incident that obviously to them didn't agree with Frank.

"He's hurtin'," Frank yelled. "Can't you fools see that?" No one replied. It would be the quietest afternoon in the history of Frank's Bar and Grill.

Paul drove to Cumming and found a liquor store where he purchased a bottle of Vodka and four small bottles of orange juice. He then drove to the warehouse where he worked and parked out back near the loading docks. He grabbed an empty Gatorade bottle from the floorboard of the rental car and poured the bottle half full with Vodka and the other half with orange juice. After switching on the radio to an Atlanta talk station, Paul began drinking. The next morning, a tap on his window awakened Paul. It was his foreman. Paul rolled down his window. With a horrible case of dry mouth and a severe headache, the foreman was the last person Paul wanted to see.

"Paul, what are you doing here? You've been here all night."

"No, I haven't," Paul replied.

"Yes, Paul, you have." The foreman was also fully aware of everything that had happened to Paul in recent days and was sympathetic to it. He considered Paul a good friend. "I saw you in this car parked right here last night before I left." The foreman paused, backed away from Paul's rental car a few feet and looked down on the ground. "Look Paul. I know you're really hurting right now. Anyone with half a heart would be. But, you can't give up on life, get drunk and sleep in a car behind a stinking warehouse. What's that going to solve?"

"Jim," Paul replied, "I'm going to need some time off." Paul started the car.

"Take as much time as you need. Your job will always be here."

Paul drove away. His hangover was so severe that he had to stop along the highway four times to throw up. He finally made it to his house. He immediately went to his room and fell asleep face down on his bed. When he woke up three hours later, he called the rental car company and asked them to pick up the car. An hour later a representative from the Dahlonega office arrived and knocked on the front door. Paul answered the door, signed a return receipt, gave the representative the keys to the car and went back to his bedroom.

Dianne had returned to the hospital. She had to keep her mind occupied during this crisis. Paul was hurting and very angry, and Dianne had no idea how to help him. For the next week, she spent long hours at the hospital. Everyone noticed the change in her. She always appeared tired, and she was short with staff members on numerous occasions. At night her only comfort was Wilson. Dianne's dog was very observant, seemingly knowing that she was in a great deal of emotional pain. Instead of sleeping at the foot of the bed where he normally slept, Wilson began sleeping next to her chest. Most nights, Dianne cried herself to sleep. On other nights, exhaustion prevented her from shedding a tear as she immediately fell asleep after crawling under her comforter and laying her head on her pillow.

Charlie and Anne knew that Paul was home but decided the best course of action was to leave him alone. Charlie had no idea what to say to Paul. He, like everyone else, knew that Paul was hurting and that Paul was angry. He just didn't know what to do about it all.

Three days later a knock came at Paul's front door. He reluctantly answered it. When he opened the door, Paul found Dr. Rodgers at the door. "Pastor, I'm not feeling well. Could you come back another day?" Paul began to close the door.

"No, Paul," the pastor replied. "I can't come back another day. Now, I'll only be here a few minutes. Then I'll leave." Paul reluctantly held the screen door open for the pastor who came in and sat on a recliner near the sofa. "Paul, you know why I'm here."

"Listen, I don't want to talk about anything right now." Paul became angry, feeling invaded. "Why can't I get that through to anyone? I don't need anybody."

"I came by to tell you that I understand, and I care." The pastor stood and headed for the front door. He stopped and turned back to Paul. "Regardless of where you are at in your life, like it or not, I love you. More importantly you have a family that loves you. You have a beautiful young woman who loves you. They won't stop loving you just because you've decided to push them away. Nor will anyone else in the congregation. We know the real Paul, and we're praying he will return."

"Pastor, please leave and take your Bible with you." Paul stood and walked into his bedroom. Dr. Rodgers walked over to the Taylor residence where he sat and prayed with Charlie and Anne. He was amazed how much it appeared they had aged in just a few days. Everyone that knew Paul was hurting. They were hurting for him. Frank, Tom, Pete, Jim, Dr. Rodgers, the congregation, Charlie, Anne and Dianne – all felt helpless to do anything for Paul. Just days earlier, he seemed happy and full of life. Now with the death of his brother, Paul seemed like he had retreated back into isolation as a way of coping.

Paul decided the only way to get away from what he thought was an invasion of his privacy was to pack a backpack and hike into the mountains. He loaded his truck and drove thirty miles north deeper into the mountainous area. In the back of his truck was Paul's mountain bike. He brought it along so that he could ride the bike from the campsite to a store for supplies. He found a hiking trail that would be close enough to a store three miles south of where he decided to hike. After finding a place to park the truck, Paul donned the backpack and hiked the trail with his bike three miles into the forest. The trail had been hiked many times and was well worn. Once Paul felt he was far enough from civilization, he moved off the path about four hundred yards and found a spot to set up camp.

Paul removed his backpack and opened it up. He pulled everything out including the small two-man tent that he brought along. He set up the tent in less than ten minutes and stored his supplies, some clothing, a small radio and his sleeping bag inside. After he was satisfied with his campsite, Paul carried his bike back to the trail and rode back out. He wanted to time the ride to and from the small store that he passed on the way up. When he arrived at the store he purchased two gallons of water, plastic utensils, extra batteries for his radio and flashlight, a loaf of bread, peanut butter, chips, beef jerky and two bottles of Gatorade. He paid for it all with his debit card. After exiting the store, Paul placed the items in his backpack, the water first, Gatorade next, then the other items, finishing with the bread at the top. He climbed back on his bike and began the ride back to the campsite. Carrying the weight, particularly the water, on his back made it extremely difficult climbing the trail, but Paul's strength and conditioning were exceptional. When he finally returned Paul looked at the watch Dianne had purchased for him. It had taken him forty minutes getting down the trail and to the store, while it took him just over an hour to make it back. He considered moving the campsite closer to the road, but decided that the last thing he wanted to hear was the noise of cars and trucks traveling up and down the asphalt.

The first night Paul put on some layers of clothing, crawled inside his sleeping bag and listened to his radio while he ate chips and drank Gatorade. He finally fell asleep at around eleven. The next morning he woke up at seven just as the sun was rising. He waited until 10:00am before he crawled out of his sleeping bag. After finally crawling from the sleeping bag, the experienced survivalist reached inside the sleeping bag to the foot of the bag and pulled out one of the gallons of water. His body's heat inside the bag helped keep the water somewhat warmer during the night. He crawled out of the tent, peeled off the three shirts he was wearing and began to wash up using the water from the one-gallon jug. As the water-cooled on the skin of his upper torso, Paul began shivering. He quickly dried off and put his shirts back on. He then shaved before returning to the tent.

An hour later after eating a peanut butter sandwich and potato chips, Paul changed into his riding outfit and took off down the trail toward the road. Once he reached the road, Paul turned left and headed north. He rode for two hours and covered nearly forty-three miles. The terrain was virtually the same as the course he rode on Saturdays from his house. The major difference on this new ride was the scarcity of houses. It was a much more rural setting. He enjoyed the solitude, the fact that there was less traffic in the area. During the ride Paul's mind drifted to thoughts about Chris. He remembered when they were kids, how Chris used to stick up for him when other kids would tease Paul for being different. He thought about the time when Chris tried to teach him how to ride a bicycle. It was at a carwash parking lot nearly a half-mile from where they lived. Paul ran his bicycle into the side of a Camaro being washed by two teenage boys. Chris had to step in to keep the two boys from beating Paul senseless. Chris was always there for Paul, even after he ran away from his foster mother. Paul wished they could have had more time together.

Paul returned to his camp refreshed. The ride helped clear his head. He decided he would stay for at least a week. On the kitchen counter at his house, Paul left an envelope with cash in it and a note that read, "Dear Charlie, The money is for my rent. Please tell Dianne that I love her and always will. I just need some time. I can't explain it all to her right now. Paul." Dianne was the one who found the envelope three days later. She had come up from Atlanta to see if she could locate Paul, but to no avail.

Paul had been at the campsite for a week. The weather stayed dry and relatively comfortable throughout the day and stayed that way most of the time he spent at his campsite. He had developed a routine of rising at dawn and riding his bike. Occasionally, he checked on his truck to make sure it was still where he had parked. It was. Paul found that routine helped him cope with the loss of his brother and the confusion he was feeling about Dianne, her parents and even his faith. The small store six miles from where he was camped served hamburgers and hot dogs so Paul ate there when he wanted a hot meal. On one particular day back at his campsite following a ride to the store for supplies, Paul heard the sounds of footsteps moving across the dry, dead leaves that carpeted the floor of the forest. He hid in the prone position several feet from the site with his buck knife and waited for the intruder.

The stranger reached the tent, knelt and looked inside. Paul snuck up behind the intruder, grabbed him and held the knife to his throat. "Hold it! Hold it, Paul. It's me."

Paul recognized the voice. "It's me. It's Ace."

Paul released him and let him turn around. It was Ace. "What are you doing here? How'd you find me?" Paul looked as though he was ready to attack. Ace was the last person, other than a certain judge, who Paul wanted to see.

"Come on, Atkinson. This is what we do. Or, have you forgotten?" Ace brushed the leaves off his pants from where he was kneeling in front of the tent. "I went by your place and talked to Dianne." Paul didn't give Ace the chance to utter another word. He planted a right hook on Ace's left jaw that sent his former team leader falling backward onto the tent. The flimsy tent didn't break his fall. Ace's weight collapsed the tent. He wasn't ready for the punch, and Paul could deliver one faster than anyone Ace had ever seen fight. He stood back up slowly. Once standing, Ace began rubbing his jaw with his left hand. "Paul, I only went there to get information about your whereabouts. She said she had no idea where you were, that she had been searching for you for over a week.

"How was she," Paul asked. "How'd she look?"

Ace was still rubbing his jaw. "You can still punch like you always did."

Paul pulled a hooded sweatshirt from his broken tent. "I took it easy on you, Ace. I thought about breaking your jaw. Now, how's Dianne?"

"She looked very tired. She misses you." Ace paused. He knelt and picked up a small tree branch off of the ground and began snapping it into small pieces. "Paul, I know about your brother. I'm sorry."

"How'd you find out about my brother? Did Dianne tell you?" Paul slipped the sweatshirt over his head, pushed his arms through the sleeves and pulled the shirt down.

"No, Paul, Dianne told me nothing. We've been keeping tabs on you for three months."

"Why? Why me? I resigned my commission, the Pentagon accepted the resignation, and I can't be touched. Why are you watching me?" Paul was ready to launch another attack.

"We need you for a mission." Ace knelt again and picked up another small tree branch.

Paul couldn't believe what he was hearing. What would the Pentagon want from him? Paul had been very clear concerning his desire to leave military service and to never look back. Now, a former team leader stood in front of him with another mission. "How'd you find me here, Ace?"

"Easy. I followed the scent of your bankcard being swiped at that store just down the road. I asked the cashier if she had seen your photograph. She hesitated at first, but I assured her that you weren't in any trouble."

Paul interrupted. "Then what did you tell her?"

"The truth, Paul. The truth."

"What happened? Turned over a new leaf?" Paul never really liked Ace and nearly three years after leaving the Quantico the feelings hadn't changed.

"You could say that. I simply told her that you are a United States government secret operative and that your country needs you for an important mission. She told me that you came to the store every few days and purchased a few things. She admitted that she, at first, thought it was strange to see someone riding a bike with a backpack, but after seeing you peel off the road and onto the trail while she was driving home one afternoon, she just assumed you were an out-of-towner doing a little camping. I think she's officially in love with you." Ace chuckled at his attempt to be humorous.

"You must enjoy pain," Paul responded.

Ace rubbed his chin, seemingly reminding himself of the punch he had received just moments earlier. "Listen, Paul. We really do need you for this mission. We feel with your knowledge of the personnel involved and your combat skills you can help us catch these guys before they create a really bad problem for our country."

"What's the mission?" Paul had no plans on going, but he thought he would at least get the intelligence information on what was actually happening.

"Let's go somewhere a little more comfortable so we can talk." Ace began heading for the trail.

"We talk here," Paul insisted. "We talk here, or we don't talk at all."

"Alright, Paul." Ace reached inside his jacket and pulled out an envelope. Out of it, he pulled three photographs and showed each one to Paul. "Do you recognize any of these men?"

"All of them. They were on our team." Paul took the pictures from Ace and examined each one.

"Correct. They were on the side of America eleven months ago before they joined a little known, highly trained and well-financed home based domestic terrorist organization. They don't consider themselves to be terrorists, but I can assure you, they are. Jacoby, Scott, and Williams left the covert unit just over a year ago, stuck together on the streets and eventually wound up in the organization I'm referring to. The organization calls themselves 'The Patriots'. Interestingly, the Patriots have legitimate government contracts for foreign security missions in places like Afghanistan and Iraq which provides excellent cover for their other endeavors. The government pays little attention to them since they hold security clearances and have supported previous administrations. The Patriots, however, have not warmed up to our new president. We aren't sure their dislike is based on the probability that they stand to lose millions of dollars in contracts, or if, as they claim, they actually believe that President Grigsby's ideas put our nation at risk."

Paul was somewhat interested. His former team members bled red, white and blue. What had happened to change them? Domestic terrorism just didn't seem to fit those three. "Patriots" – they were patriots indeed. When stateside, the three men were inseparable spending hours together debating the Constitution of the United States, the role of the military and other topics that others would have thought boring and somewhat strange for three relatively young, attractive, single men. While other members of the team – other than Paul, who was extremely reclusive – celebrated being stateside, Jacoby, Scott and Williams spent hours together in places like the Library of Congress combing the shelves for various texts on early American law and the people who wrote those laws. They were loyal soldiers, a little strange to some, but incredible fighting machines. Now, according to Ace, they were domestic terrorists. In Paul's mind, none of it added up.

"Why do you want me," Paul asked.

"Let's face it, Atkinson. You were a loner when you were in the unit. No one could quite figure you out, where you stood on certain things. If you infiltrate this organization, our three former members will never suspect you. We want you to infiltrate the Patriots and give us intel on what they plan to try to pull off. We believe they're going to try to hit a world leader on our soil – possibly the president or someone else. We aren't sure of their exact plans, but we are sure that they want to make a bold statement to America and the world, and with the money backing them along with the skilled personnel the Patriots have recruited, they certainly have the means to carry out an attack. The new president talks a lot about this idea of open dialogue with other leaders. Apparently, that idea doesn't sit well with the Patriots."

"So, you want me to give up my life here, risk my life by infiltrating what is very obviously a highly trained organization, and feed you information from inside the organization?" Paul talked as he tried to repair his flattened tent. "Ace, I'm sorry to inform you, but I'm fairly confident that the Patriots, if they recruit guys like Jacoby, Williams and Scott, have put in all of the stop-gap measures necessary to prevent infiltrators and leaks of information. If I get caught, the next time you see me will be when you find me floating face down in the Potomac."

"Where's that Atkinson confidence," Ace asked.

"Didn't you know? That sort of confidence is standard military issue. I had to turn it in when I resigned." Paul was having trouble repairing the tent. It appeared that one of the flexible rods broke when Ace fell on the small tent.

"Paul, we will have someone close to you at all times. If at any time you feel that you are in danger, we will pull the plug and get you out of there. You are the only one we believe who can get into the Patriots and get us the information we need." Ace had given up on breaking small tree branches. He pulled a pack of chewing gum from his pocket, unwrapped a stick and started chewing the gum. He offered a stick of gum to Paul, but he refused. "You've been out for over two years. You've flown under the radar the entire time. Until recently, you've been the epitome of a loner. We can get you in the Patriots, you can get the information we need, and we'll get you right back out."

"Yeah, so I can walk around with a target on my back for the rest of my life. Sounds like a great plan, Ace." Paul was able to rig the tent so that it would stand. He stood and took a few steps back to view his accomplishment. "Good enough," he said.

"Paul, you will be in no danger after the mission. We'll wipe out the organization and jail the man that funds it. You're going to have to trust me."

Paul turned and looked at Ace. "Trust you? Are you kidding me? You're the same man who tried to have me thrown into prison after our little trip to Russia, and you want me to trust you. I don't think so."

"That was a long time ago," Ace replied. "I've had a great deal of time to think about what you did since then, and I think you were right. I'm sorry." Ace was not sorry at all, but he was growing desperate in his attempt to lure Paul back into the covert unit.

"So, I will be reinstated at the rank of major, right?" Paul wanted to see just how desperate Ace was.

"You weren't a major when you resigned," Ace answered. "Your rank was captain."

"Not anymore. I'll be a major, won't I?"

"Done! I'll process the paperwork the day you arrive in Quantico." Ace was beginning to feel a boost of confidence.

"Fast-track the paperwork. I also want a $100,000.00 signing bonus. I want it the day I arrive, and I want it to be placed in Dianne's personal account."

Ace stared at Paul for a moment. "Fast-tracking the paperwork is a synch, but getting the Pentagon to cut a check for that amount and place it in a civilian's account will be virtually impossible."

"Then you can find someone else to ruin the Patriots' day." Paul had Ace on the ropes and he knew it. He knew the Pentagon had the authority to cut a check for any amount of money they chose. While in the covert unit, Paul personally witnessed numerous checks from European bank accounts owned by the Pentagon delivered to foreign informants during missions. The amount of money Paul was demanding was a drop in the bucket for the Pentagon.

"Alright Paul. I can get you the money the day you arrive and you can handle getting it to Dianne. That's the best I can do."

Paul collapsed the two-man tent he had worked so hard repairing. After placing his belongings in his backpack, he donned the pack and grabbed his mountain bike. "Let's go. It's three miles to the road."

Ace followed Paul. "So, you're in?"

"I never said that," Paul replied. "I need to see Dianne."

"Atkinson," Ace said, in an attempt to sound more assertive, "I need an answer right now."

Paul stopped and let the bike fall to the ground. He walked over to Ace and stood toe to toe with his former superior. Their noses were less than three inches apart. "I'll give you an answer when I'm good and ready. You got that?"

"Alright, Paul," Ace replied. "I read you loud and clear." The two began walking again. "I can't believe you're driving that same clunker you were driving when you got out. Why don't you join the modern age?"

"I've seen the modern age," Paul responded. "I'm not impressed."

An hour or so later Paul and Ace emerged from the forest and onto the asphalt road. "Meet me at my house," Paul said. "You obviously know where it is."

Paul walked his bike up the road to where he had his truck parked. After loading the bike in the back of the truck, he got in, started the truck on the fourth try and drove to his house. Ace beat him to his place and was waiting in his car outside the house. Paul led him inside and told him to wait in the living room while he showered and changed into some clean clothes.

After the shower, Paul walked over to the Taylor's. Dianne had taken a leave of absence from the hospital in hopes that Paul would turn up. She was losing hope, that is, until Paul walked in that day. He found her lying on the couch in the living room watching television. She appeared exhausted. Paul felt the sting of guilt pulsing through his veins and stabbing him in the heart. Dianne didn't hear him come in. Charlie and Anne were at a meeting at the church. Paul walked in front of the television and turned toward Dianne. She sat up on the couch and stared at Paul. Tears formed in her eyes as she stared at the man who she loved with so much of herself. "I love you, Dianne," Paul said, breaking the silence of the moment. "I'm so sorry I've hurt you."

Dianne stood and rushed to him, throwing her arms around Paul and sobbing. "Please tell me you're ok. Please tell me you're ready to move on. Please tell me you'll never leave me again." She looked so tired.

Paul picked Dianne up in his arms and carried her to her bedroom, kissing her along the way. The bed had not been made, making it easier for him to lay her on the bed. He laid her down on the silk-sheeted mattress and covered her with the comforter. "You need some rest."

"No, I don't, Paul," Dianne replied. "I only want to be with you."

"I'll stay until you fall asleep, but you need to rest." Paul paused. "Dianne, I have to go away for awhile."

Dianne immediately sat up in her bed. "Where? Where are you going?"

"I've been called back to active duty. I'm needed for a top secret mission." Paul looked away from Dianne. It was difficult for him to see the pain in her beautiful eyes.

"Paul, you're not that man anymore. Why would you want to go back? You've come so far." The tears were flowing now from Dianne's eyes.

"It's just something I have to do, Dianne."

Dianne reached out and held Paul's hand. "Your brother died, and you feel guilty. Instead of staying here and let me, my dad, my mom, and the church help you heal, you crawl back into that shell you lived in nearly your whole life and you hide."

Paul looked at Dianne, knowing she had everything right. He couldn't bring himself to admit it. "I'm needed for this mission. The Pentagon thinks that I'm the only one that can handle it."

"Will I be attending your funeral, too?" Dianne released his hand.

"Dianne, please try to understand." Paul reached for her hand but she refused.

Paul stood and began leaving the room. "God still loves you, Paul," Dianne said.

Paul turned and stared at her. He knew her heart was broken. What could he say to Dianne? Paul had lost faith in his self, in life and in God. He couldn't see any way of ever being what Dianne deserved. He turned, left the room and the Taylor residence, leaving Dianne behind.

Paul walked back into his house and found Ace holding a framed photograph of Paul and Dianne. He walked over to Ace, snatched the photo out of his hand and placed it back on the table. "Let's go. I want this over with. When this is done, don't ever contact me again. You got that?"

Ace stood, clapped his hands together and smiled. "Paul, you will never here from anyone in the Pentagon again after you complete this mission for us."

Chapter Eleven

The Mission

Paul packed a few things in a gym bag, wrote a short note to Dianne, left the note on the coffee table and exited the house with Ace. The two men drove to Quantico, reaching the installation at midnight. Ace showed the guards his identification and Paul's orders for active duty. After they cleared security at the front gate, Ace drove to what would be Paul's private quarters on the installation, gave him a key and pointed out the exact location of his room. "Get some rest. I'll meet you in the morning for a briefing."

Paul got out of the car and walked into his quarters. The room was nothing more than a glorified hotel room with a small kitchenette. Paul unpacked the few items that he brought with him. He didn't bother to bring too many clothes knowing that any militia-type organization like the Patriots was bound to have uniforms. His prized possession was the photograph of him and Dianne. He set it on his nightstand and stared at Dianne's incredibly beautiful face. Paul was so in love with her, but so frightened that loving her would eventually mean losing her, just as he had lost everyone else in his life.

He reached over, picked up the telephone and dialed Charlie and Anne's number waiting to hear a ring. Dianne picked up. "Hello." Paul couldn't speak. "Hello. Paul, is that you? Paul?" Paul slowly replaced the phone back on the receiver. Dianne knew it was Paul. She attempted to retrieve the number from caller identification, but to no avail. Quantico's high security prevented anyone from retrieving phone numbers from any phone on the installation. Dianne felt a surge of hope rise inside her.

Paul was reaching out. She climbed out of her bed, knelt by the bed and prayed: "Dear Lord, I ask you to hear my prayer, to know the suffering I'm enduring. Please, comfort me. More importantly, dear God, please comfort Paul. Please instill in him the truth of who you are and the fact that he has a home and people who love him more than he realizes. He is hurting, God, and he needs you. Please, reach out to him and save him. Bring him home, I ask in Jesus' name. Amen." She climbed back into her bed and slept soundly for the first time in days.

The next morning, the telephone on the nightstand by the bed woke Paul out of his sleep. Answering the phone, Paul received instructions on where to go for the briefing. After a quick shower, he put on a pair of blue jeans and a black sweatshirt. He brushed his teeth and combed his short hair before rushing out of his quarters. Just across the street from his quarters was a four-story building where most of the higher-ups worked. It was in that building where Paul would be briefed on the mission. He arrived in the conference room at 8:45am. Ace and three other officers were already waiting for him.

"Glad you could make it," Ace said with a little more bravado in his voice now that Paul was back on active duty.

"Well, you know, we civilians have to have our tea and crumpets before we leave our house to kill terrorists." The other officers laughed at Paul's sarcastic response. Each of them outranked Ace. Ace wasn't very well liked among his peers, but he was very good at what he did and extremely loyal. Hence, his career continued to flourish despite his personality.

Following the short exchange, Ace quickly realized that he was no match for Paul, and decided trying the high road would be more productive. "Good one, Paul. Now, let's get down to the mission."

Paul leaned back in his chair and folded his arms. "Let's."

Ace stood and pulled down a screen near the opposite end of the conference table. He switched on a slide projector and turned off the lights. The first slide had the mission title: "Operation Patriot Kill". Real creative, Paul thought. "Now, the mission will require you to infiltrate the Patriots and gather information on what they plan to do. We are fairly sure that they plan to strike some time within the next ninety days. You will not carry a wire or a bug - you will have to find a way to get us the information without being caught. We feel the best way will be the old fashion way. Write the information down and bury it at a designated location on their compound. We will drop someone in and pick the information up. We realize that you will be limited in your ability to go to the drop site, so we will automatically check the site every three days. I'm confident you will be able to retrieve good intel and get it to us."

"Sure," Paul replied. "If I don't get killed trying."

"Paul, you were one of our smartest operatives in the field," Ace said. "I'm confident you will figure out a way to get that information to us."

Paul sat silent for a moment. After thinking about options, he looked at Ace and the other three officers. "I need you to get me a mountain bike."

One of the other officers spoke up. He was a one star general. "A mountain bike? What for?"

"General, Jacoby, Williams and Scott all know that I have always enjoyed mountain biking. If they want me bad enough, then they'll have no problem with me bringing a mountain bike to their compound. When I go out for my rides, I'll take the written details of what I've learned and bury it at the location you designate."

The general leaned back in his chair, looked over at Ace and smiled. "Good choice."

Ace smiled. He could see a promotion in his future. "Thank-you sir." Paul let Ace wallow in his pride. He just wanted to get the mission over and done.

Ace continued showing slides, most of which were satellite photographs of the compound. He showed a map of its location in the southern section of Missouri situated in the Mark Twain Forest thirty miles west of Fort Leonard Wood. The compound looked like any other military installation, just on a smaller scale. He also showed several photographs of the drop site where Paul would bury the written information he would be gathering. Ace finally showed photographs of all known members of the Patriots before switching off the projector and switching on the lights.

"I have just one question," Paul said when the lights illuminated the conference room. "Where are the CIA and FBI in all of this? This sounds like their cup of tea."

"We've briefed both of them," Ace said. This, however, wasn't true. "We've asked them to keep it quiet and to stay out of it. The three former operatives have too much valuable information to be turned over to them. We want them."

Paul could see his point. Operatives from the covert unit had so much information a leak could keep the congress and senate busy until the second coming of Christ. If some of that information ever hit the press, it could start wars. "I'm clear," Paul responded.

The briefing continued with instructions on just how Paul was to infiltrate the Patriots, as well as how the information would be retrieved from the drop site without the Patriots knowing. The one retrieving the intelligence would parachute in at night, retrieve the information and hike back out of the compound. Paul was told that the man who funded the Patriots had actually taken out ads in various publications throughout the United States. The ads asked the question, "Do you have what it takes to be a Patriot?" Paul was instructed to email the organization from an email address that would be provided to him. After the organization received the email, they would set up a meeting at a designated location away from their compound. Paul would meet them there and tell the interviewer that a little bird had informed him that some of his former team members from the covert unit were members of the Patriots. He would go on to say that he wanted in, as well. He was instructed not to sound too eager, but to try to show extreme confidence. The organization looked for that in all of its candidates. Paul was also informed that he would be well paid by the organization, one of the reasons the Patriots attracted so many quality candidates. Most in the organization started at $80,000.00 per year tax free, paid in cash.

Paul knew he was about to venture into something that could be very dangerous. This organization was obviously extremely well organized and run as well if not better than any active duty military unit. He wouldn't be dealing with a bunch of rednecks with shotguns and rebel flags. With Jacoby, Williams and Scott in the Patriots, Paul was walking into a wasp nest of highly trained, fearless killers. He should know. He had lived a similar life just a few years earlier. Paul considered the possibility of not making it out of the operation alive and what it would do to Dianne and her parents. He had hurt them enough by disappearing and taking on the mission. If he got killed, it could push them, especially Dianne, over the edge. Paul considered backing out. He knew he couldn't, though. Backing out could land him in a jail cell somewhere on some trumped up charges or in a shallow grave. He had to see this mission all the way through to its completion. With the briefing completed, Paul and Ace headed for the mess hall for a late breakfast.

On the way Ace handed Paul a military identification card. It had the same photograph from his Georgia driver's license. Paul looked at Ace. Ace shrugged his shoulders. "Somebody has to be kings. Might as well be us up here, right?"

"What happened to rights of privacy," Paul said as he placed the military ID in his wallet.

"Are you kidding me, Paul," Ace responded. "After what happened on 9/11, the days of privacy are over. We have a system that practically allows us to know every time you flush your toilet. Tapping into a state computer is nothing."

"I guess you guys call it a necessary evil, right?" Paul didn't particularly enjoy Ace's company.

"You could put it that way," Ace responded as he handed Paul an envelope. "I called ahead yesterday from Charlotte and got everything you wanted fast-tracked."

Paul opened the envelope and pulled out a check for $100,000.00. "Ace, you pulled this off. Maybe I'll come out of this alive. Since you're so good at sneaking around personal information, I want you to get me Dianne's bank account number. I want this check deposited today before 2:00pm."

"No problem." Ace enjoyed the surge of ego he got every time he tapped into the personal information of people he was investigating. "I'll have it to you after lunch. Here, one more thing."

Paul opened another envelope that had orders promoting him to major. "There's hope for you yet," Paul said to Ace. "That makes us equals doesn't it Major?"

"You and I will never be equals, Paul," Ace replied.

"Hey, don't beat yourself up. You'll get there one day." Paul was, indeed, now equal in rank to Ace. Ace wasn't very pleased with it, but he swallowed just enough of his pride for the sake of the mission knowing that Paul wouldn't be in uniform very long.

"After we eat, I need you in uniform. You'll be here for three days before we give you a car to drive to Missouri. While you're here, the brass wants you in uniform." Ace opened the door to the mess hall and let Paul walk in first.

"Can you say déjà vu?" Paul looked around the mess hall. Once inside the mess hall Paul grabbed a tray and began working his way through the serving line. "I swore I would never wear the uniform again."

"Chalk it up to love of country," Ace said as he scooped some scrambled eggs onto his plate.

After breakfast, Paul went to the Post Exchange store and purchased two sets of combat fatigues. He got a haircut while a seamstress sowed the appropriate patches on his uniforms. He also purchased a pair of jump boots as well as all the required accessories in order to meet military standards. He returned to his quarters and changed into the uniform. The only thing about the uniform that he liked was the gold cluster on his cap. A promotion to major meant more money. As usual, all of his earnings would be placed into savings in his bank account and later moved to a CD.

Paul grabbed a quick lunch at the mess hall and returned to his quarters. He was waiting for Ace to call with the information about Dianne's bank account. The phone lines at Quantico were extremely secure so Paul wasn't worried about getting her account number over the phone. Like clockwork, the phone rang at 1:00pm. Paul picked it up, and Ace gave him Dianne's account number. Paul hung up the phone and rushed to a Bank of America on the installation to make the deposit. He forged Dianne's name on the back of the check as the endorsement and filled out one of the generic deposit slips supplied by the bank. With endorsed check and deposit slip in hand Paul approached the bank teller.

The young lady behind the counter took the check and looked at the amount. A sudden episode of coughing caused her to stand and go to her manager. "I'll need to get my manager's approval for this deposit, sir," she said between coughs.

"Sure," Paul replied. "Take your time. Need a cough drop?"

Recognizing Paul's sarcasm the teller tightened her lips and looked up at the ceiling. "No, thank-you, sir." She went over to her manager who walked back to where Paul was still standing at the counter.

"Sir, I just need to see you military identification and driver's license and we will get this deposit completed." The manager was a tall, lanky, nearly thirty year old man with a military style haircut.

Paul pulled out the requested identification and handed it to the bank manager. The manager looked everything over and initialed the check approving the deposit. "Will this post today," Paul asked.

"Let me see," the manager replied. "Yes, it will post today. It's a government check and you got it deposited before two."

"Thanks," Paul responded.

The teller handed Paul a deposit receipt and thanked him for his business.

"Take care of that cough," Paul said as he turned and walked out of the bank.

Paul's afternoon was spent mostly in further briefings and planning for the mission. After the meetings, Paul told Ace to get him set up for the rifle range. He wanted to go out in the morning and see if he could shoot forty out of forty targets on the standard Army qualification range. He once held a record in the Rangers with consecutive perfect scores qualifying his rifle. Paul's record was later broken by a young staff sergeant who had spent his entire nine-year career in the Ranger Battalion. Ace told Paul to be at the range at 0800 hours; an M-16 rifle would be waiting on him. He would have to zero the rifle first, and then qualify. Paul knew all this, but Ace liked to talk. Paul had decided that Ace's blood must have been camouflage in color. Before returning to his quarters, Paul found a computer and emailed Dianne.

Back in Atlanta, Dianne had returned to her condominium with Wilson. She was going back to work the next day. After pulling out her laptop, she logged in to her bank account. She wanted to balance her checkbook. With all of the turmoil of the previous two weeks, Dianne hadn't had a chance to balance her account. When she looked at the amount of money showing in her primary checking account, Dianne nearly coughed as hard as the bank teller in Quantico: $104,354.88. She immediately thought it was a bank error. Scrolling down the list of transactions it didn't take Dianne long to find the deposit. Fourth from the top was a listing for a deposit made that day. She clicked on the transaction and a copy of the deposited check appeared on the screen. On the front, the check was made out to Major Paul Atkinson. The on-line system allowed her to view the back of the check. She recognized Paul's signature, but it was obvious that he had forged her signature. After viewing her account, she checked her emails and noticed one had come in from Paul that read: "The money is yours. Spend it any way you like. I will always love you. Paul." She stared at the screen for several minutes before picking up the phone and dialing her parents. Charlie picked up the phone on the third ring.

"Dad, can you put mom on the line, too," Dianne said. "I have something I want to talk to both of you about." Charlie got up from his recliner and walked the other phone into the study where Anne was putting together a lesson for an upcoming Sunday school class at the church. He handed her the phone and told her that Dianne was on the other end. Once everyone was settled and listening, Dianne told her parents about the deposit she found in her account, that Paul had apparently received a check for the mission in the amount of $100,000.00 and had deposited it in her account. She went on to tell them about his email. "What does all this mean," she asked.

"It means that Paul loves you very much," Anne said. "He wants to make sure you are taken care of."

"Mom," Dianne replied as tears began to flow from her eyes. "I don't care about getting taken care of with mysterious deposits showing up in my bank account. I want Paul here, now, with me."

"I know you do," Charlie said. "I think we all want to see him back here. Time will tell if he can ever recover from the loss of his brother. Dianne, you have to get past your emotions for a moment and look at the reality of what has happened. Paul just lost his last livin' relative in Chris. He's terrified of losin' you. He is afraid that if he marries you, he will lose you like he has lost everyone else close to him. You're goin' to have to give this thing time to see how it all plays out."

"You're going to have to decide whether you want to remain committed to Paul, whether you are willing to see this whole thing through," Anne interjected. "I, for one, believe that you need to spend a great deal of time in prayer and in Bible study before you make any decisions concerning Paul."

"Both of you are right," Dianne replied. "I know he still loves me, and for now that's enough. I'm going to get some dinner and go to bed. I imagine I'll have a long day tomorrow, having been out for over a week."

"Goodnight little angel," Charlie said. "Your mother and I love you very much."

"I love you both, too. Goodnight."

The next morning, Paul arrived at the rifle range right on time for M-16 rifle qualification. A vehicle and a driver had been assigned to him for the remaining two days he would be at Quantico. He reported to the range master who directed him to a supply sergeant who in turn issued him an M-16 and forty-nine rounds of 5.56-millimeter brass ammunition. Nine rounds would be for the zero range, while the other forty were for qualification. Paul zeroed the weapon in six rounds, adjusting the rear sites only once while using the last three rounds of ammunition for confirmation. After he was satisfied that the M-16 was zeroed, he reported to the qualification range and got in line. Fifteen minutes later Paul was firing at pop-up targets that ranged in distance from his position to 50 meters and out to 400 meters. When the cycle of targets was complete, the range master got on the intercom and ordered the soldiers to ceasefire and to clear their weapons. "Lane sixteen," the range master said. "Perfect score." Paul, needless to say, was on lane sixteen. The streak continued.

The next day Paul received final instructions on his mission. The email had already been sent from a laptop issued to Paul for the mission. Paul would leave the next morning for St. Louis and wait in a hotel for the email response. Once the response was received, he would drive to the designated location where the interview would take place. Paul had never been nervous on any mission in the past. For this mission, knowing the dangers that were lying ahead, Paul was actually nervous.

Washington, D.C.

The January 2009 presidential inauguration drew the largest crowds in its history. President Nathan R. Grigsby was sworn in at precisely 11:00am in front of crowds that stretched as far as the eye could see. It truly was history in the making. He was not only the youngest president ever elected, but he was the first president ever elected with less than four years experience in any form of public office. The landslide victory and the fact that the democrats already controlled the house and the senate represented a changing of the guard in the country. The massive crowd of on-lookers mostly made up of liberal Americans approved of their new president. Every flag imaginable was being waved: flags from every state, union flags, gay flags, and even a few flags from foreign countries. The inauguration had turned into a political block party.

Following his inauguration, President Grigsby unleashed a speech meant to stir up the crowd and to get them excited about the next four years. He reiterated many of the promises he had made on the campaign trail – promises to fix the economy, create jobs, end the war in Iraq, create open dialogue with other foreign leaders who were not interested in speaking to his predecessor, and create a national health care system that would allow all Americans access to health care. The crowd loved every word, and due to the avid applause, what would have been a forty-minute speech lasted over an hour.

Following his speech, President Grigsby did something no other newly elected president had ever done. He walked down the stairs of the Capital, past the dignitaries and out into the crowd to shake hands with his supporters. Secret service was not pleased as they tried to maintain a decent level of order in the crowds of people. Of course, this act got more media attention than the swearing in and the speech. Grigsby was playing to his supporters. He had every intention of staying in the White House for two terms. Of course, the Patriots wanted him out of the White House before the new paint could dry.

Quantico

Paul woke to the sound of a ringing telephone at 6:00am on the day he was to depart for Missouri. He picked it up and listened to final instructions from Ace. A 2003 Chevrolet Silverado with Missouri license plates had been purchased for the mission. Ace told Paul that the truck would be waiting for him outside his quarters when he was ready to depart. An envelope would be inside the truck on the seat. In it he would find a Missouri driver's license, a veteran's identification card and some cash. Ace told Paul to leave everything in his wallet in that envelope and take what had been provided for him in its place. He was instructed to leave anything that could be traced in the envelope, including bank cards, social security cards, photographs, and anything else that could be checked by the Patriots. The envelope containing Paul's Georgia license and other things was to be left on his bed in his quarters. Ace told him that it would be picked up and placed in a safe during the mission. Paul followed the orders. He contemplated taking the photograph of him and Dianne. He decided it was too risky and left it under the envelope on the bed.

With $1500.00 in cash, Paul would have no problem surviving while waiting for the email from the Patriots. He placed the laptop on the bench seat of the truck, loaded the mountain bike and left the installation. He decided the best route would be south to Bristol, Tennessee, through Knoxville, and west on Interstate 40. He stopped on the west side of Knoxville for a late lunch then continued west finally northwest toward St. Louis. Once he arrived in St. Louis, Paul found a Holiday Inn Express and decided he would stay there. He unloaded his things, including the mountain bike and went to his room. Using a calling card he had purchased from a convenient store, Paul called Ace from a pay phone to let him know he had arrived in St. Louis. He couldn't call from the phone in his room. Too risky. After the call to Ace, Paul decided to dial Dianne's cell phone.

"Hello. Hello, Paul is that you? Please talk to me. I need to hear your voice." Dianne was desperate to find out if Paul was safe.

Paul hesitated, then finally spoke. "I'm fine, Dianne."

Dianne began crying, more for joy at hearing Paul's voice than out of sorrow over his absence. "Paul, I miss you. Please, come home. I got home and checked my account last night. I saw where you put money in my account. I don't need the money. I need you. Please, come home."

"Dianne, I can't. I can't back out now. I'll end up in jail or in a shallow grave somewhere." Paul regretted telling her that, knowing in hindsight that it would only make matters worse for her. "Listen, this mission will be a piece of cake."

"Will you come home when it's all finished?"

Paul couldn't answer her question. "Dianne, I need to get through this mission and –"

"Paul, why are you so scared of coming home? I know you've lost faith. I know you think you'll lose everyone you get close to. But, you have to overcome that fear and trust God."

"Trust God?" Paul was becoming angry. "Trust the same so-called loving god that took my parents before I ever had a chance to know them? Trust the same so-called caring god that allowed my brother to die in a jail cell? You want me to trust that god? I don't think so."

"So, you're going to spend the rest of your life blaming God for all of the tragedies in your life?" Dianne was standing in the kitchen of her condominium.

"It's worked for me thus far," Paul replied.

"Paul, God didn't cause that truck to swerve into the lane that your parents were in and kill them. God didn't go into that jail cell, rip a sheet in half and tie a noose to hang Chris. Please, stop blaming God."

Paul remained silent. Dianne was, as usual, correct. He had been blaming something or someone that he could not see, hear or touch. How could he blame a god that he really had no faith in? "Dianne, do you believe that I love you?"

Dianne's eyes filled again with tears. "Paul, I truly believe that you love me, but I'm afraid I've lost you forever."

"Listen, I have to go. I'm expecting some communication, and I need to check something to find out. I love you, Dianne."

"I love you, Paul." Dianne hung up the phone and laid down on her sofa. She decided to take her parents' advice. She decided to simply wait on Paul, wait to see if he decided he would come home. In the meantime, she would pray. She would pray for her own comfort and peace of mind, and she would pray for Paul.

The next morning, Paul rolled out of bed and set out for a ride on the bike that had been provided for him. The heavily congested residential area that he rode in made it difficult for him to pick up speed for any significant length of time. After four miles he turned the bike around and returned to the hotel. Following a quick shower, he checked the email address that had been provided to him. Nothing. He walked across a street and had breakfast at a Waffle House. Paul didn't make a habit of eating at the Waffle House, but on the occasions that he did, he always ordered the same thing: T-bone steak cooked medium, two eggs over-light, hash browns with onions, two slices of white toast with grape preserves, and a large glass of orange juice. He was truly a creature of habit.

After breakfast, he returned to his hotel room and checked the email again. This time there was a message. It was from the Patriots. The email read: "Drive to Springfield on Interstate 44 from St. Louis. Meet at Fred's Breakfast and Lunch. Do not bring cell phones or computers. Be there at 9:00am tomorrow morning. Confirm." Paul typed a simple "Confirmed" and clicked the "Send" icon. The website confirmed that the email had been sent. Nervous tension grabbed his gut again. He wasn't dealing with poorly trained Taliban soldiers. Paul was dealing with cream of the crop Americans most of whom had served in some form of special operations forces.

Needing to protect the laptop that had been issued to him, Paul found a UPS store and shipped the unit back to Quantico under an assumed name that only Ace would know from their days together in the covert unit. On the way back to the hotel, Paul stopped at a pay phone and using the phone card, dialed Dianne's cell phone. She picked up on the second ring.

"Dianne," Paul said, "I love you."

"Paul, I'll never stop loving you," she replied. Dianne was at the hospital when she took the call.

"I'm not going to be able to have any communication with you for awhile. I'm not sure how long. I just wanted to tell you that I'm sorry. I'm sorry that I've hurt you and I've not been there for you. I just can't –"

"What are you trying to say, Paul?" Dianne walked into her office, not wanting the staff to hear her. "Are you saying it's over?"

"No, I'm not saying." Paul was confused. He wasn't sure about anything anymore. "I'm not saying that, Dianne. I just need to finish this mission. I really believe that I'll be ok once I finish this mission."

"Paul, do you realize that my whole world has been turned upside down?" Tears formed in Dianne's brown eyes. "I don't know you. The man I'm talking to is not the man I fell in love with. Will that man ever come back?"

"I don't know, Dianne," Paul responded. "I don't know anything, it seems. I only know how to be a soldier. That, I know."

"No, Paul," Dianne replied. "You only know how to crawl into a place that hides you from reality, from people who love you, a place where you feel no one can hurt you. When are you going to realize that when you crawl away into those dark places of isolation you leave behind broken hearts in your wake?"

Her words stung. Paul felt helpless and suddenly wished he could turn back the clock and not allow his self to have fallen in love. "May I'll call you when all of this is over?"

"I'll be waiting," Dianne replied. "You may have given up, but I, with God's help, will never give up on you."

After the two ended the call, Paul phoned Ace to inform him that the email had come and that he would be leaving early the next morning for the interview. He also told him to keep his eyes open for the laptop. Paul shipped it next day air, so Ace could expect to see it before close of business the following day. After speaking to Ace, Paul returned to his hotel room and packed for the upcoming early morning departure to Springfield. Once everything was packed, he went out and found a decent restaurant for what he assumed would be a last day of real freedom for several weeks.

The next morning, Paul woke at 4:00am, showered, and loaded the Silverado with the one bag that he brought as well as the mountain bike. After checking out, he drove south on St. Louis' Interstate 270, then onto Interstate 44 for the long drive to the southwestern part of the state where Springfield was located. The nearly 250-mile trip placed Paul in Springfield at 8:25am. After stopping for gasoline and directions to Fred's, Paul drove to the restaurant. He was twenty minutes early when he arrived.

"Mr. Atkinson," a voice spoke from behind where Paul was seated in a booth, "you're early. We like that."

Paul stood from the booth to greet the man that had come to conduct the interview. The man was tall and fit for someone who appeared to be in his mid-fifties. He was completely bald and had no facial hair. His face was large and round while his eyes were blue. Paul reached out and shook the man's hand.

"I'm Lieutenant Colonel Ed Harvey. I'm second in command of the Patriots." Colonel Harvey seemed to have no problem broadcasting to the crowded restaurant exactly who he was and with what he was involved. "Why don't we sit down and have a talk. I already know quite a bit about you, so most of this will be simple formality. It appears some of our men have worked with you before." The two men sat down in the booth and began talking. "So, what is it about the Patriots that interests you?"

"Well, I found out through the grapevine that three members of a unit that I was in had joined the Patriots. I've heard about the organization, what it stands for, and I want to be a part of it." Paul knew very little about the organization other than what he had been briefed on back in Quantico, but adlibbing seemed to be working.

"You're speaking of Williams, Jacoby, and Scott," the colonel responded. "I had a long talk with them after receiving your email. They had very good things to say about you."

"Well sir, I'm flattered, but I like to let my performance in the field do the talking for me." Paul answered. "However, the four of us conducted many missions together in countries all over the world. I know their capabilities. I know how intelligent they are. I know their loyalty to our nation. I'm loyal to our nation. I want to be a part of what they're doing and what the entire Patriots organization will accomplish."

Colonel Harvey pulled out a photograph and handed it to Paul. It was of President Grigsby. "This man is one of the reasons why we're here. Our unit formed with the help of a true Patriot out of Arizona who pays our salaries among other things. We formed to put a stop to a liberal mindset that will eventually destroy our once great nation." The colonel pointed at the photograph. "That man actually thinks his idea of 'open-dialogue' with supporters of terrorism will be good for our country. That's like inviting an axe murderer into your garage and asking him to sharpen the blade of your axe. Sooner or later the blade's going to be sharp and the murderer will attack. The new president thinks that liberalism should rule the day. The Patriots are the only one's who can stop the bleeding going on in our nation. We will bring America back from the pits of hell and destruction."

"Colonel, I can't think of a better place for me to be than to be serving our nation in the Patriots." Paul sounded very convincing.

The colonel leaned back in the booth and smiled. "We treat our people very well. I can assure you, this isn't the government or the Department of Defense. We know how to treat our soldiers." The colonel was interrupted by a call on his cell phone. "Yes sir. Yes, I agree. Excellent, sir. I'll make it happen. Out here." Colonel Harvey put his cell phone back into his coat pocket and looked at Paul. "Our interviews usually take an hour, then we wait a few days to give the candidate an answer, but we have an upcoming mission that requires a great deal of training and preparation. I've been ordered to offer you a position in the Patriots. Due to your experience, I have been authorized to offer you $90,000.00 a year paid in cash. We will give you $20,000.00 just to join. The money will be held in a safe until our next mission is completed. You will not be allowed to leave the compound until our upcoming mission is complete. Anything you need, we will send someone out to get. We do provide a cash stipend issued weekly and have a small supply store on the compound. We've tried to design our compound after the military, only better." The colonel paused and stared at Paul. Paul was a picture of confidence. Everything was going better than the plan, Paul thought to himself. "So, Mr. Atkinson, are you in?"

"I'm in sir. When do I report?"

"Now! I want you to follow me in your vehicle." The colonel stood prompting Paul to stand as well. "We will make one stop on the way. Your vehicle will be searched. You will be strip-searched – one of those necessary precautions. Afterward, you will follow me to the compound where your vehicle will be confiscated and stored. You will go through three days of initiation before being assigned. Any questions?"

Paul smiled. "None, sir."

"Good," Colonel Harvey replied. "Let's go."

The two men left the restaurant and drove nearly thirty-seven miles southeast out of town to a small, gated building that was located just about a half mile from the road. Paul followed the colonel through the gate and up to some large doors that, as if on cue, slid open as they arrived. Two men in black combat uniforms with assault rifles motioned the two vehicles inside. Once inside, Paul was ordered to exit his vehicle and follow one of the uniformed men while the two other Patriots began searching the Silverado. Nothing was found, other than the mountain bike lying in the bed of the truck. Just as the Patriot was removing the bike from the truck, a voice echoed inside the open building. "Leave it." It was Jacoby, an ex-Navy seal who had been in the covert unit three and a half years before leaving active service. In anticipation of Paul's arrival, he had just come out of an office facing the open bay of the building where the truck had been parked and searched. "The man would die without his mountain bike." Jacoby's subordinate put the bike back in the truck and saluted his superior. "Find anything unusual in the vehicle?"

"No sir. The POV is clean."

"I knew you wouldn't," Jacoby said. "We're dealing with a cool, calculated soldier. He doesn't make mistakes. Dismissed." The subordinate saluted again and walked away. "Well, looks like we'll be doing a little reminiscing." Jacoby tapped his knuckles on the side of the truck, turned and headed back to the office.

Meanwhile, as expected, Paul was strip-searched. The Patriots covered every base, leaving no stone unturned and no questions unanswered. Along with his clothing, Paul was checked thoroughly for any wires or bugs. Nude and cold in the unheated building, he was forced to walk through a metal detector in an attempt to make sure nothing had been planted under his skin. Additionally, a doctor who worked directly for the Patriots examined his body. During the examination, Jacoby entered the room. Paul recognized him immediately.

"What's this scar on your upper arm," the doctor asked.

Paul glanced over at Jacoby and gave him a half smile, then back to the doctor. "Russia, doctor, Russia."

Paul was ordered to dress in a uniform. The doctor wanted to know what Paul meant by his reference to Russia. Colonel Harvey did, too, as a matter of fact. "Gentlemen, don't worry about the scar," said Jacoby. "Just consider it a gift from Atkinson to a lost Russian family. Enough said."

"Sounds good to me," the colonel responded. "Major Jacoby, I want you to accompany Mr. Atkinson in his vehicle to the compound. Get him right over to processing."

"Yes sir," Jacoby responded.

Once Paul finished getting dressed in his uniform, black combat boots and black cap included, Jacoby led him back out to the Silverado. The two got in the truck, and once the building's door was open, Paul drove out of the bay and off the property. Jacoby instructed Paul to turn left onto the asphalt road. Paul didn't speak. He waited for Jacoby to open the conversation. He knew he would. Jacoby had always been opinionated in the covert unit, and was always ready with an answer. Paul didn't dislike Jacoby, though. He actually liked the fact that he was so loyal to the unit and everyone in it. Jacoby was one of those rare soldiers that would, without hesitation, lay down his life for the safety of his comrades and for the sake of the mission.

"So, what happened, Paul? Did you begin to see what we see in the Patriots?"

Paul, despite the fact that he knew Jacoby, still needed to sound convincing. "That's exactly what happened," he said. "I'm sick and tired of these liberals."

"You know, I never could get a good bead on you when we served in Quantico. You were always hard to read." Jacoby looked out of the passenger window, then back at Paul. "I really never saw you show any emotion until the mission in Russia."

"You think I did the right thing that night?" The question was meant to gauge Jacoby.

"Yes, I do Paul. I always have." Jacoby pulled out his nine-millimeter pistol, dropped the full clip, cleared the chamber and placed the now unloaded pistol in its holster. He took the round that came out of the chamber of the pistol and reloaded it into the clip. He had an ammunition pouch on his pistol belt where he stored the clip. No personnel entering the gate of the Patriot compound were allowed to do so with loaded weapons. "Paul, the Patriots aren't cold-blooded killers. We are what our name suggests. We are protectors of everything that is right in the United States; we guard the precepts laid down by our forefathers. You represented what we believe the night you sliced your arm open and bled on the snow for the sake of an innocent family. You are who we look for in the Patriots. You are all about what is right. If we don't take a stand for our country, who will? Welcome aboard to the most lethal fighting force on the planet."

Paul reached over and shook Jacoby's hand. "So, we have a big mission coming up?"

"I don't know all the details. All I know thus far is that it will take place in New York some time in early March. That's all I've heard so far. You know how it is. The grunts are the last to know what's going on, usually not until bullets are flying." Jacoby instructed Paul to turn right onto a gravel road. "You think you still got it?"

Paul turned his head to the right and stared at Jacoby, then smiled. "What do you think?"

"After your long vacation, I wouldn't doubt it if you're better than you were before. The gate is a mile ahead. Stop at the gate and I'll do all the talking."

Paul's stomach tightened as he saw the gate just up ahead. There was no turning back now. Once they were through the gate, he asked himself if he had just written his obituary. The Patriots were very serious about what they were doing and what they planned to accomplish, and they had the personnel, the intellect, the organization and the money to make it happen. Paul knew that all other missions that he had been through paled in difficulty compared to what he was about to face.

Once through the gate, Paul was escorted over to processing while his truck was stored in the compound's motor pool. Processing took three hours and was very similar to processing at any given military installation for an active duty assignment. He was given a thorough physical examination. Following the physical, a photograph was taken of him and a clip-on identification card was given to him to be worn while on the compound. He was issued six sets of black battle dress uniforms and another pair of boots. Paul was then taken to a classroom and given a battery of multiple-choice tests and one essay to write. The essay section of the exam allowed Paul to choose one of three topics meant to gather information where he stood on certain topics the Patriots felt were critical to the future of the United States. Paul made his choice and wrote ten pages on the topic, ten pages of what he hoped would signify his allegiance to the Patriots. Following the processing, Paul was escorted to the compound's mess hall for lunch. He was amazed with the quality of the food provided to the members of the organization. The Patriot mess hall rivaled any he had ever been in while on active duty. A simple thing like an excellent mess facility proved to Paul that the Patriots were indeed an extremely well financed organization. Following lunch Paul was taken to a set of offices adjacent to the mess hall.

Once he reached the offices, his escort told him to wait outside for a moment while he went in. The escort went inside the building and was gone for five minutes. Upon returning, he gave Paul instructions on how to enter the office of the individual he was about to meet. Paul nodded, acknowledging he understood the instructions. He entered the lobby that led into the office, removing his cap once inside the building. He knocked three times on the door that led into the office.

"Enter," a voice commanded on the other side of the door.

Paul entered the office and approached the desk. He stood at attention and saluted. "Candidate Atkinson reporting as ordered, sir."

"At ease, Candidate Atkinson." Paul looked at the man behind the desk. He was a fit, possibly sixty-five year old man with tanned skin and thinning white hair. He wore a white button-down shirt with gray slacks and a black belt with a gold buckle. "Welcome to the Patriots. I'm Thomas Blair. You could say I kind of run this operation. Better said though, my money actually runs this whole thing.

"I've heard a great deal about you and your successes in Quantico. You have an excellent record. Have a seat." Blair pointed out a chair to Paul.

"Thank-you, sir," Paul replied as he sat down in a leather chair.

"Atkinson, I don't fund the Patriots because I'm some bored old man with a great deal of money and a lot of time on my hands. I do this because this country is collapsing before our very eyes. Someone has to put a stop to it. For years, I have protected this country in the best way I know how. I have served as a private corporation hired by our own government to do the jobs they can't do or won't do because they don't want the bad press. I've been involved in some way or another in every conflict since Panama. Now, I see the need to protect my own land against an enemy not foreign at all, but domestic. Where we have been seen as hired guns for our nation, we will now be labeled as terrorists. I have recruited these men, these highly trained and capable soldiers to bring an end to the madness of liberalism in our great land. I live just outside of Phoenix, but I fly here often in my private jet. We have our own landing strip here in the compound equipped with radar and personnel watching our airspace at all times.

"Like I said, we will be called terrorists with an evil cause. Well, I'm sure if they had been using such words when our forefathers rebelled against England, our founders would have been labeled terrorists also. But, you won't find any history book labeling them as such, would you? No. Nearly three centuries later, they are called heroes. They stood up against an oppressive government that had choked out their basic fundamental rights to freedom. Fast forward to 2009 and take a look at our situation as citizens of this once great nation. Look familiar to you?" Blair wasn't interested in hearing Paul's answers to his questions. He did the answering. "Of course it looks familiar. Now, we are the oppressed. Our basic fundamental rights to life, liberty and the pursuit of happiness have been stripped away by a government that is less of and for the people, and more a money grubbing corporation out to control as much of the world's finances that it can." Paul suddenly remembered the sermon given by Dr. Rodgers some months back. This sounded eerily similar – a little less spiritual, more militant, but similar nonetheless.

"I assume you've come to the Patriots because you have the same convictions about the state of our nation as we do. If so, you've made the right choice. All types of labels will be plastered on us as we begin this journey, but there will be a day when the history books will not call us terrorists but true Patriots. Are you prepared for what lies ahead?"

Paul stood to his feet and saluted. "Yes sir, I am ready to defend this once great nation."

Blair smiled and nodded his approval. "Then you will no longer be called 'candidate'. You are promoted to the rank of captain. I think you already know your pay rate."

"Yes sir," Paul replied as he remained at attention.

"Good, Captain Atkinson." Blair reached out and shook Paul's hand. He then reached into his desk and pulled out a new set of silver captain's bars. He gave them to Paul and told him to put them on his headgear after being dismissed. "Welcome to the Patriots. I'm sure you will be a valuable asset to the unit."

"I know I will, sir," Paul said.

"Dismissed." Blair gave Paul a parting salute and Paul, following military protocol, returned the salute to his commander. With slight sweat just beginning to form on his forehead, Paul turned and exited the office.

Following the interview with Blair, Paul was escorted to his quarters. He thought the living quarters would be open barracks. Much to his amazement, each member of the Patriots had his own private quarters complete with a small kitchen, private bath and television. The television, however, only allowed a member to watch DVD's that could be checked out from the recreation facility. No outside television was permitted on the compound. Paul checked the shelves, the small pantry and the refrigerator to find that his living quarters were fully stocked with food and other supplies. The quarters were very similar to the ones in Quantico but slightly larger. Paul unpacked his bag that had been returned to him by the escort and hung up his uniforms. He had asked the escort about supplies for shining his boots. The escort said that he would take care of making sure the boots were shined. He handed Paul a thick operations manual and told him that he needed to have it read within twenty-four hours. He would be tested on some of the topics in the manual. The escort picked up Paul's extra pair of combat boots and left his quarters, promising to have the boots shined and at his door by 0600 hours the next morning.

Paul couldn't figure the whole thing out. This place was nothing like what he thought it would be. Private quarters, escorts to help him get the feel for the place and to shine his boots, a class act mess hall, a landing strip with its own air traffic control facility, recreational facilities, and an incredible salary. If the U.S. military ever adopted the Patriots' way of doing things, he thought, the Pentagon would never have a shortage of soldiers. Paul rapidly shook his head. He had to remain focused on his mission. The Patriots were getting it right in their way of recruiting and keeping top-notch soldiers, but they were still domestic terrorists out to change the course of history and potentially bring about a civil war on American soil.

Paul laid down on the bed and opened the operations manual. By early evening, he had read 175 pages of the manual, two thirds of the material. Paul was a very intelligent person with a gift for retention. He would not forget what he read. A loud knock at the door stunned Paul. He stood from the bed and opened the door.

"Well, it really is true. You're not a ghost are you?"

"Williams, Scott," Paul said to his former comrades, "it's really good to see you again. Come on in."

"Good to see you, Paul. We'll all get together after chow," said Scott. "Let's get over there and eat. We're having ribeye steak tonight. You haven't gone vegetarian on us have you?"

"No, that'll never happen," Paul replied.

"Good. Let's eat." Scott held the door open for Paul, while Paul grabbed his headgear and followed Scott and Williams to the mess hall.

On the way to the mess hall, the three soldiers tried to catch up on everything that had happened in their lives since leaving Quantico. Paul told them that he initially wound up in Bessemer, Alabama, near Birmingham only to move to St. Louis less than a year later for work. He said he had heard about the Patriots from someone in a bar who had lived near the compound. Paul went on to say that he heard from a source in Virginia that his three former team members had joined the Patriots and after finding the ad in a magazine that he had decided to look into the possibility of joining. He said there was no room in the civilian world for someone like him, that he had worked menial jobs since leaving Quantico. Scott and Williams bought the entire story.

Atlanta

She was tired and frustrated. Dianne's day at the hospital had been long. One critical patient nearly died when he began choking on his own vomit. Following the episode, Dianne found out that the six year old little boy was allergic to a medication that had been administered to him post surgery. After the little boy was stable, Dianne rushed to her office and laid on the couch.

Dr. Stan Davis was at the nurses' station when Dianne rushed past the counter without acknowledging anyone. The kind and jovial side of Dianne seemed to have faded during the past month. Dr. Davis was a thirty-nine year old divorced father of two. He was known as a flirt among the nurses, but his eyes had always been on Dianne from the first day she arrived at Northside Hospital. He had asked her out numerous times, but had been turned down each time. Seeing Dianne in her emotional state gave Davis the confidence to give it another try.

The doctor walked to the door of Dianne's office and knocked. Dianne asked who it was and Davis responded, "It's Stan. Can I come in?"

Reluctantly and for the sake of doctor-to-doctor open communication, Dianne told him he could come in. Davis entered Dianne's office and found her on the couch. Despite the fatigue showing on her face, she was still stunning. He only wanted one night with her. If he could get that one night, he was confident he could win her over. "Dianne, you look exhausted."

"I've had a long day Stan, and I'd rather be alone right now." Dianne was rubbing her forehead in hopes of alleviating the pain of a severe stress headache.

"Perhaps being alone isn't the best thing for you right now," Davis answered. "Why don't we go downstairs for a cup of coffee?"

"No thanks," Dianne replied.

"Then perhaps after our shift we could just go out and have some innocent fun – a few drinks, dance a little, a bite to eat."

Dianne sat up on her couch. She could see right through Dr. Davis. She knew all about the man sitting six feet from her. His ex-wife filed for divorce after finding him in their bedroom with a nurse from one of the other units in the hospital. It wasn't the first time he had been caught, but it was the last time for his wife. She hired one of the toughest divorce attorneys in Atlanta and nearly took everything he had in the divorce. She got full custody of the children, the house, hefty child support and alimony and fifty percent ownership of a beach home the doctor had purchased near Destin, Florida. Dianne had hoped he would leave the hospital following the divorce, but he stayed on and had hounded her for nearly three years in an attempt to get her to go out with him. She knew his tactics and was in the right mood to end his charade once and for all.

Dianne stood from her couch and picked up a framed photograph from her desk of her and Paul. It was the same one Paul had when he reported to Quantico. She showed it to Davis. "This is my boyfriend. Have I ever told you what he does for a living? He's a trained assassin for the United States government." Dianne was trying to lay it on as thick as possible. "I don't think you want to make him mad. Ask the girls on the way out. They've seen him. Now, Dr. Davis, I really hope I'm not going to have to make a call to him, or can we from this day forward keep our relationship on a professional level? I wouldn't want you to disappear from the face of the earth."

"Dianne, I think you've got me all wrong." Davis was squirming in his chair as Dianne pulled out her cell phone and began dialing a number. "Really, I don't think calling him will be necessary. I'm sorry you misunderstood my intentions." Davis got up and headed for the door.

"Is that what you told your wife when she caught you in bed with that nurse?" Dianne held the phone up to her ear. Davis quickly exited her office and hurriedly walked toward the elevators.

When he rushed passed the nurses' station, one of the nurses commented to another, "Strike three and you're out."

Dianne actually had dialed a number. It was her parents'. Anne picked up the phone followed by Charlie. Dianne was in tears again. "Mom, dad, will Paul ever come back? Will he?"

"We pray every day for that very thing," Charlie replied. "God can do anything, can't he little angel? Don't forget that he brought Paul here in the first place and he can bring him back."

"I just threw a doctor out of my office. He's divorced after getting caught by his wife in bed with a nurse. Since I've arrived, he has tried everything to get me to go out with him." Dianne grabbed a tissue and wiped the tears from her eyes.

"Well, do you want to go out with this doctor," Anne asked.

"Mom, of course not. I just wonder if I was too rough on him. He only wanted to invite me downstairs for a cup of coffee."

"Dianne," Anne said, "you said this man got caught cheating on his wife. You said he has been after you since you started working at the hospital. This man sounds like a very shallow person who thinks that his status as a doctor affords him every opportunity to sleep with any woman he chooses. I only asked you that question so that you could be sure that you are standing on firm ground."

"I don't know what kind of ground I'm standing on, but I know that I would never consider sharing a water fountain with that guy. I'm sure after tonight, he won't bother me anymore."

"So, what'd you say to him," Charlie asked.

"I told him that my boyfriend is a trained assassin for the U.S. government."

"That'll usually do the trick," Charlie replied with a laugh. "That's my spunky daughter."

Dianne smiled for the first time in days. "His face turned whiter than the hospital bed sheets when I told him that I didn't want him to disappear from the face of the earth."

Charlie was laughing harder now. "Little does he know that Paul could probably make it happen."

Dianne's nerves had calmed now that she was able to talk to her parents. "Dad, I wouldn't want anything to happen to Dr. Davis. I actually pray for him often. He never sees his children. I overheard him one evening making an excuse to his ex-wife that he couldn't pick up the children for weekend visitation because he had to work. He was not scheduled to pull any shifts that weekend and was never here. I only told him those things a few minutes ago to get him to leave me alone."

"Dianne," Anne said, "it sounds like Dr. Davis has some very mixed up priorities. I'm proud of you for praying for him. Now, concerning Paul, you will have an answer in time – in God's time. He will tell you whether you need to move on or whether you need to wait. He will never leave you in the dark. Trust him."

"I know, mom. I'm trying. I just miss Paul. It seems like yesterday when we were opening Christmas gifts from each other and sharing our dreams to never be apart. Now, I hardly know him anymore. I have no idea just where he is right now, and I don't know how to help him." Dianne stared at the framed photograph. A tear from her eye fell onto the glass.

"God is a god of miracles, Dianne," said Charlie. "He can heal Paul's heart and bring him home. I'm hanging on that hope."

"Then if you can, I can," Dianne replied. "Goodnight mom. Goodnight dad. I love you both."

"Goodnight sweetheart. We love you too."

Patriot Compound

Three weeks had passed, and Paul was fully acclimated to life as a Patriot. No one suspected that he had infiltrated the organization to feed information to the Pentagon. A unit briefing was scheduled for 1300 hours that day and Paul hoped to finally gather more specific intelligence. He had been able to drop a note at the designated location only once. It read, "Initiation complete. Intel scarce. Planned operation in early March." After he had been there ten days, Paul was permitted to ride through the compound on his mountain bike. The Patriot compound was a fairly large three thousand acre area of mostly forest. Rifle ranges had been built with better systems than the U.S. military had ever developed. Obstacle courses that stretched a full one thousand meters in length were used frequently in order to keep the Patriots strong, fast and agile. A small mock town had been constructed complete with two and three story buildings, gas stations, a church, a jail, houses and other buildings one might find in a small town. Head to head training took place there to sharpen the skills of the Patriots in urban combat situations. All of the Patriots had had similar training while on active duty, but the Patriots were better equipped. With the use of satellite receivers carried by each soldier, the commander miles away could monitor the movement of every Patriot using a laptop computer that would allow him to make adjustments as necessary via advanced digital communications. Paul was impressed.

Later, Paul arrived at the briefing five minutes early with Jacoby in tow. Once everyone was seated, Lieutenant Colonel Harvey began the briefing. The lights were turned off and a slide projector was switched on. "Gentlemen, our training has been excellent. This unit is without a doubt the most qualified, most motivated, and most intelligent unit I have ever commanded.

"Now we are ready to go to our next phase of training in preparation for the following mission." The colonel clicked a remote and the projector brought up a photograph of President Grigsby. "This man's four year term has just begun and already he is putting our nation at great risk. On March fourth, Grigsby will invite this man." Another click and a new photograph came up on the screen. "Abdullah Aminadab, the president of Iran to the White House and then to New York for a rally on the streets of Manhattan, just a short distance from the site of the 9/11 attacks. Inviting a known terrorist supporter even near the site of the 9/11 tragedy sickens me. The Patriots will on that day make our statement to our nation and begin to bring true freedom and democracy back to this country. Only one person knows just who we will hit on March fourth. That individual is our sniper. He has been chosen already, and we trust that he will not compromise the mission by even telling his fellow Patriots any information. Everyone else will have other duties and responsibilities that will assist in bringing about a smooth completion to our mission. Of the ninety personnel we have, only ten will be selected for this mission. The remaining eighty personnel will stay back and guard the compound. We will not fail because we will be fully rehearsed and ready prior to moving to our area of operation.

"Mr. Blair purchased an additional 1000 acres adjacent to our compound several months ago. Since then, a scaled down mock-up of the area of operation in New York has been constructed. For the ten weeks, we will train and rehearse the operation at that site. On March fourth, our extensive training, our skills, our motivation and our loyalty to our country will catapult us to victory. Tomorrow morning, I want the entire unit formed and ready to be flown in our Blackhawk helicopters to the site by 1000 hours. Dismissed."

Paul felt like he had everything he needed to complete his mission. On the way back to his quarters, he told Scott and Williams that he wanted to get a ride in before dark. "Let's meet after chow tonight. How about a couple games of pool over in the rec room?" Paul was sure neither suspected anything.

"Sounds good, Paul," Scott replied. "We'll see you at chow."

Paul changed into shorts and a sweatshirt. Under the sweatshirt, he wore a white t-shirt that allowed him to hide a blank piece of paper inside a clear plastic sandwich bag as well as an ink pen. The bag was under the t-shirt and tucked slightly into his shorts. After retrieving his bike, he rode out to the drop point and wrote: "Mission plan confirmed. March 4th. Manhattan. Iranian president. Possibly, U.S. president. Training for mission to commence tomorrow." He dated the note, folded the paper and placed it in the plastic bag. After burying the sandwich bag, Paul hopped back on his bike for the ride back to his quarters. On the way back, he thought about Dianne. He asked himself if he could ever return to her, if he had the courage to face her and to face the fears of losing her like he had lost Chris and his parents. He wondered if Dianne had already given up on him, whether there was hope at all. He shook off the thoughts. "Focus on the mission, Atkinson," Paul said as he sped along a trail.

Paul returned to his quarters and showered. After changing into a clean uniform, he walked over to the mess hall and found Jacoby, Scott and Williams together as usual. Their plates were full, and the three were laughing at a joke told by Williams. The three acknowledged Paul when he entered the mess hall and invited him to bring his tray over to where they were sitting. Paul made his way through the line, his appetite diminished after his risky bike ride. It was worth it, though. Paul was sure the mission would be over soon with the specific intelligence he had buried at the drop point. The compound will be raided, and no one will have to die, he thought. Paul cared nothing at all about politics, but he believed in loyalty to country. He wasn't about to let the new president die or even the Iranian president die, as much as he despised the fanatic that promised to destroy Israel. Paul didn't particularly like the idea of President Grigsby bringing Aminadab to the United States for a rally, but he wasn't going to let his personal convictions get in the way of protecting the U.S. president or the Iranian president. The Patriots were intelligent. They knew that killing one or both of those presidents would create a massive uprising. The uprising, they thought, would propel them to power in the United States. Paul hoped to see the compound raided within a few days so that the whole affair could end, and so he could move on with his life, as aimless as his life now appeared to be.

Turning his attention to his former comrades, Paul took a seat at the table where they were still engaged in conversation. "I'm glad you guys left me something," Paul said staring at the mound of food on each of their plates.

"Paul, you eat like a bird anyway," Scott responded. "I don't see how you survive on what you eat."

"He's got that big heart," Jacoby said. "It keeps him full. You guys remember that time in Somalia when Paul kept giving up his MRE's to those starving kids?"

"Yep," Williams said. "We were waiting for Paul to collapse from hunger one day."

Paul looked at Williams and said, "Discipline, my friend. Discipline."

"Nothing shakes you, does it," Scott asked Paul.

"I wouldn't say that. I just don't believe an elite soldier should ever show it when he gets shaken. I've been shaken. Never forget Russia. I thought Ace was going to shoot me along with that family and leave me in the snow in Siberia. If I show fear, I'm defeated. I wasn't about to show any fear that night."

"You sure didn't when you opened up your arm with that knife," said Jacoby.

"Well fellows," Paul replied. "That was then and this is now. I feel like I'm back in the unit with you guys here. We're going to change the world on March 4th." Paul hoped that March 4th for the Patriots would be spent in a heavily guarded federal prison cell.

"Here, here," said Scott as he raised his glass to toast Paul's comment. The other three lifted their glasses for the toast.

Following their meal, Scott, Williams and Paul walked over to the recreation facility to shoot a few games of pool. Jacoby said he had some things he needed to get done and left the group at the entrance to the recreation facility. Paul wasn't much of a pool player but he gave it his best. Scott and Williams, however, were extremely competitive, betting their allowance on their games. Paul told the other two after some conversation that he preferred to leave them to their financial battle and that he was returning to his quarters. The next morning, prior to moving to the new training site, the entire compound would be engaging in a physical training test similar to the one conducted by the Army: sit-ups, push-ups, two-mile run with pull-ups added. Paul knew the next day would be long and despite his hopes that a Pentagon team would arrive soon, he had to remain focused and never allow any of the Patriots question his loyalty.

Once he returned to his quarters, Paul took off his uniform, put on a pair of sweat pants and a t-shirt. He wanted to get his mind off the situation, so he had checked out a movie at the recreation facility before returning. He turned on the DVD player and the television and slipped the disc into the unit before grabbing the remote and lying on his bed. He started the movie, but barely got thirty minutes into it before falling asleep. He awoke at 3:00am and switched off the television before rolling back over and going to sleep. Before falling asleep, Paul said, "God, if you're out there, let this be over soon."

The next day the Patriots, as ordered, were at the compound's quarter mile cinder track ready for the physical training test. The standards set by the Patriot commanders were much higher than those set by the Army. Still, Paul was in outstanding physical condition. He was able to achieve a maximum score in each event. The two-mile run became a dogfight between Paul and Jacoby with Paul edging his competition at the line by less than a second. Paul might have been in the enemy's camp, but nothing could squelch his competitive spirit. Jacoby had been a successful middle distance runner at Penn State and Paul had never been able to keep up with him on the track. This was his first time beating Jacoby and outscoring him on a P.T. test.

Following the morning test, Paul returned to his quarters, showered and ate breakfast in the mess hall. At the appointed time, he reported to the formation. Colonel Harvey announced the names of the personnel that would be going to New York to conduct the mission. Paul was confused when the colonel only announced nine names, which included his name, Williams and Scott. His confusion was abated somewhat when Harvey announced that the tenth individual had been thoroughly briefed and trained on his duties, that his name would remain top-secret to the rest of the personnel. Though Jacoby's name wasn't mentioned, Paul assumed with his talents that he was the tenth man. He was the logical choice.

The flight to the training site took less than ten minutes. Once on-site, Paul looked around and was amazed with the incredible detail of the mock-up. It had a stage with cardboard figures of the dignitaries expected to be on the stage during the rally and even cardboard figures of people making up the crowd of on-lookers. Colonel Harvey described the plan and where everyone would be during the mission. He told the nine elite soldiers that he was confident in the mission's outcome, but wanted to focus on the extrication of the team following the attack.

In the weeks leading up to the drive to New York, the team practiced again and again at the training site on the Patriot compound. Mr. Blair was present during the final ten days of preparation, and during a speech to the unit, he complimented the team for their bravery and loyalty to country. He went on to say that he was extremely confident that the team would prevail and that the Patriots would go down in history as saviors of the American way.

Paul had grown extremely concerned. He couldn't understand why the Pentagon, why Ace had not sent a team in to stop the upcoming mission and halt the operations of the Patriots. Twice he had gone back to the drop-site to make sure the last note had been retrieved. It was gone. What was happening? Where were the troops? By March 1st, Paul had all but given up hope that Ace was going to engage the Patriots on their turf. He assumed that a plan was in place to catch them in the act in New York. Regardless of what Ace's plan of action was Paul had decided that he had to find out who the tenth man on the team was and to stop him from killing anybody. The team would be leaving that night in two vans that had, "Trinity Church of Christ, Joplin, Missouri" on each side of the vehicles. All part of the plan of action.

Washington, D.C., the White House
March 3rd

The press filled the White House lawn. News crews from all over the world were present for the historic meeting between the President of the United States and the President of Iran. The world watched to see what Aminadab would say. Would he accept the olive branch offered by President Grigsby and stop making threats against the civilized world? Or, would he continue with the rhetoric of hate that he had been spewing for several years, particularly the threats aimed at Israel and the United States?

President Grigsby opened up the news conference with a short statement prior to introducing Aminadab. "My fellow Americans, ladies and gentlemen of the press, today is truly an historic day for our nation. President Aminadab and I have spent hours talking and at times debating the direction that we believe here in the United States the entire region of the Middle East must go in order to establish a lasting peace. I said it during my campaign, and I'm saying it now. Lasting peace in the Middle East will never come without open dialogue among all of the leaders, not just in that region, but throughout the entire world. With that open dialogue and a cooperative effort of every leader in the Middle East working together for a common cause, we can root out the terrorist cells that have not only plagued that region but have been menaces throughout the world, killing innocent civilians, men, women and children without remorse. Today, we will begin on a path with the help of the capable leaders of the Middle East that will eradicate global terrorism once and for all, and establish lasting peace in that region and, we believe, throughout the world. For that reason, I asked President Aminadab here today for this press conference, and have invited him to the Unity Rally to be held at 1:00pm tomorrow in New York where he will be a guest speaker. With that, I give you President Aminadab, the Iranian president. Please hold your questions until he has finished."

President Grigsby stepped away from the podium and with an interpreter the Iranian president approached the microphone. "Ladies and gentlemen," the Iranian began, "I want to thank President Grigsby and his staff for inviting me to your country. I am pleased that your new president is open to speak with me about the dilemmas we face every day in our land. Under the leadership of your former president, our women and our children have died from starvation and various diseases. Warships have blocked shipments of food, medicines and other needs into our land. Our men have no work, no income. Our nation was in the dark under your previous president. Now, we have hope. President Grigsby has reached out to us and has said that he wants to end the days of struggle we have endured in our land. He wants to allow my people to live as you live here in this vast land. I believe that we can as two nations, bring peace to the part of the world where my people have lived for thousands of years. I would like to thank President Grigsby for inviting me here. Thank-you."

The question and answer part of the news conference began with most questions aimed at the President of Iran. He had been such a polarizing figure for so long, and now, he seemed to have turned over a new leaf under the urgings of the new American president. The questions asked of the Iranian leader ranged from the nuclear conflict that raged during the previous American administration to the various embargos that had been established as punishment for Iran's defiance.

One question came from a Jewish journalist. "Mr. Aminadab, now that you have begun to establish better relations with the United States, will you halt your horrid and senseless threats of violence against the nation of Israel?"

The question infuriated the Iranian. "Israel has bombed our people and stolen are land. Innocent women and children have been murdered by the Jews. We have been called barbarians, yet they are the barbarians."

Not the ending to the news conference that President Grigsby had hoped for. Leave it to an experienced journalist to bring the best out in a person. "That's all the time we have for questions," said the American president. "We hope you will come out for the Unity Rally tomorrow in New York."

Interstate 70, Pennsylvania

With Bibles in hand the passengers riding in the Trinity Church of Christ vans were nearing New York. Paul held tightly to the Bible he had been given. It was the first time he had held a Bible since ripping the one up in his living room in front of Dianne weeks earlier. He wanted to open the book and find something that would give him hope that he would come out of this thing alive. He tried to divert his attention for a moment by picturing Dianne's face, her beautiful, penetrating eyes, her fantastic smile, soft hair and loving kisses. He missed her. He wondered if she had moved on, if she had given up on him. Paul refused to blame her. None of it was her fault. He had given up and, like a coward, had crawled in fear back into that same trash heap he felt he had lived in most of his life. How could he ever expect to be loved by anyone when he pushed people away out of fear? He longed to hear her voice, to tell her that he still loved her.

Paul's attention was drawn back to the present tense when he noticed the driver was pulling off the interstate and onto a rural road. On a two-lane asphalt road, the vans traveled ten miles before pulling off the road and onto a dirt road. The vans were halted at a gate, then motioned in after a few words exchanged between the guard and the driver of the lead van. The two vans went through the gate and back to what appeared to be a hanger. The doors to the hanger opened, and the vans pulled inside and parked. Colonel Harvey and Mr. Blair were waiting inside when the vans arrived. Everyone was ordered out of the vans for a briefing. The mission was to take place in about twenty-four hours.

"Gentlemen, phase one of our mission is complete," said Colonel Harvey with a wide grin. "This hanger and the property it sits on are owned outright by the Patriots. We will stay here tonight and fly to our designated positions tomorrow at 1100 hours. Our tenth man is here already and his identity will be revealed soon. We couldn't risk revealing his identity on the compound despite our trust of our men. He is a key to our success. Without him, we fail. I'm sure you've had some questions of just how we are going to get in and out of the area of operation without drawing any attention to ourselves. The answer is in this hanger. Follow me."

The colonel led the nine Patriots to another door inside the hanger that separated one section of the large building from another. He slid the door open and walked through. Inside the other section of the hanger were two helicopters. On the side of one helicopter, a news station logo read, "News Channel 11", and a similar news logo on the other that read, "Action News 5". One was painted white with red lettering, while the other was light blue also with red lettering. Blair was going all out for this mission, Paul thought. He hoped Ace had a team in place to stop it. He had no way of informing him of anything now, and trying to escape would surely be like signing his own death warrant.

"I want you to stay in your civilian clothing," the colonel continued. "Mr. Blair wants to treat you to a very special meal tonight in appreciation for all of your hard work and dedication to this historic mission. I'm sure everyone here likes a nice, thick t-bone steak." Everyone clapped, including Paul. He had to keep playing the role. "We thought you would. The catered meal will be brought to the gate and delivered to the hanger by our guards.

"One last thing. Before we do anything else, we will assign each man to his designated helicopter. We will also show you where the weapons will be hidden on the aircraft." Colonel Harvey assigned each man to his designated helicopter and revealed the location of the weapons. A compartment located under the belly of each aircraft had been fabricated to hold the necessary equipment, ammunition, smoke canisters, and weapons to carry out the mission. The weapons and other necessities were all in black cases with the last name of every Patriot on each piece of equipment assigned to the personnel. The colonel then opened the helicopter's side door to reveal news equipment, cameras, microphones, cords, and other equipment normally used by reporters. After looking inside the helicopters, the colonel directed the team's attention to a closet. He opened it up and revealed ten sets of clothing ranging in type from suits to semi casual pants and pull-over shirts with jackets that had the logos of the news channels on them. A tag was on the hanger of each set of clothing that had the name of the member who would wear the clothing. A successful attack of this sort required cover, concealment and the element of surprise, and Paul's experience told him that the Patriots had thoroughly covered every base. If Ace didn't get a team in place and stop this, it was going to be a very bad day in New York and possibly the entire world.

Lumpkin County, Georgia, the Taylor Residence

Dianne arrived at seven-thirty in the evening after her shift at the hospital. She let Wilson out of the Envoy first. The playful dog was now full-grown and weighed a massive seven and a half pounds. As soon as his legs hit the ground, he eagerly ran to the door of the house excited at the opportunity to spend some time with Charlie. Dianne unloaded a bag and walked to the door. Waiting at the door for his beautiful daughter, Charlie took her bag and hugged Dianne while Wilson repeatedly leaped in the air and against Charlie's leg starving for his attention. Dianne had decided to go ahead and take a vacation. She felt no desire to travel, though, but had decided instead to stay with her parents.

The look of fatigue that colored Dianne's face for weeks had faded and her incredible beauty had begun to reemerge. She still thought of Paul often, but she had begun to accept that he would probably never return. She knew that she had to let him go. He was an eagle with a broken wing, and Dianne realized that she had no ability to help him. She still prayed for him constantly, but she had come to realize that only God could save Paul and heal the broken wing that would allow him to soar again.

"Welcome home, little angel," Charlie said as he walked with Dianne to her bedroom. Anne was putting fresh sheets on Dianne's bed when the two walked in the room.

"Dianne," Anne said, "I'm so glad you're home. We have an exciting remainder of the week planned." Dianne hugged her mother, and Charlie finally picked up and held Wilson, accepting the excessive licking from the lively dog.

"It's good to be home, mom. I hear the church is starting a revival tomorrow night. I got a letter in the mail at the condo." Dianne began unpacking.

"That's right," Charlie said. "With the construction and renovation completed, Dr. Rodgers felt that a revival was in order. It'll last through Sunday."

"You know something," Dianne replied, "I think I need to attend each night."

"We certainly won't try to stop you, honey," Anne said. "We won't be able to attend Saturday night, but we will be happy to go with you on the other nights."

"Great! I'm looking forward to it." Dianne opened her closet and hung up two outfits that she brought with her. Then from a make-up bag, she pulled out the small case that held the earrings that Paul purchased for her at Christmas. She opened up the case and stared at the glistening diamonds. "You know, I can't explain it, but the diamonds have looked clearer in the last few days."

"That's because your eyes are clearer and your heart is healing," Anne said.

Dianne glanced at Anne before turning her attention back to the diamonds. "I guess you're right."

"Tomorrow at one Fox News will be televising that rally in New York," said Charlie. "I'm sure you've heard about it." Dianne nodded her head. "Well, I thought we'd have lunch here, watch the rally then drive to the outlet stores and shop for you. How's that sound?"

"Shop only for me?" Dianne's beautiful smile was back.

"Your father wants to buy a new trolling motor for the boat," Anne revealed.

"Dad, you know how to make a gal feel special," Dianne quipped. She laughed and gave her father a kiss on the cheek before the three left for dinner and a movie. Charlie and Anne were glad to see their daughter healing from the pain of losing Paul. It had been pain that reverberated throughout the family, the church and even the members of the community who had hoped to see Paul and Dianne get married and live happily ever after in Lumpkin County. Charlie and Anne could still see the pain in Dianne when Paul's name came up, but she had gotten much better. Her smile proved it.

A small aircraft hanger in Pennsylvania

With massive t-bone steaks, baked potatoes, and fresh salads on the table, the Patriots celebrated the mission that was less than twenty-four hours away. Colonel Harvey stood up during the meal and asked for everyone's attention.

"I want to again thank you men for your dedication to this honorable cause. We are embarking on a mission that will change the course of history and bring America back to its rightful place of power, honor, wealth and integrity on the world's stage. As a token of Mr. Blair's appreciation for your efforts, I have been ordered to issue each one of you a $50,000.00 cash bonus upon our return to the compound." The group of men all clapped showing their approval of this latest news. "Now, it's time to meet the tenth member of our team. Again, we could take no chances revealing his identity in the compound. But, now as we approach the culmination of our hard work, I feel that it is time. Major Jacoby, front and center." Jacoby emerged from a back room in the hanger where he had been for three days prior to the rest of the team arriving. Paul was right. Jacoby was the logical choice. He was one of the top marksmen in the world, incredibly lethal with a sniper rifle. Paul knew he had to find a way to talk to Jacoby alone, to find out just who the target was to be.

Jacoby approached his commander and saluted. "Major Jacoby reporting as ordered, sir." Jacoby was a pure picture of confidence.

The colonel returned the salute. "Stand at ease." Colonel Harvey turned to the men at the two tables. "This man will pull the trigger and send a round out of the chamber of his sniper rifle, a round that will forever be remembered by our nation and the world. We will no longer be seen as weak pawns of an oppressive government. We will, like the phoenix, rise up from the ashes of oppression and defeat the enemies of freedom." The Patriots stood from their chairs and cheered. Paul joined in. He had a sudden feeling of helplessness.

Later, Paul found Jacoby standing by one of the helicopters. As it turned out, Paul would be on the same aircraft as Jacoby during the flight to New York. Paul decided he would try to get information out of Jacoby. "You're the man," Paul said as he approached Jacoby and placed his hand on his shoulder. "The brass made the right choice. I've never seen anyone send a 7.62 millimeter round downrange from a mile away and be so accurate."

Jacoby looked at Paul and smiled. "I thought the brass might choose you."

"Are you kidding me," Paul replied with a laugh. "I might be good on a pop-up range with an M-16, but there is no one on this planet better than you with a sniper rifle."

"Steady aim, steady breathing, soft trigger pull – that's all it takes," said Jacoby. "I will hit my target with one round and be out of there before anyone has any idea the man's been hit. They'll think he passed out on stage while I'm loading up on a helicopter headed for Missouri and a $50,000.00 cash bonus."

"Hey, Jacoby, we've known each other for some time. I know the brass wants to keep us in the dark, but if for some reason, you go down, someone's going to have to step in and pick up the slack." Paul was ready to make his move. He hoped Jacoby would take the bait. "So, who's the target?"

"I don't plan on going down, Atkinson," said Jacoby.

"I'm sure you won't, but in Quantico we always had plan 'B's', right?"

"Listen, Paul. If I tell you, you keep it quiet. I'll have more than one round in the sniper rifle. I wouldn't want to have to use any more than that one round. You get my point?" Jacoby's voice had lowered.

"You've known me long enough to know that I wouldn't breathe this information to anyone else, under any circumstances." Paul's heart rate was increasing and the adrenaline was starting to flow.

"We're going to take out Aminadab," Jacoby answered.

"Nail him between his ugly eyes," Paul responded hoping he had convinced Jacoby of his intentions for getting the intel on the mission.

"Trust me, I'm going to send the man a 7.62 millimeter one-way ticket to Allah." Jacoby smiled at Paul as they shook hands.

Paul decided to try to get some sleep. Cots had been set up in the hanger for the Patriots. Paul found his and laid down without removing his shoes. He concluded, in a last ditch grab for hope, that Ace would have some intel that would allow a team to be ready to stop the Patriots in their tracks before any damage could be done. The good guys would be in the buildings waiting for the Patriots and would do whatever necessary to stop the mission. Paul decided that if it came down to him killing members of the Patriots, even Jacoby, Williams and Scott, that he would be ready to pull the trigger of his assault rifle. He wasn't going to let anybody on that stage die. After nearly an hour of considering his options, Paul finally fell asleep.

The Patriots were awakened at 6:00am the next morning. Everyone was given an opportunity to shower and shave in order to look the parts they were about to play. Breakfast was offered, but few ate anything. The adrenaline flowing through the veins of the Patriots was more than enough energy. At 9:00am, the helicopters were rolled out of the hanger and given a final check by the pilots. Once the checks were completed, the turbine engines of the helicopters were started and the Patriots loaded onto the designated aircraft.

Paul had never been this nervous. This was suddenly turning into his worse nightmare. The plan was to land one helicopter on a sixteen story building that was south of the rally location and that stood above smaller buildings that would not block the view to the stage where the event would be held a block and a half away. The other helicopter would land on another building where the other half of the team would set up. That building was to the west of the stage three blocks away and towered above the smaller buildings around it. From the twenty-sixth floor of that building, Jacoby would have a clear line of site with a scope mounted onto his sniper rifle. Paul would remain on the roof of the building with binoculars scanning the area for anything suspicious.

With the team dressed as cameramen, photographers, and reporters, the flight had begun. Forty-seven minutes later, Paul's helicopter landed on the twenty-eight-story building. It was 11:40am and the crowds were already forming in hopes of getting close to the new, incredibly dynamic President of the United States. A large number of Muslims arrived as well, carrying flags of various middle-eastern countries. Some carried two small flags – one American, the other Iranian.

Just as they had trained, the helicopters landed on their respective buildings and after the Patriots unloaded they removed the television equipment and opened the belly compartment to remove the black cases that held ammunition, weapons, smoke canisters, tear gas and the other necessities to complete the mission. Though onlookers saw the helicopters land, the news channel logos on the sides of the aircraft didn't alarm them in any way. Just another couple of news channels looking for the best spot to report on the rally, most thought.

The Patriots began setting up the cameras on tripods on the roofs of their respective attack locations. For the sake of convincing anyone that might be watching them, they made it look like they were actually reporting, with the cameraman behind the camera with the lens first focused on the reporter, then panning down to the site of the rally. Everything was going as planned. Once they were convinced that no one considered them a threat, the Patriots took up their positions. On the smaller building, three of the five Patriots took up positions on the fifteenth floor. Blair had purchased the top three floors of both buildings and had them gutted to give the appearance of being under construction. Two of the three would fire smoke canisters and tear gas into the crowd to create the chaos and confusion necessary for the Patriots to make a quick and uninhibited exit from the scene. One of the other Patriots would guard the door and patrol the stairwell, while the final two would pull security from the roof of the building.

On the taller building, Jacoby would take up his position on the twenty-sixth floor while two others guarded the door and stairwell. Williams would guard the door. Paul would pull security from the roof on the side of the building facing the rally, while Scott would guard the backside of the roof. Everyone got into their positions and waited for the radio signal ordering the Patriots to commence the operation.

Paul nervously contemplated his options. Surely, he thought, Ace and a team was somewhere near waiting for the right moment to pounce on the Patriots and stop the planned assassination. But, what if no team had arrived. Thoughts raced through his head. Maybe they never got the notes. Maybe an animal dug up the bag and carried it away. That was ridiculous. He was convinced the notes had been received. Maybe they just dropped the ball and were not ready to respond. Perhaps, he thought finally, he had not given enough intel for Ace to form a plan of action. Whatever the case, Paul was determined to stop Jacoby from firing that round, but he had to wait for the right moment.

The crowd had swelled to over one hundred and fifty thousand in anticipation of President Grigsby's motorcade. At 12:50pm cheers erupted a few blocks away as the motorcade arrived and headed toward the stage. Barricades had been erected blocking streets and access to the area behind the stages as well as a fifty-foot buffer in front of the stage where secret service and other security personnel were posted. Paul had retrieved a pair of binoculars from one of the equipment cases and with the television camera at his side he peered down toward the approaching motorcade. He then scanned the stage, hoping he might see some evidence that Ace had deployed a reactionary team to the scene. He looked at each one of the security personnel standing on or around the stage and recognized no one. Paul was convinced that he was on his own, that if anyone was going to stop it, it would have to be him.

The motorcade stopped behind the stage and President Grigsby as well as President Aminadab exited their limousines. With thundering applause greeting the American president, the two men climbed the steps of the stage and were greeted by the Mayor of New York. A Marine band played Stars and Stripes while a Marine color guard team marched onto the stage in preparation for the national anthem. With flags waving and the crowd somewhat quiet, the band played the American national anthem. Paul looked over to the opposite side of the roof where Scott was lying in the prone position keeping watch from his position. Scott turned, looked at Paul and gave him a thumbs up. Paul nodded in acknowledgement of the jester. He had no idea when he would be able to make his move.

Back down on the stage, the national anthem had ended and the Mayor of New York was at the podium greeting the crowd and welcoming the special guests to the world's greatest city. Ten minutes later, the mayor introduced President Grigsby. The president essentially repeated the short speech he had given to the press the day before at the White House, but added a few points: "The diversity of the people here today, the diversity of the flags I see waving in the crowd is the essence of who we are as a nation and as a people. We are, indeed, a nation of rich diversity where 'all men are created equal'. I want to encourage each and every one of you to get to know your neighbor, to be tolerant of another's views, whether he is white or she is black, whether he is gay or she is straight, whether he is educated or she is uneducated, whether he is rich or she is poor. That ingredient will make this nation strong. That is why I asked Iran's President Aminadab to be here today. Any nation outside our borders is a neighbor. Closing our doors to open dialogue to other nations regardless of differences in views will never promote peace. The differences we have had with nations like Iran, Cuba, Venezuela and others will never be solved unless we have open dialogue. Under my administration, we will reach out to our neighbors and seek peace. With that, I would like you to welcome Iran's President Aminadab to the podium."

Paul couldn't wait any longer. He thought he was already too late. Without knowing the itinerary of the event, he had no idea who would speak when and for how long. He got up from his position and crossed to the other side of the roof where Scott was keeping watch. "I hate to do this," Paul said as he grabbed him in a chokehold and waited until Scott was unconscious. He rushed back over to the equipment cases with his rifle as well as Scott's rifle. He packed the two rifles and grabbed a 9-millimeter pistol with a silencer. Suddenly he heard a voice in his earpiece: "Launch in two minutes." It was Colonel Harvey. "Roger that," replied Jacoby from his position.

Paul quickly made his way to the door that led into the stairwell. Standing mid-way down the flight of stairs closest to the door of the roof was another Patriot. "Hey, Paul, why are you out of position?"

Paul made his way down the staircase to the other Patriot. "Nothing happening up there. I thought I heard some commotion down here."

The Patriot turned around and began stepping down the staircase. "No problems down here. You might want to get back to..." Paul, with lightning quickness, grabbed the Patriot from behind in a chokehold using his right arm while cupping the choking soldier's mouth with his left hand. He waited until the Patriot was unconscious before he dragged him up the flight of stairs and out onto the roof. As with Scott's, Paul packed the unconscious Patriot's rifle in the equipment case and headed for the stairwell door, but stopped when he suddenly heard screams from the crowd below. He rushed to the edge of the roof and looked down on the crowd. The smoke canisters and tear gas had been fired into the crowd sending thousands fleeing in every direction. Paul stood and rushed toward the door but before he could get it open, he heard the familiar cracking sound of the sniper rifle. If Jacoby was as accurate as he had always been, there was sure to be a dead body lying on the stage below.

Paul didn't bother to look from the roof. He opened the door and rushed down to the twenty-sixth floor and pushed open the door. He quickly scanned the room and noticed that Williams was packing his assault rifle in the equipment case. Jacoby, however, was still taking aim out of the window. Was Aminadab down, Paul asked his self? He wasn't going to take time to find out. As Paul tried to get to the other side of the large room to get to Jacoby, he heard the sniper say, "One more target. Mr. President, you're mine."

"Jacoby, no!" Paul let out a yell that startled Williams. "That wasn't part of the mission plan."

"Call it a bonus," Jacoby replied as he took aim at President Grigsby who was being rushed from the stage. Williams stood still not sure what to do.

"I can't let you do it," Paul said as he aimed his pistol and fired three rounds into Jacoby's right lung. He had no intention of killing him, and he didn't, but Paul couldn't let Jacoby kill Grigsby. The rounds collapsed Jacoby's right lung sending him into immediate shock. Williams grabbed his rifle and aimed it at Paul. Paul aimed his pistol at Williams, both men ready to fire. "Williams, killing Grigsby wasn't part of the plan. Do you want to start an all-out civil war? Jacoby disobeyed a direct order and nearly pulled a trigger that would have sent a round downrange that could have destroyed this country and this unit." The sound of a helicopter caused both men to look up at the ceiling. Their ride had arrived. "Get Jacoby and meet me on the roof." Williams lowered his rifle and rushed over to Jacoby who was trying to breathe while spitting up blood.

Paul tucked the pistol under his shirt and buttoned the nylon news channel jacket prior to walking out of the room and down the staircase. Once he reached the lobby floor, he walked through the lobby and out into the chaos on the streets, quickly disappearing into the crowd. He glanced in the direction of the stage where the Unity Rally had turned into the site of an assassination that was sure to bring serious international pressure on the United States. He saw President Grigsby's motorcade speeding away. Little did the president know that less than a block away stood a former covert operative who had just saved his life. Paul looked up in the sky and saw a news channel helicopter lifting from the roof of the building he had just exited. The Patriots had succeeded, he thought.

Back in Lumpkin County, Georgia, the Taylor family watched in horror as the tragedy unfolded on the television screen. Every major network had interrupted regular programming to broadcast footage and commentary on the events of that day. Live television was unable to cut the assassination, and the viewers watching what was supposed to be a peaceful rally actually witnessed the sniper round impacting Aminadab. Dianne had an eerie feeling that Paul was somewhere in that crowd. She said a silent prayer of hope that he was not involved in the assassination. Charlie and Anne were old enough to have seen a great deal of tragedy on American soil. The events of that day ranked very high in their minds. They were intelligent enough to know that the assassination of Aminadab could spell serious trouble for the United States for years to come.

Paul walked twenty-seven blocks north from the site of the assassination and found a Bank of America. In New York, despite a tragedy like what had just occurred, life goes on. It was business as usual inside the bank. Paul walked in and approached a bank teller. "Can I help you sir," the young lady asked in a sharp, New York accent.

"Yes, I need to make a withdrawal, but I left my bankcard at home on my desk."

"No problem sir," the teller responded. "I'll just need to see two forms of identification." Paul pulled his wallet from his back pocket and showed the teller his Missouri driver's license and his veteran's identification card.

"Great! Let me pull up your account." The accent was strong. Paul could have been blindfolded and would have known he was in New York just by the teller's voice. "I have your account up, Mr. Atkinson, and how much would you like to withdraw today?"

"Six-hundred should do it," Paul replied.

"Alright, sir," the teller said as she pulled out a withdrawal slip. "I'll need you to fill this out just like a check and sign it for me. Paul quickly filled the slip out and signed it in the lower right hand corner before handing it back to the teller. She took a quick look at the slip to make sure everything was correct, posted the withdrawal and counted out the cash to Paul. "Is there anything else I can do for you today?"

"No thanks. You've been a big help. Have a good day." Paul turned and began to walk away but turned back to the teller. "You can help me with one more thing. My car's in the shop getting a new transmission and I'm going to need a rental. Any idea where I can find one close by?"

The teller thought for a moment. "I don't live in Manhattan," she said, "but I do know that if you leave the island and take the train to the city, you're bound to find one."

"Thanks again for your help," Paul said as he turned and exited the bank. When he got outside, he thought about what she said. Paul didn't want to search all over New York for a rental car, but he definitely wanted off Manhattan Island. He got on the subway and headed for the city. After finally getting off the train, Paul asked a street vendor where he could find a place to rent a car. The vendor had no idea. Finally, Paul gave up and flagged down a taxi. He got in and told the driver to find him a rental car.

The short, overweight driver with an Italian accent said, "No problem, sir. I know a place just twenty blocks from here." The taxi driver was exactly correct. Twenty blocks later he pulled into the parking lot of a rental car establishment. Paul paid the driver, adding a $10.00 tip, got out and walked inside. Thirty minutes later after paying a $300.00 deposit on the rental since he didn't have a credit card, Paul was en route for Virginia. The nearly three hundred and fifty mile trip from New York to the front gate at Quantico took seven hours. Paul pulled the small rental car up to the gate and pulled out his driver's license and veteran's ID. The military policeman at the gate informed Paul that he needed an active duty military identification card or a valid set of orders to enter the base. "Listen, I've been on a mission headed up by Major Ron Lowery and overseen by the Pentagon," Paul said.

"I'm sorry sir," but without proper identification I can't let you through the gate. I'm going to have to ask you to back your vehicle up and exit the area."

"Alright, sergeant," Paul replied in an exhausted and frustrated tone. "Pick up the phone and call Major Lowery's quarters. Tell him that Major

Paul Atkinson is at the gate. Let him know that in order for me to get in, he will have to bring my military ID card from the safe. Can you do that?"

The military policeman thought for a moment. He was sure Paul's story was true, but he couldn't compromise gate security under any circumstances. "Alright sir, I'll give him a call. But, I'll still need you to back your car up so that others entering the installation won't be held up."

"No problem," Paul replied as he shifted the compact car into reverse and moved the vehicle out of the way.

The MP went inside and searched for Major Ron Lowery's phone number. Upon finding it, he phoned Ace and told him what Paul had instructed him to say. Ace told the MP that he would be at the gate within twenty minutes with Paul's ID. After the call, the young staff sergeant walked out to Paul's car and let him know that Major Lowery was on the way.

"Good," Paul replied. "Thanks for your help."

Twenty-three minutes later a black car pulled up to the opposite side of the gate from where Paul was parked. Paul watched as Ace got out of the car and approached the MP with all of the appropriate identification necessary for Paul to be allowed to enter the installation. The MP waved for him to come through the gate. Once in, Paul got out of the car and approached Ace. "Where were you, Ace? The Patriots succeeded in killing Aminadab and were within seconds of killing our president. So, I say again, where were you?"

"Paul, quiet! We can't talk about the mission here. Besides that, it's getting late, and I'm sure you're exhausted. Go get some rest." Ace handed Paul the key to his quarters as well as the envelope that held his personal effects and the photograph of him and Dianne. "Tomorrow morning at 0900, there will be a debriefing. If all goes well, we will have you processed off this installation by 1100 hours and back to your life as a civilian."

"Sure, so I can live the rest of my life looking over my shoulders to see who's going to shoot me in the back." Paul was furious.

"I don't think that will happen," Ace replied. "Now, go get some sleep. I'll see you in the morning." Ace returned to his vehicle, got in, backed the car up, turned and drove away. Paul told the MP that he needed to leave the installation for about an hour. The MP told Paul that he would still be pulling duty when he returned. Paul got in his rental car and drove away. Remembering the location of certain places in the area, Paul drove to a Super-Walmart that was open twenty-four hours a day. He drove into the parking lot and parked the car. Once inside the store, Paul purchased several items: three pairs of Wrangler blue jeans, three large gray sweatshirts, socks and underwear, a few hygiene products, a small suitcase and a few other items. Once he paid for the items purchased, Paul returned to his car and back to Quantico. This time he cleared the gate with no hassles.

Once inside his quarters Paul showered and switched on the television to Fox News. The assassination of Iran's president was still taking up all of the airtime. Reporters were still on the scene reporting the events of the day that had already sent shockwaves throughout the world. "Well Grigsby," Paul said, "can you talk your way out of this?"

Paul pulled the photograph of him and Dianne out of the envelope. He held the framed picture in both hands staring at Dianne. He regretted leaving her and Lumpkin County. Now, he was trapped. He could never return. With the Patriots still out there, returning to Dianne and her family would put everyone at great risk. Paul laid his head back on the pillow of the bed still clutching the photograph. Finally, he fell into a deep sleep.

Paul woke at 7:00am the next morning with the photograph lying on his chest. He got up and packed it in his new suitcase. He showered and shaved before brushing his teeth. After dressing in his new clothing, Paul loaded the rental car. While outside, he noticed military personnel heading for the mess hall. Paul wasn't hungry though. He just wanted to get off the installation and to never see it or Ace again. He went back inside and waited until 8:45am before he walked over to where the debriefing was to be held in the same conference room he had been in before the mission began.

At five minutes before nine, Paul walked through the door and into the conference room. Ace was there, the same general was there as well as the two other officers that were present during the initial briefing. Paul took a seat without saying a word.

Ace spoke up. "First of all, we want to thank you for your dedicated service."

Paul looked up at Ace, wishing he had broken his jaw back in the North Georgia forest. "I don't need accolades or applause. I want to know why you didn't have a team there to stop the assassination."

"Paul," Ace responded, "we had all the necessary personnel we needed to get the job done."

"Then why didn't you get the job done?" Paul was yelling at his former team leader now. "Do you realize what this event will cost this country? Do you realize that I'm a walking dead man?"

The door to the conference room suddenly opened and a man in a blue suit with a red tie and white shirt walked in carrying a cup of coffee. He looked strangely familiar to Paul. He had seen this man before, but he couldn't remember where or when. The man walked confidently over to a television that was mounted on the wall in the conference room, retrieved the remote control and switched the unit on. On Fox News, the White House press secretary was conducting a press conference.

"Ladies and gentlemen, I want to begin by sending our nation's deepest condolences to the people of Iran for the horrible events that led to the assassination of President Aminadab. The events that took place yesterday afternoon are a sobering reminder that terrorism is still alive and well in our world today. These murderers have no desire to see peace come to the Middle East or any other part of the world, and yesterday they made a strong statement that reminds us all that they will continue their attacks on anyone seeking lasting peace. We will continue our aggressive efforts to hunt down and deal with terrorist organizations.

"At nine o'clock last night, a joint operation conducted by the Department of Homeland Security as well as personnel from the FBI and CIA received a tip that a terrorist cell that had been in the United States for five years had carried out the attack on the Unity Rally that unfortunately took the life of President Aminadab. Five men were captured last night as they attempted to flee the country. Following vigorous interrogation, three of the men confessed to being members of the Taliban as well as being the men behind the attack. They are now being held in an undisclosed location awaiting a hearing in front of a federal judge. Let the capture of these men send a message to every terrorist organization on this planet. We will not rest until we rid the earth and every nation of you and your horrible agenda of hate and destruction.

With that, are there any questions?"

The television was switched off, and the man in the blue suit took a seat at the table directly across from Paul.

"You don't actually think people are going to fall for this, do you," Paul asked as he leaned back in his chair. "Everyone knows the Taliban are poorly trained. They would never be able to pull off such a calculated attack. Their idea of an organized operation is to strap a bomb to some disillusioned twenty-five year old, promise him virgins in paradise, and have him detonate the bomb in the largest crowd that he can find."

The man in the suit spoke up. "The American public has been living in denial for years. The announcement of these arrests keeps them in that state of denial. They don't want to know the truth about the real condition of our nation. They don't want to know the truth about the bleak future that awaits this country if we don't do something about it. They only want to know what time their favorite reality TV show comes on and whether their boss will be handing out Christmas bonuses."

Paul suddenly realized where he had seen this man. "You were at the rally. I saw you standing with the other security personnel in front of the stage. Who are you? Who do you work for?"

"He works for us, Paul," Ace replied. "This is Major Anthony Mason."

Paul stared at Mason for what seemed to be over a minute. Finally, he spoke. "This was all one big set-up, wasn't it? It had to be. Everything was too easy. You used me to make yourselves look good to anyone who might have been looking into your activities. If they had looked, you could say that you were doing your best to find out the plans of the Patriots, that you had an operative on the inside. You had no interest in stopping anything. Now we have a dead Iranian president, a shaken American president who nearly lost his life, and five men in a jail somewhere facing charges for something they didn't do."

"That's America," Mason said. "It's the cost of freedom. Those five men were members of the Taliban, and they had been in this country for five years. We intercepted some of their communications. It was only a matter of time before they tried something. So, in effect, they are not innocent men."

"Paul," Ace began, "I think it would be in your best interest to go back to your civilian life and to leave this behind you. I can assure you that you will be in no danger and that you will never be contacted by us again."

"No danger because you run the Patriots, isn't that right? You are using your positions of power and your influence in the Pentagon to run the Patriots. You're nothing but lawless renegades."

"No, we don't run the Patriots. Mr. Blair runs the Patriots, but you could say that we have provided him with resources necessary to support his operation. And, as far as you calling us lawless renegades – well, we don't look at it that way. We prefer to think of ourselves as the last ditch hope of lasting freedom for our nation."

Paul looked at Ace. "Jacoby, Williams and Scott – great resources, right Ace? Jacoby nearly killed our president."

"We are fully aware of what Jacoby did," the general replied. "We were monitoring the radio communications during the operation. Thank-you for having the bravery to stop what could have been a tragic error. We will deal with Jacoby in our own way once he has recovered from the bullet wounds."

Ace slid a large envelope across the table to Paul. He opened it and found cash. Ace informed him of the amount that was in the envelope: $50,000.00 – interestingly, the same amount guaranteed by Colonel Harvey to the men who had conducted the mission in New York. "Nice bonus," said Paul. "I'm disappointed that Blair didn't send a love note with it."

"Paul, take the money and go home. Forget about all of this and get on with your life. Your military records have been altered. As far as the military is concerned, you were never a covert operative, and you have never stepped foot onto Quantico. Following your tour in the Ranger Battalion, you were reassigned as a company commander in a non-combat training unit at Fort Benning, Georgia. You processed out of the Army there, and you assumed a quiet, law-abiding civilian life. Enough said."

Paul knew that if he checked his military records that he would find documentation that would confirm everything Ace had just said. He also realized that as long as he kept his mouth shut, he would never hear from Ace or anyone else in the military again. They just wanted him to go away. With a few clicks on a computer, Paul had gone from a highly trained and highly sought after covert operative to a number in a system that defined his military career as average. "Am I dismissed," Paul asked as he stood from his chair with the envelope full of cash.

"You are," the general replied as he saluted Paul.

Paul didn't return the general's salute. "You better work on that salute, general. It's looking pretty unmilitary."

The general quickly lowered his salute and looked over to Ace. Ace looked at the general and shook his head. Don't say a word, general, Ace thought. Ace walked over to Paul. "Let me walk you to your car."

"Ace, I'm not leaving yet." Ace stepped back from Paul. What did he want? "I've done my job, now you're going to do something for me."

"Let's go," Ace replied as the two men left the conference room.

Once outside, Paul removed a slip of paper from his pocket and handed it to Ace. On the paper written in black ink was the name of a person and the city where that person lived. Ace looked at the writing, then at Paul with a puzzled expression. "Ace, I want you to get me this man's address. I want to know the layout of his house, the layout of the neighborhood, and whether he has any surveillance system on the premises. If he does, I want to know how I disable it."

Ace stared again at the slip of paper before looking up at Paul. "I love this job. You know, if you want, I can make this guy's life miserable."

"No, Ace, just get me the information. I'll deal with this guy myself."

"Follow me, Paul."

Three hours later, Paul was near an airport turning in his rental car. He caught a shuttle to the airport and checked with Delta for its flight schedules to his destination. Finally deciding on his flight, Paul paid for the ticket with cash. He checked his small suitcase and waited at the terminal for his flight. Staring out of the window onto the busy runways, Paul hoped that he would never see a military installation again. He was closing this chapter of his life forever.

March 7th, 11:40pm
Dallas, Texas – Highland Park

He was jarred out of his sleep by a scream. When he opened his eyes, a pistol was pointed at his forehead just inches away. The man with the 9-millimeter silenced pistol wore all black – military style black uniform, black gloves and black ski mask. His aim was steady and confident. The scream came from the man's lover lying next to him in bed. The masked man aimed his pistol at the lover. "Roll over on your stomach," the intruder ordered. "Cover your head with your pillow. Don't say a word. Don't scream. Don't whisper. Don't even let me hear you breath. If I hear anything out of you, I'm going to kill you. Now, do it." The intruder's voice was calm. The lover did as he was ordered.

Once convinced that the lover was going to cooperate, the intruder lifted his ski mask and stared at the other man. "I told you I'd be back," Paul said. "My brother's dead and now I've come to get his revenge."

"Wait, wait," Judge Simpson pleaded. "I didn't kill your brother. He committed suicide. How could I have stopped him?"

"By never letting your ego put him in jail in the first place," Paul replied. "Your ego will cost you your life tonight." Paul switched the pistol from safe to armed and pushed the barrel against the judge's forehead. A wet spot formed in the middle of the judge's comforter and the foul odor of urine began filling the room. "Looks like you sprung a leak, judge." The judge's lover began crying. "Shut up," Paul said. The muffled cries under the pillow instantly stopped.

"Please, please don't kill me. I'll give you anything. I'll do anything. Just please don't kill me." Tears began flowing from the judge's eyes.

"You want to live, judge," Paul asked as he pulled the pistol away from the judge's face. "Do you really want to live?"

"Yes, please let me live."

"If you want to live, then I want you to answer one question. Answer the question with an honest answer and you live. Lie to me, and you die. And, trust me Simpson, I'll know if you're lying."

"Alright," the judge replied. "Anything, I'll answer anything. I promise to be honest."

Paul looked at the judge. The ego-driven family courts judge who had just months earlier put Chris in jail looked pitiful, full of fear, and totally different from the man who Paul met sitting months earlier in the judge's office. "Here's the question judge, and I demand an honest answer. The final decree that you signed concerning custodial rights of Chris' daughter. Did you ever read that order?"

The judge looked away from Paul. Thirty seconds later he answered the question. "No. No, I never read the order."

"So, you never were able to actually see that Chris had followed the order completely, and that he was just trying to protect his daughter."

"Correct, but I've read it since, and I admit to you that I was wrong in sentencing your brother to any jail time. I'm very sorry about your loss."

Tears formed in Paul's eyes. He pulled the ski mask back down over his face. "You have thirty days to resign your seat as a judge. If you don't resign, I will be in contact with some friends in Washington, D.C., and they will be down here making your life very miserable. I let you off the hook once; if you're not off the bench in thirty days, you will not be let off again. The people that I will send here will make you wish that you had taken up typewriter repair as a trade instead of law. You see, I'm much nicer than they are. Are you clear on all this?"

"Yes, I'll do what you say," the judge replied. "Please, know that I'm truly sorry."

Paul stood and began walking to the other side of the bed where the judge's lover was still covered by the pillow. "Sorry doesn't bring my brother back, does it? By the way, I've taped your confession – a little insurance in case you back out of our deal." Paul lightly tapped the butt of his pistol on the pillow covering the lover's head. "Hey, you can come out now." The lover slowly removed the pillow, rolled over and looked in terror at the masked man. "Consider this all a really bad dream," Paul said. "But, if you don't, then when I'm gone, give Judge Simpson a big hug and a kiss. It was the first time in his life that he was honest." Paul turned and left the room, disappearing into the dark night.

Chapter Twelve

Sunday, the next day

Oak Cliff Methodist Church, AME

A man dressed in blue jeans and a white t-shirt sat quietly on the third pew inside Oak Cliff Methodist Church, less than thirty-minutes from downtown Dallas. He had never been in this church before. Services weren't scheduled to start until 11:00am, and he was two hours early. Other than an elderly woman who was vacuuming the floor just in front of the pulpit, he was the only person in the sanctuary. Fifteen minutes later, the front door of the church opened and a man in a gray suit made his way down the aisle. He gently tapped the other man on the shoulder. "I had a dream last night. I knew you'd be here this mornin'."

"Hello, Marvin," Paul said as he looked up into his kind eyes.

"You've been through quite a journey to get here today, haven't you?"

Paul looked toward the pulpit. "You could definitely say that."

Marvin sat down next to Paul. "Do you remember what I said to you in the lobby of the hotel that day?"

Paul turned his head and looked at Marvin. "Yes, I remember."

Marvin smiled. "So, the storms did come. You ran and hid from God at first. You ran to places where you thought you were safe from the storms. But, you finally came home. You knew where you had to go." Paul stared down at a Bible that was in a pew rack. "You've run from God all of your life, but he has never been far from you. You are somethin' special, son. People who know you realize that, but more importantly the Father of all knows that. He wants you to know it's time to stop runnin'. Your brother's just where God wants him to be. Your parents are, too. But, you have someone left who is waiting for you to rescue her."

Paul thought that Marvin was referring to Dianne. "How do you know all of this about me, about my brother and my parents?"

"I have a television, too. I watch the news. The stories of your brother's suicide were big, but what happened after his death was even bigger." Marvin stood from the pew.

Paul had no idea what Marvin was talking about, but wanted to know. "What do you mean about what happened after Chris died?"

Marvin began walking toward the door of the church. "I think there's someone else who can explain that better than I can. Come on, I'll buy you some breakfast."

Paul stood and followed Marvin. "But, what about your church service?"

"I think they can handle it without me," replied Marvin.

The two men climbed into Marvin's car and drove to a small restaurant three blocks from the church. Despite Paul's objections, Marvin insisted on buying breakfast. As they ate their meal, Marvin talked to Paul. "You know, when we are caught up in the storms of life, it's basically impossible to see the hand of God workin' in everything. But, after the storms are over and we look back, it's then when we see how God arranged the events of our lives for good. His word promises us 'that all things work together for good to them that love God, to them who are the called according to his purpose.' I get the feelin' you are one of the called, Paul. Maybe it's time you stop runnin' and start acceptin' his love and his call."

Paul set his fork on his plate. "So, what do I do?"

"You're not done here in Dallas. You have some unfinished business for yourself, for your brother, and for your parents."

Once the two men had finished their meal, Marvin stood from the booth and asked Paul if he was ready. Paul stood and after Marvin paid the check, the two men left the restaurant and got back into Marvin's car. Marvin drove into downtown Dallas and exited onto North Central Expressway. He drove north about seven and a half miles to Walnut Hill Lane and turned left. The further Marvin drove down Walnut Hill, the larger the homes became. He finally turned right onto another street, then a quick left into the driveway of a gated home. Compared to the other homes surrounding it, this house was a bit more modest, still large and beautiful, but more modest. The gate was open, so Marvin pulled his car behind a BMW parked outside. Paul had no idea what Marvin was up to. The two men got out of the car and approached the front door of the house. Marvin rang the doorbell.

When the door opened, Paul's confusion doubled. "Marvin, it's good to see you again. Thanks for your call last night."

"It's good seein' you again, Jensen. I guess you know this man here." Marvin pointed at Paul who was speechless.

"Paul, it's great to see you." Jensen motioned the two men inside his home. "I'm so sorry about Chris. It broke our hearts. But, we've been praying for you for quite some time." The three men led by Jensen sat down in the living room of the beautiful home. Jensen looked at Paul. "So, what have you been doing since we last talked? You kind of dropped out of sight."

Paul looked at Jensen, then at Marvin, and finally at Jensen again. "Uh, you don't want to know. Tell me something. How do you two know each other?"

Jensen smiled. "Marvin came to me after Chris' death. He told me that he saw me on the news, and that he didn't want me to blame myself for his death. He went on to explain to me just how he met you and Dianne when you were in town months ago. He asked me to promise him to never give up on you. Marvin said he believed in you, and said one day we would all meet again. The two of us have spent hours together praying. He's a special man."

Paul slowly turned his head and stared at Marvin who was sitting on the couch smiling. "So, everyone knew I was coming back to Dallas but me. Why?"

"Paul," Jensen began, "following Chris' death, the tragedy didn't end. His ex-wife was apparently riddled with guilt and relapsed. In January, she was driving her SUV along one of our surface streets. She had your two-year-old niece, Megan, with her. She had been drinking all day and had gone out for more liquor. According to the police report, the cashier at the liquor store recognized just how drunk she was and refused to allow her to make a purchase. She became belligerent with the cashier and was asked to leave. She got back into her SUV and continued driving in search of another liquor store when she drifted into the opposite lanes and collided head-on into a compact car carrying an elderly couple. The elderly couple died instantly." Paul was becoming nauseous. "She then attempted to leave the scene but was caught less than ten minutes later by Dallas police. She was charged with two counts of vehicular homicide, leaving the scene of a fatal accident, alluding, child endangerment and a host of other charges.

I did my best to contact you, but Dianne said she had no idea where you were, that the military had called you back for some secret operation.

"Paul, I know what type of man you are. I know that you would never wish harm to Chris' ex-wife or her family, but you need to know that this is the time to honor Chris by getting Megan into better hands."

Paul had leaned forward on the sofa where he sat and was staring at the floor before turning his gaze on Jensen. "What are you saying? You want me to take over custody of Chris' daughter? This sounds crazy. What do I know about raising a child?"

Marvin placed his hand on Paul's shoulder. "What would Chris want you to do? Megan is a part of you. Not only does Chris' blood run through her veins, but so does yours."

"Paul," Jensen continued, "unfortunately, Amy is looking at a minimum of a twenty-year sentence with at least ten years to serve. Now we all can agree that this is a great tragedy, but we can't let the tragedy continue by letting this child live in conditions that will only hurt her worse than she already has been. Her father's gone and her mother's essentially gone for at least ten years. The grandparents are not fit to care for this child and Chris' ex-wife has no siblings or any other relatives in Dallas. My investigator found out that Megan's grandmother is addicted to prescription drugs and has been in treatment on two occasions. Megan's grandfather was recently diagnosed with diabetes and drinks to excess on occasion. Is leaving Megan in those sorts of conditions honoring the memory of your brother?"

Paul stood and walked to the rear of the living room where bay windows allowed a clear view of a beautiful swimming pool. He said nothing at first. Jensen and Marvin looked at each other and back at Paul. Paul finally turned and smiled before saying, "My brother was one of those rare souls that could walk into any room and brighten everyone's day. If there's a heaven, there's not much happening there right now, because Chris has everyone laughing. He was never really cut out to be a Marine. He never wanted to witness another human being in pain of any sort. Chris would give you the shirt off his back and money from his pocket. That's just the way he was. He never meant any harm to anyone when he kept Megan that day."

"I am completely convinced of that, Paul," Jensen replied.

Marvin stood and walked over to Paul. "There is a heaven, and right now your brother is watchin' to see if you will take a leap of faith for his daughter. He wants you to know true love once and for all. You had a taste of it. I saw it in your eyes when I met you and Dianne. The love of a child is powerful. You can't hide from it. This is less of a task placed on your shoulders due to the tragedies that have occurred and more of a gift from Chris and from God. It's up to you to accept it."

Paul received a hug from Marvin before sitting back down on the sofa. "Alright Jensen," he said. "What's next?" Jensen and Marvin laughed. Paul finally joined in. He couldn't remember the last time he had laughed.

"Well, Paul, on Marvin's instructions – or should I call it holy pressure – I have already prepared a motion for an emergency hearing. My assistant will file this with the clerk first thing in the morning. We are going to push hard on this, so expect to be in court by Thursday. It will not be pretty, though. Opposing counsel will do everything in his power to get the motion thrown out of court. Don't worry. I will not lose." There was fire in Jensen's eyes. Paul could understand why other attorneys feared challenging Jensen in the litigation arena.

"Sounds like your proverbial ducks are in a row," Paul said. "I'll get some money from one of my CD's. What's your retainer fee?"

"No," Jensen replied. "I spent hours with Chris, and though he was often disappointed with the way everything was progressing, or not progressing, we had some incredible conversations. He was a special person. He talked mostly about you, though. He wanted you to know just how proud he was of you, particularly when he saw you with Dianne. He told me a week after we all met that he had never seen you so happy and content." Tears now flowed from Paul's eyes. "I love Chris, too," Jensen continued. "This is for him, for Megan and for you. You don't owe me a dime."

"I guess I better buy a suit," Paul said. "I hate wearing suits." The three men joined in a good laugh.

Marvin and Paul left Jensen's residence and returned to the church to retrieve Paul's rental car. Once they arrived, Paul got out of Marvin's car and thanked him for everything. "Hold on a minute," Marvin said. "You didn't think I was just goin' to let you go hide in some hotel room, did you? Follow me to my house. I have an extra bedroom."

"No, Marvin, I can't do that. You've done enough."

"Paul, don't hurt an old man's feelin's," Marvin replied. "I could use some company for a change."

Paul finally agreed to stay with Marvin and followed him in the rental to his home. It was a small, white house with black shudders and a small covered porch located four blocks north of the Veteran's Administration Hospital and not far from the church Marvin attended. Once the two men arrived, Paul retrieved his suitcase from the trunk of the rental car and followed Marvin inside. Marvin showed Paul which bedroom would be his, and Paul placed his belongings in the room on the floor. After sleeping in the rental car the night before, Paul felt a need for a shower. After showering he called Jensen and informed the attorney where he would be staying. Of course, Jensen had the number already and promised Paul that he would have a court date by lunch on Monday.

Paul sat on a couch in Marvin's living room while Marvin poured two glasses of tea. Paul noticed an old gold-framed photograph sitting on the television that was of a beautiful young woman, no more than twenty-five. She had a magical smile and crystal clear eyes. Paul walked over to the television and picked up the photograph. "Is this your daughter," Paul asked Marvin who was just coming out of the kitchen with the glasses of tea.

Marvin handed Paul his glass. "No, that's my wife."

"Well, where is she? I'd like to meet her."

"I hope you will, one day, but not here." Paul was confused. "She passed away a year after that photograph was taken. She was twenty-three when she passed on. Angela died givin' birth to our first child. The baby died, too."

Paul's head sunk. Too much tragedy in this life, he thought. "You never married again?"

"No," Marvin replied, "I spent the next fifteen years drinkin' and blamin' God for everything that happened. I'll never get those years back. But, one day, while I was sittin' out on that porch with a bottle of liquor, this man walked up to me. He told me he had a message for me – a message from God. I asked the man if he needed a drink, too. I thought he was crazy. The man said he needed nothin' from me. Then he said that God needed somethin' from me. I asked him what God wanted from me. He said God wanted me to show a little courage and to get up. He said that God told him to tell me that my wife and baby would never accept the man I had become, and that he had a special plan and purpose for my life. He said that I had to let go of the pain and the past and get on with my life. I wasn't ready to hear what this man was sayin' to me. I asked him to leave. The man turned around and began walkin' away. I took another drink straight from the bottle, and when I set the bottle down and looked each way down the sidewalk in front of the house, I couldn't see the man. It was as if he just disappeared. I thought I might have been just seein' things. I had been drinkin' for a long time. But, I was sure then, just as I'm sure now that I saw an angel of the Lord. I went inside, fell on the couch and passed out. After I woke up, I threw away the rest of the liquor and haven't had a drink since. I joined the church, later became a deacon and here I am with you."

Paul believed every word. "You know something Marvin? It sounds like that man was an angel, and it sounds like he was carrying a message that was definitely stronger than the liquor you were drinking."

Marvin laughed. "I guess you're right. Now, it's your turn. When you begin raisin' this little child, you will know that the baton is in your hand. I know you'll be a great and lovin' father."

"I'll do my best," Paul replied. "I never dreamed that I would ever have to raise a child."

"What about Dianne?" Marvin picked up the photograph of his wife.

"Marvin, she's been through enough. I've caused her a great deal of pain, and I never want to hurt her again."

"Paul, the pain she has gone through has not been what you think it has. You didn't hurt her. She hurt for you. Dianne recognized in you what God through that mysterious man recognized in me. She could see a lost, scared and hurtin' soul. That's what hurt her. She felt helpless to do anything about it."

Paul decided to change the subject. "Any decent places around here where I can buy a suit?"

Marvin decided not to push Paul. He realized that with a looming court date, Paul was under enough pressure. "The ride back into town doesn't take that long. I'll take you to a mall where I'm sure you'll find one."

That evening after Paul purchased a suit, he and Marvin sat outside talking. Marvin had a way of getting Paul's mind off of the hearing by talking about his childhood, his one tour as a supply clerk in the Army, and his life as a deacon. He was able to get Paul to open up and share some things as well. Paul told him about the success he enjoyed running track in high school and how that helped him later in his military career. He joked about the first time he jumped out of an airplane. It was at Fort Benning during Airborne School. He said that when he got to the door to make a proper exit just as he had been taught, the training and he went out the door with a shove in the back by one of the instructors. Later, as the conversation subsided, Marvin asked Paul if he could pray for him. Paul was shaky about having any faith of any kind in God, but for Marvin's sake, he said yes.

Marvin reached out and took Paul's hand. "Dear Lord, you know this young man. You know his heart. You know all things about him. You have known him from birth. I ran from you for nearly fifteen years, and Paul has been runnin' from you, too. Now, I ask you Father, that as you touched me many years ago, so to touch Paul now. Let him know now and in the comin' days just how much you love him. Let him know now and in the comin' days that your plans for him are good. Let him know now and in the comin' days that the pain of the past is in the past and the future for this man is brighter than the mornin' star. Finally, God, I ask you to show Paul that he is not alone in this world and that he is loved by many. May he find his way home. In Jesus' name, Amen." The two men stared at each other. Marvin nodded his head and smiled.

The next day, Marvin's phone rang at 1:10pm. After answering the phone, Marvin handed it to Paul, telling him that it was Jensen. Paul suddenly started feeling those somewhat unfamiliar butterflies in his stomach again. They were beginning to become a little more familiar to him. "Yes, Jensen," Paul answered. "What do you have?"

"What we have is a hearing scheduled for Friday morning at nine. The docket was already full for Thursday." Jensen sounded happy and at the same time extremely motivated, like a bull at a rodeo waiting to be released. "Everyone has been notified, and we are ready."

"Good," Paul replied. "I won't have to ask for a refund on the suit I bought last night."

Jensen laughed. "Keep the suit, and keep your chin up. We're going to win. I'll need you to come by my office on Wednesday. If you have financials, bring those. We need to show the court that you are financially sound and fully capable of providing for Megan."

"How about if I call my personal banker back in Georgia and have him fax everything to you?"

"That'll be great, Paul," said Jensen. "The sooner I get them, the better. In the meantime have some fun with Marvin, and I'll see you Wednesday."

Paul hung up the phone and looked at Marvin. "No turning back now, is there?"

Marvin walked over to where Paul was standing. "I have a feelin' that you wouldn't turn back now even if you could."

Paul smiled. "You know me too well, Marvin. There's no way I'm leaving Dallas, Texas without Megan." Paul reached in his wallet and pulled out a picture of his niece. The photograph had been taken just before

Christmas in 2007, and Chris had rushed the photograph to his brother. Paul showed the photograph to Marvin. Megan was clearly an Atkinson. Her light blonde hair and her bright blue eyes were proof in the pudding that she had been a daddy's girl. Now Paul, the youngest of the Atkinson family would be taking this little girl with him to care for in honor of his brother.

Paul arrived at 8:30am on Friday on the fourth floor of the family court. Marvin took a day off to be with Paul during the proceedings. Jensen arrived ten minutes later with his confident game face showing. At 8:50am, they entered the courtroom and took their seats. Opposing counsel was already in the courtroom along with Megan's grandparents. Jensen quickly stepped back outside and ushered in one woman and two men. Paul had no idea who they were.

The judge entered the courtroom and Paul's heart and hopes suddenly sank. "All rise," the bailiff ordered. "Court is now in session. The honorable Judge David Simpson presiding."

"Be seated," Judge Simpson said. "We are here today to entertain a motion for this emergency hearing filed by Mr. Parker, attorney for Mr. Paul Atkinson, uncle to Megan Atkinson, the child and purpose of this motion. As I read this motion, Mr. Parker, it appears that your client would like this court to order an emergency change of custody under what you term, 'conditions detrimental to the health and welfare of the child'. I'm assuming then that you have witnesses who will corroborate the claims you've made in your motion?"

Jensen stood and addressed the judge. "Yes, your honor, our witnesses are here, and they are prepared to substantiate every charge in my client's motion. Furthermore, we have gathered documented evidence that will further prove that our case is worthy of this court's attention and clear proof that a decision in my client's favor is the right and proper way to protect this child."

Opposing council interrupted. "Your honor, I object to this hearing. My clients and I were not prepared for this motion. We know nothing about Mr. Atkinson's background. My clients would request a delay in order to prepare a response to this motion."

"Mr. Hodges," the judge responded. "It is called an emergency hearing for a reason. The plaintiff in this case wishes to present evidence that will convince this court to, under a temporary order, grant custody of the child to him. The final hearing will be set for a later date at which time you can present your case. And, as to Mr. Atkinson's background, this court is fully aware of it." Paul was waiting for the judge to lower the boom. "Mr. Atkinson is a decorated combat soldier, an honor graduate from the Citadel, and has a perfectly clean record. Furthermore, if you will take a look at the exhibits opposing counsel has provided to you, you will find a financial statement that clearly shows that Mr. Atkinson is, indeed, financially sound and fully capable of providing for the child. So, based on the allegations in the motion filed by the plaintiff, I doubt if we will be spending a great deal of time talking about Mr. Atkinson. Anything else, Mr. Hodges, before we move on?"

The dejected attorney sat back down. "No, your honor."

Jensen launched into his case. Paul watched in amazement how the kind, gentle man suddenly became an attacking litigator. He presented the case in rapid-fire succession, first bringing a former family doctor up who testified that Megan's grandmother was, in her professional opinion, addicted to pain medication. She went on to say that on one occasion, the grandmother became almost violent when she refused to write any more prescriptions for her. The doctor tried to convince the grandmother to enter treatment for a third time, but she adamantly refused stating that the doctor was the one with the problem. The doctor finally substantiated Jensen's claim that the grandfather was in poor health due to the onset of diabetes.

Another witness stated that he was a bartender at a local country club where the grandfather and now retired attorney was a member. He testified that the grandfather came in when his shift started at 3:00pm on a Sunday and didn't leave until 1:00am at closing. He said he witnessed the grandfather drinking at least ten mixed drinks during the time he was at the bar, and that when the grandfather finally left he could barely walk. The bartender encouraged him to take a taxi, but he belligerently refused. He went on to say that he witnessed the grandfather scraping a pole with his Mercedes as he exited the premises.

The third witness was Jensen's investigator. It was his testimony, complete with surveillance photographs and several documents that proved the grandmother's insane attempts to forge prescriptions that put the final nail in the coffin. The two grandparents were called and Jensen had a field day with the retired attorney. Jensen, satisfied with the presentation of his case, finally rested.

"Mr. Hodges, would you like to call any witnesses," asked the judge.

Mr. Hodges whispered something to his clients before standing from his chair. "No, your honor. We will not be calling any witnesses, but my clients would like to ask the court to reconsider this hearing and to give us more time to prepare before any custodial decisions are made."

"Again, Mr. Hodges," the judge said, "that sort of defeats the purpose of an emergency hearing." Judge Simpson paused and looked down as he sifted through some documents that related to the case. Nearly a minute later he looked up at Mr. Hodges. "I'm deciding for the plaintiff. If this had been a final hearing, I will tell you that the evidence presented in this court today would have caused me to render a final verdict and a permanent change of custody. But, I don't write the laws and the procedures. Therefore, it is the order of this court that by 3:00pm today, temporary custody of Megan Atkinson, niece of the plaintiff, shall be awarded to Mr. Paul Atkinson, and that custody of the child shall be turned over to Mr. Atkinson. She is to remain under Mr. Atkinson's care and supervision throughout any further proceedings. Mr. Hodges, your clients may appeal this decision or wait for a final hearing at which time you will have an opportunity to present your case to this court as to why Mr. Atkinson should not be allowed to retain custody of his niece. The two parties may also settle this matter in mediation, but I want to be perfectly clear that this court will be paying close attention to this case, and the best interest of the child will be this court's first priority. I hope I've made myself clear. Any questions from either attorney?"

Mr. Hodges stood again. "Your honor, will my clients be allowed to visit their granddaughter?"

The judge looked at Jensen. Jensen looked at Paul who shrugged his shoulders and nodded. "My client will not prevent Mr. Hodges' clients from visiting Megan. However, my client wishes to ask the court to limit their visitation to every other weekend, under supervised conditions at his residence."

"Any objections to this offer, Mr. Hodges?" The judge leaned back in his chair.

"Yes, your honor, my clients do object to supervised visits at Mr. Atkinson's residence."

"Well, Mr. Hodges," said the judge, "based on the testimony today, I agree with the plaintiff. If she were my niece, I wouldn't want the grandparents near her without supervision. Your clients can agree to that, or wait for the final hearing to see if they are permitted visitation at all."

The further dejected Hodges sat down again. "Yes, your honor. We will accept the order of the court."

"I'm assuming you have already prepared an order, Mr. Parker, as well as copies for the court, for opposing counsel and the clerk," said the judge knowing the attorney's confidence and preparedness.

Jensen stood. "I have everything right here, your honor."

"Good," Judge Simpson replied. "Attorneys, please approach the bench." Both attorneys did as they were told. Jensen carried the copies of the temporary order to the judge. Once he signed them, he instructed the attorneys to have his clients sign each copy. Once everyone was back in place, the judge completed the hearing. "I want everyone in this courtroom to remember what this court has stated concerning this child. Megan Atkinson is this court's first priority and primary concern. Any violation of this order by either party will result in contempt charges being brought against the guilty party." Judge Simpson for the first time during the entire hearing looked directly at Paul. "Mr. Atkinson, best of luck to you."

Paul stood up from his seat. "Thank-you, sir."

With the pounding of the gavel, the judge ordered court adjourned.

After Jensen thanked his witnesses, he invited Marvin and Paul to his house for lunch. "My wife is cooking a celebration meal for us." He paused. "Alright, she's going to Whole Foods and buying a celebration meal for us."

Paul smiled and said he would love to meet Jensen's wife and would enjoy lunch. The three men exited the courtroom and drove to Jensen's house where his wife, Cindy already had the table set. Everyone took a seat at the table, and Marvin was asked to bless the food. "Dear Lord, your hand is upon us always, just as it was in that courtroom today. For this reason, we give eternal thanks to you and ask that you bless this food. In Jesus' name, Amen."

Everyone enjoyed a festive meal. Paul was anxious to see his niece. He had never seen her in person. Jensen advised Paul that it would be best if he went along with him to pick Megan up from the grandparent's residence. Marvin asked if he could tag along. Jensen and Paul both welcomed the idea of Marvin coming with them. After lunch, the three men went outside by the swimming pool and chatted. Jensen was tired from his hard work on the case, while Paul was still amazed that in just over a week, he had gone from feeling trapped in a covert operation, to gaining custody of the daughter of his older brother. So, Marvin did most of the talking.

At 2:30pm the three men loaded into Jensen's BMW and drove three miles to where Megan's grandparents lived. Paul had asked about a car seat for Megan, but Jensen informed him that he had one already in the car.

It was one he had used for his now five-year-old son. The BMW entered the gate and parked near the front entrance to the incredibly huge house. Jensen led the way to the front door ringing the doorbell once he arrived, and minutes later, Megan's grandmother answered the door. Despite the fact that the grandfather refused to come out of his study, the grandmother did her best to be cordial. "Megan, your uncle is here," she said.

Paul tried to look past the grandmother into the home to catch a glimpse of his niece, but he couldn't see her. Suddenly, from behind the door the most beautiful little girl Paul had ever seen stepped out. Paul stepped forward and knelt down in front of Megan. "Hello, Megan. I'm your Uncle Paul." He tried to pick her up, but Megan began crying and reaching for her grandmother. Paul set her back down and glanced back at Marvin and Jensen. Both men nodded and smiled in an attempt to encourage Paul. Paul looked back at his niece who had retreated to her grandmother's right leg. He reached into his back pocket and pulled out his wallet. He opened the wallet and pulled out two photographs and held the first photograph up for Megan to see. The two year old stepped toward Paul and took the photograph into her hands. She looked at the photograph, then at Paul and finally at her grandmother. A smile lit up Megan's face. It was the photograph of her that Chris had sent to Paul nearly a year and a half earlier.

"Me," she said as she pointed at her chest.

"Yes," Paul responded. "That's you." Paul carefully took the picture out of her hand and held another photograph up to her. This time, Megan moved forward and Paul picked her up again while trying to keep her focus on the photo. Megan looked at the two men in the photograph then at Paul.

"Daddy," she said pointing at Chris.

Tears began flowing from Paul's eyes. He smiled and kissed his niece on the cheek. "That's right. Daddy."

"You," she said pointing at Paul in the photo.

"Right again, angel. I'm your Uncle Paul. Can you say Uncle Paul?"

Megan tried to say "uncle" but couldn't. She was, however, able to say "Paul". Megan reached her tiny hand up to Paul's face and wiped away a tear. "Don't cry," she said.

Paul smiled and hugged his beautiful niece. "Ma'am," Marvin said to the grandmother. "Have a blessed day. I'll be prayin' for you and your family." She smiled, set a suitcase outside next to Paul, went back inside and closed the door to the house.

Paul looked at Megan as everyone turned and headed for the BMW. "How would you like to take a ride with your uncle way up there in the sky?" Megan clapped her hands and giggled. Almost miraculously, as if the little girl sensed the connection, Megan was suddenly very comfortable in Paul's arms.

Jensen drove back to his house. Paul removed Megan from the car seat while Jensen removed the seat from his car and reinstalled it in Marvin's. Paul couldn't seem to let his niece out of his arms. He was amazed with the love in his heart for her. Jensen, having finished installing the car seat, walked over to Paul. The gifted attorney kissed Megan on the cheek. "I can't explain it," Jensen said. "It seems like I've known this child from the day she was born. She's beautiful."

Paul shook Jensen's hand. "In some ways you have," he said. "Each time you saw Chris, you were seeing her. Now, we see her, and we realize that we haven't really lost Chris at all."

"You're right," Jensen replied. "God bless you, Paul. Please keep in touch."

"I don't think we're done yet," Paul replied referring to the final custody hearing.

Jensen smiled. "Somehow I get the feeling that that final hearing will never see the light of day. Expect to receive a final order in the mail within two months."

Paul wasn't quite sure what Jensen meant or from where such confidence had come, but he thanked him nonetheless. "I'm glad we met, Jensen."

"I hope this is just the beginning," Jensen answered.

"We agree, don't we Megan?" Paul began tickling his niece. She squirmed in his arms and giggled. "Marvin, are you ready, sir?"

"Ready when you are Uncle Paul." The three men laughed. Megan, not really knowing why, joined in.

With Megan safely in her car seat and her suitcase loaded, Marvin drove back to his house with Paul. Megan fell asleep on the way. After arriving, Paul gently removed her from the car seat and took her inside to the room he had been in during the week. He pulled back the blanket and laid her down onto the bed before covering her up. After giving Megan a kiss on the cheek, Paul went back outside and began to remove the car seat from Marvin's car.

"Why don't you leave it?" Marvin had followed him outside. "Let the rental car company come and pick up your car. I would like to take you to the airport in the mornin'."

"Are you sure, Marvin," Paul replied. "What about your job?"

"I've been a bellman at the Ritz for a lot of years. I've never missed a day of work. A few days off won't hurt anything at all." Marvin placed his hand on Paul's shoulder. "I'd really appreciate it if you'd let me take you."

Paul smiled and nodded. "Alright, Marvin. We would appreciate the ride." Paul followed Marvin inside and used the phone to call Enterprise to pick up the rental car. Following the call, he went in and checked on Megan. She was sound asleep. He opened her suitcase and found a child's no-spill cup designed for children her age who were graduating from the conventional bottles and heading toward regular cups. Paul walked into the kitchen where Marvin was preparing dinner. "Do you have anything I can put in this for Megan when she wakes up?"

"How about orange juice?" Marvin pulled out a gallon of orange juice from the refrigerator.

Paul laughed. "Perfect," he responded as he poured the juice into the cup.

Paul went back to his room and laid on the bed next to Megan. She had rolled over on her stomach and was sucking her thumb. Paul brushed her blonde hair out of her face, unable to take his eyes off of her. She seemed so perfect, so peaceful. Paul decided that he would do everything in his power to give Megan the life she deserved and the love she deserved. He could never replace her mother or father, but he would be the next best thing. Paul, for the first time in months, knelt by the bed and prayed. He asked God to forgive him, to accept him and to make him a great parent to this little girl. He ended the prayer by asking God for direction in his life. Marvin walked by the open door and saw Paul kneeling by the bed. The aging deacon looked up and smiled before saying, "Thank-you, God."

Megan finally woke up from her nap, and Paul fed her. This was all very new to Paul, but he was taking it in stride. Following dinner, the two played with some toys Marvin had gone to the church to retrieve from a small nursery located in the basement below the sanctuary. Hours later, when the little girl tired again, Paul bathed her and put her back in the bed. He stayed next to Megan the entire night, sleeping sparingly, fearful she would awaken in an unfamiliar place and become frightened. Much to his surprise she slept through the night. Paul woke from his sleep the next morning with Megan playing with his ears. He picked his niece up and laid her on his chest. Megan laid her head down under Paul's chin and wrapped her tiny arms around her uncle's neck. Paul had never felt this kind of love before, the kind of love one could only have for a beautiful child. Joy flooded Paul's heart for the first time in months.

Paul suddenly thought back to Lumpkin County, Georgia and Dianne. He still missed her. He asked himself what Dianne would think of this sudden change of circumstances in his life. Would she be pleased? Or, was she so hurt and angry with him that she could never find a place in her heart for him. Could Dianne ever forgive him? His attention was drawn back to Megan as she began playing with his ears again. She lifted her head from his chest and smiled.

Paul got out of bed and gave Megan a sponge bath before dressing her in a pink pants and shirt outfit that had Noah's Ark illustrated on the front of the shirt and all types of animals entering the ark. He tickled her tiny feet before slipping a pair of socks on, then her white sandals. Paul thought about allowing her to go without the socks but the new parent didn't want Megan's feet to get cold during the trip. After setting the suitcases at the front door, Paul filled two of the no-spill cups with orange juice. Marvin was already up and had breakfast on the table. Not having a child's highchair for Megan, Paul let her sit in his lap while she feasted on scrambled eggs, tiny cuts of link sausage and milk.

After breakfast, the three loaded into Marvin's car and began the drive for the airport. Marvin said little on the way to the airport parking garage. Once they arrived and parked, Paul finally spoke up. "Marvin, what's wrong? Is it that we're leaving, that you'll be alone?"

Marvin turned and looked at Paul. "Son, I'm never alone. My God is with me always, and I'm never lonely." He paused and looked in the back seat at Megan who was sipping orange juice from her cup. Marvin looked again at Paul. "Son, you are at that place, now. You have some very big decisions to make."

Paul appeared confused. "What? What decisions are you talking about, Marvin?"

Marvin smiled. "Still runnin', aren't you? If you don't know what decisions you must make, then if you will listen very closely with an open heart, God will show you."

Paul shrugged his shoulders. "I'm listening and I'm waiting, but it seems to me that God has given me a clear path. Getting custody of Megan seems pretty clear to me. I'm going to raise my niece and show her the love that Chris and I hungered for when we were young."

Marvin looked again at Megan. "She needs more than that, and you need more than that."

"Marvin, do you have to be so vague? What are you getting at?"

"Paul, you'll know soon enough," Marvin replied. "We better be goin' inside. You got a big plane to catch."

Paul opened his car door, got out, opened the back door to the car and removed Megan from the car seat that Jensen had provided. Marvin opened the trunk of the car and removed the suitcases. Paul held Megan with his right arm while he carried the car seat in his left hand. With Marvin carrying the suitcases, the three made their way inside the airport. Once inside, Paul stopped and placed the car seat on the floor before turning and looking at Marvin.

"Well, son," Marvin said, "where are you and this beautiful child goin' to land today?"

"I'm thinking Raleigh," Paul replied. "I think Chris and my parents would approve."

"Are you sure?" Marvin reached over and took hold of one of Megan's hands. "I only know this, son. If my wife were to appear right here, right now, I think she would tell me that what she wanted most for me was happiness. I think your father, your mother, and your brother would say the same thing. So, I will ask you to do one thing before you purchase that ticket."

Paul was sure about going to Raleigh, but he respected Marvin and paid close attention to what he had to say. "Alright, Marvin, what is it that you want me to do?"

"Please, pray. God be with you, son. My love and my prayers go with you always." Marvin turned and began walking away.

"Hey, Marvin." Marvin turned back to Paul. "We both love you, too."

Marvin smiled and turned again. "God bless you, Paul."

"Marvin, one more thing." Marvin stopped, but at first didn't turn. "Are you an angel?"

Paul's question prompted Marvin to turn and face him. "I'm a child of the most high God. That makes me higher than the angels. You, too, are a child of God. Never forget that." This time Marvin made it through the automatic doors and out of sight.

Paul rented a luggage cart and after stacking the suitcases and the car seat, he carried Megan to the Delta ticket counter while pulling the cart with his free hand. He looked at the flight times to Raleigh/Durham. The next flight would depart in ninety minutes. The woman behind the ticket counter asked if she could help him. Paul thought about Marvin's words, his admonition to pray prior to purchasing tickets. Paul closed his eyes and asked God what he wanted him to do. He heard nothing, felt nothing – silence.

"Sir, may I help you," the ticket agent asked again.

Paul pulled his bankcard out of his wallet and laid it on the counter. "Two tickets for the 12:40 flight to Raleigh/Durham."

"No problem, sir," the ticket agent responded. "Let me check availability. Yes, there are plenty of seats available. You will have to switch planes in Atlanta where you'll have about an hour layover."

"Do you have any window seats available," Paul asked, wanting his niece to be able to see the vastness of the earth below from over thirty thousand feet in the air.

"Let me see. Yes. There are three available with open seats next to them for your cute little girl." The ticket agent smiled at Megan who buried her shy face in Paul's neck.

"Great," Paul responded. "I'll need two tickets, and I need to check these bags."

"No problem, sir. Let me run your card and print your boarding passes." The ticket agent completed the transaction, checked the bags and gave Paul the tickets and receipt. "Have a great flight to Raleigh/Durham, and thank-you for flying Delta Airlines."

"Thanks for your help," Paul said as he turned and began his walk toward the terminal with his niece.

Chapter Thirteen

7:40pm, Lumpkin County

The Taylor Residence

Dianne had come home again for another weekend with Anne and Charlie bringing with her the liveliest dog on Earth, Wilson. As usual, Wilson made a mad dash for the door to find Charlie while Dianne unloaded a few bags from her Envoy. It was already dark but in anticipation of his daughter's arrival, Charlie had turned on the floodlights outside the garage to help Dianne in finding her way to the back door. With Wilson in his arms excitedly licking his face, Charlie made his way out to Dianne.

"Well, my little angel has arrived," said Charlie. "All is well on the Taylor farm tonight."

Dianne gave her father a quick kiss on the cheek. "You sure are in a good mood tonight," she said as the two walked inside the house.

"How could I be in any other mood when my family is together?" Charlie took one of Dianne's bags and walked inside. Anne was busy putting the final touches on dinner.

Dianne approached her mother who was stirring a homemade vegetable soup. After kissing her mother, she grabbed a spoon and tried the soup. "Oh, that's great mom, but you sure made quite a lot of it."

Anne looked at Dianne and smiled. "Leftovers, sweetheart. That's the great thing about soup."

Charlie, having placed Dianne's things in her room, walked back into the kitchen and opened a drawer. Almost recklessly, he began taking things out of the drawer and setting them on the kitchen counter. "I can't find it.

I really need to find it tonight. I'm takin' the boat out tomorrow mornin' early before church, and I really need to find it."

Dianne walked over to Charlie. "Dad, what are you looking for? Maybe I can help you."

"My flashlight, little angel," Charlie answered. "I thought I put it in this drawer." Once convinced that the flashlight wasn't in the drawer, Charlie put all the items back and stood quietly thinking with his left hand on his chin. "Wait, I remember. I loaned it to Paul back in November when his lights went out. He told me several times where it was, but I just forgot." Charlie turned and looked at Dianne. "Honey, would you go down there and fetch that flashlight? I'll be in the garage checkin' over the boat. It's in the drawer closest to the refrigerator."

Dianne hesitated. "Dad, you know I don't like to go down there."

"Well, little angel," Charlie replied. "You were raised in that house. The house is still in our family and will be yours after we're gone. You'll have to go in it someday. Might as well be now."

"Dad, please."

"I would really appreciate it." Charlie began heading for the garage. "The dinner table should be set by the time you get back." He walked into the garage not allowing Dianne to get in a rebuttal.

Dianne reluctantly walked to the other house. When she stepped onto the back porch her heart rate suddenly increased and her stomach tightened. Finally, she gathered the courage to walk inside. After switching on the lights in the kitchen she began fumbling through the drawer looking for Charlie's missing flashlight. It wasn't there. "Maybe it's in another drawer," Dianne said out loud.

"I don't think you're going to find Charlie's flashlight anywhere in this house."

Dianne screamed and turned. The unexpected voice frightened her. Suddenly, from the dark living room, a man emerged into the light of the kitchen. Dianne stood speechless at first before finally speaking. "Paul?"

"I hear this place is still for rent. Can I come home?"

Tears filled their eyes as Dianne rushed to him, and for the first time in months, the two embraced. "Please tell me I'm not dreaming. Please tell me this is real," Dianne said.

"I'm here, Dianne," Paul replied. "If you will give me a chance, I promise to never leave you again. I'm a different man, now. Please forgive me."

Dianne kissed Paul. He had almost forgotten how incredibly soft her lips were and how weak his knees became with each kiss. "Paul, I never stopped loving you. I wasn't sure you would ever return, but I refused to ever let my love for you die. You're home."

Paul smiled. "You think the church has any of that rice left?"

Dianne hugged Paul. "If I can't find any, we'll buy some. Is that a marriage proposal?"

"Yes, my love," Paul replied. "Dianne Taylor, will you marry me. I realize that from the day we met, you've always had my heart. Now, I want to give you everything." Paul paused and stepped back and away from Dianne. Dianne was confused. "Before you answer, I think you need to know something."

Dianne's heart sank. "What is it, Paul?"

"Follow me," Paul responded. Paul led Dianne to his bedroom and opened the door. He walked over to the nightstand and switched on a lamp. Dianne remained at the door to the room, but Paul motioned her over to the bed. As Dianne approached Paul, her eyes were drawn to the middle of his bed where she realized that a tiny child was there sound asleep. Dianne turned and looked at Paul. "My niece," he said. "Chris' daughter, Megan."

"She's so beautiful," Dianne whispered as she sat on the bed to get a closer look at the sleeping child.

Paul explained to Dianne what happened after he left Quantico for the final time, how he wanted to kill Judge Simpson, how he stood over the judge's bed with a pistol ready to pull the trigger. He told Dianne how the judge pleaded for his life, how he was spared after admitting that he never read the order he signed, how he admitted that he had made a very big mistake, and how the judge promised to step down rather than face an investigation. Paul went on to tell Dianne how he ended up in Marvin's church, and how Marvin led him back to Jensen. He explained how Marvin and Jensen had become such good friends following Chris' death and how the two of them had prayed often for him. He described the court proceedings, how deflated he felt when Judge Simpson entered the courtroom, and how amazed he was with Jensen, with the conviction with which the attorney presented the case to the court. He shared the joy he felt when the judge awarded him custody of his niece. Paul went on to tell Dianne about meeting Megan for the first time, how it took a simple photograph of him with her father to earn her trust. Finally, he told Dianne about how Marvin had done so much to lead him back to faith in God, the story about Marvin's wife, and the struggles he faced following his wife's death. Paul told Dianne what Marvin had said to him at the airport.

"So, you came home," Dianne said.

"Actually, I prayed before I purchased the tickets. I got no response, so I asked for tickets to Raleigh/Durham. At the time I thought I was doing the right thing." Paul turned the light off and walked with Dianne out of the bedroom. "When we arrived in Atlanta to switch planes, I had an hour to walk around with Megan. We were having fun on the moving sidewalks when all of a sudden as we exited the sidewalk my attention was drawn to one of those glass-encased advertisements. I stopped to read what it said: 'Have you heard from God today? Family first.' It was an advertisement from a local Atlanta church. I stood there and all I could do was shake my head. Marvin. I knew right then that God had just answered my prayer because I suddenly realized just where my family was. My family is right here. I turned around and headed for a ticket counter. I asked the agent if I could get my luggage, that I had decided not to make the connection to Raleigh/Durham. He informed me that it would be impossible to retrieve the luggage, but if I was willing to pay a fee, he could have it redirected back to Atlanta. I paid the fee, rented a car and came here after stopping at a store for some things for Megan. I have no idea when our luggage will arrive, but at least I kept the car seat with me during the flight. The rental car's hidden in a stall beside the tractor."

"So, dad knew you were here in the house when he sent me down here, didn't he?"

Paul smiled mischievously. "Well Dianne, he thought about trying the straggler prank but decided that it was so pathetically bad when I tried, no sense in trying it again." Dianne shook her head. Paul continued. "So, you've seen Megan. She's my responsibility, now. Will you still marry me?"

Dianne approached Paul and put her arms around his waist. "She's our responsibility. I will be your wife soon, and Megan will be mine, too, not just yours. God has made you a part of me and me a part of you. Now, that precious child is a part of both of us. Of course, I will marry you. I have one request, though."

Paul stared into his fiancé's beautiful eyes. "Alright, what is it?"

"Tomorrow morning, I want to wake up next to that beautiful angel. Is that ok with you?"

"Do you think God would have a problem if I wake up on the other side of her," Paul said.

Dianne laughed. "I think all of heaven is rejoicing right now. In fact, I have a feeling that your mom, dad and Chris are leading the heavenly celebration."

Paul reached into his pocket. "I had some time to stop at Phipps Plaza on the way here. Megan helped me pick it out. I hope you like it." He pulled an engagement ring from his pocket and placed it on her ring finger.

Dianne stared at the beautiful diamond set on a platinum band. "Your niece already has excellent taste," Dianne said as she stared at the ring. Paul agreed as the two kissed again.

"Wait a minute," Paul said as he walked into the living room, picked up the phone and dialed a number. Charlie answered on the other line. "Room service," Paul said. "We'll need three bowls of vegetable soup, some fresh orange juice in a 'sippy' cup, a bottled water and a Gatorade at our back porch within fifteen minutes."

"Comin' right up, sir," Charlie said with one of the biggest smiles of his entire life. "I do expect a big tip, though."

"You want a tip, marine?" Dianne knew the two sarcasm kings were at it again. "Don't go out in a cold rain without an umbrella."

"Good tip, ranger," Charlie replied. "My assistant and I will have the soup to you directly. But, do you mind if we bring two extra bowls?"

Paul walked over to Dianne and hugged her. "Charlie, I wouldn't have it any other way."

Minutes later, Charlie and Anne appeared at the back door with Charlie carrying the pot of homemade soup and Anne carrying a bag full of bowls, spoons, cups and other things for the meal. While Anne and Charlie set the table in Paul's small dining area, Paul led Dianne back into his bedroom. The couple knelt by the bed and stared at Megan. Her eyes slowly opened to see Paul and Dianne staring at the newest angel of the family. Paul smiled at his niece and after Megan rubbed her eyes and yawned, she looked at Paul, then Dianne and back at Paul. Suddenly, a bright smile formed on her face as she reached for her uncle and her new life. Paul carried her into the kitchen, sat down with her on his lap and following Charlie's blessing on the food the family enjoyed their meal.

Following dinner, Anne insisted on driving into town to buy some clothes for Megan. Paul reminded Anne that Megan was an Atkinson, beautiful on the outside, tough on the inside. Nonetheless, Anne asked Dianne if she would go with her to Walmart to purchase something for Megan to sleep in and a few other items for her. Dianne, of course, said yes. Paul looked at Megan and said, "Doting mothers." He began laughing, and once again, not knowing why, Megan laughed, too.

"Paul," said Dianne, "would you mind if we took Megan with us? She seems well-rested."

Paul looked at Megan who understood just enough to not want to go at first. "Do you want to go get some new clothes with your other grandmother and aunt?" Megan shook her head and held onto Paul.

Dianne, an expert with children given her profession and her deep compassion, spoke up, trying the patented childproof manipulation tactic. "You know, it's really not that late. I think we can find some toys and some ice cream for Megan while we're at the store." Megan spun around on Paul's lap and looked at Dianne. Dianne continued. "Do you like ice cream?" Megan licked her tiny lips, nodded and smiled. "Would you like to go with me and my mom to get some and maybe a brand new toy?" Another nod from Megan sealed everything.

Megan crawled off of Paul's lap and walked over to Dianne. "Now? Can we go now?" Megan reached her arms out to Dianne, and Paul's future wife found out why he had fallen in love with the beautiful child. She leaned over, picked Megan up and held her tightly.

"We can go right now," Anne said as she stood. "Men, tell war stories and wash the dishes. The women of the house are going shopping." With Megan in Dianne's arms, the three headed outside while Paul ran ahead to retrieve the car seat from the rental car. Once installed, he returned to his dining area where Charlie was giving Wilson a sample of the soup. Paul sat down at the table and stared at what seemed like a mountain of bowls, spoons, glasses, and, of course, what was left of the pot of soup. He looked at Charlie and shook his head. "I hate washing dishes," Paul said.

"Me too," Charlie replied.

"Thank God for dishwashers." Paul didn't have one in his kitchen but he knew where one was just a short walk from his house.

"Hallelujah," Charlie replied as he stood and began stacking the bowls. "Let's go."

An hour and a half later, the women returned to find Charlie and Paul snoozing in the living room in front of the television. What began as a quick trip to purchase Megan some basic things to get her through a few days until her suitcase was returned became an all-out spending spree complete with a high chair, clothing, training diapers, brushes, shampoo, lotion, toys and a slew of other things for the new addition to the family. Megan, upon seeing Paul asleep on the couch, ran over to him and crawled onto his stomach, jarring her uncle out of his sleep. He opened his eyes to find a doll less than an inch from his face. Megan squeezed the doll and as its mouth moved, the doll said, "mommy". Charlie had just awakened as well and laughed at what he had just witnessed. "No," Charlie said, "I don't think so. This man can't even operate a dishwasher."

Paul sat up on the couch with Megan still squeezing the talking doll. He looked over his shoulder at the line of shopping bags. "I should have known," he said.

Dianne walked over to Paul, sat on the edge of the couch and kissed him on the forehead. "You're losing your exercise room tomorrow after mom and I go to the mall. And, I need you to talk to Tom after church. We need an estimate on a few things."

Paul looked over at Charlie. "Don't look at me," Charlie said. "You should've been here when Dianne was born."

Paul got up from the couch and pulled Charlie out of his recliner. "Come on, marine. Looks like we have some more work to do." Everyone grabbed a bag and walked to Paul's house. On the way to the house, Dianne and Anne discussed everything they planned to purchase the next day: bedroom furniture, more clothing, more toys, and books. Paul looked again at Charlie who simply raised his eyebrows and shrugged his shoulders.

An hour later, Megan was asleep. Paul laid down next to her and her new doll. His little angel had had quite a day, he thought, as she lay sleeping with her thumb in her mouth. Paul put his arm around her, and instinctively, Megan rolled on her side facing him. Dianne had walked over to her parent's house to change into one of her favorite nighttime outfits: sweatpants and the now aging Emory t-shirt. She walked into Paul's bedroom and to the opposite side of the bed. She laid down and pulled close to Megan. Megan rolled over on her back, thumb still in her mouth.

Dianne whispered to Paul, "I usually have to look at these beautiful gifts from God in hospital beds with tubes in their mouths and heart monitors beeping away. Megan reminds me of just how precious each moment with a child is. Goodnight, Paul. Welcome home."

"Goodnight, Dianne."

Paul woke up at six-thirty the next morning. Megan was curled up next to Dianne still holding her doll and sucking her thumb. Quietly, not wanting to wake the two, Paul crawled out of bed and pulled some clothing from his dresser before leaving the room, closing the door behind him. He quickly changed into his riding clothes and walked into his soon to be converted exercise room. As if seeing a longtime friend for the first time in years, Paul stared at his mountain bike. He retrieved the bike and walked back into the living room where an envelope was sitting on the coffee table. Paul pulled some of the contents out of the envelope, found a small plastic bag in the kitchen and tucked it under his tight riding shirt before rolling the bike outside.

The course hadn't changed; the intensity hadn't lessened. Paul realized, though, that he had, indeed, changed. He decided to make this ride synonymous with putting the past in the past once and for all. With each thrust of the bike pedals, with every breath, and with every drop of sweat, Paul made this ride a ride toward the future, a future with a beautiful wife, a family, and, of course, his bloodline – Megan – his connection to people in his life who he thought at one time were gone forever.

The fifteen-mile ride to the familiar country store lasted just over forty-two minutes. He parked his bike and took a look around. With a few minor differences, everything and everyone was in place. The two little boys were chasing each other on their bikes. The two elderly men were the surprise of the day. Still chewing tobacco and debating the world's condition, the two men did so in matching gray suits and Bibles on their laps. Inside the store, the hard-working single mom was her usual upbeat self. Paul realized he was home for good. He grabbed a Gatorade from the cooler and approached the counter.

"Good mornin' to you," the cashier said. "I haven't seen you around in awhile."

Paul looked at her kind face and smiled. "Just a little journey," he replied as he looked to his left toward the door. "I need two packs of whatever type of tobacco the men out there chew; and would you mind if I bought your sons some candy and some drinks?"

"I'm sure they would love for you to do that, but you don't have to."

"I really want to if you don't mind," Paul replied.

The cashier smiled. "Sure, go right ahead."

Paul asked for a bag, then went over to the candy aisle and loaded the bag with all kinds of candy and snacks. He walked back to the cooler and bought two sodas and two pre-made sandwiches. The bag was so full the seams began to tear as Paul approached the counter to pay.

The kind cashier laughed when she saw what Paul brought to her to ring up. "Those boys will be climbin' the walls the rest of the day." She looked up at Paul and smiled. "I think I'll give them a little now and let the have some more when we get home."

"Sounds like a great plan," Paul replied. With the bill paid, Paul first went to the two men sitting on the bench outside. "You gentlemen look really sharp today," Paul said as he handed each one of them a pack of chewing tobacco.

The two men stared first at the packs of tobacco, then at each other before turning back to Paul. "Why, thank-ya son," one of the men said with the other nodding his approval of Paul's generosity.

"Have a great day, sirs," Paul said as he turned his attention to the boys. Their mother had placed some of the goodies in two separate bags and gave the bags to Paul to carry to the children. He called the two boys over to where he was standing. They rode their bikes from the far end of the parking lot over to Paul, and he gave each one a bag. Each boy peaked inside his bag and huge smiles lit their faces.

"Thank-you, sir," each said as they rode off on their bikes to dig into the bags.

Paul reached inside his riding shirt and pulled out the plastic bag that he had carried with him from his house. With a laugh at the beauty of watching the two boys feast on their snacks, Paul turned and walked back inside the store and up to the counter. He stood and stared for a moment at the cashier. She looked somewhat bewildered as Paul continued to stare. Finally, he spoke up. "Has anyone every thanked you for what you do?"

"Well," she answered, "my boss did give me a raise to nine dollars an hour a month ago. He said I'm the best cashier he's ever had."

Paul congratulated her on the raise. "I'm not really talking about what you do just here, but what you do in life. You are a great mother, a happy person, and a gift to the world." Paul handed her the plastic bag. "Thank-you for what you do. God bless you." Paul turned, walked out of the store and hopped back on his bike. He gulped down his Gatorade, and after tossing the empty bottle in the trashcan, rode off for home.

The cashier peaked inside the bag. Her eyes suddenly widened, and she dumped the bag's contents onto the counter. One hundred dollar bills fell from the bag and spread out onto the counter. She stood from her stool and with her heart racing, the cashier and single-mother of two began counting out the cash: $25,000.00 – half of what Paul received at Quantico. The cashier ran outside to see if she could catch Paul, but he was gone. Returning to the cash inside the store, she began putting the money back inside the plastic bag. As she shoved the money into the bag, she noticed a piece of paper inside the bag that had not fallen out with the cash. Removing the folded paper and noticing writing, she sat on the stool and read the note from Paul: "The world isn't always the kindest place. In fact, much of the world is cruel and heartless. But, you aren't. You are what others in this world should strive to be – kind, caring, happy, loving. This money is not a source of happiness, but a gift from God to a great mother. I hope you are blessed by it. P."

The church service at Spring River Baptist Church went from the usual traditional style service to a celebration of restoration, healing, an upcoming wedding, and the beauty of a two-year-old child. Paul spoke to the congregation, thanking them for their love and for their prayers. He introduced his niece to the church and Megan suddenly had thirty new grandmothers and grandfathers coddling her and showering her with attention. Dr. Rodgers hugged both Paul and Dianne after the couple asked him to perform their wedding. The pastor looked at Paul and welcomed him home from his journey of faith. The hand of God had been upon him all the time, he said to Paul. As directed, Paul found Tom and asked him to come to his house and talk to Anne and Dianne about some renovation. Tom promised to be there on Tuesday. Paul whispered in Tom's ear. "Listen, do you think you could build me a new exercise room."

Tom looked at Paul and laughed, recognizing that the soon to be wed eternal bachelor had been invaded by the women of the house. "Sure," Tom replied. "We'll call it a wedding gift from me to you."

Paul smiled and nodded. "Sounds great to me."

Following church and lunch along with a short nap for Megan, the adults planned their day. The women wanted to go straight to the mall and shop for the two year old. Charlie wanted to watch a pre-season special on the Atlanta Braves. But, Paul trumped everyone. "I want everyone to come with me. Charlie, we'll need to take the Yukon." The other three adults looked back and forth at each other with puzzled expressions. Once Megan was settled in her car seat, cup of juice in one hand and doll in the other, Paul drove the family south through Dahlonega and southwest on Georgia Highway 400. Eight miles later, he turned left into a large parking lot. It was the same dealership where Charlie had purchased the Yukon.

"I saw a commercial last night. They're having a clearance sale, trying to sell what's left of their 2008 trucks." Paul looked at Dianne who was smiling. "Well, I can't have my niece riding around in a truck that is on its ninth life."

Megan paid no attention to the adult conversation. Among the $447.00 of spending by Anne and Dianne the previous night, were several children's videos. From her car seat, she watched a cartoon that she had selected. "You two go ahead. Mom and I will stay here with Megan." Dianne leaned over and kissed Megan on the forehead.

Charlie and Paul got out of the Yukon and began looking around. Paul found a red, four-door GMC Canyon in the price range he was looking for. The two men talked about the vehicle when a voice from behind interrupted the conversation.

"Well, gentlemen, looks like you have your eyes on a beautiful truck."

Charlie turned around to find the same salesman who sold him his Yukon. The salesman immediately recognized Charlie, and his face lit up with anticipation. Charlie introduced Paul, and the salesman began his sales pitch with all the reasons why the GMC Canyon was such a good buy, but Paul stopped him. "I appreciate you letting me know all of these things," Paul said. "But, I just want to get the truck and drive away. Sound good?"

"Great," the salesman answered. He looked at Charlie. "Well sir, same process as last time you were here?"

"I'm sorry. I wouldn't know," Charlie replied. "He's buyin' the truck, not me."

The salesman glanced at Paul who was wearing a pair of ripped blue jeans and a wrinkled t-shirt. "Oh, well, let's go inside to my office and we'll get everything started." Paul followed the salesman into his office with Charlie in tow. Once everyone was seated, the salesman pulled out a credit application from his desk drawer and said, "Will you be trading anything in on the truck or putting any money down?"

Paul reached in his pocket and forced out a thick envelope. "No, none of that will be necessary," he said. "This should cover it." Paul laid the envelope on the desk.

The salesman peaked inside the envelope and saw cash. He pulled the cash out and nervously counted it: $23,750.00, the remaining money of what was given to Paul at Quantico minus some cash he had saved. The sticker price on the 2008 Canyon was $21,900.00. With taxes, Paul had enough with a plenty left for a new car seat for Megan and anything else she might need. The salesman quickly shoved the credit application back into the top drawer of his desk. "I'll be right back. I'll have your truck washed and filled with gas, and you should be driving off the lot momentarily." The salesman rushed out of his office headed toward his manager.

Paul looked over at Charlie who was calmly sitting in an office chair with his arms folded. "He seems a little nervous," Paul said.

"Roses," Charlie answered. "He's tryin' to figure out where he can buy some roses."

Paul stared at Charlie and shook his head. "What are you talking about?"

"Never mind," he answered. "It's not important. I like your truck. Good choice."

"It's for Megan, not me," said Paul. "I hope she likes it."

"She loves you, first and foremost, and you love her. That's the most important thing. A child would trade luxury any day for genuine love. But, nonetheless, she'll like the truck. Just make sure you tell her it's her truck, not yours."

"I get it," Paul replied.

The salesman came back into the office and sat back down. "We'll have the sales contract drawn up in just a few minutes. Is there anything I can get you gentlemen?"

Charlie leaned forward. "Son," he said to the excited salesman, "I need you to do one more thing for me."

The salesman gave Charlie a confident nod. "Absolutely, sir. What can I do for you?"

"Well, I'm assumin' you value our business, right?" Paul was listening to Charlie to see where he was going with the questions.

"Right, sir, you are an excellent customer," the salesman replied.

"And, I'm sure you want us to keep bringin' our business here, right?"

"Yes sir. Absolutely," the salesman replied to Charlie.

"Great! Then I'm sure you'll have no problem installin' one of those DVD/television systems in the truck for my new granddaughter, at no additional cost, of course." Charlie stood and began walking toward the door. "We'll pick the truck up tomorrow afternoon. Sound good?"

The salesman was, at first, speechless. He wasn't about to tell Charlie that he couldn't install the system free of charge. He was simply going to have to push his manager to do it. "Sounds great, sir," the salesman said. "I'll have the truck ready for you tomorrow afternoon by 4:00pm. Here's my card in case you need to call or if you have any questions."

Paul stood from his chair, shook the salesman's sweaty hand and followed Charlie back to the Yukon. They got in and drove south for Alpharetta and a mall.

"How did it all go in there," Dianne asked.

Charlie looked back at Dianne and responded. "Roses."

Dianne laughed. "Roses – again. His wife must really love him."

"What are you two talking about," Paul said wanting in on the little secret.

"Let's go shopping for our little angel," Dianne replied as she held Megan's tiny hand.

Paul drove to the mall, on the way thinking about his life. He realized that the hurt and rejection, the loss and the longing of his childhood and young adulthood had robbed him of the joys to be found in life. Without really knowing why as a youth, Paul distanced his self from people, shielding his self from the fears of feeling those pains that come with the loss of someone close. Where others viewed him as a complicated person, somewhat hard to read, Paul suddenly realized that he had been simply a lonely and confused soul, hiding behind whatever would cover the pain of his past. He looked in the rearview mirror as he drove and could see Dianne playing with Megan. Dianne was the antithesis of who Paul had been. She was born with a sort of buoyancy and transparency. She hid from nothing and loved without fear. Paul admitted to his self that God had, indeed, put Dianne in his life for more reasons than he could have imagined. Through his future beautiful wife, Paul believed that he would, too, know how to receive love and give love without fear, to be transparent and to live with the joy that could only come with a solid spiritual foundation and faith. He realized that though he was home and though there had, indeed, been a miraculous change with the help of a bellman from Dallas, Texas, Paul still had some hurdles to cross. Seeing the smiling two-year-old relish in the attention and love she was receiving from his future wife, brought joy and that familiar hint of fear that had plagued him most of his life. Paul had to admit that a life of faith wasn't always the easier, softer way. It was easy to hide behind an M-16 and in a military uniform. Now, he was facing real life with all of its dynamics. Paul suddenly remembered Marvin's simple plea: "Pray."

Chapter Fourteen

Mid-August, 2013, 7:15am

A back porch in Lumpkin County, Georgia

Nature's orchestra had delivered another stellar performance as the sun ushered in a new day in North Georgia, and six family members had the privilege of enjoying every minute. Charlie sat on one end with Wilson nestled in his lap. Anne sat next to him holding her husband's hand. Dianne came next, holding the latest member of the family: Joseph Atkinson who had just celebrated turning three months old. Oblivious to nature's concert, Joseph sucked on a bottle of breast milk. Paul held his six and a half year old daughter, Megan, as he watched his son feast on the bottle of milk. Megan would be starting school again soon. Paul was somewhat overwhelmed by it all, while Megan, showing signs that she was indeed much like her natural father, was taking it all in stride.

Just about three years earlier, Paul received a letter from Chris' ex-wife who had been convicted and was serving a minimum sentence of eight years in a women's prison in Texas. Her father had passed away, and she had taken a great deal of time to think about her future and about Megan. The letter stirred Paul's emotions.

"Dear Paul,

"I know that we have never really met or spent any time together, but I have had much time to think about my life, the highs and the lows. As tragic as the accident was that took the lives of those two precious people, the greatest tragedy was when I turned my back on my husband, your brother. I regretted it from the moment I signed the divorce papers and will go to my grave with that regret. I allowed myself to be manipulated by selfish people, especially my father, and in the end, I turned from the only person who ever really loved me unconditionally. I believe there is only one way to make things right and to honor the memory of my husband.

"I long for my daughter, to look into her eyes, and to see Chris in her. My addiction destroyed that. The photographs you send me on her birthday and at Christmas mean so much to me, yet they bring so much pain and regret. My desire for Megan is that she be given a home full of love and happiness, that she know God and his love for her, and that she be allowed to mature in a secure environment without the pressures that I felt as a child to be someone I never wanted to be. I know that you and your wife are giving Megan that home.

"For this reason, I'm giving you authorization to proceed with adoption procedures. Chris told me much about you. I know that you want to do what is right. What is the right thing to do is for Megan to have a father and a mother. With you and your wife, she has that, and I am so happy for her. I only ask that you never hide her from me or me from her and that you never let her think that she doesn't have a mother out there who cares.

"Paul, thank-you for loving my daughter. I pray that your life is full of joy always."

Paul went to his bedroom after reading the letter and wept. He felt such sorrow for her, such pain over her tragic losses. He was determined to honor every one of her requests. He sent her a response, along with another photograph of Megan.

"Dear Amy,

"Thank-you for your incredible letter. The depth of your honesty and the love I know you have for Chris and for Megan is abundantly obvious as the letter was read. Believe it or not, I can relate with you concerning the great loss you've suffered. Chris could, too. I will never minimize your pain or your loss in any way, and I pray that you will find peace in the one source who can free us from our past – God.

"I will honor your wishes concerning the adoption of Megan. My wife, a pediatrician and an incredible woman, agrees with you and so do I. Nevertheless, I will never be a party to, nor will anyone else in this family ever try to shelter Megan from you or the memory of her father. As she grows and as she matures, we will talk to her about the years that she will never remember. We will share with her stories about her hilarious and loving father, as well as her sacrificing mother. All the powers of heaven could never change one undeniable fact. Chris and Amy Atkinson are the parents of one, Megan Atkinson. You don't want that to change, and nor do I.

"Your life is not over, but it can begin new right now. I wandered in the dark for many years. Somehow God found me and saved me. Please, get your eyes off the past and onto your future, and you will see great things happen. I'm living proof.

"Our prayers are with you always."

The adoption process went smoothly. Jensen, with the help of an Atlanta attorney, handled everything. Megan had already been calling Paul and Dianne, "mommy and daddy", and with her young age, the transition was easier than it would have been if she had been several years older. Megan was a well-adjusted child, resilient and everyone's favorite little girl. Paul, when in public places, protected her like an attacking bulldog. Charlie joked often that Paul was the living definition of a "shotgun daddy". "The poor girl's never goin' to keep a boyfriend with commando dad around," he said one evening at the dinner table.

As a wedding gift to the newlyweds, Charlie and Anne paid for a complete makeover of the old house. Three more bedrooms were added, the kitchen was updated with new appliances, a playroom was also added, and just as Tom promised, a state of the art exercise room was built just for Paul with a special place for his mountain bike. Tom, as promised, built the room free as a gift to Paul.

The honeymoon was fantastic. Paul, Dianne and Megan flew to France finally using the Christmas gift given to Paul by Charlie and Anne in 2008. Once there, they enjoyed the sites and had incredible seats at the finish line of the last three stages of the Tour de France. Paul cheered wildly as an underdog American came out of nowhere during the final stages to win the Tour. The former soldier realized halfway through the honeymoon that the trip to France was his first time overseas without a military operation looming over his head.

Following the honeymoon, Dianne, as intelligent with her income as her parents had been with theirs, invested in a two-story brick building just off the square in Dahlonega where after some hefty renovations, she opened Atkinson Pediatrics. The sale of her condominium in Buckhead paid for most of the building while investment funds paid for the necessary equipment, furniture and other needs. Her reputation for quality and expertise quickly spread throughout Lumpkin and neighboring counties and it wasn't long before she had two more physicians and four more nurses on staff. The on-site nursery allowed her to bring Joseph with her to work on the days when Anne and Charlie had other appointments or were out of town.

Paul never returned to his job at the warehouse. With a college nearby, he decided he would go for his Masters in Education, and in eighteen months he had achieved his goal. He obtained a teaching certification and was hired at a local high school where he taught sociology and psychology and was asked to be an assistant coach on the track team as well as head coach of the cross-country teams. With a 2013 cross-country season approaching, Coach Atkinson had his boys and girls over to the farm often for summer workouts. Charlie, using a backhoe, had mowed a trail that totaled three and a half miles in distance and that stretched and turned in and out of different pastures and briefly into the forest.

Paul and Dianne were elated to receive a call from Thomas. His family had been restored and Thomas was in an executive sales program with a huge pharmaceutical company located in Atlanta. At the same time, Thomas was doing volunteer work at the Atlanta Union Mission. He and his wife had just purchased a new home in Tucker and were members of a large Presbyterian church just blocks from their neighborhood. Paul invited them for a visit, and Thomas promised to take him up on it once his training was completed.

As promised, Judge Simpson stepped down as a family court judge. Paul considered sending him a letter asking him not to step down, but instead he wrote him informing him that he would not be contacting anyone in Washington, that it was time for everyone involved to move on. The judge, however, still left his seat. He resurfaced eighteen months later as a criminal defense attorney. It seemed to fit better for him. Once he regained his confidence, the former judge became a terror to district attorneys.

Back on the porch in Lumpkin County, Paul got up and carried his sleeping daughter to Anne. "Time for a ride," he said. He kissed Megan, then Dianne and finally Joseph and walked to his plush exercise room. Tom had left nothing undone. The room had vaulted ceilings with three ceiling fans, great lighting and a built-in stereo system and flat screen television mounted on a wall in front of two state of the art treadmills. Over near a mirrored wall were two weight benches and racks with over five hundred pounds of free weights. Other equipment lined another wall, with a padded space left in the middle of the room for Dianne and her nurses. Twice a week, the ladies met for aerobics. A small locker room and shower had also been installed. Paul loved the room, but the kids on the cross-country teams loved it more. With an outside entrance added on after the construction and keys to the room given to each member of the respective teams, it wasn't unusual during the hot summer months or the cold winter days to see two or three cars in the Atkinson driveway with four or five teenagers inside the exercise room training. Charlie loved it when the kids came around. It gave him an opportunity to hang around the room telling long stories to them of his days as a high school baseball player.

Paul grabbed his mountain bike from a storage area designed by Tom and took off on his usual course. He reached the fifteen-mile stop on his ride and parked his bike in the usual spot in front of the country store. The two elderly men were in their usual spot, but the young boys weren't. Paul knew why, though. He went inside and found his favorite flavor of Gatorade before he walked up to the counter.

"Well, Paul, how are you today," said the cashier in her usual kind voice.

"Hot and sweaty, Theresa," Paul replied. "How are your two boys?"

"I'm sure they're out back playin' in their private clubhouse that Mike built for them. I'm a girl, they say, so I'm not allowed in it." Theresa had taken the money Paul had given her over four years earlier and used it all as a down payment on a new doublewide pre-manufactured home just a quarter mile away from the store. Mike was her fiancé, a hardworking man she met one Friday afternoon at the store. The two had dated for over a year and were making plans for their wedding to be held at the nearby Foggy Mountain Assembly of God Church before Thanksgiving.

The first time Paul met Mike was by coincidence. Theresa's fiancé just happened to be at the store buying bait to take her sons fishing when Paul arrived during his routine Saturday ride. When Paul first met Mike, he just stood in front of him and looked up. Mike was over six and a half feet tall and weighed nearly three hundred pounds. He was a professional welder. Paul joked with him about his size saying, "We could achieve world peace if we lined up ten thousand men that look just like you and showed you off to the world." Mike, though, was one of the kindest men Paul had ever met, and it was clear that he loved Theresa and her children.

"We'll be sendin' out invitations to our weddin' soon. I hope you and your wife can make it," Theresa said.

"We will be there," Paul replied. "I'll keep my eyes on the mailbox. I'll see you next Saturday."

"Thank-you, Paul. I'll see you soon."

Paul hopped back on the mountain bike, pressed the start button on his Garmin watch and took off for home. When he arrived, he took a shower using the one in the exercise room. With Joseph in his crib sleeping, Megan crawled next to Dianne on the king sized bed in the master bedroom and fell asleep again while Dianne read her a book. Paul walked in after his shower and found both of them sleeping, the book lying on Dianne's chest. He gently removed the book and walked outside and up to Charlie and Anne's house.

Paul walked into the kitchen following the scent of country sausage on the stove. Once in the kitchen he found a banana from a fruit bowl sitting on the kitchen island and walked over to his favorite eating spot in all the world. The sun was beaming through the tall trees and rays of light illuminated the table. "Jensen, Cindy, did you get enough sleep last night," Paul asked his friends from Texas.

"We slept great," Jensen answered. "Thanks for picking us up at the airport last night."

"Glad to do it. Dianne hasn't stopped talking about you two all month since we confirmed your visit. You are staying five days, aren't you?"

"That's the plan," Jensen replied. "Charlie's taking the three of us and Megan to a Braves game tomorrow night."

"That's right," Charlie said as he strolled into the kitchen. "I've got to teach our friends a little about how we do things in the National League."

"Don't bother buying a program," Paul said as he peeled a banana. "Mr. Baseball here knows more about the Braves than the team's manager. He's a walking stat book."

"That's good to know," Jensen replied.

Three and a half hours later, Anne, Dianne and Cindy loaded the children into the Yukon and off to Lake Lanier Islands to a water park. Charlie disappeared into his study to work on a Sunday school lesson he had been asked to teach the next day. Paul followed his Saturday routine. "Alright Jensen," he said. "It's time to see how the other half lives."

"I'm ready," Jensen replied.

The two men walked outside to the driveway. Jensen walked over to the passenger side of Paul's GMC Canyon, but Paul kept walking past the truck. Jensen was confused, but followed Paul. The two men walked through the cattle gate and out to one of the stalls. Paul pulled a large tarp off of a vehicle revealing his old Chevrolet S-10 pick-up. Paul looked at Jensen. "We cannot break tradition, my friend. Nothing will be right unless we drive the S-10. I think it could actually throw the earth off its axis, or something like that."

"Far be it from me to break tradition and risk the planet," Jensen said with a smile. He opened the passenger side door and a Gatorade bottle rolled from the floorboard and onto the ground. Jensen picked it up and along with the twenty or so other bottles, tossed it back onto the floorboard. "No explanation necessary," he said. "I'll just chalk it up to recycling."

"Great answer, Jensen," Paul replied.

The two men shared in a good laugh as Paul tried to start the truck. It finally cranked on the fifth try. Paul glanced over to Jensen as he pulled the truck out of the stall and said, "Old reliable." Ten minutes later the truck pulled up to Frank's Bar and Grill. With the ignition switch turned off, Paul hummed and stared out of the front windshield while the truck sputtered and coughed, finally shutting off with a small backfire. Paul looked at Jensen again. "That's new."

The two men got out of the truck and walked inside. Paul found his usual stool and sat down. Jensen took the stool beside him. "Well, well," Frank said. "The man has three women in his life: a wife, a daughter and a mother-in-law, and he can't get a home cooked meal. I think you need some trainin', Paul. You've got to be doin' somethin' wrong."

"No, it's not that Frank," Paul replied. "Dianne told me this morning that we were out of that gourmet Spam and said I was going to either have to go hungry or come here. You don't want me to starve, do you?"

Frank introduced himself to Jensen. "You don't hang out with this guy, do ya," he asked pointing to Paul.

Paul answered. "He's a good looking guy. It improves my reputation when I hang out with the elite."

Jensen smiled and shook his head. "Listen, I didn't bring my cowboy boots with me from Dallas, so don't let it get too deep in here."

Paul introduced Jensen to Tom. "Tom, I see the wife let you out of the house."

Tom set his mug of beer back on the bar. "Are you kiddin' me. She throws me out of the house every Saturday. Hey, are you still enjoyin' your exercise room?"

"I love it," Paul replied. He explained to Jensen that Tom had handled all of the add-ons as well as the renovation of his house.

"Paul," Pete said. "That truck must have eighteen lives."

"It's all in how you talk to it, Pete," Paul answered. "You've got to show 'old reliable' some love."

"I'd rather show it my car crusher." Peter looked at Jensen and said, "I got behind him last Saturday on the way here and thought I was goin' to pass out from the exhaust fumes from the clunker."

"That's my homemade anti-carjacking device," Paul said.

Frank came out with two plates setting one in front of Paul and the other in front of Jensen. Paul looked at Jensen and asked him if he was ready. Jensen nodded as the two men picked up their hamburgers and took a bite. Juice rolled down each of their faces. Paul and Jensen looked at each other and simultaneously responded to the taste of the burger: "Perfect."

Later that evening, Paul and Dianne stood outside by one of the fences facing the open pasture. The sun had just set leaving a beautiful orange glow peaking over the horizon. Stars had begun to replace the light of the sun and the familiar sound of crickets and bullfrogs ushered in the summer night. Paul held Dianne in his arms and stared into her eyes. "So, this is what it's like to love and be loved," he said.

"This is what happens when we turn everything over to God and let him do what he wants to do with our lives," Dianne responded. "And, Mr. Atkinson, I think he's done an excellent job, wouldn't you agree?"

"I completely agree," Paul responded. "Let's go kiss our children and tuck them in." Paul and Dianne, hand in hand, walked inside their house and turned off the porch light.

Dallas, Texas
A few days later

Another day at the Ritz Carlton was over and the bellman drove his car south toward home. Upon arriving at his little white house, Marvin got out and checked his mailbox. His steps were a little more laborious than in previous years. The hours of standing were beginning to take their toll. After sifting through a few bills, he noticed an envelope with a return address in Georgia. He excitedly opened the envelope and looked at the card. Inside the card was a photograph that included Paul, Dianne, Megan, Joseph, Charlie, Anne, Jensen, Cindy and Jacob standing by the John Deere tractor. He stared at the photograph oblivious to the traffic speeding past him as he stood near the curb. Finally, Marvin began making his way toward his front door while he read the card:

"Dear Marvin,

"We thought you would get a kick out of seeing everyone together in front of the tractor. We were all talking about you, how incredible you are, and we thought a photo in front of the tractor was appropriate. You see, you're one of those rare souls who seem to aim for one thing each day: to cultivate the love of God into the hearts of those you meet. You certainly cultivated more than you'll ever know into our lives, and we are where we're at today because of your faith. Your infectious smile, your patience, your kindness and your belief that God always has a plan for us, certainly had a profound impact on our entire family. We will not allow ourselves to forget you; in fact, I've purchased an airline ticket for you to fly to Atlanta and spend Thanksgiving weekend with us. Everyone is excited about you coming. I had a long conversation with our pastor, and after hearing how we met and the incredible role you played in God's magnificent plan, Dr. Rodgers has invited you to speak to the congregation on the Sunday following Thanksgiving. The ticket has no return date. You can leave when you are ready. Please come and be with us. Our love to you always,
Paul and Dianne Atkinson."

Marvin walked inside and picked up the photograph of his wife. A tear fell onto her lovely face and a feeling of warmth filled Marvin's heart. He glanced over his shoulder at the card lying open on the coffee table. "I'll be there, son. I'll be there."

Visit steeplesjourneys.com and share your journey or join ours!